MW01228372

A. R. MORGAN

THE HEART OF AN ALCHEMIST

TRIA PRIMA SERIES
BOOK 1

1

This book is dedicated to Kevin Harris.
For 16 years you were my mentor, my best friend.
You always told me to write, and I finally did
when all I had left was the memory of you.
So, this is for you, beloved friend.
May you fly with the angels.

A. R. Morgan

COPYRIGHT

ISBN 979-8-9873524-0-3 (Ebook)
ISBN 979-8-9873524-1-0 (Paperback)
ISBN 979-8-9873524-2-7 (Hardback)
Library of Congress Control Number: 2022922087
Illustration & Published by A R Morgan Books, Envato Elements,
and Meowlayn.art
Edited by https://getproofreader.co.uk/ & Wes Dolan
armorganbooks.com

FOREWORD

Thank you for taking the time to read this book. This story is my debut into the literary world, and I am eager to share it with you. Please note that this book is written in British English; the spelling will look a bit different if you are an American-English reader.

As you read, please enjoy the rich mythological references. I urge my readers to read more about the names, creatures, and foreign words used as they will give you, not only a better understanding of the story but will wrap you up in the magnificent culture and history I have based a lot of this story on. While Champions, alchemists, and what came of the old gods certainly stems from my own imagination, the rest is steeped in folklore, and I will continue bringing many different myths and legends from all over the world into my books. A Glossary can be found in the back of this book and a playlist for each chapter can be found on my website: armoganbooks.com.

Please take your time and enjoy this first book of mine!

TRIGGER WARNINGS:
Death, language, references to torture and rape, light sexual assault, harm and death to minors, references to abuse, violence. Meant only for **MATURE AUDIENCES.**

A. R. Morgan

TABLE OF CONTENTS

COPYRIGHT   5
FOREWORD   7
GLOSSARY   11
CHAPTER 1   15
CHAPTER 2   25
CHAPTER 3   33
CHAPTER 4   39
CHAPTER 5   51
CHAPTER 6   67
CHAPTER 7   83
CHAPTER 8   95
CHAPTER 9   103
CHAPTER 10   113
CHAPTER 11   119
CHAPTER 12   127
CHAPTER 13   141
CHAPTER 14   149
CHAPTER 15   159
CHAPTER 16   169
CHAPTER 17   177
CHAPTER 18   189
CHAPTER 19   197
CHAPTER 20   207
CHAPTER 21   217
CHAPTER 22   223
CHAPTER 23   229
CHAPTER 24   237
CHAPTER 25   243
CHAPTER 26   251
CHAPTER 27   259
CHAPTER 28   269
CHAPTER 29   277

CHAPTER 30   287
CHAPTER 31   295
CHAPTER 32   305
CHAPTER 33   313
CHAPTER 34   319
CHAPTER 35   325
CHAPTER 36   331
THE END.   337
PREVIEW   339

ACKNOWLEDGMENTS   341
ABOUT THE AUTHOR   343

GLOSSARY

Alcaeus: pronounced 'Al-SAY-us' but can be pronounced it as 'al-chaos' if you want as well.

Alchemist: A race of beings created by Mother Nature at the dawn of time, before she created humans. Each Alchemist was genetically programmed to control a singular element. Together, they could maintain and care for the balance of nature. They lived in a hidden city called The Citadel, their land extending to a great wall known as Eladaria's Wall. Their genius was renowned, their science legendary and they became hunted after the old gods fled. Yet, a little over 600 years ago, they mysteriously disappeared.

ástin mín: 'My love' a term of endearment in Icelandic Norse.Brownie: A creature that can be found in English and Scottish folklore. The Irish equivalent is the Grogan. This industrious fairy, or also known as hobgoblins, are small creatures that can be found in homes and other dwellings. They are extremely difficult to spot, silent and rarely seen. These little house elves have a mischievous side and make excellent spies and pickpockets, their light fingers a skill most valued in the Unseelie Kingdom.

Cantre'r Gwaelod: A legendary ancient kingdom, now sunken beneath the waves of Cardigan Bay; also known as the 'Welsh Atlantis'. This is where the Great Battle took place, where the Champions conquered the gods.

Champions: Gladiators created by the gods of all mythologies, to fight in their name. Each warrior possesses some aspects of their creator/s, their magic displaying the might of their master.

Dauði: Death in Icelandic Norse.

Dauði Dróttning: 'Death Queen' in Icelandic Norse.

Det som göms i snö, kommer fram vid tö: An Old Norse saying 'What is hidden in snow, is revealed at thaw'. It means that any secrets you have, will be revealed in time.

Draconus Lingua: The language of dragons.

Fae: These magical creatures were born from the magic of the Tuatha Dé Danann. Two kingdoms, the Seelie Court and the Unseelie Court. They are each ruled by a Champion created by the gods; Queen Mab, of the Seelie Court, and King Ruarc, of the Unseelie Court.

Gu leòr: Irish Gaelic for 'enough'.

Gyðja viskunnar: Icelandic Norse, meaning 'goddess of wisdom'.

Hóra: Icelandic for 'whore'.

Hybrids: A half Fae, half human.

Vampire: Stemming from the great Champions themselves, Vampires have their unique ability to regain magical power by drinking the blood of other magical creatures. Pain and suffering can increase the potency of magic, and thus their infamy was born. Extremely cunning, these creatures are known for their prowess in psychological warfare.

Ingarmr: Norse Hell-hounds.

Καλημέρα: Greek for 'Good morning'.

Megálo Kolossaío: A massive and magical colosseum that was designed by Zues and Odin. This arena is where the original Divine Games took place.

μικρός ασβός: Little badger

Otherworld: An alternate dimension existing on earth that Mother Nature, and the gods and goddesses of nature created to give a safe haven to creatures of magic.

Otherfolk: people and creatures that live in the Otherworld.

The Nightmare Court: Held in Castle Fyrkat, it is home to Queen Ragna Valdis Heldóttir, Champion to the Norse goddess, Hel. Located in Idrisid, the capital of Khaviel, which is home to all Vampire-kind.
Theïká Paichnídia: Greek for 'Divine Games'.

Tír na nÓg: The realm of the Seelie Court; kingdom of Queen Mab.

Transmutation: An Alchemist's ability to transform matter into another state or structure through the use of science, energy, and runes.

Vrykolakas: the offspring of an undead vampire and a werewolf. These creatures are cursed with endless hunger, hunting other creatures for their livers.

Were-Kind: Also born from Champions, the werewolves, werebears, werelions, etc. were created by animal gods and goddesses, their forms exemplifying their creators. They gain power through hunting and eating their prey. Fierce and brutal warriors, their strength in battle is unmatched.

Yaldā Night: An ancient festival celebrating winter solstice, or the Longest Night of the Year. It is during this time that all the powers in the Otherworld come together in peace and reenact the Divine Games.

CHAPTER I

"Ms. Melly! Ms. Melly! I can't find Ares anywhere," a child's excited voice broke through my concentration, "but I left 'im the meat scraps from breakfast. I also brought back yer favourite Forfar Bridies from McLean's Bakery. You know, the one by Old Pete's? Got some bread too. Oh, and Zephyr broke the gate... again."

The slam of the front door, a thunk, and a crash had me peeking grumpily through my towers of books. I heard a muttered 'oh shite' and then my skinny, knobbly-kneed burden appeared at the double doors of the library, dusting off the pastry in his hand. Several other brown bags were tucked underneath his arm.

"The five-second rule still counts, eh'?" Toby grinned, taking a healthy bite into the bridie.

Piles of books surrounded me on my perch atop the desk. Many lay open, revealing all the specific bits of information required. Beautiful French windows reaching from floor to ceiling were littered with equations. It was an organised path of literature all around me, the result of several alchemical theories I'd been researching. So close was my breakthrough that my ward's interruption only irritated my already surly nature. Not even Frank Sinatra's crooning notes filling the room could soften my annoyance, especially since going to the bakery had not been on today's agenda.

And I loved Frank.

Slowly, I placed my unfinished book down, replacing it with the steaming mug of coffee next to my knee; my grounding vice and saving grace.

Taking a much-needed sip, I said evenly, "Zephyr could fly out of his corral without issue, Toby, you know this. He is half Pegasus and could summon his wings if he really wanted to. He didn't break the gate. He hasn't broken any gates in over four hundred years."

Gazing over the rim of my mug, I zeroed in on my now shuffling ward. Waiting for him to confess his 245th failed attempt at riding my horse. His neck and ears reddened as the indecision of what to tell me warred across his face. My pointed stare broke his silence.

"Right so, about that Ms. Melly, I am 10 now and I think it's bloody well about time I learned how to ride 'im. I'm almost a man, ya know, and... well-" he stammered, coming to a stuttering stop as my eyes narrowed even more.

"I also don't recall giving you any money to go buy from Mc-Lean's." My tone became sharper, the calm layer stripped off to reveal I was on to him. I placed my mug down meaningfully but was careful not to spill.

Ah, there's the look. The one of the rabbit caught in the snare.

His small face went pale as his shoulders dropped with guilt. Dark, wily curls that went every which way, emphasised his wiry frame. I could see the wheels turning behind those soulful brown eyes as he grappled for an excuse.

I swung my legs off my desk, books toppling over as I stalked over to him, five-foot-two inches of vexation. I am quite average for my kind, but Toby is a Fae hybrid; his human side making him taller than the average Brownie his age, just coming up to my chin.

Snatching the bags underneath his arm, I proceeded to militantly pat down his pockets. Sure enough, my fingers encountered a small gold ring that certainly did not belong to me. I shoved it in his face.

"Care to explain this!?" As my voice rose, I sensed another precious metal calling to me from his back pocket. Toby started to back up, but I grabbed the front of his shirt to keep the little rascal from running. "And you had the nerve to take Mr. McLean's pocket-watch!"

Surprise filled his face. "How did you –"

"Alchemist, Tobias! I am an ALCHEMIST!" I snapped. "I sense elements as keenly as you seem to notice valuables! Gods! So help me Tobias Greenley steal ONE MORE THING –"

"I'm sorry Ms. Melly! I couldn't 'elp it! I just needed to –"

"Not another word, fetus," I hissed, "or I'll transmute you back into the clump of cells from whence you came!"

He clamped his mouth shut, looking down in remorse. Brownies

16

are naturally prone to sticky fingers, as it were, but with him being a hybrid, I had assumed the itch would not be this bad. Clearly, I was mistaken. Breaking him of his kleptomaniacal tendencies continued to be an uphill battle and, on more than one occasion, I debated the ethics in transmuting hands into fin-shaped appendages when we went out into public.

"You," I stuck my finger into his chest, "are going to march straight back down to poor Mrs. McLean and pay her for the bridies and any other baked goods you've pilfered. That woman slaves away making her goods and you treat her efforts with stealing! And I will absolutely know if you don't give Mr. McLean back his watch! So, if you value a peaceful life, child, return it. Though, I suggest doing it discreetly. The man is an avid golfer; I can just see him trying to hit a hole-in-one with his cane and using your head as the ball." I released him with a huff, disappointment clear in the shake of my head. I tossed the baked goods onto a nearby chair. "And give back the damn ring as well. For shame, Toby." I stuffed the ring back into his pocket.

Irritated, I walked back over to my desk and picked up the book I had been sifting through. Toby didn't move. So, after a moment, I sighed dramatically, peeling my eyes away from the pages, only to find a cheeky smile blossoming on his face.

"What?" I snapped.

"So... that means we still get to eat them, right?" I narrowed my eyes at him, having realised he saw the loophole in my demand.

Oh, Great Mother, why hast thou forsaken me to this level of cheek?

Pinching the bridge of my nose, I fought the twitch of my mouth at his cleverness. I'd been had. By a ten-year-old, no less. My pride would never accept visible defeat and I certainly would not be letting him off the hook that easily.

"Get your troublesome arse out that door, young man, before I decide to thrash it too! Or perhaps a bit of time on those bony things you call knees, scrubbing every floor in this house, might finally break this criminal habit of yours, hmm?!"

Brown eyes went wide, and he vigorously shook his head.

"No! No, no. I... um won't happen again, Ms. Melly. Ya 'ave me word."

Your word. Indeed. Until the next time I catch you.

When Toby began to leave, I stopped him, remembering the incident with my horse.

"Oh, and Toby?"

"Yes, Ms. Melly?"

"You'll learn to ride Zephyr when I say you are ready, and not a moment sooner. You are not doing yourself any favours by continuously breaking rules. You are lucky you haven't been stomped to dust with your failed attempts. At this point, you would rightly deserve a good kick in the arse. He's not a normal horse. Remember that." The boy opened his mouth to argue, but thought better of it when he saw my pointed look. "And since you believe yourself so close to maturation, let me tell you something about being a real man – a real man has capable hands. He fixes what he breaks. The tools are in the shed. Once you're done, head on over to the bakery and return those items. Every. Single. One."

"But Ms. Melly, can't you just transmute the gate back to normal? Being an Alchemist and all?"

I looked back at him, my face wistful as it struck me with a memory; one where an eager Alchemist harassed her surly old mentor over silly questions.

"Just because one has the power to do something does not mean one should always resort to it. You must rely on personal skill before you rely on any powers or abilities, Toby. And skill is something one learns through repetition and overcoming many failures. Go fix the gate." I motioned in the air as I pointed out, "At the very least, learning how to repair everything you break will certainly make my life easier." At his eye-roll, I grinned. "Besides, fixing things with your hands instead of stealing with them is a far more productive pursuit, don't you think?"

Walking over to my desk, I pulled open the drawer where I kept several pounds. I knew I'd never see the change, so there was no reason to ask as I handed the money over to him. When he grabbed for it, I held on as a silent understanding passed between us before letting go. Toby folded the money and put it in his pocket.

Eager to get back to my research, I moved towards my desk, picking up several texts from the floor along the way. Instead of the expected sounds of Toby exiting, my ward's presence could still be felt.

The little brat was still here.

My sigh ended with a bit of a growl as I turned to him, cocking my head to the side with the silent question of what? on my face.

He started walking backward, hands behind his back, and replied, "Right but, I mean, the speed at which you fix things is, well, amazin' and it would mean I could run down and pay Mrs. McLean faster... whoa!" Toby dodged the book I threw at his audacity.

He laughed and said, "Yer still a terrible shot Ms. Melly!" Dodging another tome, he made a run for the door. "Okay, alrigh' I'm goin'! Leave a bridie for me too!" Toby ran out the door as another book smacked the door frame, his tinkling laughter echoed through the house.

Cheeky child.

As I watched him fly down the path on his bicycle, a tender warmth filled my heart. For all his mischief and troublesome ways, he still managed to endear himself to me. As he had since the moment he first came into my life.

∀∇ ♂ ☖ ♂° ᔕ°

Three years ago, I was making my way through London, visiting Burlington House on my quest to hunt down some rare texts. I hated leaving my home, my cosy literary paradise with my baker's kitchen and laboratory; the best part being the complete absence of anything that speaks. It rested on the border between the human realm and the Otherworld, somewhere in your Scottish countryside. I'm not one to admit to its location, you understand, as I'm very inclined to my privacy, but suffice it to say it's deep in a forest of my own making and wonderfully concealed from nosy busybodies from either realm.

It was dark, wet, and chilly as I made my way out of Piccadilly station. The cluster of bodies, despite the late hour, only furthered my ill temper. Reaching the main road, I had stopped for a moment, letting others walk by as I orientated myself. My Alchemist staff, a mix of platinum, tungsten and iron, was currently transmuted into an elaborate cane and I leaned on it lest I succumb to the urge to smack someone with it.

Suddenly, I caught movement just beyond my peripherals. A brief, almost imperceptible pressure against my pocket. I snapped my hand out, catching a tiny wrist that was followed by a yelp.

"A bit handsy are we?" I growled.

Ready to unleash a verbal beating, I looked down into big chocolate-brown eyes, filled with fear and panic. The rest of him halted all words as my anger evaporated.

The little boy in front of me was sheer heartbreak.

Underneath the ragged cap were greasy brown curls, falling wildly around a pale face covered in bruising; some were old, tinged yellow, while others were deep purples assaulting his pale skin. A lip that was badly split, and his nose crooked from a break. One eye held a bit of swelling which emphasised cheeks that were sunken in from malnourishment. His jumper and trousers were ripped and dirty, clearly hand-me-downs.

Sudden jerking brought me back to the present.

"Please, I was just jokin'! Let me go! Oi!"

I frowned harder and my grip remained firm. My nails dug into my own palm; it was like holding onto a skeleton. I would have expected to see a child in this state maybe a hundred years ago, but not in this current age of 2021.

"Ya gotta let go, miss! Me mum will 'ave me hide! I won't do it again, I swear it! Please!"

He pulled and tugged, but I couldn't let go as the utter state of him caught me out. As if letting go would render me just as guilty of subjecting him to the fate that no doubt awaited him. I may be a rightful curmudgeon, but I had a soft spot for the weak and broken, the poor and downtrodden.

I closed my eyes and with a deep sigh, I asked, "Boy, when was the last time you had a proper meal?"

He continued to tug and beg.

"Food, boy! When was it?" I snapped.

He stilled. "Um.... a few days ago. But -"

My hand went up and he fell silent. I did not bother asking about his parents as I very much expected they were the cause of his injuries. If they could allow him to pickpocket and beat him like he was their welcoming mat on a spring-cleaning day, then they could deal with me giving this poor child some charity.

I refused to stomach this situation any longer. "Come."

His wrist still in my hand, I began heading towards Steak & Co. Haymarket. Or tried to. He didn't budge. His eyes were glassy and fearful. Socialising was not my strongest characteristic, but showing him that I meant him no harm was a good start. So, I crouched down to his level as I did my best to soften my perpetual frown.

"What's your name?" I asked gently.

"T-Tobias...Tobias Greenley, but everyone calls me Toby, miss." He wiped his nose with his sleeve, sniffling.

"Well met, Toby. My name is Melisandre. Melisandre Von Boden. Now, you tried to pickpocket me, child, and theft is wrong, no matter the reason–"

"You're gonna call the coppers, aren't ya? You're draggin' me there. Please miss, I'm beggin' ya!" Tears started to form again, and I softened my voice even more.

"Shh...shush now. I'm not going to call them. As I was about to say—while theft is wrong, your circumstances are clearly provoking your actions. Your penance will be in the form of eating a nice hot meal and an escort home. So, wipe those tears boy, and follow me." His eyes widened, surprise filling his mottled face.

"R-really?" He sniffled.

I smiled gently and nodded. Jerking my head in the direction we needed to go, Toby gave a shy smile in return and his body relaxed. We took off towards the restaurant where I watched him eat his body weight, and my wallet, in food. All the while chiding him to slow down lest he make himself sick. He was a chatty one, once he felt comfortable. Toby's intelligence also shone through, far too wise for a boy his age.

I learned he was 7 years old and caught somewhere amid 13-odd siblings. His father spent most of his time around the drink and gambling. His mother smacked around the children if she herself wasn't unconscious from drugs. If Toby couldn't bring back anything shiny or useful, he'd be 'dealt with' by his drunk father. The more I heard his story, the more I was less inclined to walk him back home. I wondered if I'd be able to let him even go inside, knowing the abuse would continue.

No dinner would be complete without a bit of ice cream for dessert, and I'll never forget the joy in Toby's eyes when I said yes to his two scoops instead of one. Nevertheless, I could only procrastinate for so long. So, heart in turmoil, we walked towards Toby's flat as he chatted animatedly about what he wanted to eat next. When we arrived, I was not the least surprised by what awaited us.

Toby walked ahead as I lingered in the shadows. Within a moment of nearing the door, it burst open to show a portly and dishevelled man staggering outside. He took a long swig from the bottle that dangled in his grip. A wall of stench smacked me in the nose as he came closer; alcohol and cat piss permeated around him like a cloud. Judging from his bloodshot eyes and the yellow pallor of his skin, his ticket was close to being punched.

"Where tha fuck ya been Toby?" He slurred; Birmingham accent thick as syrup. Swerving a bit, he noticed me. "Bringin' strange bitches 'ome now are ya?" His drunken gaze assessed me, crawling up and down my figure.

I resisted the urge to gag at his approval.

He smirked. "Strange emo bitch, but not 'ard on the eyes. Not 'ard at all. Well..." He let out a chuckle before looking back at his son. Mr. Greenley's expression instantly morphed into anger. "What did ya do? What 'e do this time, the little shit? Always causin' issues!"

He took a step forward and grabbed Toby's scruff.

"No, she's a friend Da, don't call her tha-" the sound of a smack and the shatter of a bottle resounded in the quiet corridor.

I stepped forward.

"Ya made me drop me gin, ya fuckin shit."

Toby curled his body away and his father raised his hand again, seemingly oblivious to my presence. His mistake. Before his fist fell, I held my cane to the man's throat. What his weak human eyes didn't see was the slight transmutation of a blade at the end of it, now pressed firmly into his rapidly beating jugular.

He stiffened. "What tha fuck-"

"Hit him again and see what happens, Mr. Greenley," I said with a deadly calm. Jaundiced eyes were wide as saucers as he shoved Toby away.

He flushed red and spit, "Who tha fuck do ya think ya are telling me what I can do wit me own boy! I'll call the coppers for pulling a knife to me throat, ya fuckin' cunt!"

"Don't waste my time, Mr. Greenley. We both know how that would play out; the moment law enforcement arrives is the moment you would lose your entire family and possibly spend the rest of your waking hours behind bars. Tell me, how well do you think the 'coppers' would take to the sight of your beaten son's face? If I go into your home, how many of your children sport similar bruises and broken bones?" My voice rose, controlled rage mounting with each word.

I could see when he got a good look into my eyes because fear finally formed on his features. My eyes make even creatures from the Otherworld uncomfortable, for they were so strange. One eye was bright molten gold. The other, a striking silver, like tinsel. They swirled, the colours in constant motion of liquid metals. Only true-born Alchemists have eyes like mine. As I am the only one left, they were an impossible sight indeed. The irises were so vibrant that it gave my eyes a haunting glow. Heterochromia at its finest.

Now, while I may have thoroughly enjoyed calling Mr. Greenley's bluff in regards to the police, the attention that would draw if he had followed through left me at a crossroads internally. I was hiding from both realms. The significantly muted imagination from modern humans made it much easier to mask my true race, but falling under the scrutiny of their government was a line I refused to cross. So, I was left with only one solution.

"Unfortunately, I cannot stop you from tormenting the lives you brought into this world. That's between you and your god. However, you will allow Toby to come to me if he ever decides he wants a better life than being subjected to your abuse. I will see to it that he is properly cared for, for as long as he needs a respite." I slammed my cane down, discreetly transmuting the blade back into the solid metal.

I leaned forward, staring down at this deadbeat tub of lard with terrifying sincerity.

"I will know if you've kept him from doing so. I. Will. Know. And by my word, you will rue the day you ever laid a hand on him." Holding his attention, I waited until he nodded his head violently. My face softened as I motioned to Toby to come closer. Red-rimmed eyes looked at my hand warily, then glanced at his father, who moved to stand at the base of the stone steps of their home. The little boy came toward me and sniffled, still holding his cheek, which was red and smarting from his father's slap. I took one of my rings from my right hand and held it up to him.

"As I told your father, if you ever need respite, you come to me." He stared at the ring and then looked at me.

"But...how will I find you again, Ms. Melly?"

The nickname made me smile slightly, and I instructed, "Go to the British Museum and ask for Solomon. Show him this ring and he will contact me; you can stay with him. I will come for you."

He gave a shaky nod and smiled. Suddenly, he threw his arms around my neck, whispering, "Yer an angel, Ms. Melly." But just as quickly, his father grabbed his arm and shoved him inside, slamming the door.

It only took him three days. I do believe I said 'respite', meaning temporary, but the little bugger is still here. So thus began my journey with my troublesome little ward, from whom I never did get my ring back.

If someone told me that I would someday play a motherly figure to a child, I would have laughed in their face and suggested they drink only water from now on. Yet, Toby brought out an unexpected softness in me. Insanity as well, if I were to be completely honest, but somehow, this little boy manages to steal away my heart by the end of each day.

How could I know that this child's actions would set in motion a most epic adventure? Where the lines between life and death, friend and foe, were in a constant blur. A journey that would define us all. Or break us.

CHAPTER 2

For the 823 years I have been alive, sleep was always a struggle. We Alchemists have a mind in constant motion and are burdened with an insufferable desire for knowledge. Sleeping has such a bothersome habit of getting in the way of that pursuit. I am naturally inclined to the night and particularly despise early morning hours. The conundrum of hating sleep but also abhorring the process of waking, was never-ending in the Von Boden residence.

This particular day, the setting sun found me as a small lump in the middle of my bed. Buried amidst a multitude of oversized, deliciously fluffy duvets and an army of pillows, I awoke to voices and the general sound of activity.

Wait, voices? There should only be one voice, I grumbled to myself.

My head emerged from my cave of duvets with a scowl painted on my face. My billowy raven-curls were a tangled sort of chaos, falling past my shoulders to mid-back, brushing against my silk nighty.

"Oh, Melisaaaaaandraaaaaahh!" A singsong voice I knew all too well, called out. "I brought you gifts, sleepyhead! It's almost 7 o'clock! How could you possibly still be in bed? It's an absolute sin."

Elis, who embraced all colours of the rainbow in everything he wore, burst through my bedroom door. I ducked back under, nearly growling at the assault of colour and disgusting cheeriness.

"Oh no you don't!" He grabbed the top cover and flung it away only to reveal a second. "My god woman, how thick is this cocoon!?" He began to frantically grab the blankets until I all but exploded out like a landmine. "Ah, there she is!"

I glared at him as I jerked my robe on, tying the sash.

"What the hell are you doing here, Elis?" I growled.

25

Unfazed, the colourful Vampire grabbed a cup of coffee off my side table and walked over to me.

"How you sleep without suffocating under all that chaos, only the gods can know. Speaking of, I have brought an offering lest you sacrifice me for dragging your adorable little ass to greet the night's eve." He shoved the hot coffee into my hand. "Oh, and by the by–you're nearly out of sugar."

It smelled divine. I glared grumpily at him but took it. The rich scent of coffee with hazelnut and chocolate accents wafted up my nose. Upon exhaling, I let go of all murderous intentions and slowly dragged my gaze back up to him.

Beautiful, colourful, and sinfully devious was my Vampire friend. He was slight of frame, with honey bronze curls perfectly framed around his youthful face. The bright lavender eyes with lashes that would make women weep with envy, always had a twinkle of mischievousness and sharp wit.

Elis was a perfect balance of effeminate and masculine. At first glance, one would take him to be around 26 years of age, not his actual age of 467. He was a young Vampire, lithe and graceful, built like a dancer. Even still, he had a fair bit of height on me compared to my short stature, as most did.

"You still haven't answered me, you annoying ball of happiness. Furthermore, you have efficiently ruined what little rest I was able to glean, you inconsiderate ass," I grouched.

"Did you truly forget what today is? My darling Mels, you were the one who asked me months ago to take our hybrid child on a week-long stint of educational pursuits. The very adventures you implored me to put him through so that he may better understand the world his ancestors came from, remember? Is your age finally catching up to you? Should we get you tested for dementia, Granny dearest?" He laughed as I shot him a look.

Pinching the bridge of my nose, I exhaled. I had forgotten.

"Yes, I'm sorry, Elis. I did forget. I've been wrapped up in research as of late."

"Ah, yes, the never-ending research of Melisandre Von Boden. Honestly, you should just live at Oxford or the British Museum. I'm sure you're considered curio and relic at your age by now," he teased.

"I'll have you know that right now, this cup of coffee is the only thing standing in my way of testing the myth that the only way to slay a Vampire is by beheading, staking, and immolation."

"First of all, there is a reason that is a myth and not fact. Second, you'd have to catch me first, old hag." A dazzling smile filled his face as his eyes twinkled with merriment. Unfazed by my threat, he glided to my wardrobe and swung it open. "One day, my beautiful grump, I just might let you test that theory. Certainly not today, when all of this," he threw his arm out, displaying my all-black wardrobe, "threatens the limits of our friendship and your position in a civilised society. Utter travesty. Every time I come here, my hopes and dreams are dashed at your lack of improvement. This has now become a charity case for poor Toby and saving him from exposure to your horrific sense of fashion. No child should go through this kind of suffering."

I almost pulled a muscle rolling my eyes.

"I have yet to even warm my hands from my coffee and you're already bitching about my wardrobe. Charity case for Toby, eh? If by that you mean you'll pay for all of his clothing then by all means," I lift my mug at him, "alms for poor Toby. Also, feel free to stop coming by. Perhaps then I could get some work done."

He let out a dramatic huff as he rolled his eyes. Not one to give up, he began rifling through my clothes, picking out an outfit for me. I made no move to him. I have tried winning that battle and have come to accept it is not a hill worth dying on.

I sat on the edge of my bed, pondering.

It was upon first meeting Elis and his mate that we discovered my little ward's true origins. I thought it was only fair that I educated him. Toby had assaulted me with questions ever since, questions with answers he should experience instead of being told. It also explained his kleptomaniacal tendencies; Brownies were notorious for their light fingers which is why they preferred to live among humankind where the consequences for getting caught were so much less severe. True to Fae culture though, the Brownies do not see it as stealing, for how is it stealing when you allowed them to take it in the first place? An item easily taken is an item of no value. Or so any respectable Brownie would argue.

They had evolved over time and, had Toby grown up in a Brownie city, he would have learned more control. The last time I was in an Otherworld city, the Brownies had turned to more domestic ventures and worked in households instead of thieving. They also make superb spies, or so Llyr informed me.

Which leads me to the other reason I was asking Elis, a Vampire, to oversee the boy's education; Elis' Chosen Mate, Llyr, was a high-ranking Fae noble of the Seelie flavour. A duke, in fact, of the Summer Court and ambassador between Fae and Vampire courts, no less. Their union was much frowned upon, as both species valued purebloods and, theoretically, intermixing led to weakened bloodlines. For this reason, Elis and Llyr resided mostly in the human realm when Llyr wasn't being called to either court. Llyr himself was an excellent scholar and patient teacher; he would be good for Toby to learn from.

"I'm surprised Llyr isn't with you. His blessed sense of propriety usually keeps you from bursting through my house like a cavalry charging into battle."

"Oh, pish posh, you love it when I visit despite your endless growling. Especially since I bring goodies. Alas, my love was called away to the Vampire court two nights ago. Some issues regarding loose Fae creatures in their forests or some such." He walked up behind me and began fussing with my hair. "These lovely curls on such a grumpy little troll." My hair tightened as Elis spun it around a hair-stick. Once in place, he secured it with a second one. Where he got them, I had no idea, but that's Elis for you.

"There," he said, pulling a strand down the side of my face, "positively lovely. Sans the perpetual glare, of course. Ah, the things I could do with this canvas if you would only let me! Ah well, we make do. Whatever would you do without me, I wonder?" Opening my mouth to tell him, I was quite eager to answer that question, when he quickly shushed me. "No! Not a word! I almost witnessed the end of our friendship as we know it. Now, get dressed while I go help Toby pack and we can discuss the details." With that, he glided out of my room. Vampire speed and silence are quite real, but Elis is nothing but graceful and poised.

I sighed, a hand to the back of my neck as I rolled out the kinks. Begrudgingly, I dressed and made my way to the kitchen, knowing I'd need significantly more caffeine to deal with Elis' abundance of energy. Toby's giggling could be heard from downstairs, followed by Elis' teasing voice. After a few more moments, my friend came down the stairs alone, each step like he was making a royal entrance. Sinking onto one of my rickety stools, I leaned against my counter, taking in his baby-blue silk shirt and cashmere sweater vest.

"Where do you plan on taking him?"

"Just to the town of Glenmorach, on the west boundary of the Summer Court. Llyr did say he had to stop by the Guild of Antiquities for a few manuscripts, but I am quite sure it won't take us too long."

"Isn't that in the capital of Idrisid?"

"Yes? You of all people should be familiar with that."

"That's Vampire territory though." At Elis' look of confusion, I explained, "I haven't been to the Otherworld for centuries and the last place I would go is Idrisid. Just last month you would not cease your insufferable complaining about the political unrest. Not only that, but I've also heard a rumour that the Sickness has spread quite rapidly there."

Many years ago, with the rise of modern religions, the ancient powers were forced to reside in the Otherworld. But forcing gods from different realms into a single dimension could only lead to one thing–bloodshed and destruction. The old gods went to war among themselves. The divine from all earthly religions vied for what power was left after leaving the human realm. Zeus and Odin devised a grand solution in which peace was briefly achieved when Zeus created the Megálo Kolossaío where the Divine Games, gladiator-styled battles, took the place of real conflict instead. Grievances were handled by pitting creatures of legend, Fae versus Were or Vampire versus Changeling, against each other until either first blood or, the popular choice, to the death. Many gods created Champions; warriors created in their image.

Yet, it did not take long for one betrayal, one uprising, to destroy the balance.

During the great and final Battle of Cantre'r Gwaelod, the gods suffered grave losses when their own Champions entered the foray and rose against them in mutiny. Legend says all the divine vanished after that.

In the wake of their disappearance, a strange darkness began covering the land, and a sickness spread. Immortality waned, and those who contracted it lost their sanity, turning into rotting, mindless beasts. I had my theories as to why it had happened, but I kept them to myself.

Nevertheless, it was one of many reasons I avoided the Otherworld and its growing chaos.

The great land of Khaviel, where the shining capital of Idrisid stood, was home to the dark and terrible Nightmare Court. It had well earned its name and, while Elis might be given a pass, I was not inclined to Vampire culture. Hell, I wasn't inclined to the rest of the cultures in the Otherworld, but the Vampire society left me with disdain.

Elis crossed his arms with a sigh, considering my concerns. I went to take another swig of coffee only to find it empty. I glared at the ceramic bottom staring back at me.

"Well as insidious as Vampires can be, honestly it is safer than going to Tír na nÓg; Queen Mab has increased her violence towards hybrids," Elis replied. "Glenmorach is far enough away from there but if we do encounter issues, Toby will be protected by our court standing alone and Llyr has made significant efforts in creating several backup plans in case we misjudged. But Queen Mab isn't going to bother with a little boy, my darling. There is little to fear. We shall not linger more than necessary, I assure you. My queen has employed the best mages in the land to keep the Sickness at bay and, from what I understand, they have been quite successful." He moved to grab my empty cup and began to refill it. With a splash of cream and a drop of sugar, the Vampire held it out to me. "Besides," he said, leaning back against the counter, "the Guild of Antiquities is quite impressive and a perfect place to take an eager young student." He paused, examining his nails, and sniffed. "Even if it is more suited to yours and Llyr's interests as opposed to mine."

I tried to mask the anxiety crawling up my stomach by frowning harder and bringing the mug up to my face. It took me a delayed moment to register that Elis had moved directly in front of me; that sneaky Vampire movement of his. My body stiffened in surprise but relaxed quickly as he rubbed my arms up and down soothingly.

"Look, I may be the Lord of Flowers and Foppery but we both know that I would protect Toby AND you with everything in me. I've got this, Mels. For once, relax."

I sighed, letting go of my pervasive concerns. He was still a creature of the Nightmare Court and that was something. Being the Lord of Flowers may seem laughable but if one knows anything of botany, their beauty often hides their deadly nature.

"Alright, but one day and one day only in Idrisid. I also have some business I must take care of at the British Museum. I expect Toby back in two weeks, Elis."

"You have my word," he said solemnly. Suddenly, he pushed a finger between my eyebrows. "These wrinkles Melisandre! It's a marvel your skin is as smooth as alabaster when you frown so much. I demand to know your secrets, oh grouchy one! Confess your beauty secrets!"

I raised an eyebrow at him, a half-smile forming. "That's rich coming from an immortal. I would think wrinkles are the least of your concerns."

"With a friend like you?" He grinned and winked.

I'd give him that one.

"Yer goin' to the British Museum, Ms. Melly?"

I looked past Elis and saw Toby all packed and ready for his trip. "I am indeed. Solomon needs assistance in restoring some ancient items."

"Oh. Will ya tell him I said 'ello?"

"Of course. Now, before I send you off on your little adventure we must have a wee chat, you and I."

Elis moved towards the door. "I'll wait outside. We will contact you as soon as we reach Idrisid."

Nodding, I watched him take Toby's bag and walk out the door. I turned to Toby.

Before I could begin my prepared lecture, Toby spoke first with a rush of words. "I know, I know, don't steal nuthin' and listen to mister Elis and don't do nuthin' you wouldn't do, or I couldn't tell ya."

Helpless against the grin creeping up my face, I replied, "That's right. More so, Toby, this is your opportunity to learn your history and embrace your roots. As well as to learn some impulse control, hmm? Hopefully, you will meet a nice Brownie Fae who can help you.

"Nevertheless, heed my words, Tobias." I placed my hands on his bony shoulders, staring down at him. "You will see things you could have never dreamed of, both amazing and terrifying. What dangers you thought were in the human realm, are tenfold in the Otherworld. Even words have consequences far greater than you can imagine. Stay close to Elis and Llyr, they will protect you and teach you how to protect yourself. Please be mindful."

"I understand, Ms. Melly. It's alright ya know; ya can tell me you'll miss me."

I chucked my knuckle against his chin and said, "Cheeky thing, you."

With an answering grin, he went to leave but stopped. He whipped around then, small arms linking around my waist. Caught off guard, I hesitantly returned the boy's embrace.

"I'll miss you too, Ms. Melly. It's only for a couple o' weeks. I'll be alright."

There was no time for a response because he quickly let go and, with a smile, bolted out the door. Moving to the kitchen window that overlooked the front, I silently observed their departure. A beautiful Dapple-Grey horse stood still while Elis hoisted Toby onto the saddle, then handed him his bag. After tightening and checking a few bits here and there, Elis gracefully settled behind him, taking the reins. With one last wave, they rode off.

Yes, Otherfolk are still stuck on horseback; iron, anti-Fae, machinery, and all that. Besides, who needs that when you have magic and portals? While I am considered Otherfolk, I cannot do magic. Nor am I affected by the elements as they are, rather I am the master of them. Still, I am partial to horseback, and nothing beats a winged steed.

CHAPTER 3

The house was so quiet. Not that I was complaining at the blessed silence; I could almost weep with joy.

"Now then, best check on poor Zephyr and Ares," I said aloud to myself. "Speaking of which, where is that damned dog?"

Putting on my boots, I headed outside. Inhaling deeply the smells of the forest, I took in the birds chirping and the trees teeming with life. Chickens squawked and ran away from me as I made my way to the stables to check in on Zephyr. The feed on the ground let me know that Toby had at least done his chores before he left.

I looked around, trying to find signs of the massive wolf that showed up at my door two winters ago. Nothing. The trees only revealed three barn owls peering down at me as I made my way to the barn. No doubt keeping an eye out for mice. Strange, though, to see so many of them at this time of day. Yet no sign of the mangy wolf.

Initially, I almost thought to put him down; his sudden appearance while Toby and I were outside made me fear he was stalking us. Toby wanted to pet him right away, but I grabbed the little idiot before he got his fingers bitten off. But when the big bad wolf laid down and began belly crawling toward us, it was clear he was at least mildly domesticated. Thankfully, Ares was gentle and showed no signs of aggression.

He's been here ever since. Just like Toby. I do seem to have this annoying habit of attracting strays...

As I neared the stable, a big black head popped out, munching away. To the human eye, one would assume he was a great Friesian stallion from some epic tale. His origins were a bit more sinister, however. He had wings he could summon at will but, being in the human realm, we trained vigorously to hide them.

"Hello, gorgeous. Glad Toby fed you before he left. Maybe you'll stand still for me this time."

His bulky head leaned down, velvet nose rubbing against my outstretched palm, looking for a treat. I rubbed the side of his sleek face as I gave him several kisses.

"That's my boy."

Zephyr was massive, standing well over seventeen hands, so I grabbed a stool while I was in the tack room. He had been my companion for nearly half my life. An abandoned foal I had come across in my initial escape from the Otherworld. The one nice thing about other-world pets is they don't have that irritating tendency to die as quickly as animals in the human realm.

I was brushing out his mane when a Familiar whine came from outside. I turned to see the wolf in question finally appear.

"Ares, where have you been? Your breakfast is probably rancid at this point." I put the brushes down and went up to him.

He whined again but pushed his nose into my hand. The fur my fingers sank into was soft and thick, if a bit dusty from whatever he had been up to. I scratched the top of his head where he had an intricate white marking, a stark contrast to his midnight fur. Golden eyes gazed up at me with an intelligence that always made me suspect that he was an Otherworld wolf. His past was a mystery, but he'd been a surprisingly enjoyable companion these last two years. It wasn't uncommon for me to wake up snuggled in his fur. I tended to sleep in the middle of my bed and yet somehow, he'd find his way into my little cocoon, making the best pillow. Ares came and went as he pleased but always came back.

The stillness in his large body was sudden as his head snapped towards the dense brush. Letting out a quiet growl as he watched the trees intently. I, too, felt as if I was being watched. Standing slowly, I looked deeply into the darkening forest but saw nothing. Shaking my head, I leaned back down and tried to soothe my wolf. Dismissing any threat, he leaned into my scratches.

"I'm off to London tonight. I need you to watch the house while I'm gone, yeah?" He gruffed and with a lick to my palm, he trotted off in the direction of his food bowl.

I finished brushing down Zephyr and got him ready for the trip. I would only ride Zeph to Old Pete's, a surly old farmer whom I had befriended years ago. He never asked questions or tolerated small talk for that matter, and in exchange, I would fix anything on his farm that needed it.

Walking back into the house, I began to pack minimally. Grabbing my bag, I snatched my staff as I turned to leave but then doubled-back and grabbed my violin; Solomon loved it when I played. The instrument's case was specifically designed so I could hook it onto Zeph's saddle or sling it onto my back.

A small measure of excitement filled me as a picture of whiskey, song, and friendship flashed through my mind.

I had very few friends in either world and Solomon Ives was unique. He was a hybrid of human and satyr, hiding in the human world. Most human hybrids were hunted and killed since mating with a human was taboo. The dangers of Toby's own heritage were not lost on me, but my trust in Elis and Llyr was absolute.

Locking up, I walked to the stable, saddled Zephyr, and away we went. The ride was smooth, if a bit cold, and it was dark by the time we arrived at old man Pete's. After checking in and dropping off a few pound notes to Pete, I walked my way to the nearest station and in no time, I was London-bound.

Eleven hours later, I checked into my hotel. As soon as I was settled in my room, I picked up the phone to call Solomon. Two rings in and the rich bass of his voice greeted me.

"This is Solomon."

"Hello, Sol. It's Melisandre."

"Melisandre! Glad to hear from you. I take it you've checked in at your usual spot?"

"Do I ever change Sol?"

"Ha, I suppose not. Will you be coming in tomorrow? The shipment from the Nile Delta contained some most exquisite finds but was disturbed on the journey."

"Actually, I can come in tonight if it's not too much trouble?"

"Of course not! I'll see you soon then. Oh! Did you bring it?" He asked eagerly.

"What do you think?" I could almost hear his grin through the phone.

"Excellent. See you in a bit then." The phone clicked.

I hung the phone up and grabbed my jacket and cane.

As I neared the door, I noticed two flowers there that weren't there before. Clover and a yellow rose–protection, and friendship. It was Elis; his power of conjuring flowers anywhere was lying on the side table. Flower language was what he used to send messages across the realms.

They had arrived safely, then.

I touched them gently and then out I went, closing the door behind me.

☌♂°☿☌◇⊕

A week and a half later, I was nearing the end of my stay, having helped Solomon restore precious and ancient artefacts from Egypt. Pottery, combs, and even a statue of Bastet, were among the many terrific finds that I was asked to restore. History of all kinds was something I delighted in, and it was times like these I enjoyed myself the most.

I tried my best to avoid transmuting anything, but for some of them, it could not be helped. It would be a greater sin to allow these precious bits of human history to disintegrate into dust. No one would know it was fixed by alchemy, of course. Only I could see the Alchemist mark a transmutation left behind.

Crystal tumbler in hand, Solomon closed his eyes as I played through a gentle version of My Funny Valentine. His deep voice rumbled softly as he hummed along. The song flowed through me, and I let myself get lost in the colours. Reaching the end of the song, my fingers gracefully let off the neck of the violin. The last note, its gentle vibrato, still echoed in the air as I was brought back to reality.

"Ah, I so look forward to this whenever you visit, my dear. You play so beautifully, those dainty hands are perfect for that fiddle," said the satyr, taking a sip of his drink.

If you looked close enough, one could see the stub of horns hiding in his thick curly hair. Warm chocolate skin glowed in the light, his amber eyes mystical. A full beard that would do any Viking proud jutted out from a proud face.

"I should hope so; I've had over three hundred years of practice." I grinned, loosening the horsehair on my bow as I put my violin back in its case. I took a cloth and wiped the rosin off the strings on the instrument before closing the lid gently. "It would be rather pathetic if I was not able to play with a modicum of skill after all this time, wouldn't it?"

"Oh, you play with more than a modicum of skill and you know it." He winked and I laughed, humbled.

"Any news from the Otherworld?" asked Sol, though the keen look of concern told me what he was really wanting to know.

Shaking my head, I told him, "No, other than the Sickness becoming even more rampant. I've asked Llyr to keep me updated on your family but no word since you and I last spoke." My hand squeezed his. "I'm sorry. I wish I had more to tell you."

Disappointment was a quick spark on his face before vanishing under the warm smile that was usually in place.

"It's alright, my dear. No news is good news, as they say. Oh, don't fuss over me, Melisandre; what a mother-hen you are underneath all that prickle," he teased and it rendered a disagreeing snort from me. "You can't fool me. There's a heart of gold hidden in that fortress you've erected; I've seen it. I'll say it now - There is a very lucky man out there somewhere, someone who will sweep you up and make you forget the meaning of being a grump."

The violin case swung to and fro gently as I pulled it off the table after having donned my coat. "Save me from the romantic delusions of satyrs. I have a better chance at finding a unicorn, Sol, and they went extinct thousands of years ago. But if I do find such a specimen," I grabbed my staff as I headed for the door, my friend following politely behind, "you will retain the right to say 'I told you so'."

He opened the door and called after me as I walked out, "I want that in writing, Ms. Von Boden!"

Shaking my head, I called back "Not a chance!". With a hearty laugh and a wave, Solomon bid me goodbye.

Stepping further out into the darkened streets, I was overcome with unease. Though I may be a scientist through and through, over the years I have learned to trust that inner sense. That gut feeling, as it were. And it crawled like a thousand spiders inside me.

Frowning, I upped my pace.

Rushing to the hotel, I ignored the concierge completely, taking the elevator to my room.

My apprehension nearly swallowed me as I neared the door. When I swung it open, the feeling became full alarm. The heavy hotel door clicked shut behind me as I took several slow steps in, surveying the chaos inside.

It was like someone had detonated begonias and rhododendrons.
The meaning of each flower screamed at me.
Danger! Beware!
Amidst the sea of red was a bouquet of purple hyacinths.
Sorrow and regret.
I am sorry.

CHAPTER 4

Ominous foreboding sunk deep, like raw meat in the gut. As if a thousand spiders crawled up my back, the knowledge that something bad happened had me getting on the train back to Inverness without delay. I hit the ground running to old man Pete's where he stood waiting with Zephyr. At the urgency of the situation, I had rung him immediately, asking him to ready my horse at the hour. Pete did not disappoint.

Zephyr knew something was terribly amiss as soon as I sat myself in the saddle, and he sped away like the hounds of Hades chased us. As we neared the forest, a grey mist took hold. I urged him to be faster, coaxing his Otherworld stamina forward.

My heart sped up when I saw the peak of my manor house nearing. Reining Zephyr in slightly, he whinnied and snorted in annoyance and fear; there was a foreign, decaying smell that assaulted the air.

I jumped off him before he even came to a stop, skidding to a halt to see the wreckage of my home. Windows were smashed, papers and random things strewn about the empty space where my front door should be.

Something flitted by, like snow. Holding my hand out, the substance gently landed on my open palm. It was not snow... but feathers. That was when I noticed all the dead chickens strewn about.

Nothing stirred.

Ares! Where was Ares?

My gut clenched in concern, but I had to focus on the possibility of intruders still in my home.

Without taking my eyes off the front entrance, I dropped my pack and unhooked my cane from the saddle. With a small flash of light, I transformed it into a short spear and held it behind me. I walked slowly and silently through the door. I went through the house like this, taking in the destruction. Anything that could be broken, was. Even the walls were blown through, and the floors were cracked.

The moment I knew I was alone, the perpetrators long gone, flames of anger began to trickle through me. Every break, every item out of place fuelled the fire. I slammed my Alchemist staff down in the middle of the floor, the runes on my skin coming to life beneath my clothes. I closed my eyes and imagined all that was, how it should be. I drew upon the circles of change, repair, and time. With a flash of transmutation, a jolt of energy and light, the house was how it should be. All that was broken, fixed. I looked around, the new repairs doing nothing to calm the anger still humming in my veins.

I took a step but then I heard it: a haunting, soul-chilling howl. I rushed to the entryway just to see the dark shadowy figure of my wolf trotting towards me. He was covered in blood and other questionable matter. I reached for him.

"Ares, thank the gods! What happened to you? Are you alright? What do you–Oh, sweet Mother," I cringed as Ares opened his mouth, plopping something onto the palm of my hand.

A finger with a signet ring. Disgust crossed my face.

"That... that is just... foul." Swallowing back bile, I still had to give it to him. "Well, at least you seem to be in good health as that blood is not yours. I cannot imagine what the other one looks like."

It was a potential lead, so I did not gripe further. Removing the ring from the mutilated appendage, I held it up in the moonlight to examine it.

Suddenly, Ares growled so deeply that the hairs on the back of my neck stood. He had moved past me and was snapping violently at the pillar connected to the archway of my house. There was something I had not seen before–a piece of parchment with a dagger through it, blood dripping down in ominous warning.

The blood effect must be magic since the blood would have already coagulated by now, I thought to myself.

Straightening from my crouched position, anger once more built within me. Walking slowly up to it, a flutter of movement had me snapping my attention up to where the gutter met my roof, where a Great Horned owl stared unblinkingly at me. Watching me.

Not to be distracted, I ripped the parchment away from the dagger, quickly scanning its contents. The bottom had a gold and green seal with a black hound in the middle. My breathing slowed to a stop. This could be none other than the Queen of Khaviel's sigil. The Vampire Queen of the Nightmare Court.

The note itself read:

In the name of Queen Ragna Valdis Heldóttir
Ruler of the Khaviel Kingdom, Protector of all Vampire-kind,
Her Royal Council hereby demands the presence of Melisandre Von
Boden
To answer for the crimes of her ward, Tobias Greenley
Against Her Majesty and the laws of Khaviel.
Tribunal is set at the beginning of the first
Quarter Moon.

My heart plummeted. The Vampires had Toby. I ripped the parchment away and crumpled the letter in desperation. Their penchant for torture and suffering made the Inquisition look like a sleigh ride.

They have Toby.

I put my hand up against the pillar, supporting myself, trying to contain my rising panic and dread. According to the summons, I had three days. My fist slammed into the pillar as I cursed loudly.

Every effort into hiding from their world, to be invisible to the eyes of the mystical, was now in vain. I desperately tried to avoid setting foot into the world where the laws of nature and the magic of the Otherworld creatures were constantly at war with each other; a world that wanted nothing more than to enslave me. Control me.

My eyes squeezed shut as I attempted to slow my heart rate. Yet there was no calm to be found. There was no letting go of the ever-present frustrated anger that began to bubble, to fester.

Mel... you cannot let the sins of the past repeat itself. Not again.

An indomitable resolve to protect what was mine, flared to life. I went back inside and headed to my room.

This would not be a legal court session like in the human realm, no fair trial or impartial judge. Sentencing was executed swiftly and without mercy, the verdict never in the favour of the accused. Mediaeval and primitive, Toby's life was dependent on me and my ability to fight for him before the gavel swung in condemnation. There was every possibility he may not make it out alive. Failure was not an option.

I opened my wardrobe and reached into the far back, grabbing a bundle. Clothes I hadn't worn for many years but would serve me now, nonetheless. A black short-sleeved shirt with an opening cut in the centre showing just above my cleavage where several alchemical runes could be seen. The shirt met at my neck and continued upward, covering all the way to my nose so only my eyes could be seen. An under-bust corset-like vest that strapped around my shoulders connecting to the front, went over it. Tight fitting pants slipped under black leather boots, coming to the knee. I snapped my leather utility belt around my waist and right thigh.

On my way to the laboratory, I wondered where Elis and Llyr were in this present predicament. Unfortunately, speculation was all that was left to me. I grabbed several different items for transmutation purposes, putting them in the pouches at my waist. My black cloak with an oversized hood was the last item. Fashion was quite different in the Otherworld but that was the farthest from my mind; my clothes were specifically designed to repel the one element I had no control over–Magic. This was also why I had not sensed the bloody dagger and summons; objects covered in magic were difficult for me to see, let alone sense, and impossible for me to manipulate.

No other supplies were needed. My only goal required me to travel straight there.

I passed Ares in the front yard, who was still sniffing around as if to look for more clues. Grasping the dagger still lodged into my doorframe, I yanked it out. It was a bit small and the blade was ornate, no doubt belonging to the same owner of the ring Ares so diligently took from him. It reeked of nobility. I tucked it into my boot and walked to Zephyr who stood at the ready. Once mounted, I looked at Ares, his golden eyes at attention.

"I'll bring him back. I promise."

Just as I'd turned to leave, Ares trotted ahead, leading the way. A smile tugged briefly at my lips, but then I closed my eyes, remembering Toby's cheeky grin. I breathed deeply and nudged Zephyr into motion.

Hang in there, lad. I'm coming for you.

⚕☉♀☿⊕♀☿

The path to the door of the Otherworld was shrouded in an unnatural fog. It was meant to ward off humans, confuse them, and make them lose their way. It was a path I'd hoped I wouldn't have to take ever again. Ares continued to lead the way. After a time, he slowed.

We were here.

To the naked eye, there was nothing there. Just a path that continued and, perhaps for humans, it would. I brought Zephyr close to the wall I knew to be there, could feel, but couldn't see. If I had been magic-born, like everything else beyond this wall, I could have whispered the incantation to lift the veil. We Alchemists, however, are from a far more ancient line. Only our blood will let us pass. Not wanting to use the dagger infused with magic, I transmuted a sharp point from the metal on my reins, cutting my palm.

I used my blood to draw my own sigil into my hand and press it against the glass-like wall. It shimmered and then parted, revealing a much darker wooded path before it. Ares went first then Zephyr and I followed a short distance behind.

As we passed through, several things happened. To my surprise, Ares almost doubled in size, his true form revealing itself in our natural realm. My previous suspicions of the black wolf being a creature of Other was now confirmed. Zephyr also transformed and I leaned back to accommodate the massive black wings that spread from his shoulders. Zephyr is a Pegasus and thus how his name came to be. Pegasus are typically white, but Zephyr's sire was a Kelpie, a mischievous one at that.

The human realm dampens the essence of magical creatures significantly; once you passed through into the Otherworld, it was like watching a sopping wet dog drying instantly into a fluffy one. Almost unrecognisable. For an Alchemist, passing through the gate was like taking steroids for my senses. I could sense it all, every element of everything. It called, no, sang to me. Shutting my eyes, I felt the wind whipping past me. A steady breath helped as I tried to adjust to overwhelming sensations. It had been so very long. My senses were so much more acute here. Like I could reach out and touch the heartbeat of Mother Earth herself.

It was empowering.

Zephyr's wings flapped in excitement but I reigned him in, patting his neck. "No flying tonight, Zeph. I cannot chance being caught by a gryphon or wyvern patrolling the skies. We stick to the ground until daybreak. Onwards Ares! We must hurry!"

The wolf howled, bolting down the path. Zephyr took no urging to follow, forcing me to squeeze my knees around the saddle as I held on tightly. While there were dangers in the sky, the ground was no more safe.

We continued well into the night. Haunting wails, screeches, and keening screams in the distance chased us in the darkness. The brush was so thick it was impossible to see into the wood, the trees overhanging as if attempting to cage us in. I kept a close eye on any movement towards us, but I knew Ares would hear danger far before me and trusted him to act accordingly.

Finally, we reached a breakthrough on the path leading into an open field. Immediately my attention went skyward to its star-studded canvas. Three moons lorded over the realm. Only afforded a moment to enjoy their beauty, Ares howled, breaking from the path and headed through the field, dipping back into the woods, with Zephyr and I right on his heels.

Further in, I felt it. Water.

The trees broke away, revealing a large lake. The water was so still, the stars reflected on its mirrored surface.

"Good thinking boy. We'll take a quick rest here, eh?" I hopped off Zephyr, who let out an excited whinny and trotted over to the water. He began making a lot of high-pitched sounds and splashing, his Kelpie half eager to be near the lake.

"Dammit Zeph, keep it down! You're worse than Toby! You'll bring a damn mountain troll on us at this rate. A quick rest and then we're off again. No playing! No!" I said sternly, finger pointed at him like any irritable mother. He snorted and shook his head, stomping his foot in the water but quieting down.

Rolling my eyes, I took my Alchemist staff and transmuted it into a metal whip and wrapped it into a coil. Hooking it to my belt, I stretched and plopped down on the bank. Ares also took a quick drink but then moved to scout the area around us. Breathing deeply and taking a moment to slow my mind, to finally allow myself to enjoy the night sky.

Ares came back, bumping into me before plopping down beside me. He dropped a stick full of goji-like berries on my lap before resting his heavy head on my knee. I curved my arm around him and kissed the white mark.

"Look at you, taking care of me. Thank you, sweet boy."

The berries were a burst of sweetness in my mouth as I enjoyed the warmth of the wolf curled up against me in the cool night breeze. After a time, I started to feel anxious to set off again. Stretching from my former pose, I suddenly froze as a teeth-rattling roar resounded behind me.

It all happened too fast.

Only just grasping the handle of my whip, something ungodly strong grabbed me around the waist and legs before I could turn around. With an 'oof', the breath was knocked from my lungs. The world swung and spun.

"Ares!" I shouted, struggling in its hold.

Ares' vicious growling and snapping seemed distant and Zephyr flew off in a panic. I tried to turn in the steel-tight grip only to be thrown from it and into the wood. I went airborne, trying to unfurl my Alchemist whip, waiting for the crunch of impact against my back.

Time slowed and I could see it now - a massive forest golem.

Before I could question who created the damn thing, I collided with something hard... and warm. A masculine grunt followed. My breath was again knocked from me, but strong arms wrapped around my torso, holding firm at my waist and chest. The pressure on the front of my neck that kept me from whiplash was a large gloved hand, one I grasped with my own.

We slid backward from the momentum, but he held fast. I knew he towered over me because my feet were dangling like a child's. Warm breath tickled the shell of my ear. The hood of my cloak had come down, and my long hair had come loose during the chaos. The strength of him made me feel incredibly small.

A rich timbered voice that reached the depths of me asked, "Are you alright? Are you hurt?"

Goosebumps exploded over my skin at the barest feel of his lips as he spoke, and a very strange feeling of rightness came over me. As if this was exactly where I should be. My own nature took over as suspicion rose up in lieu of it.

What is this feeling?

"Y-yes," I gasped, still trying to catch my breath from colliding with him.

Another roar came and the stranger's arms tightened around me. My gaze shot to see Ares dodging and then lunging toward the branchy golem, taking a chunk of bark-like flesh from its arm. It roared again and smacked the wolf away. My body jerked reflexively. Then the golem turned and looked at us. My eyes widened as it began to charge.

The stranger set me down, pushing me slightly behind him, and ordered, "Stay here!"

He drew a longsword that was so bright it was almost blinding in the darkness. Instantly, I knew the metal was not of either realm; I would have sensed it and it made this stranger even more intriguing. And suspicious. I could not see his features, as he too was cloaked, and the large hood masked his face.

Yet, if he thought I was going to stand back and watch, he was poorly mistaken.

He became a blur of speed as he met the charging oaken golem. The brilliant sword arced, the golem roaring as its arm went flying. It reached for him with the other. He ducked, slicing the creature at its knees, causing it to fall. Piercing through its back and all the way through its chest, the tip glowing incandescently.

My eyes widened when I watched the sword burn brighter as the golem began to shrivel and shrink, its magic leaching into the blade. When the creature was nothing more than a husk, the man smoothly yanked the sword out and the monster turned to dust.

The stranger turned sharply, just in time to see a second golem crashing in. Its roar pierced the air as it backhanded the man, who went flying. He landed with surprising grace. Readjusting his stance, he readied for the oncoming attack. Multiple rumbles echoed behind. Three more golems had joined the onslaught.

I had no idea what he was capable of handling, but I wasn't willing to wait around to see how skilled he was. Throwing my cloak to the ground, I flicked the length of my whip out. A thunderous crack struck the air as I snapped it above me, walking forward. The forest became still at my command, and then the energy of life began to buzz.

I had nature's attention.

The earthen monsters turned to me and roared. Branchy trunks hit the ground in agitation as they smashed the foliage and trees around them, but they made no move toward me. Even mindless golems could recognize who had power here.

Cracking the whip again and raising my arms in a challenge, I continued walking towards them. Another echo of roars and then they started to charge.

"That's it," I whispered, "Come play."

When magic goes wrong, feral golems are born. Or oftentimes, when a magic user has too much magic, they store it in these creatures made of organic materials. But those golems are tame and controllable. Feral golems were wild magic, extremely unpredictable and violent; but they were still made of elements that I could control.

"What are you doing? Stay back!" The stranger shouted.

I ignored him, transmuting my whip back into a staff.

Just as the golems were about to close the distance, I swung my staff into the earth. A huge transmutation circle activated beneath them. Spears of light shone, stopping the golems in their tracks. In a flash, an earthen cage of stone and iron wrapped around them, imprisoning them. They roared with rage, struggling against their confines.

I put my hands out, targeting the iron, then shoved my hands together by linking my fingers. The iron responded to my command, forming stakes that went through the golems. They screamed.

The stranger walked slowly up to the trap. I also approached, never taking my eyes off the golems.

"Do you know what elements make up the majority of trees?" I asked, getting closer and closer to the roaring, struggling wild magic. The stranger looked at me but said nothing. "Carbon, hydrogen, and oxygen. Basic but oh-so-useful." I stopped, unflinching at the enraged monsters within. "And do you know what that can become with just a little bit of adjustment?" I asked him once more, reaching out to touch the nearest golem. The man thrust his hand out as if to stop me but froze when I pinned him with my stare. "Fire."

My fingers touched the rough bark of the nearest golem. Lighting up, the symbols on my skin flashed as the golems were consumed in a roaring blaze of flame. The stranger jumped back, staring at the caged bonfire as he slowly sheathed his weapon.

The flickering firelight illuminated him, giving me a little more detail of his visage. He was tall, well over six-foot, I imagined. Though, from my perspective, once someone is over six feet, it's all the same.

The black hood of his cloak covered most of his face. He looked built for battle, all leather and sword and daggers. His shirt sleeves were rolled up, hands were clad in black leather gloves cut at the wrist. There was no crest or symbol to indicate who or where he'd come from.

"Are you alright?" I asked, the irony of our reverse positions not lost on me.

His head turned to me then and while I could not see the upper part of his face, the lower part suggested he was quite handsome. There. There it was; that strange pull once again, a distant song calling me.

He walked closer and before I could react, he took my chin between his fingers and thumb, pulling my attention to his shrouded face. The strength of his arm was a strong pressure at my waist, pulling me against him. My normal distaste for being touched by strangers was nowhere to be had, nor was my typical snappy bite at my personal space being invaded without invitation.

I was so taken aback, defenceless against the strangeness of what was happening. Confusion at my own reaction and disbelief at my inability to comprehend this pull to him, rendered me motionless. Unable to do more than place my palms against his chest and let the moment unfold.

I could see his lower face clearly now. A straight, strong nose. Full lips. The closely trimmed beard along a strong jaw. A peek of sun-kissed skin.

That mysterious pull morphed into a low thrumming, the closer this cloaked stranger and I were. Fascination and unease crept around in my mind, one warring with the other.

"Beautiful." His voice was a velvet rumble as the soft leather of his gloved thumb stroked my cheek.

All the breath left my body. Engulfing me with his presence, my eyes locked on his mouth as he spoke.

"Not in all my years have I seen eyes such as yours." He leaned closer. "How I have longed to see them up close."

I looked up at him questioningly.

What an odd thing to say... Had we met before?

"I'm sorry, have we met? Who are you? How do you know me?" I was met with an annoying bout of silence. Instead, I felt his finger hooking on the fabric that covered half of my face, pulling it down slowly. My breath caught in my throat. "Wait—"

Voices called out in the distance. We both started, and his arm tightened around my waist. Looking back down at me, I saw the muscles in his jaw tighten as if he was reluctant to let me go, when he suddenly released me. Finally feeling as though I could breathe again, I took advantage of it, exhaling deeply.

He stepped back. "I fear our time together is up, my lady. Thank you for your assistance with the golems; the Fae have been releasing many of them into this territory. We have been hunting them for the past week, but they continue to prove to be a nuisance. The spreading sickness is no doubt at work here as well. I would tell you to stay safe but after what I just witnessed; I should probably save that warning for the golems themselves." The corners of those full lips curled upwards slightly and, tilting his head, he reached up to touch me again. Gently, he dragged his hand down my cheek. Butterflies tickled every part of me. "I will dream of these eyes as sure as us meeting again. Be careful, my lady, and keep watch. There are creatures in these lands far more powerful than golems that seek more than your demise."

With that cryptic message, he turned and disappeared into the night. I stared into the darkness, and then back at the flames still blazing. At least two minutes passed before the reality of what had transpired hit me, my face falling into my hands.

What... just happened? What the bloody hell was that?! What did he mean? He... Who? Why...? I'm on Vampire land so he must have been... Oh, Great Mother take me! Pull yourself together Melisandre!

My thoughts became chaos and my embarrassment drowned me, but a suspicious warmth still brewed within. I shook my head, clapping my cheeks hard enough to leave red before picking up my cloak and staff. I had no time for thoughts like this. There was a troublesome brat to save from a vengeful Vampire queen. Getting flustered by some tall, mysterious stranger was nothing but a distraction I couldn't afford.

Ares padded towards me, probably just having revived from the blow he took from the golem. I looked up and saw Zephyr in the air and called him to me. He glided down and landed, prancing around and nuzzling me as if checking to see if I was wounded. I caught his bridle, steadying him as I rubbed his nose and made calming sounds to him. Looking over both, neither seemed worse for wear. Zephyr nudged at me.

"I'm fine Zeph, it's okay. Let's go. No rest until we reach Idrisid. We cannot risk another delay."

I hopped on his back and away we went. It had been over 400 years since I had been to the Vampire capital, but I could never forget where it was. We galloped towards the rising sun; the memory of the stranger tucked away deep within my mind.

CHAPTER 5

Dusk was setting by the time the sparkling towers of Idrisid came into view. I tugged my hood over my head. A massive stone bridge, miles long and wide enough to fit an entire brigade marching through, connected the city to the outside. The mighty Sanguine River roared underneath. The setting sun's light sparkled along the water, adding to the shine of the already twinkling city. It would be breathtaking if it weren't for a ten-year-old's life hanging in the balance, pushing me forward.

Deceptive beauty hiding untold horrors was the main castle that stood high above the massive city below. Its huge, spired towers reached for the heavens, their points like the sharpest of blades. Proud flags displayed the monarchy well—black, gold, and green banners with a stark image in the middle: Queen Ragna's sigil of a black hound with flaming green eyes. It had two screaming skulls on either side of its head, each of them with swordlike incisors. The hound itself had one skull in its mouth, consumed by green flame. The Norse symbol for the goddess Hel encircled all of it.

As we neared the city gates, they eerily began to open.

They were expecting us, was among many of the grim thoughts that scuttled across my mind.

We hurried through, not slowing for a moment. Winding and weaving through the empty streets. Only merchants and shopkeepers were about, setting up for the coming night as we made our way to the castle. The town would come abuzz once nightfall set.

I pulled the fabric on my face over my nose, securing it.

The castle parapets came into view and the embers of purpose began to blaze in my chest.

Zephyr's hooves pounded the cobblestones as we rushed through the castle gates, passing the guards standing at attention. No one made a move to stop us.

Nearing the castle's main courtyard, I reined Zephyr in and stopped him in front of the steps to the great hall. A row of guards and footmen stood waiting, along with what appeared to be the castle's steward. His livery was a vibrant blood red with gold brocade and immaculate. Posture impeccable.

I hopped off Zephyr as the footman took hold of his reins. My steed flared his wings in agitation at the predators before him, but settled when I patted his neck.

"Lady Von Boden, we have been expecting you. I am Oweyn, seneschal to Her Majesty. Welcome to Fyrkat Castle, home of Her Majesty, Queen Ragna Valdis Hel–" I grabbed my alchemical whip from the saddle with a snap, the tip cracking into the air and sharply cutting off his irritating welcome speech.

I began coiling my whip to hook onto my belt as I said brusquely, "I am quite aware of who presides over this castle, Oweyn. If you would?" I gestured for us to move forward.

The shock at my abruptness was quickly masked with the typical haughty but controlled look one would expect a steward of a castle this size would have. His lip twisted with disdain as he nodded curtly to Ares behind me.

"I'm afraid the... wolf will have to wait outside."

I looked back at Ares, who was on the verge of charging any of the Vampire guards surrounding us, their spears partially lifted off the ground in anticipation. His massive head bared teeth and he growled so deep, it resonated to the bone. He was Fenris in the flesh and the air sizzled with tension. Golden eyes flicked to mine, and I gave him a curt but reassuring nod. He snapped several times but backed down and followed Zephyr as the groom led them away.

"I must also request that the lady relinquish all weapons and instruments that could be considered a danger to the court."

Oweyn gestured towards the guards, who suddenly pointed spears at me just as one stepped towards me. I reached for my whip and transmuted it into its natural state of a staff. Twirling it around me defensively, I slammed it down.

"That will not be necessary, Oweyn, as I carry none. I am here by order of Her Majesty, and I would strongly advise you not to delay me further for I will be going in there," I said through gritted teeth, "whether it's by mutual understanding or me stepping over your headless corpses. Choose." We held each other's glares unflinchingly until the steward made a small sound and looked away.

"This way, my lady," Oweyn sneered as he whipped around and began marching up the large castle steps. I followed him up and through the archway leading to the great hall. Four guards fell into step behind us. My back itched at their presence, but I kept my attention forward.

Yet, despite the perilousness of the situation, I could not help but look up and take in the splendour that was Palace Fyrkat. The granite arches and brilliantly painted ceilings in the great hall were a wonder to behold. The room was so spacious that there was no doubt several fully grown dragons could fly around with little effort. It seemed the entire place was built with granite, limestone, and marble floors. Massive tapestries with epic battle scenes, and emerald and metallic gold rugs and furniture filled the room; the Queen's colours.

This palace was filled with thousands of years of history, and it showed even in the smallest details. Vampire culture was hard stuck in ancient traditions which explained why even the lighting was still in the form of huge bronze braziers atop stone pillars, some hanging by great chains and wall sconces.

Brownie servants were quiet and swift, doing their best to remain unseen. Courtiers milled about by tables, some sitting and lounging and posing, as if for an artist. Ministers and scholars were gathered in small groups; their heads bent, deep in discussion. As we passed, those that looked up and noticed us either went completely silent, staring in shock, or quickly began whispering behind cupped hands.

As we reached the end of the hall and the large wrought iron doors leading to the throne room came into view, I began to steel myself for what was to come. Four more guards stood at the door. Oweyn stopped suddenly and turned to me.

"This is where I leave you. I strongly advise you to not keep her waiting," he hissed my own words back at me. Without so much as a bow, he just vanished as Vampires are apt to do.

Putting thoughts of transmuting him into an ashtray aside, I looked straight ahead as the guards opened the doors.

Big breath, I said to myself as the grip on my staff tightened, gathering the courage to step towards a dire but unknown fate.

Like the great hall, the throne room was enormous with a gleaming marble floor streaked with gold and black veins. Colossal granite pillars lined the path to the throne and chandeliers seemed to float in the air as if held there by magic. Great iron braziers blazed along the walls. The room was full of mystique and splendour, mystery and shadow. The chatter and buzz of Vampire nobility filled the room. Their haunting beauty barely concealed the dark predatory nature that lurked so close to the surface.

I walked with purpose, such purpose that my cloak billowed behind me and my staff echoed in the room with each step. Heads turned to me and those in my path began moving quickly out of the way, glaring and baring teeth at my intrusion. I could hear the whispered insults and stares, but I paid them no heed.

Suddenly, the pathway cleared and there she was—Ragna, Vampire Queen, sitting on a solid gold throne. A Champion of the gods.

The pure obsidian throne was curiously vacant beside hers. She wore a blood-red gown with an elaborate gold brocade bodice and what appeared to be matching gold fur along the neckline. The skirt had a slit all the way to her thigh, revealing strong and shapely legs. Black diamond-studded stilettos glinted, like the obsidian throne next to her. She sat idly back yet still was the epitome of regality. Her blonde tresses were perfectly situated and braided to hold the elaborate spiked bone crown on her head. The crown itself was encrusted with rubies and diamonds with gold accents.

Every bit of her was painfully beautiful, majestic, and terrifying. She was the perfect combination of the modern and old world; both in dress and power. Above her throne were twin battle axes that were mounted in front of a large tapestry which depicted a graphic scene of the goddess Hel surrounded by the dead.

Suddenly, I felt an ache in my bones and my skin tingled and buzzed like a thousand spiders crawling over me. While I could not use magic and was typically insensitive to its presence, her power overwhelmed me. She was ancient; magic so old that the mind could barely comprehend. My discomfort only fuelled my anger, my resolve. I stood fast, allowing no waning of confidence as I approached her.

Several nobles and advisors stood beside the queen. The closest whispered in her ear; she smiled wide enough that I caught a glimpse of fang.

Guards standing at the bottom of the steps tensed as I approached, so I stopped, landing my staff rather loudly and purposefully. The sound echoed loudly in the hall, announcing my presence. The entire room went silent and stilled. In a deliberately slow motion, the queen looked at me, a knowing smirk on her face. She was aware the moment I had entered her domain, yet only now deemed to gaze upon me. Glittering emerald eyes bored into mine, her ageless face sculpted by the angels themselves.

"Ah, the mysterious Melisandre Von Boden has arrived." Her voice was liquid gold and threatening. She leaned forward, her eyes narrowing as she took in my shrouded appearance. "Mysterious indeed. Smaller than I expected. Tiny, really. The way your ward spoke of you, well," she scoffed, "I expected...more. Oh, did I say 'spoke'? I meant screamed." She leaned back, a vicious smile on her face, "The young ones always crack so easily."

While a deep dread for Toby sliced through me, I didn't rise to the bait. It was better to lie in wait, waiting for your enemy to make a mistake before striking.

"My informants were certainly not far off the mark in their information about the lone Otherworld creature hiding in the human realm, so close to the Veil. How intriguing it was when the darkness whispered to me of a woman with the strangest eyes meeting with one of my own. Even more so to discover a very interesting phenomenon that seems to occur around you, Lady Von Boden. One that used to be considered the stuff of legends. One that should. Not. Be." A gold-manicured finger tapped on the armrest of her throne with each of the last words. Her stare intensified, as if trying to peel away the layers with her eyes alone.

I had no doubt she could hear my elevated pulse, the drum in my chest. My eyes narrowed but I remained silent. How foolish I was to not consider Elis' position and how it could expose me. He tried to involve himself so little in court affairs that, I think, not even he calculated it would catch the attention of his monarch, subsequently tying him to me.

"In fact, my most trusted spy would not cease in talking about the woman who had one eye that was platinum silver, the other pure gold. 'They were so brilliant that they shone in the dark,' he said. There was only one creature in all of Otherworld's history that was ever reported to have eyes like those. Do you know of this?" She asked, raising an eyebrow at me.

I made no move to answer, waiting to see the verbal trap unfold that she was attempting to snare me in.

"This creature belonged to a race that had incredible mastery of the elements. Not magic, no. Something more," She paused, searching for the word, "organic. These beings had the power of Mother Nature herself. Some say that they had the power to change lead into gold and even bring the dead back to life. That they could control time itself with a mythical stone. And yet," She cocked her head at me, "They were a mysterious people, never leaving their Citadel and severely limiting trade or interactions with the outside world. Suddenly, several hundred years ago, they just disappeared. Presumed extinct. Not a single sighting since. Even so... I wonder..."

Queen Ragna's look changed, like the cat who noticed there was a bowl of cream. Thankfully my face was hidden, so she could not see how deeply I frowned. Unease so great that it was a pile of snakes in my gut. I had been found out, it would seem. She was just waiting for me to admit it. This is the game that both Fae and Vampires play; herd you, ensnare you, break you.

The Fae were powerful in elemental magic. Their politics were deeply rooted in old laws and duels, rites, bargaining, and ceremonies. Vampires were the masters of the psyche, the body, and nightmare. They lived for the intrigue, the mental prowess of surviving The Game. Battle was a mental art form, done by seeing who could break the other's sanity and willpower first.

While their powers manifested physically, many had abilities that could break your mind like a quail's egg; they would do it so subtly that you would not know what happened until it was too late, and you were nothing but lobotomized flesh. I was an Alchemist who had neither the time nor patience these immortals had. It was plain to see where this conversation was headed, and I was having none of it. Refusing to be baited, I would not dance to her tune.

Reaching down to my boot, I took the dagger, which was still magically covered in fresh blood, and tossed it towards her. It landed with a loud clatter, the echo bouncing off the walls of the room. The queen's eyes darted to it, narrowing. The guards around her tensed, waiting to intervene.

With all the sophistication of a fishwife when rent was due, I snapped, "I am here for my ward, Queen Ragna, not petty small talk. Do not waste my time. You have accused him of a grave offence. I have come to answer for it. Where. Is. He?!"

Several gasps and hushed whispers rippled around the room. A wicked grin crossed her face even as a dangerous glint of malevolence danced in her eyes.

"A woman who strikes at the heart of things. How refreshing. Alright, lady Von Boden, I will allow your insolence for the moment. Something tells me the truth behind your origins will be coming to light sooner rather than later. And I do so hate waiting." With the promise of that threat in her eyes, she motioned to what I assumed was the captain of her guard. "Bring the accused before us!"

She made another hand motion and Oweyn suddenly appeared beside her. He leaned down and the queen whispered something to him I could not hear.

The doors to the right of the throne opened and the sound of chains and cries filled the room. Toby was dragged by a massive guard, Elis stumbling behind him. I thanked the gods for my hood and the fabric covering half of my face, hiding my pained expression. Their clothes were ripped and bloodied, and bruises marred Toby everywhere. His right hand was almost blackened, shaking badly. One eye was swollen shut.

Oh Toby, my sweet boy...

My heart clenched at the sight of him. I was not surprised but it didn't make the state of them any less distressing. I had no doubt Elis had seen to his own beatings, but Vampires healed faster than hybrids. Also, his position in court probably kept him from seeing the worst of it. Elis being Elis though, I would not be surprised if he sweet-talked his way into gentler treatment. As it was, he was scuffed and pale but otherwise visibly unharmed.

His violet eyes widened at the sight of me and gasped my name before he was shoved to my left and to the side with Toby. Both were thrown to their knees before the throne.

Toby finally looked up and saw me. Desperation filled his face as he struggled to get to me, tears running down his face.

"Ms. Melly please I'm so sorry I didn't mean–Ah!"

The guard smacked him, "Quiet!"

I made no move towards him, lest I incite the queen's wrath, but every fibre of my being was torn between reaching out to him or killing his guard first.

"Elis! My sweet Elis!" A desperate cry and the crowd parted.

A tall Fae with long fiery-copper hair pushed through, stopping at the sight of his chained and dirty mate. Llyr, Fae noble of the Summer Court and a favourite ambassador of High Queen Mab, covered his mouth with his hand and began taking a step forward. I held my staff out in front of him, warning him to remain where he was. Llyr would not have been imprisoned due to his political status but I had no doubt he was beside himself.

Llyr grimaced, looking back at Elis and then at me. I gently shook my head, pleading with him. His olive green and gold eyes darted to his mate once more, face littered with emotions.

After a moment, Llyr straightened his shoulders as the mask of Fae nobility fell into place. I could tell he was about to address the queen, to plead his case for Elis, but I stopped him by speaking first.

"Your majesty," I began, swinging my gaze back to the throne, "Elis had no part in this beyond my request of his assistance in the boy's education. Whatever fault you believe he had in not controlling my ward lies with me in not preparing him adequately. He has no fault here and should be released."

The queen raised an eyebrow, "The boy was in his care when the crime was committed. He almost left the capital. I fail to see how negligence and ignorance excuse him from liability."

"You have yet to state what my ward is being accused of. What possible crime would warrant the life of a child and the life of one of your own ambassadors?" Anger finally took over the queen's face and for the first time, I felt a sliver of fear.

Slamming her hand down on her throne, Ragna cried, "Theft! Thievery, Lady Von Boden!" A damning finger pointed at Toby, "He stole a ring of power, Lord Abhartach's ring! One of the Twelve! Just to touch any object of power belonging to a Champion is a thousand years of slavery!"

The breath left my body and my stomach landed somewhere in the seventh layer of hell. I closed my eyes. I assumed he'd steal something; it's always stealing. How he even got his grubby hands on something so powerful, so rare, I couldn't fathom. To steal from a Champion no less...

Oh, gods. Oh, by the fucking gods this is bad.

The Twelve were the great houses of Vampire royalty. All were created as Champions for the Divine Games. It was how they absorbed their magic that differentiated the races; Vampires by drinking the blood of their victims, Were-people by eating them, and so on. As Champions were created and not born, magic was the very thing which kept them functioning. According to the history books, of course. Items of power acted like a catalyst; a tool given to these gladiators to absorb magic more efficiently.

Lord Abhartach was created by none other than the Celtic deity and leader of the Tuatha De Danann, Dagda. To steal from Abhartach was to steal from the great god himself.

The possible outcomes of this suddenly became far grimmer. My goal of whisking Toby away to freedom, died swiftly. Now, there was nothing left but to pray we lived through this.

I knew better but I still had to ask, "And you have proof of this crime?" Ragna glared at me, a clear warning I was treading on thin ice with her patience.

One of her advisors stepped forward, nose turned upward. His voice was as condescending as his glare. "As soon as the ring was taken, Lord Abhartach awoke prematurely from his thousand-year slumber. All relics of power are left in the care of the Guild of Antiquities until they are reawakened once more. As the ring is tied to Lord Abhartach's soul, he was able to locate it almost immediately. It was found in the possession of your ward who was close to crossing into Seelie lands. It has cost the lord's house greatly at this interruption, offsetting the balance of power between houses!"

I caught movement and saw Elis jerking at his chains leaning towards me, his lavender eyes frantic and stark against his pale skin. "I swear to you Mels, I had no idea! I would never have allowed us to leave! I never left him alone! I have no idea how -"

"SILENCE!" bellowed the queen.

All eyes focused back on her. Something did not sit right with me, something was missing. Still, my first goal was to get Elis released before I focused on getting Toby out of this with his life.

"Your majesty, there is no possible way Elis would ever have allowed Tobias to steal something so important and attempt to run away let alone use the boy for something so nefarious. Between his family's political standing, their nobility, and that of his mate, it would defy logic that he would jeopardise that over a relic he cannot even fathom using. He's more likely to run off with one of your gowns before he takes a ring of power that he has no hope of wielding."

Some soft snickers could be heard at my last statement.

I would apologise later for using his own lack of power later and foppery but right now, it was his strength.

With confidence, I laid my own trap. "Even still, Elis is mated to a noble of the Seelie High Court. Would you risk open conflict when Yaldā fast approaches?"

The queen scoffed. "Even Queen Mab would not fault me for punishing the mate of one of her own for this. Elis may have concurrent standing in both courts but he is still one of mine. His life is mine to take as I see fit."

From the corner of my eye, I could see Llyr's breath hitch. Elis stayed completely still, waiting to see if the axe would fall.

Time for the finishing blow. "Yet we both know Queen Mab would use this as the opportunity she has been looking for to break the peace. Killing Elis is a death sentence to Llyr; an invaluable asset to her court. You would be handing her the war she has wanted on a silver platter, and you know it."

While I may have been living in a self-imposed exile and in hiding, I was not ignorant of the politics between kingdoms. I made it my business to know; as they say, keep your friends close and your enemies closer. Even I knew the importance of Yaldā, the longest night of the year. A neutral time when all the primary kingdoms came to celebrate, negotiate treaties and trades, and hold a court of justice. Where each court could openly spy on the other. It was also when the re-enactment of the Theïká Paichnídia, the Divine Games, took place; where the kingdoms would choose their own Champions to fight for glory and, sometimes, to the death.

To incite conflict so close could lead to open war, destroying the tradition. That simply was not done.

The queen's eyes narrowed, boring into me, her power making my skin crawl. She looked at me like she was seeing me for the first time. The Norse Queen underestimated me; her arrogance would be her downfall. I felt now the game had truly begun.

Ragna clicked her tongue and motioned to the guard. I released the breath I was holding. Elis pinned me with a look that held a thousand words of gratitude while the chains were released. He leaned down and whispered something to Toby, probably encouragement, kissing his head before he stood shakily.

As he made a move towards me and Llyr, Ragna's words froze him.

"Your mate's position in court and the cunning words of your friend may have freed you this time, Elis son of Taranath, but you are still of my court. You are but a fledgling, your pretty flowers and little thorns are easily crushed. You would be wise to remember that." He bowed low and when the queen waved him off, he backed away slowly, head still bowed in deference.

When Elis was about a foot from me, he straightened and turned. Exhaustion pulled at his face, along with a thousand unspoken words, but he merely brushed his hand against my shoulder before going to stand by his mate. I could only hope we would have time to speak later. If we survived it.

I turned my attention back to the queen.

"As for the actions of my ward, I would beg mercy for a child who only just recently discovered his Brownie heritage. Had he grown up in a Brownie village, he would have learned to control his impulses by now. Tobias grew up in the human realm, having no knowledge of the customs or even the creatures he's related to. This crime was committed while trying to educate him. Not. Premeditated." I emphasised.

One of her ministers stepped forward, shouting angrily down at me.

"Justifiable ignorance, is it? Stupid girl! Ignorance has never and will never be a valid reason for a crime of this severity! Theft is still theft, regardless of what realm you exist in. Even if one were to entertain your poor attempt at justifying criminal behaviour, then clearly the fault should therein lie with the guardians, should it not?"

I gritted my teeth. "He is my ward, not my flesh and blood, having only come into my care three summers ago. Nonetheless, I acknowledge my responsibility to him and perhaps I did fail him in lack of discipline. Even still, I question how it is that a child could have possibly been able to commit such a crime. How could something of such value be so unguarded that a ten-year-old could swipe it unnoticed?!" I snapped back.

This fact was eating at me; while Toby was a clever and wily pickpocket, to steal something so valuable was beyond his abilities.

It didn't make sense.

The queen stood, indignation filling her frame.

"Your implications at the ineptness of the crown only deepen the hole of his grave!" Ragna said darkly. Her voice steadily began rising. "For to suggest such a thing only convinces me of the necessity to execute swift justice! I will not have such a nimble-fingered thief in my kingdom! Even that Seelie farce of a queen would not have thought twice to have him beaten and made an example of in the face of such disrespect. No! Punishment is absolute for those who intend on stealing power from us!"

She walked closer to the edge of the dais, looking down at me. I saw her resolve; there was no more room for negotiating.

So be it.

"You seem to enjoy going straight to the point, dear Melisandre," she hissed. "So, hear me now: the boy dies. I will not suffer this insult idly. Here and now. Let his head roll!" Her eyes were filled with green fire, her power vibrating the room.

I acted, throwing my cloak to the floor. In the blink of an eye, I transmuted the bottom of my staff into a jagged point, slamming it into the face of the guard holding Toby. He screamed as it ripped through metal, flesh, and bone, before falling with a thud. I grabbed Toby, pushing him behind me as I swung my staff, now a spear, in a circle in an attempt to ward off the soldiers quickly surrounding us. The room darkened, shadows creeping in. A buzz filled the air and a massive pressure pushed against me as Ragna unleashed her power, making it hard to breathe.

"You DARE bring violence to a court hearing?!" she bellowed.

I faced her once again. People started running, trying to escape the wrath of their queen. I pointed my staff at her.

"This is but answering violence with violence! I told you I was here to answer for his crimes! If you want to kill him, you will have to go through me first!" I twirled my staff behind me, my body poised for the strike.

"And so I shall!" snapped Ragna. Thrusting her arm out, she cried, "SEIZE HER!"

Black-armoured guards filled the room, answering their queen's call. I slammed my staff down again, transmuting the quantum state of the electrons in the air around me from particles to waves. A shockwave formed around me, blasting back air and guard alike. With a path to the door cleared, I backed in its direction, careful to keep my eyes on my biggest threat.

In the next moment, time slowed. A guard, sword held high, came to my front. At the same time, I felt a carbon steel sword come down at my back, where Toby stood. Twisting, I swept Toby around me in a one-eighty-degree turn, and I dropped to one knee.

My staff whistled through the air, in a twirl, reaching behind me and above Toby's head. A blade caught against its grooves. At the same time, my left hand rose to meet the one previously at my back. In a brilliant flash of light and alchemical runes, thousands of carbon steel beads exploded through the air, falling to the floor in a rain of metal. The guards stumbled back, gaping at the shattered things that had once been swords. I stood up, whipping around to see the shocked faces of those around us, including the queens.

It didn't last but a moment when an unimaginable weight slammed into me, knocking me backward. My staff was sent flying, the unknown force launching me into a granite pillar like a rag doll. I hit the ground with a gasp, feeling the cracking of bones as pain exploded in my chest. A blood-curdling scream had my head snapping up. The queen was holding Toby, his head wrenched backward, eyes wild with terror.

"TOBY!" I screamed. I tried to get up but the weight was back, crushing the life out of me.

"One move, Alchemist, and he is gone forever!" The queen's teeth were visible now, incisors long and deadly, her eyes a pitch black. "Yes! I know *what* you are! We hunted your kind for years, trying to tap into the secrets of the earth itself but your people were hidden away, untouchable. The power was lost to the Otherworld in the great extinction of your kind but here you are. The gods have smiled upon me with this opportunity!" Her eyes were crazed with power.

Her elongated incisors poised over my ward's tiny neck. I could smell his fear from here.

"You say you are here to answer for his crimes, Alchemist? Yes, you will! But I don't want you dead, oh no. You are far too valuable for dauði. As tempted as I am to consume that powerful soul, I have a better use for you."

Toby struggled and her grip tightened on him.

She looked down at him then, slowly licking his neck. He cried out, shaking. I fought against the invisible weight, shouting obscenities, to no

63

avail. Ragna looked back up at me, satisfaction all over her face, knowing she had me cornered. She continued laying down her demands.

"Become my consort's Familiar and I will consider his debt paid. Fight me, and he dies!"

"Kill him, and I will shred every last one of you down to the atom! I will destroy you!" I raged.

I slammed my hands to the floor and activated the power within me. The whole room shuddered and shook. A huge crack in the marble floor appeared with a boom throughout the room. Transmutation circles appeared everywhere, glowing and crackling. I could see everything down to its atomic level, ready to tear it apart.

"No! Melly, no!" Elis screamed.

He and Llyr suddenly appeared next to me, reaching for me, but the shine of my runes and my eyes stopped them. The queen laughed victoriously.

"The power of the alchemical divine still lives! But your ward will not be granted such a fate! One bite from me and he will never see the gates of Hel for his soul, his essence will be mine for eternity. Choose wisely, Alchemist!" Tears streaking his face, Toby shook, reaching his hand out to me in a pleading gesture.

Elis lay on the floor, inching closer to my pinned form. He was shaking, itching to touch me but refrained. "Oh, gods! Mels heed me please!" He begged, "Ragna is the goddess Hel's Champion! She has the power to steal someone's essence, their soul! He will never reincarnate, never know the afterlife. He will cease to exist! Mels please!"

"Melly!" Toby screamed.

Indecision tore through me, Toby's cries awakening something primitive within. But...

I could let him die. Escape from here. Gather my things and go back into hiding. Is one life worth the risk of being enslaved to this deranged demon? To allow her to use me at the destruction of entire kingdoms?

The cracks deepened in the floor, and the room shook as the circles pulsated, awaiting my command; I held fate in my hands. I didn't break my gaze from Toby, nor did he from mine. All the trust and hope in those eyes. Elis' words reverberated through my mind like a thousand gongs.

That little boy would cease to be, never to be reborn. Never to laugh again, never show me that dimpled grin. His presence, extinguished for-

ever.

Taking in that sweet face, I remembered. Remembered my greatest sin; my greatest failure. A haunting agony I knew too well washed over me. A sin I never would repeat again.

My eyes closed at the knowledge that I would relinquish my freedom a thousand times if it meant I didn't commit Toby to my same sin twice. There was a debt to be repaid to those I had wronged so many years ago, seeking a forgiveness I shall never receive.

This left me with only one decision to make.

While there was a dire possibility my submission gave the Vampire queen an insurmountable amount of power by becoming her prisoner, there would still be time to fight it to my very last breath. But for now, Toby would live.

With a cry of defeat and an alchemical flash, I righted the crack in the foundation of the castle. I let go. The glow of my runes went dormant once more, the secret of my power going quiet within me. Instantly, the weight pushing me down was lifted.

Elis and Llyr scrambled to me, trying to help me stand. With fussy and trembling hands, Elis pulled me close and swept the hair off my face. Yet my need to get Toby away from the queen had me pushing away from him.

Quiet but deadly, I bit out, "You have what you want, Vampire. Now get your fucking hands off him!" I took a threatening step toward her.

With a triumphant smirk, Ragna shoved the sobbing child towards us, his chains causing him to crash to the floor. She stood and sauntered her way back to her throne. Utterly pleased with herself.

With a cry, Toby crashed into me, and my arms went around him as his legs gave out from under him. We slid to the floor. I pulled Toby onto my lap as one hand threaded through his dirty curls, holding his head to me, and the other around his back.

He's here. He's safe. He's going to be okay, I told myself.

"I'm s-s-s-ooo sorrryyy Ms. Mel-ly," he hiccuped, "I s-s-should have l-l-listened to you," Toby sobbed.

"Shhh, my boy. You're okay, Toby. I've got you. It's alright now. Let me see that hand."

I gently picked up his broken hand, seeing the damage. For all I can do, I have never been the best healer. Healing bodies takes an immense amount of focus and just the right circles. For now, I just transmuted the worst break into place, earning a cry from Toby who hid his face in my shoulder.

Elis' arms went around both of us, and I noticed he held my staff.

"I failed you, Mels," he said tearfully.

Adamantly, I shook my head and clutched his arm. "No, Elis. Do not lose yourself to our present circumstances. We both know there is a larger game at play. There must be. Hold fast."

Llyr crouched in front of us, gently pulling Toby from my arms. His long copper hair fell around his shoulder as he picked him up, coming to a stand.

"I'll get him cleaned up and treated, Melisandre. We should get him out of here. And..." he whispered, "thank you. We owe you a great debt." Tears rimmed his pale gold eyes.

Looking up at him, I nodded back and then unfurled myself from the floor.

I looked over at the queen, who was motioning to her captain of the guard. Armed soldiers seized me by both arms and began dragging me away, towards the doors.

Toby cried out for me, but Llyr's hold was firm. Stumbling, I righted myself and jerked myself away from their grasp; I may have just signed over my freedom, but I would go with dignity. I looked back at Elis, hugging my staff. Then at Llyr, whose arms were around a broken and sniffling Toby.

I gave them a reassuring look.

The three of them looked back forlornly, but with a hint of hope. I followed the guards to the dungeons to await my fate.

CHAPTER 6

For three days I sat in the drippy, grimy dungeon cell. At least, I believe it was three days. There was nothing but darkness, save the torches that burned low.

Drip. Drip. Drip.

I stewed in the darkness.

Electricity is a thing... How can one live this long yet still be so chained to the blatant inefficiencies of the past? The invention of toilet paper should have been enough to instigate change, but no, these idiots would rather wipe their pompous asses with gods know what.

My thoughts were nothing but murky pools of pessimism, my mental words the biting edge of sarcasm. Quite befitting of my dreary surroundings.

As much as I griped, objectively, I knew why creatures of the Otherworld were still stuck in what felt like the human realm's sixteenth century. Beyond the fact that nothing seems to die in this place unless it was violent and purposeful, change was not a welcome thing. I won't even discuss the elements that technology requires that have an adverse effect on magic and its users.

So, torches it was. I could only hope these Vampires embraced some other modern conveniences.

Screams and moans of agony echoed through the dungeon, blood-curdling and chilling. But I couldn't be bothered to care; the darkness was welcome to any alternatives Queen Ragna might have and I was just grateful those screams were not coming from me.

I shifted my legs so one knee was up, and my other leg stretched out. Arms raised above me, my hands hung from iron manacles. My hair was limp, strands clinging to my face. Everything was damp and cold.

Drip, drip, drip.

I looked up at my bound hands and snorted.

As if binding me could keep me from transmuting anything. That was, however, a card I would hold close to my heart. It would be folly to reveal my aces before I discerned the hands of everyone at the table.

Kicking at some rubble at my feet, I sighed. Irritation and frustration ate at me.

"You knew the boy had this issue, Mel, you knew! And still, you let him go with Elis. I should have put up more safety measures. Bloody should have gone with them! Fantastic job, you idiot. Well fucking done." I say out loud to myself, scowling at the mouldy stones.

Yet, even as I chastised my stupidity, there was a niggling feeling that all was not as it seemed. The queen never did answer my accusation. How could a child possibly break into a heavily warded chamber, steal a powerful relic, AND get as far as the Seelie border before getting caught? Let alone get past Elis' watchful eye and his Vampire sensitivities.

She knew. She had to have known. It wasn't about Toby. Not really. But how?

None of this made sense. There was a crucial part of the formula of this problem that was missing. Now, I had to contend with staving off a power-hungry queen and this consort of hers. I groaned, leaning my head against the stone wall. I had no idea what becoming a Familiar entailed and was dreading finding out. Since I was dealing with Vampires, it most likely would involve biting, body fluids, and a lot of pain.

I shuddered, grimacing at the thought.

Drip, drip, drip.

"I should have gone with him..." I whispered in the darkness.

I should have, but deep down, I knew I could not risk it. For hundreds of years, I hid from the powers of magic, powers like Queen Ragna or the Fae Courts, for they sought to control and possess the one thing that I could–life. Alchemists were the love children of Mother Nature, each born with a unique ability to draw upon an element of her. Far before humans, we were her original caretakers. We kept balance and order; her laws were written into every gene of our makeup. Even in our own creations, everything follows the balance.

The Tuatha Dé Danann had the magic of the elements and could force the earth to bend to their will, but even they could not control the seasons or stop her power should she become enraged. We Alchemists were often mistaken as such but even among our own race, Alchemists were limited to control of a single element, not multiple. Not like I could.

At the thought, haunting faces I've tried to forget flooded the forefront of my mind. Squeezing my eyes shut against the pain and grief that shot through me, distorting my face. The fingers of Familiar darkness crept across my heart and mind. I shoved those thoughts aside, shutting down the sucking black hole of my emotions. There was enough to worry about; dredging up my darkest secret and greatest sins wouldn't help me. Especially now that I would be at the mercy of a Vampire elder, a queen and Champion, controlled and caged.

NO! I roared in my head. I will not be. I cannot be! You owe it to them to fight! Think, Melisandre, think! There is always a way. Do not succumb. Calm your mind and think!

My thoughts raced but were met with nothing but dead ends. As any good scientist knows, one could not come up with a solution for success without enough information. I had so little to work with, too many missing variables.

Kicking myself internally, I had allowed my fear of capture over the years to keep me ignorant of the finer details of Otherworld creatures, and their key players. Master Kian, my former mentor, would have smacked me with his favourite book a million times over for such folly.

"Knowledge is everything, Melisandre! Never let your emotions keep you from expanding your mind!" His gravelly voice echoed in the chambers of my heart; the memory was as clear as if it was yesterday.

I took a deep breath, exhaling slowly. Despite my courage, the reality of what I was up against weighed heavily upon me. My inner fire dimmed but did not diminish. For now, I could only wait for the opportunity to turn the tide.

My stomach growled loudly, and I glared at it. My own body was determined to remind me of my unfortunate situation.

"Gods, could you be any louder—"

A loud clunking and creaking echoed through the hall, and I could hear footsteps coming in my direction. I craned my head to see two tall guards in black armour, one holding a torch. They were followed by a woman who was dressed simply, with her hair covered. She was young and far shorter than me. They stopped at my cell and one of the guards unlocked it. They both came in, the one with the torch standing farther back. The woman remained outside. The other guard started toward me, and I looked up at him. He stopped, hesitating.

The guard holding the torch asked, "What's wrong Dev?"

"Those eyes...fuckin' eerie. You don't think she'll turn me into something, do you?"

I leaned my head back and raised an eyebrow, daring him to come closer.

Dev frowned, looking me up and down. If he had a stick, I think he would have poked me with it. He stank of unease and fear. The guard with the torch came forward and kneeled in front of me, pinning me with his beady glare.

"Try anything, freak, and the queen said she'll happily send over your ward's fingers in a box." He smiled, his incisors flashing.

I glared back at him. His eyes slowly travelled over me as he licked his lips.

"Oi, she's a bit of a looker, eh? Once you get past the eyes. Too bad you ain't down here longer; always had a thing for the exotic. Put a blindfold on 'er and we woulda 'ad some right fun." Leering, he leaned closer, reaching out to touch me.

I started to lift my foot to give him a swift kick in the face when the other guard, Dev, grabbed his wrist, saying "Ain't worth it Sevil, she's goin to the Lord Commander and Prince Consort. Don't want 'im smellin ya on 'er."

Sevil jerked his arm away, spat at the ground next to me, and stood.

"Tch, fuck it. Get 'er up. Ain't got all fuckin day."

I felt the chains release and my arms fell to my sides, the blood rushing *back into my hands. The guard grabbed my upper arm* and hauled me to my feet, pushing me towards the open door and the waiting woman. I snapped around, jerking my arm out of his grasp. The guard glared back but stopped touching me. Rolling my shoulders and neck, they cracked as I walked stiffly to the cell door.

The woman gave me a small smile and a curtsy. "My lady, I've come to take you to your chambers. My name is Ada. I am at your service. Please, this way." I frowned, but followed her lead through the dungeon. The guards followed, uncomfortably close.

Had the consort returned? My chambers, she had said.

Apparently, I wasn't making the dungeon home sweet home. There was no denying my relief, but I was wary, nonetheless.

She set a brisk pace, and I tried to keep up with her, but my healing ribs and muscles screamed at me. Taking stock of my surroundings was crucial, but the lack of food and water left me feeling dizzy and light-headed. While I wouldn't die from the needs of the body not being met, it didn't save me from suffering the effects.

We passed elaborate halls and rooms and flourishing gardens filled with fountains and statues. The smells of freshly baked goods and spices filled the air; my mouth watered as hunger hit my gut like a sledgehammer.

After what felt like miles, we arrived at cream-coloured double doors. Ada opened them and ushered me inside. The guards remained outside, to prevent any escape, I assumed.

I wanted to sneer at my new gilded cage; to curse it and verbally tear down its opulence. But I couldn't, because it was truly lovely. Instead, I took my time admiring the elegance of the room. It was like a mesh of seventeenth-century French castles with heavy influences of Islamic architecture; open yet homely. The decor itself was a hunter-green and gold. The ceilings were arched and high, decorated with gold and emerald filigree.

The room we had entered was clearly a sitting room. To my left, an enormous fireplace was set ablaze, with intricate and cosy couches facing it. A writing desk with several built-in bookshelves to the right. Between the couches and the open veranda was a little dining table set for two. Directly past the sitting room gave way to three open archways, leading to a spacious balcony. The balustrade had thick marble pillars attached to a matching railing, the top wide enough one could comfortably sit.

Ada led me to the right of the sitting room, to another set of double doors, which she opened to reveal the bedroom. It was large and spacious, while still embracing that comfortable ambience. The canopied bed to my right was huge, beautiful, if not a bit over the top in my eyes. Its footboard was parallel to another roaring fireplace, albeit smaller than the one in the previous room. Two hanging flower pots with beautiful vined-plants hung on either side of the mantle, making the room that much more homey.

The bed's woodwork of stags and wolves caught my attention; the carvings were so detailed, the animals seemed to come to life if you looked long enough. I tore my gaze away, instead seeing a tempting cushioned bench that sat flush against the end of the bed, desperately wanting to relax on it. Instead, we walked past the fireplace to a door across the room, which I suspected was the bathroom.

"Please tell me that the queen has at least upgraded the castle to modern plumbing." She glanced back at me, failing to withhold her grin. "Ada, if there is a chamber pot behind that door, so help me–"

She let out a giggle and replied, "Yes my lady, we do have proper plumbing, rest assured."

Ushering me through the opened the door, I eagerly walked into the bronze and marble bathroom. Like the sitting room, it was large. To the left, there were archways that led to an identical balcony. A huge bronze clawfoot tub stood in the middle, like a centrepiece. A drain to the left of the tub sat under 8 circular shower heads hanging down over the tiles. An open shower, no curtains, no privacy.

I frowned. "How do you turn it on?"

"Oh, I'll do it for you, my lady. I figured you'd want to refresh yourself after spending several days down in the dungeon. The Royal Consort is returning on the morrow, and you are to be presented to him in the throne room. I will prepare your bath and then return with your supper. Will my lady be needing assistance in undressing?"

She'd already begun running the bath, putting scented oils into the water, and checking the temperature. She was shorter than me, maybe coming to my shoulder, thin, and had tight brown curls. Based on her bone structure and the point of her ears, I'd wager she was a Brownie hybrid, like Toby. Interesting.

"No, I'm fine. Thank you, Ada."

I moved towards the bath slowly, waiting for Ada to leave before undressing. Nudity was nothing to Vampires, or Fae for that matter. I was neither. A hermit through and through, my pale arse was for no one's gaze.

"When the water is filled to your liking, just turn those knobs there, my lady. Let me turn the shower on for your initial wash and then I shall let the kitchen know to start your supper. Right here is the knob." After engaging only one of the large flat shower heads above from the nearby wall, she set out soaps and oils before she headed to the door.

The complete change in my surroundings and the events of the last few days hit me then, and an overwhelming weariness settled into my bones. So, I took a moment to look around me, taking it all in. The calming sounds of falling water and the general silence beyond it, grounded me. I shook my head and began to undress. The cool breeze hit my naked skin and goosebumps raced along my body. Stepping into the rain of the shower felt like being enveloped in a warm hug after a hard day; I almost groaned from the pleasure of it. Taking a moment to allow the water to run off me, I then began scrubbing days of travel and incarceration off my body with stubborn determination.

Once several layers of skin had been adequately scrubbed off, I turned off the shower as she had shown me. The fragrant bath was calling to me, the steam rising from it promised a level of relaxation that was absolutely deserved. I was also grateful for the marble footstool. Vampires were naturally tall and graceful. I doubted my short legs could clear the tub without falling and knocking myself unconscious. I put a toe in, then, without further ado, melted into the water with a big sigh. Heavenly. I dunked myself fully under the water and sat back up. Putting my arms over the edge of the tub, the open balcony. The hot water felt wonderful against the chilled air. It was dark but I could sense the rise of the sun not far away.

My mind was riddled with anxiety, desperate for solutions I didn't yet have. Yet, even through the heavy yoke of the burden I carried, thoughts of him drifted to the forefront. I finally allowed myself to indulge in those thoughts, the heat of the water and the romantic view in front of me making it impossible to resist. My eyes fell closed as the memory took hold.

I remembered everything—the strong lines of his jaw, proud chin. Perfect, tempting lips. Broad frame, tapered waist. The strength of his arms... how I felt in them. The memory of how his voice resonated deep against my ear, caused a visceral reaction and my legs clenched together. Oh, how badly I wanted to see his face. I have never been so drawn to a stranger, as if something about him called to my soul. Curiosity overcame caution in a way that would truly be the cause of my downfall someday.

Shaking my head, I tried to clear the lust that hazed my ability to think. Warmth continued to pool within me despite me reciting elements in alphabetical order. Giving up, I let out a frustration. Perhaps I've gone too long without release, without another's touch. There would be no indulging now though; who knew who was watching, listening.

I finished bathing and got out of the tub. There was a stack of fluffy white towels on the counter, so I began drying myself, then wrapped the towel around my body. Just as I was about to grab another to pat down my hair, Ada opened the door. Her perfect timing was suspicious to me.

"I've brought your supper, my lady. I've laid a shift and dressing robe on the bed for you."

There was no hiding my look of incredulity, but she turned and walked away, leaving the door to the bedroom open. I haven't worn a shift in several hundred years. By the gods, these people were outdated. I walked into the bedroom and sure enough, a flowing white shift lay on the bed. A snort escaped me.

"Absolutely not," I grunted, placing my hands on the gown. A simple transmutation in readjusting molecules and they were now pants and a shirt. The fabric was lovely against the skin though. Next to it, was a simple dressing gown and it was equally as soft as I pulled it tightly around me.

When I left the bedroom, I came to find Ada setting my food out on a table for two near the balcony but still inside. The roaring fire emitted a wonderful warmth that was surprisingly not lost in the open air, making the room exceedingly cosy. The succulent smell of dinner led me to quickly find my seat at the table.

"Thank you, Ada. It smells delicious." Mouth watering, I quickly laid my cloth napkin on my lap before attacking a seasoned potato. It was piping hot but I would happily burn my mouth to a crisp if only to feed my aching belly. A small groan of pleasure escaped me.

Ada noticed, giving me an amused smile. "Glad you like it, my lady. I'll be sure to give the cooks your regards." I gave her a silent nod. She put the lids and serving utensils back on the little metal trolley that had carried up the food. "I will leave you now and be back to clean up. Is there anything else you may require, my lady?"

"No, Ada, I'm quite al—actually yes, do you know if Lord Elis LeGervase remained at court?"

"I do believe he did, my lady."

"I see..."

"I'll leave you to your dinner then, my lady."

Ada opened the door before grabbing the trolley to push through it, but halted abruptly when met with arguing just outside. A sharp, familiar male voice cut through and Ada gave me a quick nod and disappeared, leaving the door open. Swinging one leg over the other, I waited with a look of expectancy on my face.

Elis shoved his way in, slamming the door in the face of the objecting guard. He whipped around with an incredulous look on his face. To my relief, my Alchemist Staff was in one of his hands.

"Speak of the devil." I finally grinned as I begrudgingly placed my fork down.

Tossing my staff onto the couch, he slapped a hand to his cocked hip. "How dare you, my beauty far surpasses that of any demon."

As if by a trick of the light, Elis appeared before me, pulling me to my feet.

"You never do miss a chance at inflating your own ego, do you, Elis?"

He wrapped me in a firm hug, holding me close.

"I daresay it's a necessity when my dearest friend is a grumpy little troll who loves to shatter it," Elis said softly against my hair. He pulled away slightly, his fingers lifting my chin to meet his eyes as his thumb brushed my cheek. The smile on his face lessened and his eyes filled with concern. "Are you well, Mels? Were they cruel to you?" He tilted my head from side to side, checking for injuries. "My little buds have remained silent until they gave an image of you moving within the castle."

"Your buds? A new facet to your flower power that involves more than simple symbology? I think I'd like to see that. But no, I am quite fine, Elis. They left me alone for the most part. But look at you! You seem to be in peak condition. One would never know you were at the mercy of your rabid queen just days ago, ragged, wrinkled, and smelling of a dungeon."

"Oh, gods don't remind me," he groaned, "I must have looked a terrible fright when you saw me."

"It certainly was not your most attractive moment, no." Elis snorted but then I frowned, a thought irking me. "But Elis, why are you here?"

"I told you, my flowers—"

"No, no," I corrected, waving him off, "Why are you still in Idrisid? I would have thought you three would be long gone by now, seeking safety in the arms of the Seelie court. To get Toby out immediately."

He sighed, saying, "That was what we intended to do but the queen stopped us. She forbade us to leave. Llyr is free to come and go because he is a Fae Ambassador, but I am still a Vampire and a subject to Her Majesty. I can be compelled." Putting his hands on my upper arms, he gazed down at me in seriousness. "I think she's trying to keep leverage over you by keeping Toby hostage here."

I pulled away from him, needing to sit down, walking quickly over to the sofa in front of the small fireplace. Sinking into the cushions, I stared unseeing into the flames, trying to analyse this turn of events.

Elis moved to sit across from me. The movement dragged my attention away and I took that moment to take in his visage. The lavender linen shirt brought out his beautiful eyes. Buckskin breeches and boots finished the outfit. Simple for Elis, a clear indication how stressed he has been when he sways from his normal elaborate fashion choices. He still had a modern flare, though, and it suited him.

All my thoughts from the past three days came rushing forth and I could no longer hold back my frustration as the questions without answers continued to pile up in my mind. "She said she would release Toby if I became her consort's Familiar. I agreed. So why the bloody hell won't she let him leave?"

Elis waved a finger at me. "No, no. She never said she would set him free. She said she would let him live and forgive his crimes. Besides, the debt is only considered paid once you become the consort's Familiar. So, it makes sense why she's leveraging Toby. And..." he cleared his throat, "she is very much aware of how close we are and will undoubtedly exploit the hell out of it, my dove. Welcome to the Nightmare Court," Elis said with a little smile that didn't match the defeat in his eyes.

I'd been had. "Damn her." Annoyed, I rubbed a hand over my face.

"It's been days since you've eaten, Melisandre. Please," said Elis, motioning to the dinette filled with food.

Indeed, it had been. Obeying the rumble of my stomach, I sat down to my lovely plate of roasted rosemary chicken, potatoes, and seared asparagus. My ire at the queen simmered as I stared down at the beautiful sight. Food made by her cooks. In her castle. That I was now imprisoned in.

I positively seethed.

"Vile. Scheming. Malicious. Bitch." At each word, I stabbed my chicken.

"It's already dead, my dear."

I tossed my fork down. I would eat, but needed a moment.

Then a thought occurred to me, "Why didn't the queen just mark me herself right then and there? Why bother giving me to her consort at all?"

Elis frowned, considering me. He folded his arms and put a finger to his lips. He tapped them gently, thinking.

"I'm honestly not sure," he said after a moment. "My knowledge is limited with the finer details in regard to the ritual of binding a Familiar; I'm not powerful enough and I've never witnessed it being done. It's extremely rare and most Vampires aren't powerful enough to bind another person, let alone an animal. However, I do know one thing: it must be consensual. There must be an utmost willingness by the Familiar. I can only speculate that the queen knew you'd reject her till the very end, making the binding impossible. I know a failed binding kills the intended Familiar. Perhaps she thinks Prince Alcaeus has better chances at winning your affections?"

I snorted at the absurdity, but asked, "So that's his name? Alcaeus? Perhaps we should start there. May as well gather what information I can about my new captor; tell me about him."

He leaned back, a flirtatious smile glossing his features.

"Alcaeus Pallas," Elis said the words slowly, savouring the words as if they were as sweet as chocolate. "Champion of the goddess Athena, Lord Commander of Queen Ragna's armies. He is a master tactician and brilliant strategist but ruthless in battle, so the history books say. Even the queen is cautious in her demands of him, and the council fears him. After all, it is said he brutally slayed two gods in the arena and then four more in The Great Battle at Cantre'r Gwaelod. That is how he got the moniker, Godslayer.

"Yet, the people love him, for it was through his wisdom and diplomatic skills that Khaviel is the most diverse nation in all of the Otherworld. Khaviel experienced a huge economic boom because of his talents in agricultural management, opening trade between the kingdoms. Even the state of peace between the kingdoms falls to Prince Alcaeus' genius. Now, many view our nation as a safe haven for hybrids and misfits. He is what stands between Ragna and ruin, as our *beloved queen*," he sneered, "has no mind for politics nor economy. But that is a conversation for another time. Where was I... Ah! And last, but certainly not least," he leaned forward as his smile deepened, eyes becoming dreamy, "our *extraordinary* prince truly is one of the most exquisite Vampires the gods have ever graced us with. Athena certainly knows how to make a man, despite being a virgin deity." Elis placed a hand over his heart. "If the circumstances weren't so dire, I'd be downright jealous of you.

It's no wonder the queen trapped him into being her consort, his divine abilities aside." His eyes twinkled and he leaned back into his seat.

I rolled my eyes at him, taking a deep drink of wine. Then he suddenly became serious, a warning upon his lips. "So do be careful, Melisandre. It is well-known Prince Alcaeus did not come into his position willingly so anything powerful enough to control the commander of Khaviel's army..." Shaking his head, visibly trying to find the right words, "Just... Please, be cautious in trying to challenge Ragna. Everyone who dared stand up to her has met their demise by bloodshed, torture, and their very souls being ripped from them and swallowed whole. You know as well as I do that Toby and I would be the first on her list if she wants to punish you."

If my best friend were talking about anyone else, I'd have teased him for being melodramatic, for drama was indeed his cup of tea. Yet one look at his ashen face and the trembling of his hands, told me that he had most likely witnessed these horrors first-hand. I took his reaction and the dire warning to heart.

Maybe I couldn't tease him for being a diva, but I would never resist a jibe. "Well, it would certainly relieve me of two burdens, so perhaps it wouldn't be so bad."

He gasped and eyed the table, to toss something at me, no doubt. Finding nothing, he settled for stealing my wine. My reaction was too slow as he snatched the goblet out of my reach and drank it down noisily. With a satisfied smack of his lips, revenge was had.

"You're a wretched troll," he said.

"So you keep calling me. There's more wine behind you." I pointed to the small side table. While he refilled my glass, I wanted to bring the conversation back to something he had said. "If Alcaeus didn't choose to be the royal consort, then what was he before? Not only that, since he has the favour of the people and even the loyalty of the military, how has he not usurped her? If he's so brilliant, how is she still in power?"

Elis pointed a finger at me. "Worthy questions but, alas, I only have answers to a few. What happened between our queen and the prince was long before I was born, making it a history lesson we have little time for. So, I'll attempt to give you a small breakdown." He snagged a bread roll from the basket between us, talking between bites. "Now, rumour has it a great battle took place. Victory was assured to Alcaeus but one day, all fighting stopped, and the Lord Commander was now engaged to the queen. Many just assumed it was an effort to stop the bloodshed. We all have our suspicions but only the queen and prince know what really happened. I have heard whispers that the queen is getting impatient and that does not bode well for you; perhaps by giving you to him.... Well, I shouldn't speculate."

My fork stilled above my plate, then I lowered it slowly; it was evident where he was going with that statement, and disgust filled both of our faces. Was I meant to be a bribe? Was all of this some sort of attempt to seduce her intended? We sat in a moment of pensive silence, the mood turning dour.

After a moment Elis sat up straight, crossing one leg over the other. Clearing his throat, he said, "As far as your other questions, that is the elephant in the room. There are many who would rather see Prince Alcaeus as the high king and Ragna forced to abdicate and sent to her thousand-year sleep. Most of the Elder Twelve have taken their rest, as was agreed by the First Council, but Ragna refuses. Yet, so far, our prince has not made a move towards overthrowing her. His motives and ambitions are a mystery to the entire court." He stole a piece of chicken off my plate and continued, "Even the council is fed up with Ragna's madness and tyranny, though the last councilman who spoke out is now abiding with the rest of the souls the witch has devoured. She wields insanity like a weapon." With a big sigh, he ended with, "I think your best and only chance is trying to win Prince Alcaeus over to your side."

I considered his words, taking a bite of roasted potato. At this point in time, I wouldn't know anything until I met said consort, observed, and interrogated him myself. The fact the Familiar needed to be willing could possibly play into my favour; or destroy my chance at saving Toby. Even I could admit I wasn't exactly known for my pliable and amicable nature.

Also, the fact that I was coming into this situation that had well over a thousand years of pre-existing issues made me want to grind my head into dust to avoid all its complexity. My hands were tied in more ways than one so I needed to let it go for now. Which meant I now needed to address our most recent events and hopefully get some answers.

"So, what happened, Elis? How could Toby possibly steal a relic of power while evading detection?"

It was a moment before Elis shook his head slightly, saying, "I honestly have no idea, Mels. We were only at the guild for a couple of hours at most. Llyr went to speak with the curator, and I took Toby to go look at some manuscripts on Vampire history. At no point did he leave my side. Imagine how positively confounded I was when the queen's guard crashed through our rooms at the inn near the border, three days later! When I saw what he had taken, I truly thought we would be executed on the spot." The last part ended in a whisper, his eyes sombre. "I've wracked my memory countless times and at no point did he have an opportunity. Yes, we looked at the ring and several other objects of power; that was part of our history lesson. We BOTH walked out together, though." He looked down at his hands, guilt and regret were evident in his slouched shoulders.

I frowned hard, letting out a sound of exasperation.

"This just doesn't make sense, Elis! None of this does. This almost feels like," I shake my head, struggling to find the words, "I don't know, like a setup. The probability of that is so unlikely, but it's the only logical conclusion I have at this point. There are too many facts that do not line up for this to be a coincidence. It reeks of intrigue and power plays."

My jaw tightened with frustration. I leaned into my hand, rubbing my temple. I couldn't stand ignorance and the helpless feeling gnawed at me. I heard a shift of a chair and Elis knelt before me, taking both of my hands in his with a gentleness that made me look at him.

"Hey." Amethyst eyes gazed into mine. "It's going to be alright. We'll figure this out. Even if Llyr and I were able to go, I wouldn't want to. I could never abandon you. Or Toby. While my standing among the nobles was shaken, I'm perfectly confident I'll be back in their good graces by the end of tomorrow." He winked but his face became serious again. "You have allies, Mels. You're not alone," he said gently.

I gave him a slight smile, squeezing his hands in return.

"I know," I responded quietly.

Elis stood and gracefully plopped back into his seat. "And, from what little I know of the ritual," he grabbed a dinner roll from the basket, "I'm pretty sure the process of binding a Familiar takes time. In which case, we will most certainly use every moment to our advantage."

I nodded, my eyes flicking over to the blazing hearth. Fatigue seeped into me and I yawned. Elis took that as his cue and he rose, coming to stand in front of my own seat.

He pulled me to a stand, wrapping an arm around my waist.

Caressing my cheek, he whispered, "Trust in yourself, Melly, no matter how dark the night falls here. Oh, and before you ask, Toby has been on full bed rest and healing beautifully."

Guilt swarmed me, "Oh gods, I should have asked but -"

Elis put a finger to my lips, stopping me. "YOU, my dear, have more weight on your shoulders than Atlas, so none of that feeling guilty nonsense. Toby is fine, we've seen to that. Your one job is to focus on you right now, alright?"

Deflating, I leaned into him, staring up into his beautiful eyes. "I couldn't ask for a better friend, Elis."

He gave me a brilliant smile and tapped me on the nose with an elegant finger.

I frowned.

"Ha! There's my grumpy little troll! No, you couldn't, and you'd do well to remember that." He winked and released me, making his way to the door.

"I will let you rest. Try to enjoy the luxury and don't transmute anything I wouldn't. Oh, and tomorrow I'll bring over a violin for you. I'm sorry I can't bring Sinatra or Bennett over; I know how much you love your human music, but at least you'll have something." He cast a glance around the room. "As beautiful as we could both agree these lodgings are, knowing you, you'll be bored out of your mind within the hour without your precious books."

Perhaps Elis did know me a little more than I have given him credit for. "Thank you, Elis. Oh, and tell Toby that everything will be alright, and to stay out of trouble and that...," I hesitated, "well to stay out of mischief. If he so much as touches something that does not belong to him, I'll... Just, please keep him safe."

He smiled with understanding, opening the door. "He won't. And I will. *And* that you love him. It's okay to use the 'L-word, my dear!" He said, shutting the door softly behind him.

I stared at the door for a moment longer before standing and making my way to the vast balcony beside me. Wrapping my arms around myself against the chill, the breathtaking view beckoned me closer.

The tower my rooms were in was one of many, high above the twinkling city. The powerful Sanguine River wrapped around, defining the divide between the town and the dark, thick forests that lay beyond. Mountains silhouetted in the distance, meeting the edge of a sky that had so many stars the night held light despite the disappearing moons.

81

If I had learned anything on my path to maturity over these eight hundred years, it was to be still in moments of conflict when there is an absence of a solution. To take in the present and simply be. So, as my eyes took in that star-filled sky, I did just that. I cleared my mind and just existed in the moment.

My eyes scanned the forests before me. The memory that now continued to fill me with warmth and fascination, replayed in my mind, and I wondered if he was still there now. Eventually succumbing to the exhaustion that plagued my body, I made my way to the bed and fell into a fitful sleep; dreams that were riddled with chains, lurking threats, and a voice that called out to me–the same one the stranger in the forest had.

CHAPTER 7

I begrudgingly awoke just as dusk was settling. A lump in the middle of my bed, I felt my way to the edge of the mattress, only to then bonelessly slide to the floor and come to a stand. To have slept so long, my body was clearly in need of it and my ribs no longer burned with sharp pain with any movement. My biological regeneration was nothing near the speed of Vampires or other Otherworld creatures like Fae or Were, but I do heal remarkably fast compared to my own kind.

Searching around for my clothing, a twinge of alarm ran through me when they were not there. Overturning bedding, opening drawers, even checking the bathroom, came up with nothing. They were gone. I cursed and took my ill-tempered self, back to the bathroom. I had just finished ripping a brush through my wild dark curls when there was a knock.

The door opened to reveal Ada, her gaze respectfully lowered. "I brought your outfit for this evening, my lady. I am also well equipped to dress your hair as well."

"Where are my clothes, Ada?"

"Oh! I took them for washing, my lady."

"Bring them back, please Ada. They are not meant to be handled by magic folk. I will wash them myself."

She frowned slightly and hesitated but reluctantly nodded. My clothes were the only armour I had to help nullify magic and I couldn't afford Ragna taking that from me. I followed the Brownie maid back to the bedroom.

"Here we are, my lady. The black lace is lovely, don't you think?"

I did a double-take, eyes bugging out of my head while my jaw hit the floor.

"W-w-what...h-how...What is THAT, Ada?!" I sputtered, pointing to the bed where an outfit better suited to an expensive whorehouse was displayed. The corset was the most concealing bit, the 'skirt' was sheer gossamer silk. The same material appeared at the shoulders, trailing into long sleeves with detailed lacing stitched into it. Ornate silk stockings, garters, and a belt with black lace underwear. While one could never accuse me of being a prude, far from it, there was still no way I would be caught dead in something so lascivious.

"I-It's... It's your outfit, my lady. Specially picked by the queen!" The excitement in her eyes died instantly at the sight of my fury.

I crossed my arms, taking a defensive stance. "Not by all the seven hells am I wearing that, Ada. You have a better chance of saddling me and putting a damn bit in my mouth to pull the queen's fucking carriage," I growled.

She looked down again, fiddling with her hands nervously.

Barely above a whisper and with a trembling voice she said, "M-my lady, Oweyn warned me that you would probably refuse and told me to tell you that Toby will be sitting in Her Majesty's personal sitting room alongside her favourite torturer. She wanted to remind you of your agreement."

My gaze turned murderous as fear for Toby fuelled my rage. Ada shook but didn't move or look at me.

I slammed a fist into the bedpost

That fucking cunt!

Runes lit up in my eyes and across my body in answer to the torrent of emotions; the black tattoos morphing into a glowing purplish white that indicate when my abilities are activated.

Never had I been so manipulated, and I knew this was just the beginning. Swinging away from the bed, I made my way to stand in front of the fire, gazing deep into the flames. The elements chirped at me, giving me focus. I took a resentful breath to force the rage down, then proceeded to have a right chat with myself.

You cannot let your emotions rule you, you know this. She is going to push you, try to strip you of everything you know, everything that you are. Reacting to every little thing she does will only ensure her victory over you. She may be the queen of this game, but you are the queen of your own. This is nothing compared to what you have already been through. Be smarter, wiser; do not let her break you.

"Don't let her break you," I whispered as a new purpose blossomed within me. With a pained but politer voice, I acceded, "My apologies, Ada. The fault does not lie with you. I will..." I cleared my throat, "I will wear it. But the corset looks like it will need two pairs of hands."

Ada cautiously peeked at me and gulped but nodded quickly and said, "Of course, my lady." She stood there, waiting expectantly.

"Oh. Um, a moment." Grabbing the scraps of fabric, as it were, I fled to the bathroom. It was bad enough being paraded in such a humiliating manner; I didn't need to add getting naked as a babe in front of Ragna's own.

Dressing only took moments, and I held the corset closely to my breasts as I came back into the bedroom. Ada only looked a little curiously at what had once been my shift but did not comment. But her eyes widened at the sight of my runes and circles covering my body; ancient alchemical symbols and circles covering most of my body, though the tops of my shoulders, face, and neck had the least amount.

As she began lacing up the corset, I said to her, "Based on the style of clothing you laid out last night for me, I find this surprisingly modern."

"Oh, the Queen enjoys both traditional and new fashion, my lady. The latest styles seem to incorporate a mixture. I think when you've lived as long as them, even the traditional looks can become rather repetitive."

"So, asking for some pants and shirts would be possible?"

"Of course! Although, it would need to be cleared with Prince Alcaeus. You belong to His Highness now."

I scowled at her wording.

"I belong to no one, Ada." She paused, but then continued yanking at the strings.

"Indeed, my lady," she replied noncommittally.

By the time she was done, my breasts were almost spilling out of the top, my hips flaring out from my tightly cinched waist. I might as well forget about breathing. I'd always had curves with a delicate frame, but I denied the 'delicate' part; I could break a man's jaw with a solid punch if I needed to. Right now, I wanted to.

The stockings were black with lace at the top but somewhat transparent, giving my legs sexy lines. They were tied to a delicate garter belt that had tiny roses stitched around it. My thighs were otherwise exposed, and I could feel a draft on my rear that shouldn't be there. I glanced around for shoes but saw none.

Ada noticed and said, "Oh, the Queen wants you in just stockings. Let me do your hair, my lady."

Of course the queen does.

I don't think my eyebrows could go any lower on my face, or the disgust be any more apparent.

With arms crossed, I sat stiff-backed on the stool placed in front of the glowing hearth.

After intricately braiding the top half of my hair, Ada attached a black lace choker to my neck. It had a platinum studded chain leading to a glittering diamond teardrop that rested right above my decolletage. She then placed a delicate silver chain headpiece on my head. Four chains, two on each side, were gently wrapped on either side of my head. It met a chain in the middle of my forehead that went over the top of my crown. Where the chains met, another teardrop diamond settled right above my eyebrows.

"Oh, my lady, you look beautiful!"

It took everything in me not to roll my eyes in disgust. I looked like a courtesan and Elis was never going to let me live this down if he saw me; there'd be no living with him if he did.

Catching a glimpse of myself in the mirror halted me. The woman staring back was someone I hardly recognized; all the cinching and restriction gave my body a heart-shaped look. Even partially braided, my dark hair billowed, framing my pale face before coming to rest at my low back. The diamond on my forehead only accentuated my bi-coloured eyes. The runes on my skin were on full display, giving me the air of a priestess. Perhaps Elis was right about the queen's intentions; the woman staring back at me screamed seduction.

A knock on the main door and someone traded whispers with Ada. She turned and nodded to me. It was time. I stood and the sleeves of the outfit flowed down, just touching the ground. The outfit also had a short gossamer silk train that trailed behind it. Absolutely ridiculous.

We thankfully made our way to the throne room in record time. The not-so-sneaky peeking from our retinue of guards, made me want to rip this outfit off and burn it along with their roaming eyes. Every step was sheer discomfort but my chin was high and dignity intact. I walked confidently, my hips swaying.

As we came to a stop at the throne room doors, I cracked my neck while giving myself a mental pep talk. Ada moved aside and I walked forward, two guards falling in behind me.

The room was the same as the last time I'd been here, except there was a buzz of excitement and anticipation in the room. All around, the courtiers were beautifully dressed. Some were elegant, others scantily clad like me, sex appeal oozing from them. There was something new, however.

Slaves. Young naked men and women with collars around their necks, sat at their master's feet. Some were being played with and others were tied in some sort of bondage. Not all were human either.

Unused to the sight, I kept my gaze forward, the scowl on my face hardening. As we neared the dais, a flash of movement caught my eye and I turned to see Elis and Llyr with shocked faces. Both blushed but Elis was the first to recover and gave me a reassuring smile and mouthed 'wow' to me. I shook my head at him and continued forward.

I approached the Queen, who was speaking with a finely dressed man that was leaning to whisper in her ear. A lean but muscled young man leaned against her legs, his curly brown head laid against her lap, and she stroked his hair. A naked girl, nipples clamped with a chain connecting them, knelt next to him with her gaze to the floor. Ragna turned to look at me, her mouth lilting into a satisfied smile.

"Ah, Lady Von Boden. You've arrived. I daresay, that look suits you." She grinned at my scowl. Her eyes travelled downwards and then back up and I felt exposed. It took everything in me to not hide. Or attack her.

"For being so small in stature, you are quite lovely of figure. Ethereal, even. No match for Vampiric standards, I dare say. Too bad the tattoos mar your beautiful skin. No matter, my consort will be most pleased, from what I can see." She continued to examine me like an insect on display.

I didn't respond and instead crossed my arms and raised a challenging brow. Deviousness played on her smile, and she licked her lips. A movement to my right and Oweyn appeared out of thin air, whispering in her ear. Ragna then turned to me with a full smile blossoming on her face.

"My consort has arrived! It's time! Oweyn, will you make Lady Von Boden more presentable?" She smirked at me.

"Yes, Your Highness." He straightened and nodded to the soldiers.

They grabbed my arms firmly and led me toward the obsidian throne. I tried to glance back at where Elis was, but the guards shoved me forward, my stockings slippery on the marble floor. Upon reaching the black throne, they turned and lifted me up, nearly throwing me into it. The throne was so tall that my feet couldn't touch the floor.

Suddenly, chains shot at my ankles, wrapping around them and pulled my legs wide. I struggled against them and managed to force my knees together. The guards raised my arms above my head. Chains shot from above, wrapping around my wrists, yanking up and behind the throne which forced my back to bow, and my chest pushed out. Where the chains came from I hadn't a clue.

Fucking magic, the bane of my existence, I mentally cursed.

I managed to keep my legs from being completely splayed, but my breath heaved. I could sense the chains were made of carbon steel with traces of iron. But magic crawled up them like a spiderweb, blocking me from accessing the elements. How easily I could turn this into a weapon if only magic was not in play. Yet, even if that were the case, it was too soon to make my move. Still, I felt my resolve crack ever so slightly. I shot the queen with a venomous glare.

"There, my pet," Ragna cooed, "You bind so beautifully! I cannot wait for Alcaeus to see you; what a gift you make! Perhaps I can convince him to let you take part in our entertainment one of these days. Once he has trained you, of course." She chuckled, sliding a gold-painted fingernail down my arm.

My self-pep talks in my room went straight out the window. I jerked at her, chains clanking together but remaining taut as she just laughed and leaned back against her throne, watching me. Regaining my composure, I looked away, focusing my stare on the floor. I refused to think about what she meant by 'entertainment'.

"Oh yes, breaking you will be most enjoyable." Ragna purred, then turned to face her court.

I was already hating this Alcaeus with every fibre of my being, his name the embodiment of my imprisonment. Needing a stronger focal point, I searched for my dear friend's face. When I found him, his face was filled with trepidation, but he tried to give me a reassuring nod. Next to Elis was the lithe and copper-haired Llyr, who had an arm around his waist. He looked at me with concern, perhaps even anger at the sight of the chains.

My arched back and tight corset made my breasts heave with each breath, annoying me to no end. Before I could focus on the strain the chains caused and the clawing humiliation, a deep horn sounded. The doors opened.

Everyone turned and cleared the aisle. A tall, heavily armed man entered, followed by a retinue of his men. All were similarly dressed in black and silver. His cloak concealed him, billowing as he went. The clank of armour and boots resounded through the hall. In my current position, it was difficult to get a good look, but his power suddenly swept through the room. Unlike Ragna's which seemed to seep into your bones, his came in like a stampede; images of charging cavalry and war drums came to mind. An irrational amount of fear cloyed my throat, threatening to suffocate me. I scowled and tamped it down.

Power that plays on fear. Can't say I am surprised.

As they came closer, I subconsciously struggled against my bonds. I refused to give my attention to the person who would be ultimately responsible for securing my servitude. Locking onto Elis' lavender eyes, they filled with apprehension and worry. His face softened and he gave me a gentle smile and nod that said it's going to be alright Mel, I'm here.

Armoured footsteps came to a halt before the dais and from the corner of my eye, I sensed his slight bow. His deep baritone voice filled the room.

"Greetings, Your Highness. I bring news of the success of our ventures in the Trillium Forest."

That voice...

"Excellent news, Prince Alcaeus. I had the utmost confidence you would. But first, I have a gift for you, my dear." She stood and the boy at her feet moved as she sauntered over to her consort.

Still, I kept my gaze away, finally closing my eyes as I continued to strain against my bonds. Only holding onto the image of Elis and Toby lest I give in and turn this entire room to dust. My patience edged closer to breaking. Not even when I heard the soft steps of his boots nearing close, metal clanking against metal, did I give in. Suddenly, all my thoughts stopped. This feeling. I knew this pull.

No no no...

Then his presence was before me and the demand to see him became too much. I opened my eyes. Black leather and linen, chainmail, and daggers filled my view. I didn't look up initially, for something caught my eye. Even in its sheath, the sword that was strapped to his left side, glowed brilliantly. I knew this sword; the same one that tried to come to my rescue several nights ago.

It's him!

A gloved hand grabbed my chin, forcing me to look up. I saw the moment recognition hit him, his brows rising in disbelief. At that moment, there was no one in the room but us. Towering over me, midnight eyes pierced me to my soul. Dark chestnut hair, half pulled back, hung straight around his face and shoulders. The rest of his face was just how I remembered it. We stared, trapped in each other's gazes.

Fear, shock, and warmth pooled in my belly. His leg pressed against the throne and between my knees, forcing them apart. I couldn't look away. Alcaeus reached up with his other hand and held the chains at my wrists. My heart raced as his large, gloved hand wrapped around both of mine. His warmth contrasted so clearly against the cold obsidian beneath me.

"Oh, little one..." he whispered.

Did he truly not know? I tilted my head at the possibility.

His eyes took me in, moving slowly down my body, desire evident in them. My own body responded, tightening. A growing heat trickled into my lower belly. His eyes shot up to my face and, for a moment, his gaze softened. His hand cupped my cheek, thumb gently moving back and forth underneath my eye. My breath caught in my chest, taking in the beautifully masculine face I had seen only a glimpse of by the fire.

"To see these eyes again." His voice was so quiet I almost didn't hear.

Without thinking, I closed the very ones he spoke of, leaning in. As if we had never left the forest.

The queen spoke, breaking the spell of the moment. "While you were gone, Melisandre Von Boden's ward was caught stealing Lord Abhartach's ring of power. In exchange for his life, she has agreed to become your Familiar." His attention snapped to Ragna. "Yes, my love, I am giving her to you. Am I not the most thoughtful lover?" She grinned when he didn't reply. "But what is even more fascinating is what we discovered during our little... chat. My spies were indeed correct." His brows lowered but he waited for her to continue. "She is the last Alchemist, my prince! We now control the power of Mother Nature herself! Not even Queen Mab would dare challenge me now. The Norns have smiled upon us." She laughed, clapping her hands together as her beautiful and cruel face filled with delight.

Alcaeus turned back to me, a look on his face dark and indiscernible.

Ragna walked up behind him, and whispered in his ear, "Now even the council cannot deny me." The look on her face as she looked down at me caused a dark tendril of dread to snake its way around my heart. Alcaeus didn't look at her, instead his face hardened as he beheld me. The queen's slender hips swayed as she made her way back to her throne. Her face suddenly became serious. "As such, my prince, I expect her to be broken and bound to you within the next three months. I want the first seal to be done by the end of the week. I have leverage if she attempts to give you issues. I trust you to not keep me waiting, my darling."

An underlying menace threaded through her voice, and I watched Alcaeus stiffen, his face a mask as he pulled away and faced the queen.

A stare-down ensued. But before tensions could rise, Alcaeus inclined his head and said, "I am unworthy of such a gift and I am grateful for your generosity, my queen," he spoke with a commanding softness, the rich tone sending butterflies through me. "Consider it done. There are other aspects of this issue I believe we must still discuss. For now, I am weary from my journey and eager to enjoy the comforts of home."

She waved him off, "Yes, yes of course. We can sort the details later. Take her with you for now; I placed her in your quarters to do with as you wish. Enjoy her, my love." Ragna became comfortable on her throne once more, though she watched us keenly.

My stomach plummeted. Alcaeus bowed his head stiffly, then turned to me once more.

Holding a hand above the chains, he whispered something. The chains pulled me to a stand and then released me with such force I was thrown forward. He caught me against his chest, his arm around my waist as he hugged me to him. For an instant, I felt sheltered from the enormity of the room and even the queen's insufferable schemes. Yet, just as abruptly, it ended when he turned, pulling me roughly down the steps of the dais just as Oweyn appeared.

"Oweyn, take Lady Von Boden back to her chambers. I have some other matters I need to attend to first. I will request her later."

"Very good, Your Highness."

Without sparing me a glance, Alcaeus walked past me, his men following behind him and disappearing into a room to the left of the throne.

My mind whirled, desperately trying to make sense of what just happened.

"This way my lady." I began to walk behind him until someone called my name. I stopped but Oweyn grabbed my arm and kept walking.

"Mels!" Elis moved through several courtiers and tried to walk with us. "Are you alright?"

"I'm fine, Elis. Just –"

The seneschal halted and turned to my friend.

"My lord Elis, please speak with Lady Von Boden at another time. She is commanded elsewhere."

Elis raised an eyebrow, full of contempt, but turned to me. "I'll come by in twenty minutes. I have clothes for you as well."

"Yes, please hurry. I'm burning this thing the moment I get the chance."

Elis grinned but before he could respond, Oweyn tugged me along. As we reached the doors of the room, I tugged my arm back and shoved a finger in his face.

"Grab me again and you'll be without a hand." I rubbed my arm. "I can walk just fine without you pulling my arm from its socket."

He sniffed, glaring down at me.

"Then do so, my lady," he sneered. "This way." Oweyn turned sharply, walking away briskly.

I stared at his back, entertaining violent thoughts. I started walking, almost at a run, to catch up.

When we reached my quarters, the doors were slammed shut behind me. The lock clicked home and I rolled my eyes at the uselessness of it.

My hand pressed against my corset, ready to turn this vulgar monstrosity into confetti but stopped when I realised that I had nothing else until Elis showed up, since Ada had also removed my bedclothes. So, going to stand in my favourite spot on the balcony, I gazed out at freedom like the caged bird I was.

It's him. The stranger in the forest. I shook my head. Did he know then? Did he know what I was that night? Why wouldn't he take me then? He must have suspected... and yet, he let me go. Perhaps he didn't know...

I sighed, pinching the stress of my chaotic thoughts from the bridge of my nose.

Yet warmth filled me recalling the moment we recognized each other. From the light of the pyre I had made, I knew there was a handsome face underneath that hood. Oh, how much it was and more so. His eyes were deep, dark pools that pierced right through me.

But not once in our encounter did I feel the depth of his power the way I had in the throne room. He had hidden it well; for me to feel it as much as I did, meant he was as frighteningly powerful as Elis had said. The worst part was that I was no closer to discovering a possible solution to this issue than I had been before I met him. It was quite possibly even worse. Sigh after sigh, there was nothing in me but feeling a twinge of hopelessness.

Thankfully, distraction came to the rescue as the door burst open. Elis glided in, holding a violin case. He was followed by several servants with clothes and boxes in their hands.

"Come, my lovely courtesan! As much as I love how ravishing you look in that 'tie me up and spank me, Daddy' outfit, we need to see you properly dressed." I snorted and couldn't help the laughter that escaped.

"You're incorrigible!" I laughed as I jumped down from my perch and walked into the sitting room.

"Oh, I am just getting started! But first—alcohol! After that whole," Elis waved one hand in a circle in the air, "whatever that was, I daresay our nerves need a bit of steadying." One of the servants approached him and handed him a very nice bottle of scotch, at which point Elis wiggled it at me. "As the humans would say: On the rocks or neat?"

"Neat," I replied quickly.

Thank the gods for Elis.

A. R. Morgan

CHAPTER 8

Servants filled the room, laying clothing, hats, shoes, and other accessories on the couches and the coffee table. Ada came in with the clothes I'd worn to the castle.

"I'll put these on your bed milady."

I nodded, making my way to the bedroom to change when Elis stopped me with a backbreaking hug.

"Oh, my darling Mel! When I saw Prince Alcaeus, I felt true fear... I'm so sorry, my dove. I wish I had more power in court; even I won't dare stand up to royalty." He pulled away, forlorn.

"Calm down Elis," I wheezed, wiggling against him, "it won't do to have the fabulous," I pushed at him until he released me, "and gorgeous Lord LeGervase losing his confidence right from the start. You're my anchor - if you're in hysterics, then that means we're positively fucked, old boy."

Sadness dissipating, Elis let out a laugh. With a twinkle in his eye, he said, "Well, I never thought I'd see the day when Lady Von Boden compliments a plebian like me! I want a full recording of you calling me gorgeous AND fabulous all in one sentence. You are quite right though: you are nothing without your right-hand man in charge of damage control in High Society."

He winked and laughed when I slapped his arm as I walked past him.

As soon as I entered my room and shut the door, the queen's 'gift' became nothing but shreds of fabric on the floor. Quickly changing into my own clothes, an immense amount of relief rushed over me as I regained a semblance of control. Returning to the sitting area, I found Ada laying out tea and small plates of food at the table. Elis was already

95

sipping his. I joined him, looking out over the clothes.

Yet my thoughts wandered back to Prince Alcaeus, attempting to process what happened.

"...and honestly, I really cannot believe you didn't turn those chains into paperclips. I mean, the look on your fa—Mel? Hello? Are you even listening?"

"Yes, Elis. I'm sorry. I'm just still trying to wrap my head around... everything." I waved my hand dismissively, reaching for my tea. He looked at me curiously, considering me.

"Indeed. Yes, our prince is quite something to behold, is he not? I did warn you."

"By 'warning', you mean he is as powerful as you claimed? Significantly so. It would be invaluable to know the extent of it."

"You're evading. You know exactly what I mean, don't pretend. And it sounds like you'll be learning the extent of him as well, according to our queen."

I rolled my eyes to stare at him, giving him a deadpan look.

"Only that which is necessary to secure my freedom," I said.

"Oh, come now, Mel. I've known you for hundreds of years and if I know anything about your weaknesses, well... devastatingly handsome men are at the top of the list. Prince Alcaeus certainly fits that description. He is Athena's Champion, after all."

I sputtered. "First of all, what would dear Llyr say if he knew you were talking up another man? Second, that is an absolute lie. I will deny it until the day I die. I am not weak against male beauty. Gods, Elis, if I didn't know any better, I'd say you were trying to get me into your prince's bed."

"It could certainly have its advantages." He considered. At my open-mouthed stare, Elis smiled mischievously and continued. "Llyr would agree, though. We both know that he would have welcomed a man such as Prince Alcaeus to our bed without a second thought. I'd have happily joined in, too, assuming the warlord didn't slay us in our sleep afterward." He paused, giving me an admonishing look. "Jealousy is for humans, my pet, and we are certainly in the twenty-first century. Besides," he said, taking a delicate bite of cherry tart, "in five words I can prove you wrong." I scoffed at his claim. He grinned. "Edward, Jericho, Callum, Henry—"

"Enough! I get it." I interrupted, trying to stave off additional embarrassment. "They were years apart though and they were but fanciful flings when my biology demanded company." It was a weak argument but true.

This time, Elis rolled his eyes. "Biology demanded company... God's teeth woman, it is a wonder you ever engaged in anything involving 'biology' or 'company' at all! Regardless, every single one of them probably made Narcissus green with envy. Wasn't Jericho a model?"

"Actor, but I believe it's the same thing. That was a weeklong romance, mind you. I couldn't risk media attention, you know that. Anyways, I should probably tell you," I paused, suddenly overcome with shyness, "that, well uh... Alcaeus and I met already."

Elis dropped his tart. "WHAT?! How? When?"

"On my way here, I was set upon by forest golems while taking a rest by Isolee Lake. He helped me kill them, although I didn't know who he was. Everything was so dark. Although, it was... quite strange."

"Strange? How so?"

I shook my head, cheeks warming. The words struggled to come to me. "He... well, just how he behaved."

Elis leaned closer.

"Oh, come on, Mels! Explain! Did he try to kill you? Stab you? I vaguely remember his power lies in the ability to manipulate ill will. Did he turn your powers against you?"

"No, no nothing of the sort. Um, he... well he..." I stammered, still struggling to find the words.

"He what, Melly? Spit it out!"

"He... put his arms around me and mentioned something about having wanted to see my eyes up close. For a moment I thought he was going to kiss me. He... acted so familiarly. It was almost as if he had known me before, although I'd never met him, and yet... och," I blustered, my whole body turning crimson.

Too uncomfortable for Elis' reaction, I became far more interested in my tea. For a brief moment, I considered telling him about this 'pull' inside my chest whenever Alcaeus was near. But there was little point; knowing my friend, he'd have me married the next day over this 'feeling'.

When I finally chanced a glance at him, Elis' eyebrows had climbed up, almost to his hairline. For once, he didn't have a teasing reply, giving me the courage to continue.

"Alcaeus recognized me in the throne room when he made me

look at him, mentioning my eyes once more. Though, for me, it was his sword that gave him away. The metal is not of this earth; its radiance almost blinded me. I had thought him maybe a high-ranking Vampire soldier or a noble at most. Certainly not royalty, let alone a Champion."

Silence fell on both of us, and I found shelter from further embarrassment behind my upraised cup of tea. The china clinked as I placed it down in favour of some of the sandwiches and fruit arrayed in front of me.

Finally, Elis straightened. "Yes, you would notice that sword. That is the legendary sword of retribution, Nemesis. Forged by Hephaestus and gifted to the prince by his maker, Athena. Nevertheless, this is most unexpected. While I certainly cannot blame him for being enraptured by your beauty, I agree with you, his reaction is quite strange. This could either pose a huge risk or work in our favour."

"How could this possibly work in our favour, Elis? If anything, his behaviour so far complicates matters entirely."

"Yes, you would see it that way. However, you don't know the depth of drama and intrigue that riddles the Vampire court. I told you before - beneath all the pretty words, Alcaeus and Ragna are not the happy couple the queen wishes them to be. Yes, indeed, this could very much work to our advantage..."

I could see the wheels turning behind those amethyst eyes.

"I don't like your face right now, Elis. What are you scheming?" I asked warily.

"What do you mean 'right now'? Are you implying you normally do?" he asked but then thrust a hand out the moment my face gave my answer away. "Exactly. We both know that's a lie. Anyways, I shall not be distracted! Now, I will need to spend more time around the Lady of Gossip, not to mention pick Llyr's brain. I have been away from court for too long. Regardless, I did tell you that Prince Alcaeus is not the Royal Consort by choice, remember? Ragna trapped him somehow. There is no love lost between them."

Realisation dawned on me. I could see the path Elis was taking and I snorted incredulously. "You think we can make him an ally through... what? Seduction?"

He paused, choosing his words carefully. "I think it's worth testing that, yes. Indeed, desire is a powerful tool. Wielded appropriately, even the head of a king can be turned. Yet there is a risk. Desire is a double-edged sword; anything less than surefootedness and precise planning would see you bleeding; you would need to play your cards right." He took a sip of his tea. "You could lose much if Prince Alcaeus proves loyal only to his own ambitions."

"So, what you're saying is I either lose my freedom to the queen or potentially lose both my dignity and my soul to her consort."

He sighed. "Precisely."

"No, I'm not sleeping with him, Elis. This is me we're talking about! When have I ever been that... that..."

"That what?" Elis asked, exasperated.

"Manipulative!" I snapped, shooting out of my chair to pace back and forth. "All of this scheming and plotting! There must be another way. I will find a way."

"In case you haven't noticed, we are very limited on options. We could not have asked for a better chance! You could have the Prince of Nightmares on your side! You have the beauty for it! Your personality, um, well..."

"I will not trade my dignity, my values, for a slim chance at freedom. That is not who I am. You of all people should know that!" I snapped. "I would rather be true to myself as a slave than forsake all ethics and honour, my own integrity, as a free woman!"

"I would never doubt your code of honour Melisandre. Nor would I ever suggest you jeopardise it under any other circumstance!" He stood, facing me. "But this is an opportunity we mustn't ignore! Our only opportunity. Surely you see the possibilities! If there is even a remote chance we can sway Alcaeus to our side, we'll have the best chance of seeing you free from Ragna—Oh, don't look at me like that. I would do anything to see you free and Toby safe, even scamming the very Prince of Nightmares."

I shook my head, my passionate defence extinguishing as a reluctant smile tugged at the corners of my lips. Elis' tender love for us was undeniable, his passion at seeing me free putting out my own inner fire. Despite my whole tirade, the seed that Elis planted took root. Aggressively. The thought of getting to know Alcaeus provoked excitement and dread in equal measure. Perhaps it would even guarantee a measure of security for Toby.

Dropping the smile, I grimaced.

"It's not your worst idea, Elis. Consider it duly noted but no more than that. Not tonight. There is still too much we don't know. It would be foolish to decide anything, right now. I have a few days before he is supposed to give me this first 'seal' that the queen spoke of. I need to research. I need to find the library. If only I were permitted to go to the Guild of Antiquities; I might have found some useful information. Besides, dare I say discussing this openly in the queen's castle... who knows who could be listening."

Elis stood, giving me a nonchalant wave. "Only my flowers, my dear. They would alert me if we had company. Plants do so make the best spies. Anyways, I'll have Llyr visit and see what he can find. He's with Toby right now; I promised I'd come to relieve him once I'd brought you the clothes and we'd had time to talk." He waved at all the clothes in the sitting area. "Go through any of this you wish and anything you don't want, have Ada send it back to me. I would stay and help you, but I already know the pieces you are going to choose. I am far too emotionally drained to bear witness to the funeral attire you claim as your wardrobe. I'm three bottles of wine too short for that, I'm afraid."

He gave me a quick kiss on the forehead and made his way out, leaving me to ponder the impossibility of what he had suggested. To navigate the one thing that I remained wilfully and deliberately inexperienced in – seduction and romance. If it were such a simple matter of lust, perhaps I could do it. However, this wasn't a human man I was dealing with; this was the prince of Vampires. A Champion. Conquering their body was not enough, for lust is but a flame with little fuel, burning out quickly. You want the lasting heat of coals. You want the heart of the fire.

The heart of a slayer of gods.

I shuddered.

Books were so much simpler. Elements, transmutation circles, physics, science and knowledge... all of which I could bury myself into and know what to do. The chemistry between two living organisms for the purpose of procreation? Understandable. But not this; this psychological game of ensnaring another's mind and heart.

I was out of my depth.

Turning my attention to the gifts Elis had left behind, I walked over to the couch where the violin case sat. I trailed my fingers over the smoothed wood. A twinge of homesickness filled me. Gently opening the case, I gasped. Elis didn't just bring me any violin–he brought me a Stradivarius. Truly, one of the pinnacles of human craftsmanship, the violin was exquisitely made. Who he had to off or what museum he robbed to get his hands on such a rare instrument, I didn't want to know. I took several moments to appreciate this genuine piece of human history. Finally, I grabbed the bow. After several minutes of tuning and putting resin on the fine horsehair of the bow, I placed it on my shoulder. It felt so right.

The moons shone brightly against the night sky, so I went to the balcony. The night was perfectly quiet as I began to play. The sound was incredible, melting away any thoughts but the musical notes dancing through the air. I glanced upward, into the eyes of two Barred owls perched along the castle parapets. I smiled. My heart was on my bow, my emotions conveyed with every press against the board. The night was my stage as I serenaded the moon and stars, and my winged audience.

CHAPTER 9

It wasn't until the following evening that Alcaeus summoned me. Unease churned my stomach. The reality of my impending doom threatened to swallow me as I walked behind the queen's steward. Oweyn had come rather abruptly to my door right after I awoke, finding me drinking a steaming cup of coffee on the veranda. His distaste for me, along with my foul mood and few choice words for him made the walk awkward and unbearable.

Much to Ada's dismay, I dressed in the clothes I arrived in, although I had my face uncovered. I wanted all the protection I could afford; I had no idea of the depths of Alcaeus's magic, and I couldn't allow our recent interactions to blind me to its potential. I tried to focus on my goals, and on gaining any information that could help my cause. But my heart felt like it was stampeding out of my chest. Nerves on edge, I scowled at Oweyns's stiff form.

I have never been as socially adept as Elis; his cultured smoothness and charming energy make him a flame among moths. I cared little for social niceties, preferring brutal directness and productive conversation. Truly, I preferred no conversation at all; thus, why I try to keep it efficient. And short.

Perhaps I should consider trying to emulate Elis. But the image of me attempting to flirt my way to Alcaeus's good graces only made me snort, shaking my head.

I only had time for several possible scenarios and planned speeches in my head as we walked down the corridor. Based on our direction, Prince Alcaeus' personal quarters appeared to be in the opposite wing of the tower. We took several turns before coming to a stop at another pair of double doors.

Oweyn knocked.

"Come in." A deep voice beyond the door answered.

103

Whatever plans and confidence I had, flew to oblivion. Oweyn opened the door. I stared through to what appeared to be a study but didn't enter.

"My lady. If. You. Would," Oweyn said through gritted teeth, his patience gone. He motioned sharply at the open door.

I slid my eyes to him in annoyance but walked forward. The door shut behind me with a snap, causing me to jump a little.

I hate that man, I thought as I glared back at the door.

After entering, I avoided looking at Alcaeus, focusing on my surroundings instead. The walls were lined with ornate shelves, filled from top to bottom with books and manuscripts. Unique bookends and baubles sat in the nooks and crannies, among other random items on display. A marble chess table with two chairs sat next to one of the walls. A roaring fireplace with a lounge area. The room itself was about as large as my own sitting area similar to my own down the hall, The colours were warm mahogany, gold, and burgundies. The smells of cinnamon, parchment, and wood fire filled my nose. A balcony lay behind him and there were a pair of doors on the far-left side of the room. Under better circumstances, this would be a literary paradise for me; cosy, warm, and full of books. But I couldn't let my guard down when the prince of Vampires sat before me.

My eyes finally fell on him. The prince had yet to look up at me, finishing what he was writing. He sat at a huge carved mahogany desk; the intricate woodwork breathtaking. Alcaeus was a large man himself, however, so the desk did not dwarf him. Quite the opposite; it made his presence even more imposing.

His long-burnished hair was half pulled back in a dishevelled, sexy sort of way, some pieces having escaped and framed his face. Dressed simply, in a white linen shirt, sleeves rolled up his arms. His sword glinted, resting on the wall behind him.

Putting his pen down, he leaned back in a slow and deliberate manner, finally acknowledging me. His gaze was calculated but curious. I watched him keenly. Alcaeus stood and moved around the front of his desk, leaning against it and crossing his arms. His face was unreadable.

The prince motioned to the chair in front of him.

"Please, sit."

Looking at the seat and then back up at him, I ignored his command. Instead, I turned and nonchalantly moved toward the nearest bookcase. I set about perusing, giving an air of disregard, despite my every sense being tuned in to the Vampire behind me.

"So," he said with a deep softness, "Melisandre Von Boden – the mysterious beauty in the wood. The last living Alchemist. Soon to be my Familiar, if the queen gets her way. We meet again." Alcaeus cocked his head at me. "Tell me, how could such a mythical creature like you get trapped by the likes of Ragna? After what I saw in the forest, I know you're more than capable of handling yourself."

Not answering right away, I held his gaze for a moment, ignoring that pulsating feeling within me, encouraging me to step closer. "Why don't *you* tell me why, Prince Alcaeus? Masked stranger who suspiciously failed to introduce himself that night. I would wager you know exactly how it happened. And why." I said pointedly. I grabbed a book written in Old Norse and flipped through it. When he did not respond, I continued without looking at him. "What is there to say? Ragna manipulated and blackmailed me, using the life of my ward as collateral, over some trumped-up charges. Even now, that witch holds Toby hostage in order to guarantee my submission, despite agreeing to let him go." I sneered, angrily snapping the book shut. "What I want to know is this: how do you play into all of this? Did you know who I was when we met that night?"

His eyes narrowed, my abruptness causing him to straighten. Ignoring my questions, he instead asked, "Trumped-up charges? Do you deny your ward a thief? Claim the queen a liar?"

Pushing off the desk, he walked over to me. I turned to face him, back pressed against the shelves. Alcaeus stopped less than a yard away, eyes boring into mine.

"I don't deny that the Brownie hybrid that is my ward struggles with kleptomania and has, on frequent occasions, rendered a few pockets and wallets lighter. He is half Brownie— we both know it is in their nature! I do, however, find it highly suspicious-no, mathematically and physically impossible that a ten-year-old boy could somehow get past who knows how many wards, a double-locked, secured display case, AND the crime going unnoticed by a Vampire noble who never left his side AND nearly got to the Seelie border before being apprehended. Ragna insults my intelligence if she really thinks I am fooled by her obvious ploy. It was a set-up. Toby was just bait." I gave him a pointed look. "We both know why."

Hand rubbing his jaw, he gave a slight inclination of his head. "Indeed, rather blatantly I might add. This then begs the question as to why you did not just leave the boy to his fate. The moment he was taken, surely you knew it was not about him?"

I looked away, crossing my arms. "I accepted responsibility for him three years ago; I will not sacrifice the few values I have just to hide away in cowardice," I snapped. Turning to look at him, I asked, "What hand had you in this, Alcaeus? Did your plans of capture fall through so you used my ward to give you the upper hand? Are you that much of a coward?"

At my accusation, the prince's eyes narrowed and his back straightened as he took a measured step towards me. That baritone voice hit deeper than before. "Careful, Melisandre. While your anger and suspicion are not unwarranted, being accused of cowardice is not something I take lightly." We held each other's stare, neither backing down, but he continued. "Now, I am not surprised over Ragna's schemes, but I played no part in them. The queen tends to rely only on her own personal council in all that she does. My mission in the Trillion Forest was exactly as I had told you—rampaging golems and other wild Fae wreaking havoc in our lands." He took another step towards me. "I was just as surprised as you when I saw you chained to my throne." The look on his face sharpened, making my heart race. "Had I known what she had planned, that night in the forest would have ended quite differently." A dark promise coated his words and warmth threatened to suffuse my cheeks, held back only by sheer will.

With a frown on my face, I lifted my chin.

"Perhaps. Perhaps not. Either way, it would not have ended the way you think it would."

The prince smirked. "The little Alchemist has a bit of fire in her. Good." Then his grin deepened as a brow lifted. "Or, perhaps, that night would have shown you exactly who and what you are dealing with."

I narrowed my eyes at him. "I believe that is precisely what I am trying to see now."

A calculated hunger sparked in his eyes and Alcaeus leaned against the bookcases, crossing his arms. It was impossible not to watch the muscles tense at the movement; strength emanated from him. The tension unnerved me and I broke away, facing the books once more. Grabbing another tome in Arabic, I flipped through it before settling on the page.

I stared. And stared.

When had Arabic been so difficult to read?

Where my brain had gone, I dared not wonder, instead asking the question I'd been dreading.

"So then," I began, clearing my throat, "Would you care to explain the exact process of becoming a Vampire's Familiar?"

He didn't answer right away and I could feel his stare, but my attention was committed to the book in my hands. Just as I started to feel the itch to look at him, he answered.

"A Familiar," he said, "must desire to become one with its master and the master with the Familiar. The seal itself requires three marks, each taking several weeks to manifest itself. The closer the bond, the faster it takes hold. Your mind, body, and whatever powers you possess will be at my sole command. It's an intricate bond that entwines our souls, chaining yours to mine." His voice was velvet against my skin, rumbling deep at his last words.

Even so, goosebumps broke out over my body and my hands tightened around the book. Fear and panic nibbled at my stomach at the idea of being chained to anyone like that for eternity. I pushed it down, my breath shallow.

"And I take it this 'seal' involves..."

"My bite, yes." He sounded amused.

I swallowed, clenching my jaw.

"Touch me with those," I flipped the page, "and I'll transmute your canines into fountain pens." Throwing him a challenging look, I held it long enough to get my point across. Then I turned my eyes back to the text.

In one swift movement, Alcaeus crowded me, and I dropped the book.

"W-What are you doing?" I looked around rapidly for escape but there was none.

I backed up into the corner of the bookcases, plastering my arms against them. The prince towered over me, arms caging me in. Alarm shot through me as my heart rate spiked. Too long had I spent in the human realm, among modern human men. I realised my folly and carelessness too late.

Discomfort and rising anger bubbled inside me. For once, the eeriness of my gaze had no effect, as Alcaeus refused to budge. This position forced me to look up at him. My head reached his mid-chest, and the width of his shoulders blocked my view of the room. A quiet, deadly strength radiated off him. His beard and moustache were so closely trimmed, slightly longer than a five-o-clock shadow, that I could see a small white scar on his cheek and upper lip. A matching scar could be seen cutting through his left eyebrow. The battle scars only added to his raw masculinity.

The intimate proximity also revealed that his eyes were not black like I had first thought, but so deep a blue that it was like looking at the edges of a midnight sky. A loose piece of dark chestnut hair hung in front of his face as he bent his head towards mine, brushing his lips, causing my eyes to flicker towards them. The memory of that night in the forest burned in my mind.

Humans always portrayed Vampires as tall and thin. No, true Vampires were the gladiators of the gods and built as such. Majestic and statuesque, with the arrogance and possessiveness of their creators to boot.

Eyes holding his attention, my fingers slowly locked onto the spine of a book, getting ready to transmute it into a spike depending on Alcaeus's next move.

"I'm warning you-" I whispered.

Before I could finish, he snagged hold of my wrist that held the book, with threatening strength. It tumbled to the ground. Without thinking, I tried to slap him with my other hand. He caught my wrist an inch from his face and gave a laugh of disbelief.

"Do you always try to slap a man more than twice your size?"

"Who said it would end in a slap?" I challenged him back.

Jerking me closer, I felt his breath across my face. "I do not believe you understand," his voice deepened, "the gravity of the situation, little Alchemist. Neither of us has a choice in this matter. Fight me all you want but what Ragna wants, she will inevitably get. She will stop at nothing to break, twist, and wring you of all life to get what she desires. So, your willingness is paramount to making this work." He stared at me with such intensity that I couldn't look away. "For if you value your ward's soul, you'll uphold your end of the deal."

Incredulous, I scoffed. "Neither of us has a choice, you say? Are you really telling me that you would not go through with this if given the choice? To pass up the opportunity to control the powers of nature itself? Why do I find it difficult to believe a Champion of Athena is just as chained as I?"

Alcaeus's face turned to stone; his grip became bruising. "Even Champions of gods are not without their weaknesses," he hissed through clenched teeth. He grabbed my chin between his thumb and forefinger. "Make no mistake, Melisandre: Ragna's time is at hand, but her end will not be today, tomorrow, or even a month from now. So, until then, we do as she demands. To do otherwise would put everything at risk and countless lives would be lost."

Warning bells rang and questions abounded in my head at his words. I opened my mouth to let them free. What he did next stopped me in my tracks. His muscles flexed, then relaxed a bit. Eyes travelling downward, they stopped at my chest. The outrage that blossomed was quickly snuffed out when I realised it was the rune above my cleavage that had caught his attention. The hand holding my face released me. Then the tips of his fingers caressed my jawline and the sensation seemed to amplify across my skin. Those long fingers followed the line of my neck and chest, finally coming to a stop at the rune.

"What does this mean?" he asked, voice almost a rumbling whisper.

"I—Uhm," I struggled to respond as the back of his knuckles moved lower, brushing the top of my breasts.

A stab of desire speared my core. Breathing was becoming unnecessarily difficult. His eyes came back and captured mine again, waiting for my response. A knowing look crossed his face; he knew full well what he was doing to me.

"It's...it's my primary r-rune," I said, annoyed at how breathless I sounded. "All Alchemists are born with one. It, um..." his fingers continue tracing a path on my chest, "it is how we transmute our fundamental element, the one genetically linked to us."

Once again, that thrum between us pulled at me; calling to me like a lighthouse in a storm. I couldn't think. Nor did I make any move to pull away or fight him. I was caught, weak, in the moment. Even as my fight-or-flight response went off in my head, I waited.

"And what," he murmured against my neck, just below my ear, "is yours?"

Fingers delicately traced across my face, knuckles dragging along my cheek.

Just as I was about to give up all sense and reason, I remembered the very intimate connection he had with the queen of this kingdom. I stiffened and jerked my neck away; he still didn't release my wrist, but he was no longer touching my face.

"I know what you're trying to do, prince," I sneered, "and it won't work. Go seduce your own wife if you're going to play that game. Let go of me."

Not releasing me, Alcaeus's eyes narrowed. A sly smile bloomed on his handsome face.

"Not married. Engaged. Quite unwillingly, I might add. Queen Ragna wanted her claim on me to be incontestable so Royal Consort I became, despite it being rather untrue. Semantics, really. So, you can save your jealousy for the moment." At my look of outrage, he grinned, jerking me back to him once more, this time wrapping an arm around my waist.

I pushed against him, but he had a firmer grip on me than the damn forest golem.

"Release me!"

"Not," Alcaeus leaned down and nuzzled my cheek, sliding to my ear and whispered, "until you realise that this is no game I play. I will not deny that I, too, have my own ulterior motives, but I can assure you they are not aligned with the queen." His breath blew into the shell of my ear, causing me to hold my own for a moment. "But you are correct—I am trying to seduce you."

Releasing my wrist, his hand slid into my hair, grasping it firmly. He pulled. I resisted but still, my neck was vulnerable. A rush of wetness pooled inside me just as fear clawed at my throat. With a powerful combination of rising panic and desire, my mind clouded as I scrambled to think of a way to transmute a Vampire. It was then that I remembered my conversation with Elis.

This was my chance.

Alcaeus just admitted he was not on the queen's side and that his engagement was a farce; while I couldn't afford to trust him, neither could I pass up this opportunity. So, for once, I gave into desire, allowing it to overcome me. This allowed me to actually take him in. I stared up into the midnight galaxy that was the royal consort's eyes.

He searched my own face with a heated look, seeing my surrender. Lips brushed against my cheek, finding their way down to the line of my jaw.

His next words whispered against my skin in a gentle caress.

"Breathtaking," kissing the corner of my mouth.

He pulled back slightly, "Oh little Alchemist, that fire in you. The Nightmare Court of Khaviel may be filled with deception and intrigue. We dance to the tune of blood and death. Ragna will surely drag you into the depths of night; and when she does, may that flame burn so bright it renders the darkness obsolete."

My breath caught at his words. His lips hovered over mine. I waited for him to close what little distance there was.

But it never came.

Alcaeus turned his head slightly as if he heard a noise; I heard nothing. Releasing me abruptly, he reappeared instantly next to the desk. I was so disoriented that I stumbled, catching myself against the bookcase.

What just happened?

"You will join me for dinner in two days. Unfortunately, I have other matters to attend to. We can discuss more then, including any other questions you have about the ritual. My steward, Tomwyl, will see you back to your rooms."

He still had his back to me, fiddling with what seemed to be a pipe. Suddenly, the door opened, and a well-decorated soldier stepped in. The first thing I noticed was a wicked scar slashed across the entirety of his face.

He moved to the side and a black-cloaked figure came in holding a gnarled oak staff. Static finger-like branches held a large resin sphere with brilliant sapphire shards that seemed to float inside. Curious.

"Sire, I have information about—" he stopped, noticing me. He shifted his stance and said, "We must speak, Your Highness."

Alcaeus tossed me a look over his shoulder. "You may go now, Melisandre."

Dismissed. Just like that.

Fury and embarrassment exploded within me. I swear my stare could have burned the arrogant prince's body to ash. But being the dignified scientist that I was, I straightened my shoulders and made my way to the door.

I glanced up at the soldier as I passed. Heavily decorated, his armour shone bright and gleamed with his helmet tucked under one arm. Winter-blue eyes looked at me warily, but curiosity was hidden beneath them. Yet the moment his gaze met mine, they widened and jerked away, clearly unnerved.

The hooded figure said nothing but, like a phantom, moved around me until it was several feet away to my left as I faced the door. A coldness prickled my skin as I peeked a glance at the wraith-like figure; it was all magic and darkness, its mysteries filling me with unease.

I glanced over my shoulder and said, "I will do what needs to be done, Prince Alcaeus. Be sure you do as well." I shut the door, not waiting for a reply.

Once outside, the door locked behind me. A straight-backed, greying Vampire was standing there in black livery. His face was professional but when he saw me, his eyes softened, gently motioning for me to follow him. Tomwyl was the opposite of Oweyn in every way. He had a kindness that radiated off him that made his presence quite comforting, especially after all of the previous stimulation.

We did not speak, but after all that had happened, I embraced the peace.

CHAPTER 10

"Is that...? Is she...?"

"Yes, Sotiris, that was the Alchemist," said Alcaeus. "Last of her kind." He took a long puff from his simple, hand-carved pipe. He was leaning against the open archway that led out to the balcony, staring off into the distance.

"Her eyes... I have never seen the like. And those... What were those symbols?"

"Hmm," grunted the prince, the only answer he gave.

His second in command hesitated for a moment before coming to stand across from him. It was clear Sotiris wanted to say something, but he waited for leave to do so. While his commander was considerably saner and more patient than the queen, Alcaeus was still the most fearsome warrior Khaviel had ever seen. He was the embodiment of the goddess Athena, whom even the other gods of war respected and feared. Yet he was, above all, wise and thus Sotiris waited upon his council.

"Did you look into the matter with the boy?"

"Yes, Sire. It was as you suspected." After a moment, Sotiris continued, "If it was not for Cillian noticing the little bit of magical residue, I do not believe we would have noticed it. He has placed the signature wards, as you commanded." He shifted his stance, glancing out onto the veranda. "The queen's resources are impressive as always, along with the ingenuity of her lackeys."

The Lich from Ebroriath spoke from the shadows of his cloaked head.

"Ilirhun disrupted the ley line that runs through the Guild to put a displacement enchantment upon the ring and the glass surrounding it. When the boy touched the glass, it transported it onto his hand. He had to have been there to ensure the ring would go specifically to the boy;

that was where he made his first mistake. I could smell that rotten mage leagues away. The Sickness grips him."

Sotiris' lip curled in disgust. "Ilirhun should have been put down like the rat he is before he infects the rest of court!" He shook his head. "I just do not understand this; the queen has been obsessed for months over this woman. How powerful can this...this Alchemist truly be? They are but a myth! They should be extinct! Ragna must be infected as well, as that is the only explanation for this ridiculousness." Seeing Alcaeus's expression, the general swallowed his tirade and continued with his news. "Also, there has been word that the queen plans on hosting Yaldā here. For what reasons, I do not know. It is not even the Vampire's turn yet the Kings and Queens of Were have given up their right to host. With tensions rising with the Seelie..." Sotiris shook his head, "it is quite the risk."

Alcaeus blew several smoke rings, one arm tucked around his chest. He remained silent.

"Is it because of...?" Sotiris asked.

The prince looked at him, although he still did not reply. He did not need to; Sotiris already knew. Rubbing a hand over his scarred face, the general sighed.

"The Alchemist... The queen wants to show off her new toy."

"It is more than that, Sotiris. Yes, it is a power play. I also believe she desires to see the extent of Melisandre's abilities, using her enemies as test subjects." Smoke curled around the consort, casting him in a haze. "Unusually predictable for Ragna, but her point has been made. We are closer to war than ever; the recent golem attacks are just a petty distraction. With Lady Von Boden under her control, she is sending a clear message to those that seek to destroy her. Would you challenge a queen who not only possesses the power of soul-tethering but now controls the might of the last Alchemist? It would be most unwise," he took a puff, exhaling, "to underestimate this 'toy' and the destruction Melisandre could wield if Ragna truly has her in her claws."

Sotiris considered his prince's words, fiddling with the pommel of his sword at his side. He knew little of the mythical species; only that they didn't wield magic the way the other creatures in their realm did. He had heard stories of some Alchemists being able to change objects and structures into something else or perform unbelievable natural feats without magic. But it was all legend, hearsay. Many different kingdoms went in search of these creatures, hoping to capture these 'branches of Yggdrasil', but they remained shrouded in mystery. And yet...

"Sire," Sotiris began, gathering his courage. "You have known of Lady Von Boden's presence for some time now, even before Her Majesty got wind of her. If she is as dangerous as you say, then–"

"She is," interjected Cillian, "dangerous. I have seen a little of what this Alchemist can do, Sotiris. This one is more than what the rest of her species was, and I believe Ragna and our Commander know this."

"You are also wondering... why did I not take her for myself before Ragna could, using Von Boden's powers to overthrow her? Or just kill the Alchemist before she was discovered?"

The general swallowed nervously, then nodded. Even Cillian held his silence, waiting for his lord to answer.

Alcaeus looked back at them with a calculated stare, taking a deliberate inhale and exhale. Loose tendrils of dark hair moved gently in the wind, brushing slightly past his shoulders and some whispering across his chiselled face. He was broad; not ox-broad but taller and slightly wider than his general. Sotiris knew through years of sparring matches of his commander's long and lethal reach, the strength in the swing of his sword, and being at the mercy of his profound agility. Thousands of years of leadership could be seen in the strength of his posture. Pushing off the archway, Alcaeus moved toward the outside.

Gazing out over his kingdom, he said quietly, "Some things are just not meant for our world, Sotiris. Their beauty, amplified only by their ignorance of it. Melisandre is an innocent, inevitably caught up in a battle between the Nightmare Court's most powerful leaders. A war that will soon spill over, if it has not already, and include many other kingdoms. Now that she is here, she has become the most valuable of all pieces in play. As I knew she would if she came. I was content protecting her location from afar, but when I caught wind that Ragna discovered her, I knew it was only a matter of time." He sighed, tapping the tobacco out of his pipe. He tucked it away and turned to face Sotiris. "As for killing her–No," Alcaeus shook his head, "Death was not meant for one such as her. It would be neither mercy nor justified. That is not her fate. The Fates themselves have brought Melisandre here to me; their motives only I am privy to and it will remain that way until the time is right. So, we let Ragna play her games. Only until our own plans have time to mature, to come to fruition. To have expedited them in an unlikely endeavour to convince Melisandre to side with us, with me, when she otherwise had no incentives would have only backfired in the end." He looked away again, arms crossed, gazing out across his kingdom. "Now, she has just cause to. She has no choice," he said softly in the gentle breeze.

Sotiris leaned his head thoughtfully. It was not lost on him, the slight change in inflection, the softening in his tone when the prince spoke of Lady Von Boden. He and the Lich were the only ones who knew of Alcaeus's mysterious interest in the strange little Alchemist, and it puzzled him now as much as it did when she was discovered by his lord.

For weeks at a time, the prince would disappear; it was not uncommon for him to venture occasionally to the human realm. His love for their artistic culture was well known. However, when Sotiris braved questioning him, he did reveal the existence of the woman, but otherwise kept her race and any other of her mysteries to his own counsel. He swore Sotiris and Cillian to secrecy, which his general understood.

At first, Sotiris thought it was merely a matter of keeping her safe from the queen's jealousy, but over time, it became evident it was something more. When he offered to send guards to watch over her, Prince Alcaeus shut him down completely. Cillian tried next, providing tracking and protection spells. He too was disregarded, and they wisely did not bring it up again with their liege.

In the fifteen hundred years of being at the prince's side, never had the Champion set his sights on a woman the way he did with Lady Von Boden.

Armoured fingers tapped his lips as Sotiris asked, "Did you know what the Lady Von Boden was, Sire?"

"I had my suspicions. Alchemists have always been legends and I was never blessed enough to meet one in the flesh, in all my years. They were right to conceal themselves from hunters. The rare ones that were captured expired too quickly to be studied, from what I understand. When I first saw Melisandre, it was also the first time I witnessed a real transmutation; it only reaffirmed my convictions on hiding and protecting her. I believe she is unique to her kind, however, just as Cillian suggests."

"What do you mean?"

"I need more information before I can answer that, Sotiris. On your way out, stop by and ask Sage Kevyn to send all manuscripts and

116

texts on Alchemists that we possess."

"Of course, My Lord."

Sotiris turned but stopped, hesitating.

"My Lord, I must say: the queen played right into your hands; she practically gave the Alchemist to you on a silver platter. I still cannot work out why she does not take Lady Von Boden for herself. Is she finally succumbing to her madness? I cannot help but be concerned at Queen Ragna's ulterior motives."

Alcaeus did not answer. Instead, he straightened and went back inside. Going over to the book that Melisandre had dropped during their encounter, he picked it up and brushed his fingers over the cover before placing it back on the shelf. He knew why the queen did not take his little Alchemist as her Familiar but kept the truth to himself. Without a doubt, the petite silver and golden-eyed woman was a key piece in Ragna's twisted game, but not her end goal. His scheming fiancée had only ever wanted one thing–him.

It was always him.

While he trusted his Second in Command the most, there were some truths better left hidden in shadow until they were ready to come into the light.

"Cillian," Alcaeus said, turning to the cloaked figure. "Listen closely to the shadows; Melisandre is our singular goal; keeping her safe is our prerogative. Put whatever wards you see fit on her chambers and that of her ward's. We must complete the mark at all costs. Try to keep Ilirhun and his lackeys one step behind."

"Yes, my liege. Your wish is my command."

Shadow consumed the Lich, and he was gone. A soft knock at the door interrupted the silence left in his wake.

"Come in."

The door opened to reveal Tomwyl, Alcaeus's valet. The Vampire was slight of frame, but the black and silver uniform was clean-cut and form-fitting, giving him a fashionable air.

"You called for me, Sire."

"Yes, Tomwyl, I did. Could you please invite Lord Elis LeGervase and his mate, Lord Llyr O'Cananach to join us for dinner in two days' time? Make sure they bring the boy, Tobias Greenley, as well. Have the servants ready my private dining hall and bring the guests to the blue room while we wait."

"Very good milord. Will that be all, Sire?" At the prince's nod, Tomwyl turned to leave.

"Wait a moment, Tomwyl."

"Yes, Sire?"

"If the queen asks for me, tell her I am indisposed. I am not to be disturbed this evening."

"I understand, Your Grace."

"Thank you, Tomwyl. You are dismissed." The valet bowed and left.

Alcaeus turned to his second as his demeanour shifted to his natural commanding presence.

"Stay sharp, General. Now that Melisandre is caught in the queen's web, the battle is about to begin. We must be ready."

"Yes, Your Highness. My sword is yours." Sotiris bowed deeply.

Alcaeus dismissed him and turned back to the night sky.

CHAPTER II

Tick. Tock. Tick. Tock.

My mind was beginning to run out of new things to contemplate, having spent hours mulling over all my current problems so many, many times. The pads of my fingers were sore from playing the violin for too long, and I pressed them into the cold stone beneath me to find relief.

Tap, tap, tap went my feet as I swung them in a monotonous tempo that matched the tedium of the situation. It may have only been a day but for an Alchemist, a day of nothing was the worst kind of torture. The chilly marble of the veranda against my head, back, and legs was a welcome distraction. Boredom consumed me to the point of insanity. Elis had not visited. Guards refused to let me leave. The writing table was completely empty, with nary a piece of parchment. Not a book in the room.

"What I wouldn't give for a book," I said to the deafening silence. Not even the damn birds sang, nor crickets chirped. The sky, too, refused to entertain me; a dreary grey, darkening as the hour grew later.

Suddenly, I stopped tapping. Then shot up to a sitting position as an idea formulated in my head. Mischievousness no doubt filled my face as I said, "You know who has books? The fucking prince."

Getting up and moving further into the room, I paced around, devising a working plan of escape. Picturing the architectural structure of the tower and then piecing the information I had gathered when we walked to Alcaeus' office, I was able to calculate its location. As we hadn't taken any stairs, it was on the same level which gave this plan a higher probability of success. Unfortunately, the guards had full view of the corridor both ways, so emerging from a room further down wasn't an option. Alcaeus' office was also undoubtedly locked, assuming he wasn't in there.

Now, while I couldn't 'see' through walls and solid objects, I could differentiate molecular structures from that of the living and that of the inanimate. For the most part. Briefly, I entertained the idea of just creating a walkway around the tower to the balcony. But who knew what guards were below and too many might witness the flash of transmutation. So that left me with one option.

Making my way to the bathroom, I went to the farthest wall. Closing my eyes, I formulated the correct transmutation circle while also activating my Alchemist's Vision. Nothing living showed on the other side. Placing my hand on the wall, light flashed as the circle drew energy as I rearranged the molecules. Now, there stood a door where the solid wall had once been. Opening it, I took in the room's contents: boxes, crates, canvas, and a boatload of cobwebs that denoted it could only be a storage room. Carefully stepping inside, I repeated my actions.

I continued this way until, at last, the final door revealed the top of the tower's main staircase. Peeking past the wall, the guards could no longer be seen. Quickly making my way forward, I tip-toed down the corridor, constantly checking over my shoulder. Every corner I looked both ways, but it was suspiciously empty. Not a servant in sight.

Finally, I spotted the double doors of Alcaeus' study. Treading carefully, I used my Sight to see if anyone was inside. Blessings be upon me, it was empty.

Hesitation was replaced with relief and eagerness as I placed my hand on the handle, testing it. Unlocked. I smiled with delight. It was then that I felt a firm nudge directly between my arse cheeks, pushing into a place that shall not be named.

"Yeeeeeeeesssshit!" I squealed, plastering myself against the door. The noise alone made me cringe in fear of alerting someone, anyone, and I whipped around to see who or what had violated my dignity.

"Ares!" I hissed. "How-? You little shite, you're going to get us caught! Hurry!" I opened the door to the study and slipped inside with him.

He whined, sniffing me and licking me, as if to check for injuries. I did a quick look around before crouching down and wrapped my arms around him. His thick fur was soft and coarse at the same time and a sense of homesickness filled me. The big wolf laid his head against my shoulder, returning the affection. Pulling away, I scratched behind his ears and his eyes closed with satisfaction.

"How on earth did you get here? I would have bet my life they had locked you away in the stables or run you off. Where did you come from, you sneaky thing?" I asked, at a complete loss in trying to understand his sudden appearance. "Absolute lunatic," I grinned, kissing his head. "Well, no time to question it now. We're grabbing books and then making a run for it. So, keep your nose and paws to yourself. And stay quiet!" Walking swiftly to the bookshelves, the memory of Alcaeus pinning and holding me against them flashed through my mind. Tendrils of desire curled within me but I frowned, willing away the distraction.

Grabbing a couple that looked interesting, I decided to grab two more books for good measure.

"Hmm... Oh, this one looks interesting," I said to Ares, who had wandered off behind me. *"The Memoirs of Asclepius: The History of Healing*. You know, out of all the many different mythologies, the Greek Gods are always quite fascinating to study." The book of healing stacked on the other two thick tomes in my arms, my eyes now searching for one more text. "Perhaps another Greek text; maybe it'll give me more insight to Alcaeus—"

"Then I would strongly suggest *Theoi, Diamones, Theres: The True Tales—*"

I screamed. The deep voice penetrated my focused mind, my amygdala reacting before the rest of my brain. Books flew into the air along with what was left of my dignity after Ares' scare. My right arm swung to the presence behind me but a strong warm hand grabbed my forearm. Steel seemed to wrap around my waist, keeping me from turning. So, I looked up. Straight into the amused eyes of the Royal Consort. Like he had appeared out of thin air.

He raised an arrogant brow, laughter playing on his face. "Lady Von Boden. Sneaking into my study without permission, stealing my books no less, when you are supposed to be in your rooms. Whatever shall I do with you, my little thief? Are you sure you do not possess the same Brownie heritage as your own thieving ward?" he teased.

Glaring up at him, I struggled in his grasp but to no avail. "Do not speak to me about my ward. Besides, I was borrowing books, not stealing them. You've left me with nothing but the furniture in the room! What kind of psychopath has bookshelves in a room with no books? Or a writing desk without paper–let me go!" Hot breath caressed my right ear and I sucked in a breath. His body dwarfed mine and though I felt angry and mildly panicked at his sudden presence, deep down, one feeling defied all logical reaction to the situation and was completely inexplicable. I felt...

Safe. The very realisation scared me more than anything and it had me renewing my efforts to break free from his hold. Unfortunately, it only succeeded in trapping me further as Alcaeus took the opportunity to bury his face in my neck and shoulder. My movement ceased as a wave of unexpected desire crashed into me. A small gasp escaped me at the shock of his lips against my skin.

"Mmm." Alcaeus' voice vibrated against me as he placed a firm kiss at the crook of my neck and then on the side of my head. "My apologies, Melisandre, for leaving you bereft. Take whatever you would like. My library is yours." He released me, reaching past and up to grab a large text from the top shelf. "This one will hopefully keep you quite occupied, I imagine."

I gave him a wary look and took a step away. Cautiously, my hands grasped the heavy book he handed to me. The book took both hands to hold and I relished the feel of it. Based on the bindings and vellum, it had quite the history itself. The gold lettering was all in Ancient Greek, and despite its age, had not faded over time.

Bending down, Alcaeus gathered the books that had gone flying from my hands when he startled me. Hefting the book further onto my left arm, I sank down to pick up a book next to my feet. Alcaeus reached it before me and my fingers brushed over the top of his. Strong hands with long fingers and pronounced veins. Part of me wondered how rough the underside would be against the more sensitive parts of me.

Hopeless, Melisandre—there's no hope for you. Stop this idiocy! I shook myself mentally, frustrated at how my biology responded to this Vampire.

As we both stood, I put a hand out to take the rest of the books but Alcaeus shook his head. "Allow me. I will escort you back to your rooms." He took in my hesitation and motioned to the room. "Or you are welcome to remain here for a time; I have some correspondence to finish before I must meet with the council and would very much enjoy your company."

Much of me did want to remain here, if only for the change of scenery. If not for the circumstances that overshadowed my enjoyment, this study was a dream and I would not mind in the slightest enjoying the comforts the room offered. As long as he did not continue speaking to me. Or look at me.

I glanced around as indecision ate at me, hugging the big book to my chest. Seeing this, the prince gave me a gentle smile before walking over to the leather-studded couches by the fireplace. Placing the books on the round ebony coffee table, he motioned for me to sit.

"Please," he said warmly. "Make yourself at home, my lady." He made his way to the desk and sat down, setting up his stationary. Movement behind him caught my attention as I noticed a Great Horned Owl perched comfortably on the balcony railing. Which reminded me...

I paused, looking around for Ares but he seemed to have disappeared into thin air.

What on the Mother's green earth...?

"Is everything alright? Are you looking for something?" asked Alcaeus, noticing my confusion.

"I-I, um," I tipped my head to see if I could see him underneath the furniture, a table, something. "My, uh, wolf..."

"Wolf?"

"It's nothing," I replied, deciding against revealing Ares' to the prince. One less loved one to worry about being used against me.

Walking swiftly to the couch, I sank into it, curling up against the arm rest. Removing my shoes, I curled my legs under me and opened the massive book. My eyes scanned the first page. Then again. And again.

Just ask him, Mels. It's been eating at you since he said it.

Slipping the book to the cushion next to me, I sat up and turned so the prince was in view.

"Alcaeus... you said something to me, that night in the Trillian Forest, that I found rather odd," I ventured. He looked up from his work. "You said 'how I have longed to see them up close' when you mentioned my eyes. And you didn't answer my question if we had met before."

Leaving it at that, I eyed him expectantly. I half expected my interruption of his work would have annoyed him; I, myself, despise being interrupted. Instead, he seemed to consider my question for a moment before answering, giving no indication he minded.

"No, we had not met before. If we had, I certainly would not have allowed you to forget." I reddened slightly, but my eyes rolled heavenward for a brief moment at his flirtation. Amusement had a way of dancing in his eyes that was completely captivating, even if the rest of his face was stoic. "I will confess having noticed you from afar on my way out of the Veil and into the Human Realm. Most especially in the darkness, where your eyes glow like the brightest of stars in the night. It was a little difficult to ignore, as was the rest of you."

Speaking of ignoring, I did just that with his flattery; he had just confessed to seeing me yet did nothing. His answer threw me so I asked, "For how long did you know I was there?"

"Long enough."

"That's ambiguous." He shrugged, remaining silent. So, I probed further. "And you never thought to come after me? Capture and enslave me to do your bidding, just as your queen has done, and others before her, or would have done had they known I was there and what I am?"

Placing his pen down, he folded his hands, linking those long fingers together. "Why would I? You were a creature at peace and it is that very peace that I seek for my people and this kingdom. What right would I have to such a gift if I were to gain it only through the act of stealing the individual liberty of another? If I cannot attain tranquillity without the enslavement of others, then it is neither the peace I want nor deserve. Blood may very well be the price to pay for freedom, for peace, but only from those who seek to oppose it. Not from the innocents who stand to gain."

Silence fell between us as his words soaked in, marinating in my mind. A suspiciously perfect answer.

"Do you truly mean that?"

Unblinkingly, he replied, "Every word."

I stared at Alcaeus then, really studying him. His statement gave him a new dimension and, as much as I hated it, a small tendril of respect wound its way into my heart. This prince seemed to show great care and consideration for his people and, from what I could tell, it was sincere.

Still, somehow, his response left me at a loss. Had he just been another Queen Ragna, I would know what to expect. Now, I felt as if there was a door in front of me and I had no idea what was behind it.

"What do you want from me, Alcaeus?" I whispered.

He looked at me tenderly. "For now, all I want is this: us conversing. I want to get to know you, Melisandre Von Boden, the Alchemist. Then, it is my sincerest hope we can find a semblance of friendship and trust. Eventually, I hope to get to know Melisandre, the woman, in every sense of the word." A teasing lift at the corners of his mouth betrayed his intentions and I fought a grin of my own at his silver-tongue.

"Quite the wordsmith, aren't you? Well, you're certainly ambitious, I'll give you that," I teased back, curling into my former comfortable position as I dragged the book onto my lap. "But like all ambitions that involve two consenting parties–prepare yourself for the state of unrequitedness, for just as peace requires preparation for war, so too does romance require a preparedness for pain and rejection," I said with a saccharin tone. I was met with a masculine chuckle.

"We shall see, my lady."

I gave a small shake of my head but dove headlong into the text in front of me, letting the world tune out.

⚜ ☿ ♀ ⊖ ⊕ ♀ ☿

My subconscious picked up that I was being carried, bundled up in strong arms just as my nose filled with the warm masculine scent I had come to attribute to Alcaeus. My feet bounced slightly as we walked but I was too tired to open my eyes. My pride alone couldn't take waking up in the enemy's arms so I clung to the vestiges of sleep instead. And, I was so very tired. This calling pull from my chest seemed to buzz with delight at the closeness and I snuggled deeper into the chest that held me. Insomnia had been my constant companion since I had first met with Alcaeus in his study and my body and mind were finally paying its toll.

Alcaeus slowed down. The clinking of armour indicated we were in front of my door with my two guard dogs faithfully by it.

"Your Highness! Is that–?" The sound of a door opening. "Please, Your Majesty, I swear she did not come out! I don't know how–"

"Truly, Sire, we've been at our post all night–" Suddenly, both fell silent.

Alcaeus must have given them a look not to wake me, for he said quietly, "Your orders to guard her door are not to guard others from her but to guard her from others. She is allowed to come to my study if she so wishes and, soon, I shall make several other places available to her. Is that clear?"

"Yes, Your Majesty," they replied in unison, albeit quieter than before.

The prince continued walking and, in no time at all, I was placed gently down on my bed. For a moment, nothing happened and I wondered if he had left. But then I felt the trail of fingers up my arm, stopping where my neck and shoulder converged. It was one of the only places that was free of alchemical runes. He caressed the spot with his thumb, making small circles. Then they ventured to my face, barely a whisper over my cheekbones and lips.

"I will try to keep you safe, sweet one." His voice was barely a whisper, so much so I questioned if I had heard him correctly. The rough feel of his beard along with warm dry lips pressed to my temple and he held it for a moment. I felt him pull away and a strange sensation of disappointment flashed within me.

After enough time had passed, I cracked my eyes open, only to find myself alone. Getting up slowly, I padded my way to the closed door leading to the sitting room and opened it slightly. It was empty. I shut the door, but not before noticing the books Alcaeus had allowed me to borrow along with a few more, stacked on the previously empty bookshelves.

Smiling, I stripped myself of my clothes, washed, and then crawled into the oversized bed with a sigh of contentment. Sleep came swiftly and dreams of strong hands and warm lips kept any and all nightmares away.

CHAPTER 12

When Tomwyl opened the door to the sitting room where we were to wait prior to dinner, I was shocked to see Elis and Llyr standing there, holding champagne glasses and speaking together quietly. I took the time to appreciate the pair. Llyr was dressed in creams and pale greens, perfectly complementing his rich red locks and fair skin. He was taller than Elis, a little broader in the shoulder, but still had that same lithe grace that most Fae do. Elis too, wore pale creams but with gold; a perfect match to his mate. The room itself was like all the rooms, beautiful and elegant, although this one had a masculine air to it. Yet the pair in front of me made the room dull in comparison. Would I tell my dear friend that? Not a chance.

I walked towards them when I stopped suddenly at the small figure that appeared from behind Elis.

"Ms. Melly!" Toby bolted for me.

I caught him and he almost bowled me over. My heart clenched in relief as his skinny arms circled my waist in a crushing grip, head pressed against me.

"For God's sake lad, let up a little!" I wheezed. He eased his grip, but I returned his hug. He looked up at me then, mossy green eyes rimmed with emotion. My heart clenched at the affection that looked back at me. Despite everything that had happened to him, the lad still possessed that inexplicable capacity to trust and love without question that only children seem to have.

I gave a quick kiss to his forehead. Gone were the bruises and swelling, nothing but youthful freckled skin. The power of Fae healing.

"I thought I'd ne'er see ya again Ms. Melly! I've been good, I ha' been! Just ask mister Elis; he even says that I get to work in the kitchens since Cook is Brownie." His eyes widened and his voice dropped to a hissed whisper, "There's a fine lass, a kitchen girl, a Brownie 'ybrid like me! And she's been 'elpin me wit' me impulses and the like. 'Er name's Sophie."

I wiped his tears away, then tucked a wily brown curl away from his face.

"Oh really? Well, I'm glad it seems you've made a friend, Toby. They are true treasures in a place like this." At this, I glanced up at Elis; he winked at me over the rim of his glass. "It also seems you're healing nicely by the looks of it. How's your hand?"

He held it up, wiggling his fingers. Faded yellow was all that was left, his movements were neither stiff nor limited.

"Mister Llyr did a great job, eh? Didn't he, Ms. Melly?"

Smiling then, I gave Llyr a look of appreciation. He saluted me with his glass and then turned back to Elis.

"Aye, lad, he did. The Fae are full of spectacular talents." I extricated myself from Toby and led us over to where the men stood.

"Elis, why the hell are you here?"

"Bitch, I am nobility, why wouldn't I be here? Good eve to you too, by the way." Elis put a hand on a hip, one perfect brow raised. "Glad to see your signature characteristic of being the local grump has not been lost to all the recent excitement."

I rolled my eyes, a teasing glint in them. "That's not... I am just surprised to see you here. He made no mention of inviting you. Or Toby. But why he would invite you out of all his subjects, is what truly baffles me."

He let out a gasp of indignation, "Oh the ego of this woman, I swear, Llyr." Llyr hid his smile behind the glass, as his mate continued. "Careful, you spiteful gremlin," Elis pointed his glass at me. "Your diminutive stature can only handle so much of your own self-importance before it leads to your downfall. Luckily for you, the ground will meet your face quickly and, being the loyal friend that I am, shall be there to laugh at you when it does."

"Oh, I think my *stature* has plenty of room to spare. Perhaps it'll give me the height boost I've needed these past 800 years."

Elis laughed at that. "Ha! We could only hope."

I passed by him smacking his arm on my way to the couch, "Brat."
"Troll."

I finally allowed a grin, shooting my best friend a look that only we share.

"Alright you two," interjected Llyr, always assuming the role of adult whenever it came to myself and his mate. "Let us sit and at least pretend to be the summation of our ages." He followed Elis who gave him a 'don't look at me' face, but his mate wasn't having it. "No, you are a repeat offender, my sassy flower. Sometimes I wonder if you two aren't secretly siblings the way you unceasingly bicker." Before my best friend could respond, Llyr was quick to turn to me, saying, "I must say though Melisandre, you look positively stunning this evening."

"Thank you, Llyr," I replied as Llyr sat across from me with Elis to my left. Toby took a seat by the fire with a book in his hands. "This outfit is obnoxiously uncomfortable but the lady's maid strong-armed me."

Elis snorted, letting out a dramatic sigh. "If beauty were comfortable, I fear ugliness would no longer exist and we need ugly people to make someone, like myself, validate our self-confidence."

I rolled my eyes. "You're terrible, Elis."

He winked at me. "Truly though: you are breathtaking when you try."

Giving a rather indelicate snort but unable to hide my blush at their compliments, I smoothed the front of my black gown, the black corset perfecting my hourglass figure. I had lost the hour-long debate with Ada about appropriate dress, and I feared she might hide the few pairs of trousers and shirts I still had. The memory of my own mother's voice reminded me that while I came from humble origins, I certainly didn't need to dress the part in the presence of royalty.

The corset itself had silver embroidery with ornamental chains on the sides. The neckline of the dress was more of a halter, leaving my arms exposed, showing off my runes. I left my hair down, soft billowy curls trailing to mid-back. I had a simple silver chain across my forehead, and a teardrop-shaped pearl dangled in the middle. Make-up had never been necessary for me, so I forewent it.

Looking around, there were only two footmen and our party; the prince had yet to arrive. The furniture we sat on was a deep sapphire blue, its richness making it a treat for the eyes. A servant came to my side discreetly, offering me a glass of what looked like champagne. I accepted.

Elis scooted closer to me and Llyr leaned forward, elbows on his knees.

"So," whispered Elis as he darted his eyes around the room, "tell me how your meeting with prince Alcaeus went?"

"How did you know about that?"

"I have my ways, you know this. The fact you failed to tell me is not lost on me either, traitor. Now spill, before he comes."

I took a long pull of champagne to cover the blooming blush suffusing me. My memory of the study and finding myself a prisoner in Alcaeus' arms, on both occasions, was so vivid that it distracted me for several damning moments. I cleared my throat.

"Well... we met. We talked. Learned a bit about the mark. Not much ha-"

"Sweet gods! Something happened!" Elis grabbed my arm, eyes twinkling like it was Christmas.

"Oh, for fucks sake, Elis!" He always knew and it was beyond irritating. The Vampire was a starving terrier, able to smell the blood of my drama without fail.

"I would apologise but that would make me a liar. Something happened. Spill. Now."

With a flustered sigh, I recounted what happened in Alcaeus's study on both occasions. When I had returned to my room after my initial visit, I had probably paced a hole into the floor of my bedroom in an attempt to rationalise the mysterious pull I'd felt to the Royal Consort. Just as I had when I woke this afternoon, reminiscing in the feel of his embrace for a little too long. Much to my utter dismay, I was nowhere close to understanding the draw between us that seemed so beyond physical attraction.

Rushing over the intimate encounter as discreetly as I could, I avoided their curious stares. By the time my tale was concluded, I was more than ready for something far stronger than champagne. I braved a glance at the two men who sat in shocked silence.

Llyr leaned back and sipped his drink thoughtfully while Elis looked like he'd just witnessed the biggest scandal of the century. Elegant ringed fingers covered his mouth, the wheels ever turning behind those pale purple eyes.

"This is good fortune indeed, Mels! I told you he wouldn't be under Ragna's thumb! This is it, my dear, our answer!"

"Calm yourself, Elis. Yes, he made his interests, albeit dubious, known. However, he also admitted to having his own ulterior motives... That's as far as I'm willing to trust him. I'm still an exotic bird in a cage." Sighing, I set my glass down. "I will say, Alcaeus did make mention of allowing me access to 'other areas' so it's probably safe to ask to use the castle's library, maybe even a laboratory if they have one." Still feeling the discomfort from revealing the intimacy between Alcaeus and myself, I quickly asked a bit louder, "Does this place have real drinks around here? Whiskey? The lady doth needs her spirits, lest she lose her own."

"Have I driven you to the drink already, my little Alchemist? Surely, you are made of sterner stuff than that?"

We all spun around to face the Familiar baritone voice that filled the room. The fact that a Vampire and a Fae were just as surprised at the prince's sudden appearance was cause for concern. Their senses were far more heightened than mine and should have noticed his presence immediately.

Elis and Llyr stood quickly, bowing low and murmuring the proprietary greetings of 'Your Highness'. Toby jumped to my side and bowed clumsily, keeping his gaze to the floor but stood half behind me. I had risen as well but did not bow; he was no prince of mine.

Alcaeus stood several feet away, looking sharp in a black jacket, his rich mahogany hair tied back in a Viking sort of fashion. His double-breasted vest had a silver filigree design, which laid upon a black velvet background. A platinum-coloured cravat graced his neck, and he wore a white shirt beneath. Completing the outfit were a silver pocket watch and a sterling silver chain belt. My eyes narrowed. We were awfully close to matching. Ada's insistence on my wardrobe this evening suddenly made sense.

I flicked my eyes up to him. "You have no idea what I am made of Your Grace."

Alcaeus lifted a brow, accompanied by that masculine smirk. A small heated flame danced in those dark eyes. "Indeed, μικρός ασβός, but I'm very much looking forward to the process of its discovery."

His moniker for me had me frowning; *mikrós asvós*—little badger.

From my periphery, I could see Elis stare at me in astonishment at his prince's open flirtations. I could also see his herculean effort in not losing it at the Consort's new pet name for me. Elis lived for drama and romance, especially around me, and Alcaeus just delivered an abundance of ammunition I would never hear the end of.

"Dinner is served." Tomwyl declared.

Alcaeus motioned to the door, holding up his arm slightly. "My lady?"

I stared at that arm for half a moment, struggling with my inner re-bellion, before stomping over to him as best one could in heels. I detest-ed my corset even more the closer I got to him as breathing was already a struggle and his presence seemed to suck the air right out of the room. Uncomfortably aware of him, I slipped my hand in the crook of his el-bow. Alcaeus tightened his arm slightly, his other hand coming on top of mine. I narrowed my eyes at our hands, looking up at him. His eyes were filled with merriment, stern lines softened in knowing amusement.

"You are stunning, Lady Von Boden. Perhaps it was my mistake inviting your friends; I would have very much liked to enjoy this view privately. I take it you slept well?" he whispered. At my silent glare, he chuckled, "Yes, I think mikrós asvós suits you very well."

I tried to jerk my hand away, albeit discreetly, but he may as well have nailed my hand down to his own arm. My barely masked strug-gle only incited an amused chuckle from my companion as he led us through to the next room. Our height difference was such that I would have to take several steps to match his own, but the prince was ever a gentleman and walked gracefully at my pace.

Inside the dining area, the long table was set to perfection. Sterling silver tableware gleamed in the candlelight, and several footmen stood in waiting. Compared to the overall size of the palace, this room was considerably more intimate.

The prince led me to sit to the right of the head of the table while Llyr and Elis took the seats across from me. Toby sat next to me, his book hidden in his lap. Any other person would have scolded him for be-ing rude to the host, but I am the last person to chastise him for bringing books to the table; I envied him fiercely. A crystal tumbler with amber liquid was placed in front of me and I went for it.

The first course was served. Contrary to modern human belief, Vampires do eat food and require sustenance, although not as frequent-ly. They also require blood, not for nutritional purposes, but to replen-ish their magic. Blood is where magic is found, or so they say. And before you think to ask, no, I have never witnessed Elis take blood. Despite our closeness, it would feel more like an invasion of privacy, as if watching was an act of unwelcomed voyeurism. The scientist in me had always secretly wondered, however.

The prince began to engage Elis and Llyr in light conversation, gen-tly prodding about Fae politics. I watched this verbal dance silently. Llyr was a clever hand at this, saying everything and revealing nothing. The more I observed, the more Queen Mab's most eloquent diplomat shone through.

Even so, I became surprisingly enraptured by Elis, who handled the interrogation and conversational nuances with ease. He was charming, amethyst eyes holding the flicker of the candlelight. This version of him was new, having never seen him in this kind of environment. Our dealings together were casual, typically in my home or out in the human realm. Conversations usually revolved around witty banter and keeping the other's ego in check.

Elis glanced at me, giving me a curious look, eyes whipping back and forth, but his words never faltered. Following his line of sight, I realised Alcaeus was no longer paying attention to them. He had leaned back in his seat, resting on one arm as his hand thoughtfully stroked his jaw while observing me.

Warmth curled within and I shifted, mentally trying to focus on my goals for this evening. He had this intensity that made me feel like he could see beneath all my layers and a confidence that he believed I'd reveal all to him of my own volition. Having enough of being intimidated, I stared back with equal purpose. I couldn't deny he was something to behold and the longer I stared the stronger the pull of him became. So much so, the fear of getting lost in his gaze became greater, forcing me to look away first. For the life of me, I could no sooner discern the emotions on his face than I could admit to what was stirring in mine. What was this draw?

"So, Melisandre tells me you two had met previously in the Trillion Forest?" Elis' voice broke the crackling tension in the room, my head whipping to him.

"She's spoken of me then, has she?" asked Alcaeus. At Elis' nod, the prince's grin widened.

If my stare had hands, they'd be wrapped around Elis' pretty little neck and wringing the immortal life from him. Alcaeus continued stroking his beard, never breaking eyes with me.

"Indeed. We had been hunting golems and cú sídhe, running rampant on our lands. We discovered a breach in the wards. Melisandre was kind enough to lend me assistance."

"If I recall from our conversation, I believe it was you who initially saved her, Your Highness," suggested Elis.

"It is not every day Alchemists go flying into my arms, that is true. The cage and following blaze, however, were entirely Lady Von Boden; it was quite remarkable and certainly saved us from the true peril of the situation. Truly, my only part was merely to catch the heroine."

I cleared my throat, taking a deep swig of whiskey. Elis' smile deepened at my reaction towards the Nightmare prince.

"Yes," Elis said, grinning over the rim of his wine glass, "our Mels is quite capable of handling herself, I dare say."

You would do well to remember that, you traitor, is what I wanted to say but instead, I allowed my face to do the talking as I continued nursing my scotch.

"Indeed." The prince swirled his wine glass, then tipped it forward, taking a drink. "Ah, that reminds me, I have been meaning to ask–how did the two of you meet? An unlikely friendship considering our little Alchemist has been so effective in hiding her presence from the rest of the Otherworld."

My normally chatty friend seemed to finally bite his tongue for once. Llyr suddenly became engrossed with his soup. The question seemed harmless on the surface but by the look Elis and I exchanged, we both understood the depth of it. Elis and I met under rather epic circumstances. To reveal it all would also expose some depth of my ability; I wasn't ready for Alcaeus to know that yet. My biggest weapon against the Nightmare Court was ignorance. If people knew that I was no ordinary Alchemist, then any hope for escape would be gone.

I also did not trust him or his motives yet, despite our last conversation. The prince had only seen a simple transmutation. I was inclined to keep it that way.

"Oh! I love this story! Ms. Melly saved the 'ell outta mister El- Ow!" I smacked my hand down on Toby's thigh.

"Why don't you leave the conversation to the adults, Toby, seeing as you've hardly touched your plate?" I said with force.

Toby frowned. "Aww, but the soup is cold Ms. Melly..."

"It's supposed to be cold, it is like a gazpacho," said Llyr.

"Gaz-wot?"

I squeezed Toby's thigh hard. "Just. Eat."

He made a face and grumbled but picked up his spoon. Llyr was trying to hold back a smile but failed and Elis shook his head at me, clearly blaming me for Toby's lack of refinement. I was about to use it to change the subject, but Alcaeus wouldn't be swayed.

"So, saving Lord LeGervase?" the prince grinned. "Why does that not come as a surprise? I feel as if I am in for an interesting tale."

He set his wine glass down and leaned on his hand, waiting to hear our story.

"I wouldn't quite call it 'saving', that's a bit of an exaggeration... There's really no point in telling it–"

"No, Mels, do not be humble. You saved my life that day," Elis said softly. A gentle look of admiration came over his face. "I will never forget it, you see. I was travelling to the Veil on business. I used to own a lovely little floral shop in the human realm. Ah, I so loved that shop." As nervous as I was about Elis revealing too much, I couldn't help the memories flooding back from that fateful day. "Anyway," Elis continued, "as I passed through, I didn't realise I was being hunted by a vrykolakas–"

"Wots that?" Toby interrupted.

"It's what happens when an undead Vampire mates with a werewolf, creating an equally undead creature that only lives to hunt. Incredibly dangerous and one of the many reasons mating between those species is strictly forbidden and enforced. The fact that Sir Elis encountered one is rather interesting," replied Alcaeus. His finger stroked his chin thoughtfully.

"And unfortunately for me, they only eat the livers of their prey." Elis shuddered, taking a strong gulp of his wine. Llyr placed a hand on his back, but Elis motioned he was alright.

"So, there I was, pinned down, being gutted like a fresh catch at the market, watching this demon take a chunk out of my liver when suddenly it was thrown from me. I saw a flash and heard it scream; that's when I saw iron rods coming up from the ground skewering it. Then–"

"Elis." I implored him not to continue. He had already shared too much. I didn't care if Alcaeus knew I was trying to keep Elis from telling the whole story.

My friend gave me a long look, one that told me we were not on the same page.

"Then what?" asked Alcaeus.

"Then, I heard a great clap of thunder. The flash of lightning was so sudden I thought myself permanently blinded. When my sight recovered, it was to see the beast incinerated where it stood, impaled. That was also when I saw her. There I lay dying, blood everywhere, no saving the lovely jacket Llyr had made me. She knelt beside me then, looked at me with those beautiful molten eyes of hers and healed me," he said, his voice almost a whisper. Then he chuckled and finished with, "Terrible bedside manner though."

I watched the metaphorical cards in my hand go up into flames. Anger stirred within me. Not even nostalgia could dampen my frustration. The more he talked, the more I realised Elis was taking the gamble in trying to convince Alcaeus to our side by buttering me up like a Christmas potato.

On one hand, there was no fault in his logic and it was what we discussed. On the other, I still had yet to determine how safe and likely that plan was. It hadn't even been a week yet and already Elis was pushing the agenda as if the world was ending tomorrow.

"I merely sped up the growth of your liver and sealed the wound. Your body did the rest." I bit out.

"Nevertheless, you saved me that day. Took me back to your place and nursed me back to health for several weeks."

"Several weeks too long. I thought you'd never leave."

"See? And now we are the closest of friends."

I glared at him. He grinned back. The bastard knew I wasn't happy with him and he didn't care.

"That is quite the story," commented the prince. "The fact that you survived the vrykolakas attack is a feat in and of itself. But calling the power of the elements to such a capacity? Now that is interesting. I would very much like to see the extent of that." I could feel the burn of Alcaeus's gaze.

Oh yes, Elis and I would be having words.

"It was a long time ago," I said quickly, finishing the rest of my drink.

Before he could inquire further about my abilities and with anger fuelling my courage, I snapped, "Prince Alcaeus, I was under the impression this dinner meant answers to what is to come, primarily regarding the Familiar's Mark. If you don't mind, I'd rather we no longer waste time with idle small talk and reminiscence."

Both Elis and Llyr's eyes widened, and I thought Elis' jaw was about to hit his plate. Not a sound could be heard, not even the sound of breathing. I'd probably broken a hundred rules of etiquette, but I was out of fucks to give and my patience all but spent.

136

"Melisandre! He is a prince, r-royalty...you shouldn't speak –" sputtered Elis.

"It's alright, LeGervase. She is quite correct; I did promise to discuss these things at dinner." Alcaeus looked at me with a hard edge, despite the understanding words. He motioned for his steward. "Tomwyl, would you see the boy safely back to Lord LeGervase's rooms? Also, we shall be taking digestifs in the blue room in a few moments."

"Very good, Your Grace."

Tomwyl, motioned for Toby to follow him. Toby looked reluctant but didn't argue. He bid us a quick goodnight and followed the steward out the door.

I stared after them for several moments even after they were gone. Steeling myself, I turned and faced the Royal Consort. At some point, the dishes had been cleared. He was sitting straighter, although still in a relaxed repose.

Perhaps it was the build-up of all the events this past week, the confinement, the never-ending threats to those I cared for, that stoked the fires of trickling rage deep down. This was my freedom, my soul on the line and his calm arrogance, this stupid pompous dinner, was oxygen to those flames that were quickly building.

"In your office, you told me that you were on my side. Is that true?"

His eyes narrowed slightly. "Yes, it is."

"Then put off the mark for as long as we can. Allow me access to the libraries and the Guild of Antiquities. I know I can find something that can at the very least, stall Ragna in whatever nefarious plans she has."

"Lady Von Boden, I thought I made it quite clear in my office why we cannot delay." His voice hardened at this, becoming sharper.

"Not even a week? A few days? I can hardly imagine the Champion of Athena, the Master and Commander himself, incapable of negotiation! Have you truly no sway over your future lady-wife?" The sarcasm in my voice bit deep, judging by lines of anger now forming on that beautiful face of the prince.

"She could just as easily demand it be done in three days if it did not kill you! I have already pushed for the longest allotted time the marking allows but there is nothing stopping her from shortening it! There is a delicate balance here you know nothing of, Melisandre! So, unless you want the blood of everyone you love on your hands, I suggest," he leaned forward, eyes glaring in warning, "you quickly accept the inevitable and work with it, with me."

"Perhaps we should retire..." Llyr said timidly. Both of us ignored him. I shifted in my seat to fully face Alcaeus.

"And what you do not know of is what I am capable of given the opportunity and resources, which you continue to deny me! I may not be of this court, so yes, there is much here I cannot even fathom. But you cannot sit there and tell me that there isn't another way when you have yet to even calculate me into the equation! You fear Ragna and what she is capable of; I get that. But stop letting–" The words were lost in my throat at the reaction of the prince, whose face became shrouded in darkness.

From my periphery, Elis was violently shaking his head at me, face half hidden behind his cloth napkin as if he couldn't watch but dared not look away. Llyr' had his face in one hand, thumb and forefinger rubbing his temples while his other arm was outstretched in front of Elis to keep him from tackling me, no doubt.

"Fear?" growled Alcaeus, his voice like iron dragging on concrete. He slowly came to a stand, eyes aflame. The room seemed to shrink as he straightened to his full height. While my dull sense of magic only felt the ripples of his power, I could tell Elis and Llyr felt the full brunt of it as they both shrank away, bowing their heads. "You think it is because I fear the queen? Do you think it is because of fear that I am obeying her commands? This is the Nightmare Court and I," his voice dropped an octave, as he came around the table to stand in front of me, towering, "am its Commander. Prince of Nightmares. Do you think that a nightmare *feels* fear?" He leaned in closer, forcing me to bend my neck painfully in order to continue looking up at him. Darkness seemed to rapidly close in, as if all the candles in the room had been snuffed out. The cold claws of magic pierced my skin, powerful enough for me to feel it directly. "I am the hunter in the night, the *Great Owl* that strikes its prey in swift silence! You will never hear me coming, for death rides upon my wings! I am the chill down your spine, the reaper in the shadows! Do not *think* of speaking to me of fear!" His voice had reached thunderous depths and tendrils of cold terror began to creep along my insides.

Yet, at the implication of ignorance, fury blazed through me. Standing so quickly my chair flipped over, I met his stance and piercing glare unflinchingly. "Do not try to intimidate me with talk of death! If that is what you are then we are birds of a feather, you and I. For life cannot exist without death, nor death without life! And we Alchemists are the stewards of both!" I snapped back. "So, if not fear, what then? The more I reason with you over a delay, the more you push me away from it! A wordsmith you may be but a man of action you are clearly not!"

"The audacity of you, Alchemist! You speak to me of actions? It was you who agreed to this, Melisandre, not I! *You* agreed to this! Becoming allies is the wisest choice and you would be a fool otherwise. You gave your life for the life of your ward, or did you happen to forget your vow? Reneging so soon? Is this what your word is worth? And you speak to me about actions not taken! See to your own integrity before casting mine in judgement!" His words hit me like a punch to the stomach. I reeled back as if I'd been hit. I could not reason through the torrent of volatile emotions coursing through me.

Alcaeus saw the change in me, his magic completely receding and the room filled with the subtle lighting once more. Even his gaze softened as his own anger cooled. My pride ruled me to the bitter end, however, not ready to show defeat.

"Ally? Don't fuck with me," I choked out, "Everyone has a game to play." Seething, I nodded at the prince. "Especially you."

Stepping away from the table, I stalked out of the room.

A. R. Morgan

CHAPTER 13

Coming to a stop by the fire in the blue room, I stood there, trembling. My arms grasped my torso desperately, as if to try to contain the turbulence within me. Breathing came in short, shallow intakes before I took a deeper one to try to calm my stampeding heart. The moment I was alone, guilt and rationale flooded me as my anger became nothing but the smoke from a fire, put out by the cold water of reality.

The truth angered me. It ate at me. I wanted Alcaeus to bear the brunt of it. To hate him for it. Rage at him. To blame these invisible chains leading to my destruction on him.

Yet, here I stood, the epitome of hypocrisy. For I was the one truly afraid. Terrified. Grasping onto the last straws of my freedom like they were my last breaths of air before I drowned.

Caught in the cruel grip of terror at the reality of being bound for eternity like a slave. To be broken by the will of another.

Knowing the truth but refusing to accept it had led to such an internal struggle that left me weary. This fight was fast proving to be futile and it was becoming a useless expenditure of energy. There was no getting out of it without sacrificing the life of my friends. That was a fact. And it was a sin I would not commit again.

You have to accept it, Melisandre. One mark does not a Familiar make, but three. You have time. How bad could the first one be? Alcaeus has shown you kindness; perhaps there is something to work with here.

Even so, I shivered. The fire could not warm me fast enough.

But one must also accept I was still naught but a pawn in this game with Ragna... but would I be as such to him?

Of course you are, Melisandre. What else would you be? That you would bring sentimentality into this at all is laughable. Alcaeus himself reminded you quite clearly that this is a contract, nothing more. Yes, he desires you. But anything else would leave vulnerabilities. Wield the knowledge, not the heart.

I should have known better and continued to berate myself internally. Disappointment and bitterness at my foolishness continued to eat at me. Staring but unseeing, I compartmentalised my emotions as logically as I could. Accepting that dread would be a constant companion for the foreseeable future, I begrudgingly accepted the situation.

Soft voices echoed in the hall behind me, and doors closed. Then silence once more. Then I felt him standing behind me, making no move to break the silence.

When the tension became too thick, I took a deep breath followed by my confession.

"You're right," I said, barely above a whisper, "I am afraid."

"Melisandre—"

Shaking my head, I gathered my courage to face him. "I don't trust you. I am fully aware that I am just a pawn in this stupid game of power between Champions. For hundreds of years, I knew what would become of me if someone like Ragna, someone like you, found me. So how could I not fear? How could I not fight? A mad woman holds the lives of the only people on this earth I care for, holding my own like a weapon she wants to wield. I am facing giving up my very existence as I know it and the secrets of Mother Earth to you, to Ragna. And for what? To slay thousands? To be king or queen of corpses? Because that's what she wants, your fiancée, and she seems to think that whatever abilities I possess will help her succeed in her power-hungry endeavour!

"But I am an Alchemist, not a marionette; I will not dance to anyone's tune no matter how you pull my chains. Her biggest mistake is believing that I am a pawn at all and can be manipulated as such. Can you truly find fault for my rebellion, my instinct to fight back and delay all I can? Does a horse not buck when you try to break it? Does the wolf not snap and bite, rending flesh from bone when cornered? We have known each other for a week at most, Alcaeus, have met even less, and yet you ask for a trust you have not even had the time to earn." My eyes were rimmed with emotion. "To not fight this, to not do everything I can to remain free would go against everything that I am. And right now, that is all I have."

His brow was set deep as he studied me. There was no pity or anger in his gaze, only understanding and perhaps a bit of sorrow even. I hated it as much as I needed to see it.

"Although the situation may demand otherwise, I am not expecting your trust right away, *mikrós asvós*. As a creature made for war and commanding others, so does it come with the deep understanding that trust must be earned as much as one must be worthy to receive it. Believe you me—I will never stop working to earn yours nor cease making myself worthy in your eyes." Alcaeus's sincerity was blatant in the intensity of his gaze. He walked so much closer as he spoke. "I cannot deny that you are a pawn, but we are all pawns in someone else's game. Having one's wings clipped for the ulterior motives of another, is a reality I know intimately. In that, we are the same. Would that I could allow you to return to your life, your freedom. You must know I would. Even now, doubts plague me in the success of what we're about to do; nature's forces themselves are a testament to how powerless we are in attempting to contain her. Unfortunately, freedom is a privilege that is afforded to no one who possesses power in the Otherworld." He moved closer, taking my hands in his. Looking down at them, he said, "We both know that delaying the inevitable will only put Toby's life at risk, your life at risk." He took one of my hands and placed it against his cheek, placing a gentle kiss against my palm. "And I cannot allow that. Not when it comes to you."

The act was so intimate yet felt so right. My heart was pounding, and I held my breath at the touch of his lips against my hand. The smooth warmth of his skin, the rough bristles of his trimmed beard. I stared at my hand against him, not wanting to pull away. Finally, I looked up at the midnight sky in his eyes.

"I would have a promise from you, Prince of the Nightmare Court."

"What would you have of me?"

Stepping into him, I cupped his face with both hands.

"I would have truth and honesty between us, always. I'm not a Vampire. I'm not Fae. Nor am I a Were or Changeling. I am a foreigner in your lands. No games. No dancing around half-truths. If you want my cooperation, then no lies. You were born of Athena; surely honour means something to you. If it does, I call upon it right here, right now." I implored him, trying to see any tell that his sincerity was false.

He placed his hands over mine. "I swear to you, on my honour, that only the truth will pass my lips in your presence. But I will not hide that there is much you are not yet ready to hear nor have we had the time to establish it. But with you, my truth is yours."

I wasn't going to get more than that, but it was enough. I dropped my hands from his face, but he wrapped his arms around me and lifted me up in a warm embrace.

"Thank you, Melisandre." His relief was evident.

I didn't push him away. Resigned, I could only nod against his shoulder. It was a step.

"Tomorrow, I will have Tomwyl take you to the libraries and introduce you to the head sage there."

Before I could thank him, the tip of his nose brushed the side of my head, and I felt his kiss there. I stilled. Gentle breath blew against my ear, causing pleasure to trickle down me. He felt so strong, so tall against me. Warm cinnamon, pine, and leather with a hint of smoke; his scent made me weak. My hands clutched the fabric against his chest, and I closed my eyes. With the settling of emotions, I was reminded once more of the siren's call deep within, enticing me to do... something with him. I knew not what.

My body went soft against him as his lips made a path down the side of my face. When his kisses reached my neck, I couldn't help the small gasp when his tongue darted out, licking me. He pulled back slightly.

"Melisandre..." He breathed. Then he kissed me.

I moaned gently and wrapped an arm around his neck, wanting to pull him closer. Instead, he lifted me against his chest, our height difference forgotten. When his tongue flicked my lips, I opened in invitation. His tongue darted in and searched me deeply, with so much passion that breathing felt unnecessary for a moment. I matched his movements, my tongue dancing and circling his, soaking up the warmth of his mouth and the masculine smell of him. A floodgate of desire burst through me; my body awakened with a vengeance as his tongue danced with mine.

"Well, well, well, what have we here?"

The sneering voice shot ice into my veins.

We broke apart and Alcaeus set me down and shoved me behind him. The queen stood at the doorway, arms crossed, icy gaze piercing through the shadows that gathered around her. Even the fire seemed to dim in fear.

I was only half-hidden, so I saw the queen's eyes dart to where his hand still held both of mine.

"Enjoying my gift? Without me? If I was any other Vampire, I think I would be jealous," Ragna whined, pretending to pout. "Yes, yes, I did give her as a gift and you should enjoy her flesh on your own time, my dear. But saying you are indisposed to me *because* of her, well..." Her beautiful face turned to stone, a cruel edge along her lips. "You clearly need to be reminded that this does not apply to your queen, Consort. A lesson is in order."

She stepped aside as two guards came in and unceremoniously deposited a limp Vampire in front of us. He was bloody and unmoving. I couldn't see Alcaeus's face, but he stiffened almost imperceptibly, his hand tightening in mine. It took me a second, but my eyes widened in recognition; it was Tomwyl, Alcaeus's steward. The one who escorted Toby.

Fear for my ward snaked through me, but I took care to not show it.

The queen glided closer, and it was then I realised she wore very little. Wrapped in precarious bits of gold and black embroidered cloth that somehow covered all the important bits and ended by trailing down, causing a floating effect. Her golden tresses were piled high with a few tendrils hanging down.

"You're missing the Gathering, my love," she purred, coming almost chest to chest with him. She was only a hairsbreadth shorter than him.

Trailing a long and elegant finger down his cheek, she said, "And you know how much I require your presence during my Gatherings. Especially since I've given you the Alchemist; all must know to whom she belongs. Our nobles demand it."

She looked at me over his shoulder then. What I saw in her eyes made my skin crawl.

Alcaeus tilted his head back slightly, so she was no longer touching him and carefully grabbed her wrist.

"My queen, it was by your own demand that I begin the process of the Familiar mark. Why else do you think I was indisposed, even to you? You're spoiling your own fun by interrupting me. You know how sensitive this process is." He spoke quietly but with no less authority. Even his quiet volume demanded respect and attention.

Suspicion filled me when I heard his words, but I quickly tampered it down, reminding myself of our moment just prior. I had to believe he

145

had been honest; the consequences were unthinkable otherwise.

But seeing the queen touch him so familiarly, stirred something rather nasty in me. It took me by surprise but then I ignored it.

"Perhaps I was a bit too impatient to see if you had followed through; I'm eager to see the results." She leaned closer and kissed him. I looked away. It probably looked like I was giving them a moment, but I couldn't stand it. The dark stirring escalated within my chest.

"Come. You can finish the mark later. We are expected." She barked her command as she turned away abruptly and left the room. Silence fell upon us as we watched the guards leave. As soon as the last guard's cloak disappeared, I pushed past Alcaeus to have a look at the broken and still unconscious Vampire in front of us. But before I could fully kneel beside him, Alcaeus was pulling me back up.

"Alcaeus what—he needs help! Let go!" Ignoring me, he dragged us to the door. Suddenly, the scar-faced soldier I had seen when I had left Alcaeus's study appeared.

"Sire, I tried but somehow she broke through the wards –" The prince put his hand up, stopping him.

"We'll speak of this later, Sotiris. Take Tomwyl to his chambers and call for Cillian; the lich will take care of anything permanent. Also, bring several willing bloodslaves; Tomwyl will need them; I have no doubt Ragna drained his powers."

"At once, Your Grace."

Before I could so much as blink, Alcaeus was pulling me through the door by the hand and down the darkened corridor. His stride was long and deliberate, with an intensity that I presumed to be anger, which radiated off his broad shoulders.

"Please, Alcaeus slow down—Oh!" I stumbled; my own shorter stride combined with these silly heels causing me to lose my balance.

He turned suddenly and caught me, steadying me. I glared up at him.

"My apologies, *mikrós asvós*. I miscalculated, I didn't anticipate—" He shut his eyes for a moment, taking a deep breath. Consternation filled his face briefly, but he quickly composed himself. "I had planned on preparing you for the Gatherings, but I didn't expect her to demand your presence so soon. I will try to prepare you for what is to come as we walk there. Testing her patience in this will only end in bloodshed." He turned, hand still in mine, and began to walk forward. I didn't move.

Alcaeus looked back, questioningly. "My lady?"

I swallowed hard before whispering, "Do you and the queen... are you intimate with her?"

I had no right to ask that of him. They were engaged. It wasn't my business. Memories of our own intimate encounters flooded my mind. But I recoiled at the thought of touching him if they were. It all seemed too messy.

It's not my business... right?

Surprise, understanding, and then his face transformed into the biggest smile I had ever seen. You could even see the length of his incisors, which I had yet to see in their full form. My breath caught at the transformation. At that moment, I knew I'd give anything to see that smile as frequently as possible; he was breathtaking.

Alcaeus shook his head and pulled me closer to him, resting a hand along my cheek as his thumb lifted my face to his. "No, my dear little Alchemist, we are not. I have avoided her for over a thousand years. That's not changing. Yes, she tries her tricks, plays her games. All have failed. So, worry not, Melisandre," he leaned down, kissing my cheek and whispered in my ear, "you are the only woman I desire. With vigour."

He pulled back with a self-confident gleam in his eyes. When I rolled my eyes and scoffed, I was met with a soft chuckle. We started walking again. With his back turned to me, I couldn't help the silly smile that took over at his confession. I barely noticed where we were going, so focused on what Alcaeus was telling me.

"...not sure what your experience has been with Vampire customs and traditions but this one is considerably more primitive than you are probably accustomed to. Try not to stare. Just stay at my side and I ask you not to do anything that could cause Ragna to –"

"I am no fool, Alcaeus."

"No, you most certainly are not. However, when was the last time you have ever been subservient to another? Been owned? That is the behaviour that is expected of you at Gatherings. It is a show of status and power; a place and time where greater Vampires, elders, and Champions can feast and replenish their magic."

The words 'subservient' and 'owned' made my lips curl in disgust. Over 600 years I had been successful at avoiding capture or ownership, blissfully free. Admittedly, my fears were few, but they ran deep; enslavement and subservience could be counted among them.

The last portion of what he said had me asking, "Replenish magic? By feast? Is it not just taking blood or is there more? Dare I ask what that means?"

"Either by blood slaves, through sexual acts or by violence, or even through their Familiar if they have one. Has Elis shared anything with you at all about how Vampires replenish themselves?"

Oh, sweet, blessed gods. The image my mind procured at his description had the blood draining from my face.

"I knew the general gist of it, but Elis only explained how he and Llyr replenished each other; we never went into any of the finer details. I felt it too personal to ask, even in the name of science..."

"Ah, yes, that's the beauty of being mated–both become a vessel of power that never empties. Chosen Mates are a powerful thing. Those who are Fated, are almost unstoppable," he said the last part so quietly I almost didn't catch it, as if deep in thought.

"So then, how will you...?"

"I will not. I do not need to."

"But then how—?"

"Another time, I answer that, or rather, show you. For now, let us deal with tonight first. Nevertheless, I will make a show of it as is expected of both of us. If we do not, Ragna will get creative and that is the last thing either of us want to be subjected to. So, I beg you, mikrós asvós." He came to a sudden stop and turned to me, placing his hands on my shoulders. His voice dropped and he pinned me with an earnest stare. "Do not question, do not fight. No matter what happens, know this: You. Are. Mine. No one else's."

The burn of desire I felt when we kissed burst through whatever apprehension I had, igniting every nerve at each word he growled out. At that moment, I believed him.

"Alcaeus—" A door behind the prince opened, revealing Oweyn.

"We've been expecting you, Your Highness. The Gathering has already begun."

Alcaeus clenched his jaw but gave me a questioning nod, asking if I was ready. I inclined my head in confirmation.

He turned and I saw as he morphed into the Royal Consort of the Nightmare Court, settling his shoulders before walking through the double doors. There was nothing left but for me to square my own and follow him.

CHAPTER 14

What we walked into could be described as no less than an orgy of epic proportions. That is, if you could consider the element of horror as part of an orgy. Alcaeus told me not to stare; I stared. I had enough awareness not to let my jaw hit the ground, but nothing could have prepared me for this.

There was not a place in this room where people weren't either fucking, sucking, or both. Many of the nobles were lounging on chaises, some were partially clothed; most were naked. Chains hung from the ceiling, tables, and other torture devices were spread around the room; many were occupied. In the far corner, I glimpsed a body in pieces, several thrall-like creatures feasting.

The smell of sex, blood, and meat filled the air. Moans and screams overshadowed whatever the musicians were playing in the background.

Alcaeus's hand gripped mine almost painfully as he dragged me through the throng. The strength of his pull was the only thing keeping me from bolting out of the room, although it didn't stop me from digging my heels in and leaning my entire body weight backward.

"Mmm-mmm. No. Absolutely not," I stated, shaking my head, desperately wanting to bleach my eyes after witnessing the scene in front of me. "I'm not doing this."

Alcaeus stopped, whipped around, coming nose to nose with me. "You must! Courage, Melisandre! Ragna will not accept your refusal and will likely try to punish you for it!" he replied, his voice quiet but nonetheless demanding. I had always considered myself relatively comfortable around sex and kinks, confident in my own abilities. It was a natural part of the biological cycle, after all. Yet, it quickly became clear I was but a frog living in the well, the ocean so much more vast than I had imagined. An ocean full of horrors that had no business being in the same sentence as 'sex'.

"Well, I've changed my mind and she can certainly try; Ragna can go fuck her nasty, obscene self into next Thursday. I refuse. This is grotesque! I am not one to shame others for their natural instinct but this... this is..."

"This is natural in the Vampire Court. You were warned. And remember: it is not you who would bear the true brunt of her ire." He meant Toby or Elis, and it took everything in me not to march straight over to her and let her have it. "Please," pleaded Alcaeus. "I will get us out as soon as possible. Bear with it, *mikrós asvós*. Save your fire to get through this." My eyes darted around at the horrors surrounding me but when they came to rest on his imploring face, my resolve weakened. "Please," he asked once more.

"'Primitive' was how you described this. It's a bit more than that. You give shite warnings, Alcaeus."

He grinned. "Fair enough and duly noted. I shall endeavour to be more explicit next time. Now, shall we?" After a deep sigh and a begrudging nod, he kissed my forehead and took me by the hand once more.

Leading us to the centre of the large room, it had a massive stone stage, too tall to be considered a dais. Several stairs led up to its platform, soft rugs placed where the seating area was. The most ornate couches and pillows were spread out and servants holding refreshments kept vigil at the four corners of it. Even they were more scantily clad than normal.

The queen lay on her side, propped up on her elbow. Golden locks now loose, it looked as if she was sucking the face off one of the many boys that surrounded her. Several women lay naked on the floor, as if they'd slid off her chaise: glassy eyed with bite marks at every major arterial point, blood trickling down. They looked... empty, devoid of life.

Dead.

Noticing our arrival, she grabbed the back of the boy's head she was kissing and yanked, inciting a yelp from him. Blood trailed down her fingers and I knew she had pierced his scalp with her talons.

"Ah, finally! You are late, my prince. Do sit and enjoy yourself, show off your *gift*," she said, a suspicious undercurrent present in her tone. Alcaeus said nothing, his face now the epitome of noble arrogance and boredom.

A male Vampire on another couch, who was getting sucked off by a painfully skinny and petite female slave, glanced at us but addressed the queen.

"My Queen, with utmost respect, do you not have a dress standard for these gatherings?"

Alcaeus turned his head slowly to stare at the audacious noble. The lesser Vampire quickly lowered his gaze and made no more comments. Though I could have sworn I saw a look of animosity flash across the man's face. His discomfort was obvious, and the Vampire slapped the girl between his legs and then began to skull-fuck her. Disgust and anger filled me like wildfire in the middle of August.

"Indeed, you are quite right Lord Cyto. Even my dear consort is not above the laws and expectations of this court. Besides, this is Lady Von Boden's first gathering - she should be dressed for the occasion! Or should I say...undressed?" She chuckled, sharing a look with the others. "Mage Ilirhun, if you would be so kind?"

A hooded figure, who I didn't notice before, appeared behind the queen. Before I could question why I hadn't, he lifted a gnarled hand in my direction. In my culture, to raise your hands toward an Alchemist is a direct challenge and the power within me flickered. Runes coming to life, I moved to a fighting stance. He flicked his wrist and suddenly my clothes were gone. Instantly I tried to cover myself only to see that I was wearing fine silver and gold chains, weaved around my body. They covered my nipples and private areas but nothing else.

I slowly raised a scathing glare at the mage. Runes alight, I touched the gold and silver chains and transmuted them. By heating the molecules, causing them to expand, mould, quench, and tempering them into wider bands, they wrapped and curled around my body tightly, so they covered a bit more. It still wasn't much but it would do. I may have inscribed *futue te ipsum* during the transmutation on the band at my chest. The queen narrowed her eyes at my small act of defiance.

I had defeated mages before, and I was almost jumping at the chance to take this one out in my rage. I took a step, but Alcaeus quickly moved in front of me, blocking out the queen as he faced me.

"Look at me, *mikrós asvós*! Look at me!"

I didn't, closing my eyes instead, jaw clenching. Remembering his words earlier, I tried to calm my fury.

Then there was a pressure at the nape of my neck, long fingers threading into my loose hair as he fisted it, yanking my head back. Just enough force to elicit pleasure and pain, teasing me with his strength.

151

My eyes shot open. A gasp escaped me as I instinctively grabbed the arm holding me, my other hand gripping the front of his vest. To everyone else, it may have seemed like he was reprimanding me, and I believe that's what he wanted people to see. Only I was privy to the tender, beseeching look he gave, underlined with desire as he skimmed over my mostly naked form.

Closing his eyes, a small frown crossed his face before snapping them open. A glowing silver geometric pattern appeared in his irises and around his pupils.

With an intensity that made me weak, he trapped me in that stare. A gentle whisper of presence, then his voice caressed my thoughts as he spoke into my mind.

"Remember what I said - you are mine. Head high, my little Alchemist - do not let them goad you. Focus on me."

Never before had I experienced telepathy and nothing could have prepared me for that level of intimacy. So much of me wanted to be upset but my own body burned with need, my mind with fascination. But there was no time, for he moved me back to the lounge and gently nudged me to sit. Alcaeus swung his head sharply over to the mage who began lifting his hand towards him. The Nightmare Prince only had to raise a regal brow at the motion. The sorcerer quickly put his hand down and bowed low.

Ragna said nothing but looked beyond pleased with herself. Taking the head of the boy she still had her claws in, she shoved her tongue down his throat. A choking moan came from him.

I looked away from her, swallowing hard. Gathering my wits, my gaze was drawn back to Alcaeus. An absolute mistake. Whatever wits I had gathered left me instantaneously.

The Royal Consort was looking down at me, clearly soaking in my reaction, as he slowly removed his jacket and then began unbuttoning his waistcoat. Letting that drop to the floor, he removed his cravat. Untucking his shirt, he pulled it over his head the way men do. There may as well have been no one in the room for all I saw was him, the cacophony of wet noises completely tuned out.

I could not hide the look of wonderment or desire even if I wanted to and he was enjoying every moment of it.

Golden skin, not quite bronze, was smooth wherever it lacked hair. Muscles in all the right places, contracted with every graceful movement.

His long torso was perfectly sculpted with a cut Adonis belt that left my mouth watering.

There is a difference between a man who lifts excessive weights and a man who trains and breathes for battle. Every movement was like watching a tiger saunter, confidence in every step as if ready to attack should the need require it. Indeed, it was the confidence within him that exacerbated that masculine sensuality.

A smattering on his chest and a thin line from the navel to below his belt was all the hair that could be seen. Scars gleamed in the firelight, one slash across the right side of his chest, another on his shoulder, and one more across his abdomen. Alcaeus pulled the tie from his hair and ran his hand through it, letting it fall forward; a thick mane of amber chestnut that made me want nothing more than to sink my own hands into it.

Before I could embarrass myself by drooling or creaming the poor cushions, he swiftly picked me up and took my place on the couch. Placing me on his lap, Alcaeus positioned me so I sat sideways against him. I tried to relax into the safety of his arms but the warmth of his skin against mine almost burned me. Awkwardly, I folded my hands in my lap, trying to calm down. Then he quickly pushed his face into my neck, breathing me in. My breath hitched and my hands clenched.

Reaching around with his right hand and sliding it underneath my breast, he gave a teasing caress before slipping it underneath the band.

"I beg your pard–ah!" I squirmed, my hand slapping against his to push the intruding hand away. But my words were lost and my strength left me as he firmly massaged my chest, his thumb flicking over my nipple several times before fully palming it, then expertly pinching it once more. I sucked in a breath at the sudden action. Alcaeus' eyes held mine, watching my resolve shatter and lust for him take over.

Somewhere in the back of my clouded mind, I knew I should slap him away, but the prince moved his other arm to rest against my thighs, hand playing along my hip until it slid underneath my cheek, squeezing it. Hard. Then gently massaging. When his fingertips nearly brushed my folds, I almost became undone.

My body was small enough in his arms that he could reach me anywhere he wanted. Through the haze of lust, also came the realisation Alcaeus was doing his best to hide me from curious stares; though the bastard was clearly going to enjoy himself while he did.

I was so unbelievably aroused, the thrum between us was near vibrating. Where my sense of disgust had gone was beyond me; whatever magic Alcaeus was playing on my nerves was working. Or maybe it was the moans, the smells of sex but I subconsciously ground against him, feeling his desire for me. It pressed against me in earnest, the size of him making my eyes widen as it occurred to me what I was doing.

"Oh! I—" I gasped.

Alcaeus's arms tightened around me as he nuzzled my neck.

"I did not lie when I told you it was you that I wanted," he rumbled in my ear. "Be a good girl and try not to move so much. Because when I have you, mikrós asvós, it will just be us—the rest of the world be damned, for it will cease to exist for you and me." He squeezed a little harder as he said this.

I let out a hard exhale, pressing against him, my core throbbing and wet.

"Gods, I can smell your desire for me, little one." Kissing and nipping at my neck, my shoulder, and my collar bone, I felt the scrape of his teeth.

Just as I was on the verge of losing myself to the sensation of him, I cracked my eyes open to see the deadly stare of Ragna, watching us. Her smile did not match the calculated coldness in her gaze, which made me stiffen in Alcaeus's arms. It was more effective than a tub full of ice water, my lust evaporating.

Alcaeus pulled back slightly, sensing the change in me. He didn't ask me what was wrong, just shifted us so one arm remained curled around me, the other coming to rest on the back of the couch. For the second time, I sensed his presence in my mind.

"A little more time, Melisandre, then we can leave. It needs to look as if I am taking power from you. Tis but a power play by the queen, nothing more. Bear with me."

Having zero magical ability, let alone psychic aptitude, there was no way to respond to him in kind. So, I sat up and leaned into his chest, wrapping my arms around his neck. I let my hand slide through his thick hair.

Putting my lips against the shell of his ear, I whispered, "Don't get used to being in my head, Vampire prince. That is a privilege I afford no one."

I felt him smile against me. "Then I shall endeavour to not take it for granted. Though I must confess, you might regret not allowing me to 'get used to it'."

Snorting delicately, I shot back, "You know no shame, silver-tongued fox." Then I shut my mind, throwing up a mental wall.

Feeling his sigh, Alcaeus didn't press me and relaxed more into the couch, observing the sexual chaos of the room. Over his shoulder, I looked around, both hoping and dreading seeing my best friend. My initial shock had worn off and I began to take a more scientific approach in observation. Many of the power exchanges had already taken place, it seemed, as many of the slaves were passed out on the floor or over furniture. Their Vampire lords and ladies chatting, lax and drunk off the power exchange.

At the end of the room, however, several slaves hung spreadeagle, their flesh stripped as the butcher who held the whip kept going. Disgust filled me but I understood it for what it was - this Vampire must regain power through pain and suffering. Having enough of that, I continued to scan the room.

"Looking for someone, my lady?" A smooth, cool voice said.

I looked up into opal, almond eyes. Long, pearl white hair hung long but he had the front half in an ornate topknot. It was held together with a gold headpiece and a golden stick running through it. If he were human, I'd say he was an Asian royal. Bare-chested, he was dressed in nothing but trousers with a strip of blood-red linen wrapped around his waist like a belt. Both nipples had silver rings and a silvery-white phoenix tattoo ran down one shoulder all the way to his wrist. Fine boned but muscular, not a hair could be seen. His face was sharp but beautiful.

"Ah, Zhenbai," Alcaeus said, motioning with his hand, "please join us."

The new Vampire came around the couch and reclined on the other end. I shifted too to look at him, but I curled into myself slightly, subconsciously trying to hide my lack of cover. A slightly darker white brow lifted but his eyes looked over me curiously.

"Melisandre, meet Lord Zhenbai, a long-time friend. Champion of the goddess Jiutian Xuannü, goddess of -"

"War," I answered softly. Both of them looked surprised but before they could ask, I added, "I can see why you two would get along. Are you one of the Twelve?"

At this, Zhenbai smiled, canines flashing.

"What a curious little thing you are. Technically, yes. Although, my mistress had little interest in the wars of the Western gods. I did not compete in the games."

"And yet she created you." I stated plainly.

"One must always be prepared," he replied without hesitation. "Commander, if I may?"

They shared a look, but Alcaeus said, "You must ask the lady, my friend."

Seeing my confusion, Zhenbai leaned forward slightly.

"I just want to look at you, for it is a great honour to be in the presence of a child of Hou Tu. Your symbols are a great testament to your power. May I touch your face?"

Hou Tu, the spirit of the earth. It had been so long since I had heard that term and I had loved it the first time. Still, suspicion swept through me. I glanced at Alcaeus, but he gave me a reassuring nod. Hesitating, I finally scooted off his lap and onto the couch, facing Zhenbai. He gently lifted his hand to my cheek. Without thinking, I jerked back slightly but in the face of his patience, I leaned forward again.

His touch was cool and gentle, softly caressing my cheek but then sliding up to rest next to my eyes. Those opal spheres of his glimmered like the very stones they mimicked. His brows drew together as if seeing far more than my face.

"Silver and gold, refined by a great fire and purified from it. Like the deepest of oceans is the depths of your knowledge, your intellect the blade you wield. I can see it - the vines of Yggdrasil wrap around you, child of earth. Oldest of your kind and yet...there is no sense of time around you; you do not age. These eyes," he whispered, sadness crossing his porcelain features, "have seen such sorrow. Such... suffering. I can see faces -"

I jerked away, shutting down the tendrils of memories that were flooding to the surface, as if being called forth by his gaze. Memories that I kept hidden, locked deep within me for over 600 years.

"Enough!" I snapped.

Breathing heavily, I moved to stand but Alcaeus grabbed me once again and settled me against him. Finding sanctuary in his arms, my head tucked into his chest, he stroked my head as if I was a child in need of calming.

"My sincerest apologies, my lady. I meant no—"

"My Queen! Royal Consort! A messenger from the Unseelie court!"

We all turned to see Oweyn speaking quietly with the messenger that just barged in. Ragna sat up, throwing her victim to the ground past the dais, and there was a slap and crunch as the slave's face hit the marble floor.

Licking the blood delicately from her lips, she said, "The royal consort and Lord Zhenbai will receive the messenger. Prince Alcaeus is most skilled at foreign relations, and I have had enough of politics for one day." She wasn't looking at Oweyn when she spoke.

She was looking at me.

I felt the tension between us, and Alcaeus stiffened. Gripping him a little harder, I was reluctant to let go.

"As my queen commands," said Lord Zhenbai, tilting his head dutifully.

Alcaeus squeezed my hip and I stood, giving them both room to rise. Taking my hand, he began to lead me away.

"The Alchemist stays."

All went still in the room, an invisible authority sitting heavy in her words.

"She stays."

Ragna pinned Alcaeus with a look that left no room for disagreement. Zhenbai's eyes darted between the royals, his gaze finally landing on me with a face filled with concern. Power began to grow, nearby lesser-Vampires and still-conscious slaves shrinking away. Dread filled my stomach. The prince stared hard at her, his face a mask and indiscernible. Slowly he inclined his head. I couldn't help the niggling feeling of betrayal. He let go of my hand and I watched the two men walk out of the room. Slowly, I sat back on the couch, stiff-backed. Something was about to happen; I could feel it. But I would not be cowed.

So, I waited. Ready.

A. R. Morgan

CHAPTER 15

Crossing my legs, I scooted back, draping my arms across the couch. I waited thus, outwardly uncaring of my near nakedness. Ragna wanted subservience but she bowed to power and we were equals in that respect. No. No, my abilities were so much more. I knew it. So did she. But she also knew she had the upper hand until I decided the lives of my friends meant less than my own. And that would never happen.

But maybe, just maybe, there might be a chance to provoke her and take her focus off Toby. She was going to do the same, attempting to lead this psychotic dance we played. Ragna would continue to push me and poke at me until she could see the cracks. Then, she would strike like the viper she was.

Ignoring moans and muffled screams, the sounds of tearing flesh, and the cracking of bones that echoed behind me, I continued to stare unflinchingly at the door.

Please hurry back, Alcaeus. Before I try to finish this. But my mental plea went unanswered.

"Come, Alchemist, let me taste you. I am most eager to see how you play," crooned the queen, a beckoning hand reaching out to me.

"Taste yourself, Ragna," I replied coolly, foregoing her title as my eyes stayed glued to the door. Yet, I could not help glancing to the floor at the four dead slaves near her chaise, my lip curled in disgust. "You've clearly had your fill, Queen of Corpses."

"Your insolence will only be tolerated for so long, Von Boden. Your defiance tests the limits of my patience! Obey me!" she demanded.

Slowly, I turned my head towards her.

"And you continuously make the mistake that I am one of your subjects, to cow and tremble before your might. To be a puppet to your every selfish whim. I am neither a Vampire nor a citizen of your kingdom—you command me by blackmail alone. By your own contract, my deal is now with your Consort. Not. You."

Those around us who heard became as still as stone. Ragna's green eyes glittered, soulless and maniacal. She sat up slowly, dangerously. The boy she'd been holding onto tried to slink away but she grabbed him by the throat and, without leaving my gaze, tore the flesh right out. Her nails had grown to 5-inch talons, now dripping with red and bits of tissue. Blood spewed as a look of shock crossed the man's face. He dropped like a weighted sack.

I merely lifted an eyebrow at her, unimpressed. Tyrants were always the same.

"You care little for the life of your ward, do you not, Alchemist?" She asked, licking the blood off one of her fingers.

"Imagine having to threaten the life of a child to get your way with me. Tell me, who is truly the powerless one here?" I baited her, done with her psycho babbling, tyrannical shit.

"ENOUGH!" Ragna screamed, her eyes going black.

Green smoky tendrils of flame snaked around her and pierced the bodies lying at her feet. Jerking her hands, the dead convulsed, coming to life. Except their eyes were hollow, a green flame emanating from them; the same colour as the queen's own. It would appear Ragna, Queen of Nightmares, was a necromancer.

"This could have been so easy for you, enjoyable even. You cannot say your queen is not considerate, however. I am also graciously abiding. You chose strife today, Lady Von Boden, and I am more than happy to oblige. Besides, force is usually necessary to break even the strongest of beasts. Mage! Restrain her!"

Instantly my runes came to life, even the ones that circled my irises. Adrenaline shot through me as I stood quickly, placing my hand on the side of the couch. Calling forth the mahogany and granite of the floor, I transmuted them. A wooden staff with a thin vine of granite wrapped around it to reinforce the mahogany, formed in my hands. Twirling it behind me, I jumped off the stage to face off with the mage.

People began to clear, the nobles getting behind their queen. The hooded Ilirhun walked forward, like a grim reaper. Whispering words I couldn't understand, magical chains shot out. This time, I was ready for them.

Dodging three, I rolled, closing space against the mage. I needed to disrupt his incantations. I went for a strike, but a thrall grabbed the end of my staff before it could reach the sorcerer, its strength keeping me from moving the staff. Ducking under it, I stepped into him and touched his chest. I called upon the power within me, and it answered back. As if time had stopped, every cell of this Vampire's body came to life in my vision. Every molecule. Every atom. Freshly dead, its cells had yet to accept their fate. Transmutation circles appeared on his chest where my hand was, and I accelerated the speed of his molecular structure. The thrall screamed and burst into flames.

I shoved it away from me just as another made a grab for me from behind. Twisting, I shoved the staff towards its body, the end I had turned into a point just as it pierced flesh. It slid through the thrall like butter but the zombified Vampire was unfazed.

"Dammit," I cursed as it slid towards me, my staff completely going through it.

With flailing arms, it reached for me. This time, I let it grab my hand. Circles appeared all over him. Speeding the molecules of his body to heat almost to the point of combustion, I then rapidly cooled them. The thrall froze as I vitrified him into glass. With a violent yank, I withdrew the staff and the thrall shattered.

Turning to face the mage once again, I ducked as another chain came after me. Ilirhun was wise enough to not throw elemental spells at me; something I noted. He made a motion of his hands and suddenly my staff was gone. I stumbled slightly but went at him. Suddenly, that same force that threw me the first time I was in the throne room slammed into me, knocking me off my feet.

A chain wrapped around my neck, and I grabbed for it, but several other tethers shot around my wrists. A magical coating drenched the metals, keeping me from transmuting them. Interesting.

I struggled to my knees, my head bowed over the floor, but the chains pulled in opposite directions, keeping me from standing. The one around my neck flipped to the ceiling, almost choking me. My spine stretched.

"Useless, the lot of you! Even in death, you have failed me!" snapped Ragna as she stared at the still-burning body of her thrall. "As they say, if you want to get something done…" Suddenly, the queen was before me. Leaning over, she smirked down at me and whispered, "You do it yourself." Smug satisfaction rippled through her cold Norse features, and I felt as if I were staring into the eyes of Hel herself. She straightened, turning back to her court.

"Now, where were we? Ah! Yes, enjoying our Consort's Familiar. Did you all enjoy a taste of her power? Magnificent, is it not? Now," she shot me a look over her shoulder, "shall we see how well Alchemists can fuck?"

My whole body went cold, and fear hit me in the gut. Torture, I expected. Sexual depravity I did not.

Where the hell was Alcaeus?

The queen's beautiful form made her way back to her couch, the thralls on their knees and staring blankly at the floor. The man who was getting his cock sucked earlier stared at me like I was the mouse and he the cat. He helped the queen sit, bowed, and then rounded the couch, waiting eagerly for the show.

I glared back, rage and hatred filling my gaze. Breathing hard, my muscles strained against my restraints. By the end of all of this, I made a vow I was going to bind Ragna and choke her until those sewage green eyes popped from the force of her own damn chains.

"Lord Saelish, would you mind getting my Consort's Familiar... prepared for engagement? You are one of the best in seduction psychosis. I have always admired your work."

"Anything for you, My Queen. I thought you would never ask."

The man that answered pushed forward through the crowd; curly brown hair flopped over crystal blue eyes. He only had on brown breeches, unlaced in the front. Dark bronze skin gleamed in the candlelight. With high cheekbones and an arrogant set to his chin, he would have been devastatingly handsome under different circumstances.

Lord Saelish sauntered towards me, and it was then that I saw two leather leashes clenched in one hand. Two male slaves crawled on all fours behind him. Both slaves were hard and eager to please their master.

"Ragna! You-" My words caught in my throat as an invisible force stole my voice.

My eyes darted over to Mage Ilirhun who had a blue orb floating between his hands as he mumbled incantations. The power inside me began to thrum, sensing a threat and desperate for action.

"Stand, my lovelies, assist your master," the lord Vampire commanded. His slaves obeyed and began to walk around me.

I eyed them warily.

"My Queen, are you sure it's...safe? After all, she is a..." He stank of anxiety, flinching under my gaze. A quick look at the impatience on Ragna's face and his noble mask fell back into place, and Lord Saelish clapped his hands. "Well! What is pleasure without a little risk? Indeed, she is a beauty. Her figure is stunning. Perfect size for a plaything, don't you think? Those markings make her pure exotic. Her eyes though, I think they'll haunt me for the next millennia!" Saelish laughed and several chuckles could be heard around the room.

"Mage Ilirhun is my strongest sorcerer; I trust his abilities, as should you."

Lord Saelish turned slightly, bowing his head in deference. Turning back to me, he looked down with lust and curiosity, though a healthy dose of fear peeked from the depths of those crystal blue eyes. My stomach rolled. Never in all my years have I been unable to defend myself. Oh, I have been subject to many a violent person's ire. Many have tried to capture me when I first fled the Otherworld and some almost succeeded. I've been fighting and hiding my entire life. But for the first time, I felt my self-confidence crack. I felt vulnerable in a way I'd never known.

That's when I felt them, hands snaking around me to cup my breasts, fingers trailing along my hips. I closed my eyes, trying to think of a way out that did not include bringing down the entire city of Idrisid. One of the slave's hands trailed towards my inner thigh. I tried to buck him off, but he pressed his groin against my rear, causing me to freeze and stiffen away at the firmness of his cock between my cheeks. I started to shake, the Vampire mistaking my rage with fear.

"Shhhh, my lovely, do not be frightened. I will make this feel so very, very good for you." Lord Saelish's voice whispered against my ear like honey, and I felt the pressure of his power crawling on me like a warm viscous liquid. Suddenly, every nerve tingled as desire shot straight to my core. My nipples tightened and I clenched my pelvic floor hard in a subconscious effort to fight the magic off. It took a powerful amount of magic to affect me like this.

I need... I need to be... No! Don't let go!

"There, you see my sweet thing? Much better." Lord Saelish kissed me gently on the lips. "Oh, you were made for fucking, I can tell."

My jaws snapped at him like the cornered wolf I was and he jerked back, letting out an uneasy chuckle. Squeezing my eyes shut against this vile man, his slaves, and their touch, internally fighting a losing battle.

Crack.

My runes began to brighten as power begged to be unleashed, wiping out the room. The castle. The land. Uninvited fingers grazed over my lower lips.

Crack.

"Are you sure it's safe, My Queen? Her markings are glowing brighter...?" Concern marred the noble's voice.

"Lord Saelish, I assure you she is well in hand. You are safe from her," snapped Queen Ragna, her voice exasperated, clearly eager to get on with the show.

The Vampire lord hesitated, then trailed his fingers down my face and my body. My heart pounded in trepidation and horror. He leaned down to kiss me again, but I looked away at the last minute and his mouth met my neck. Baring such a vulnerable area was probably very unwise but I could no longer tolerate him near my face. His slaves were trying to work the band around my waist off, fondling me in the process.

Crack.

For the last time, I closed my eyes as a single angry tear tracked down my cheek as I began to let go.

Alcaeus...

Thu-thunk.

The sound of wet heavy flesh hitting the hard ground caused my eyes to shoot open. The slave directly behind me sagged against my back before sliding to the floor. Warm liquid dripped down my shoulder blades and spine; the tell-tale odour of metallic copper indicating blood. I glanced down at the body lying next to me—his head was gone. Without looking, I knew the same fate befell the other slave. I stared at Lord Saelish but before I could blink, the tip of a sword came through his mouth, mere millimetres from my face.

Alcaeus's broad form appeared behind the Vampire lord. He leaned in, fangs brushing the noble's ear. Dark rage coated his voice as he whispered, "It is not her you should have feared. Death has come for you, Saelish—and *I* am its reaper." Wrath contorted the Royal Consort's face.

Lord Saelish's eyes were a myriad of emotions; terror, regret, disbelief, and finally, acceptance. The prince's sword, Nemesis, began to glow brighter and the Vampire's powers, essence, and everything that made him living were absorbed into the metal. Like vines on a tree, the former lord's power snaked up Alcaeus's arm through the hilt, his dark eyes glowing as he received it. What remained of the lord seducer was swept away with the draft in the room.

"What have you done? Stop at once!" cried Ragna but he ignored her.

With a few words from its master, Nemesis disappeared. Alcaeus then whispered an incantation and I found myself once again released from the chains. Falling forward, relief hit me so hard my legs almost gave out from under me. Without hesitation, the prince swept me into his arms. I couldn't stop shaking. His warmth and his scent had me burying into his chest, my face turned into him.

"I am here, *mikrós asvós*, I will not let anyone hurt you," he whispered into my hair. "We must get you out of here."

"What did they do to her?" I heard Zhenbai ask.

"Whatever they did," growled Alcaeus under his breath, "they died for it."

He started walking towards the exit.

"Stop! Stay where you are, Consort! You slay one of my noblemen and take what is mine and think to walk away? I would have words with you, Prince Alcaeus!" Queen Ragna demanded.

Alcaeus whipped us around.

"You gave me a direct order to make this Alchemist my Familiar, My Queen, and yet you continue to jeopardise the very process that you sought in the first place! Yes, we will have words but first I am going to take Lady Von Boden back to her rooms. I will gladly seek an audience with you once she is settled."

Silence. All I could hear was the pounding of my own heartbeat.

"Get out. Do not mistake my acquiescence for reprieve–there will be consequences for this insolence, and you will hold an audience, My Prince," Ragna hissed.

Giving her a hard look, the Prince of the Nightmare Court turned, with me tucked tightly in his arms, and stormed out of the room.

The moment we emerged from that room of horrors, Alcaeus let out a heavy breath and he raised me up just enough to kiss the top of my head. His steps quickened and everything seemed to become a blur. The prince's Captain, Sotiris, fell into step with several guards behind him.

"Double the guard tonight, Sotiris. I do not want anyone, and I mean anyone, disturbing Melisandre tonight. Is that clear?" The command in his voice made even me want to straighten up and obey.

"Yes, Commander."

Zhenbai caught up with Alcaeus and the prince turned to look at him, not breaking pace.

"Zhenbai, I need you to see into the possible outcomes of what just happened and how they could have impacted our plans. Once I am finished settling the lady in, meet me in the arena."

"The arena? Sparring so late?"

Alcaeus stopped, turning to face the white-haired Vampire.

"No, but I have just acquired newfound abilities and I have no intention of going before Ragna without knowing the full extent of them."

"Ah, I understand," Zhenbai's gaze fell to mine, full of concern. "My lady, if the memories of what has happened become too much, I may be able to ease them for you."

My heart softened slightly at his thoughtfulness. Still too raw, I could only shake my head. I'd had enough of Vampire manipulation, no matter how considerate the intention may be. He nodded back in understanding. Bowing to Alcaeus, Zhenbai disappeared.

The prince kept a strict pace and before I knew it, we had arrived in his wing of the castle. Upon reaching my doors, they were promptly opened by Ada.

"Oh, milord! Is my lady—?"

"Quickly Ada, a hot bath for the lady."

The prince walked us right by her, straight towards the bathroom. I began to wiggle in his arms.

"Please, Alcaeus, let me down, I can walk."

He didn't respond, but once we entered the bath chamber, he reluctantly set me down. As soon as I was out of his arms, the reality of all that happened hit me. I had been violated, vulnerable...and weak. I couldn't be strong anymore. Not right then. I needed to break, even for just a moment.

He reached for me, trying to help me. "Melisandre, I—"

"Please Alcaeus, just go." I pushed away from him, walking towards the shower part of the room.

He grabbed my hand. "I tried to get to you as fast as I could; the queen—"

I broke.

"I said go! Leave me alone for one goddamn minute! I don't give a fuck about why you weren't there or what the fucking cunt of a queen did! Just," breathing hard and shaking as tears finally fell, I choked out, "leave me alone."

I turned away, waiting and hoping he did what I had asked. When I was greeted with nothing but silence, I peeked back. He was gone. Only Ada remained.

"My lady, did you want a bath then? And would you like oils or—"

"You too, Ada."

"Milady?"

"Please...leave." I looked at her then and it was also then that I realised she understood the haunting look in my eyes, as her own face filled with empathy.

"Yes milady," she replied gently, "And if you do need anything, I'm 'ere. I will send up some nice hot cider for you. I'll be on my way then." And with that, she left.

I was alone.

My hands shook on the knobs, releasing the cascading waterfall from the showerheads. Steam drifted in the air, and I ducked under the spray. Transmuting the bands around me into a solid gold and silver ball that landed with a loud *thunk* against the stone floor, I grabbed it and threw it over the balcony with a broken cry. Then, I curled up into my own little ball, pulling my knees to my chest. I wrapped my arms around myself, letting the water cleanse me of all the violations my body and mind had endured.

It certainly could have been worse and I had never been more grateful in seeing Alcaeus but... I shook my head; this game with the queen was so much darker and more evil, going beyond any of my previous expectations. My own imagination could not even begin to fathom the depths of depravity Ragna was capable of and I needed to remember that. Tonight had been a sore reminder of how far our thoughts were from one another.

Cerulean eyes flashed across my mind, and I began to scrub my skin in earnest. Finally accepting that no matter how hard I scrubbed, one could not wash away a memory. I dropped the rag with a sob. My skin was raw and angry red but clean. A deep cold seeped into my very bones despite the water cascading around me like a warm hug.

You're okay, Mel. They're dead. They're dead. You're not.

Repeating this mantra over and over in my head, I shut the water off. The fluffy white towels felt good against my extra sensitive skin as I dried off. Exhaustion set heavy, both emotionally and physically and my lids became heavy.

Making my way to my bed, I forewent bedclothes, slipping underneath the soft sheets. But the moment my eyes were closed, all I saw were them; the queen's satisfied smugness. The lust and power in Lord Saelish's eyes when he saw me at his mercy. Lord Cyto's predatory gaze. My voice, silenced. The helplessness at my inability to escape from wandering hands. Tears escaped my eyes and I cried out in frustration.

"Stop it! You're stronger than this...than them! Don't let them... break...you..." I choked back a sob, and I gripped my head in my hands. Pounding the mattress, my anger flooded my body just as grief consumed me. "Why... did I not fight back? Why did I allow this to happen? Why—"

Suddenly, I felt *him* then; a calming warmth, like coming home after a long and horrifying trip away. A soft caress, a sense of safety. Before I could tell Alcaeus off again for invading my mind, I heard it—the notes of a piano. A beautiful, gentle song began to play in my head. All memories of what had just happened vanished, replaced by the sweet melody.

My hands gripped the covers as I pulled them up to my chin, wiping my face of tears. The anger and regret that had ruled my entire being just moments ago, dissipated, leaving only a calm exhaustion in its wake.

That's when I realised why Alcaeus had connected his mind with mine—so he could soothe me. The tune was one I'd never heard, so this must have been something he wrote. I relaxed into my pillow, gazing into the fire across the room. Each note brought comfort, easing my anxiety, and healing my soul. Never did he speak or share anything else–just his playing. Alcaeus continued to play until I could no longer fight sleep.

I closed my eyes and dreamed. Not once did I wake from the nightmares I surely should have had. No, that night, my mind was filled with only dreams of him and his beautiful lullabies.

CHAPTER 16

The moment he felt Melisandre fall into a deep slumber, Alcaeus retreated from her mind, his hands slipping away from the keys. Picturing her room clearly, he appeared there, silently by her bedside. A tender smile played on his lips when all that greeted him was a small lump in the middle of the huge bed. Careful not to wake her, he gently lifted the covers, revealing only her face which was surrounded by pillows. Curled up in the fetal position, Melisandre's billowy curls were a halo around her. She was so very beautiful, he thought to himself, delicate features hiding a fierceness and resolve rarely seen, even among the greatest warriors he had battled.

Guilt still lingered from having left her, the death of Lord Saelish a mere bandage over a deep-rooted conflict that festered between himself and the Queen. The game had begun and Ragna had made her move. The first of many to come.

Delicately placing his fingers on her temple, Alcaeus whispered an incantation, a protection spell to ward off nightmares. Slowly, he removed his hand.

Sighing wearily, he whispered to her sleeping form, "My brave little Alchemist, soon you will discover why I cannot save you from the wrath of Ragna. But by all the gods, let the Fates hear me now: I vow to always be there to catch you if you fall. When the darkness threatens to swallow you whole, reach out and I will grab your hand so that you know you are not alone."

Placing a delicate kiss upon her brow, Alcaeus gave one last look of longing before he vanished. Arriving inside the arena, he was met by a now-clothed Zhenbai. His Hanfu robes were a simple black and red but nonetheless regal as he stood patiently, hands clasped behind his back.

"Is she alright? I sense she is sleeping."

The prince raised an eyebrow at that. "Connecting to her already? That is rare for you."

Zhenbai stroked his chin thoughtfully. "The lady is the tree in which we birds are meant to find shelter in her branches. She is the key to bringing true peace to the Otherworld that we have not known since her own race was alive. But... she is not quite what I had expected. Unusually powerful, is she not?"

Alcaeus nodded. "Behind those eyes is a bottomless ocean we cannot even begin to comprehend. The show of her restraint is something I believe we should all be immeasurably grateful for. I believe it is safe to assume Melisandre is not only the last of her kind but the only one of her species that is capable of something greater. This much Athena did prophecy. How or why," he shook his head, "only she knows. My past dealings with Alchemists involved all of a singular period of time when a correspondence took place with a rogue Alchemist, in the time of the Great Drought. My understanding was they were capable of manipulating only a singular element; Melisandre's abilities overshadow that a hundred-fold. And we have yet to even breach the surface."

A frown marred Zhenbai's flawless oval face. "I should tell you, my king—"

"Careful, Zhenbai. The dead may be listening."

His friend looked around briefly but continued, "I should tell you what I saw when I looked into the soul-gate of Lady Von Boden. I have pondered this deeply and I do not understand it."

"What is it? What do you mean?"

"I... I did not see her soul. If it was there, it somehow hid from my sight. There was an immense amount of soul energy, however. And the power... I sensed it hiding deep within her, but she cut me off before I could see it in its entirety. But it filled me with both terror and wonderment."

Alcaeus stared at Zhenbai, frowning at this unsettling bit of news.

An accomplished soul-seer and master of light, not many had the ability to block out Jiutian Xuannü's Champion.

"What could this mean?" asked the prince.

The other Vampire shook his head. For a moment, they stood there silently. Finally, Zhenbai spoke.

"I can only speculate the obvious: Whatever your lady is hiding, she is determined to keep it there and has the power to do so. It is with honey you should tempt her, not force nor the psychological dance that is our way. Like the elements she was born from, that is how you will gain her trust; simply and organically."

Remembering those piercing silver and gold eyes brought a grin to Alcaeus' face. "Undoubtedly, she would see through my ploy even as the thoughts came to fruition in my mind. No, I would never consider doing anything but, my friend." He scratched his beard thoughtfully, recounting when he first entered her mind and discovered the strength of her psyche alone. "Her mind is a fortress, sealed so tightly it was a wonder she let me in the little that she did. Melisandre was even able to control my presence enough to push me out. Telepathy has never failed me thus until now."

"Seeing even the *Great Owl* having difficulties with this tiny woman is truly a wonder. What fascinating creatures these Alchemists are."

"So they are. Considering this, the odds of the marking going well are becoming less in our favour, Zhenbai. There is a considerable amount of concern for the unexpected to happen."

"You know well that is a risk you both must take," said Zhenbai, "You know the queen will demand it after this. It is also your best option to keep her safe."

Alcaeus grinned at this. "Who, Melisandre or the queen?"

His friend smiled back. "Indeed."

"I will give my *mikrós asvós* a day to recover; I fear if I press her too soon the mark will not take. Possibly even backfire. You are right, however, once the first mark is in place the queen will have little reason to continue to harass Melisandre."

Nodding in agreement, Zhenbai's opal eyes were still filled with concern, his brows pulled together in consternation.

"Come, my friend." Patting the Vampire on the back as Alcaeus walked past him, the prince came to a stop in the middle of the arena. "Let us see what Lord Saelish was capable of."

Zhenbai inclined his head and opened his arms wide. "I am ready."

▽▽ඊ௳ൎ༠

Alcaeus came to a stop before the queen's personal sitting room. He hesitated, gathering his thoughts and schooling his features. Before the guards could announce him, the door opened. Oweyn stood back,

171

allowing the prince entry.

"Welcome, Your Highness. The Queen has been expecting you."

"I am sure she has," Alcaeus mumbled.

Walking further into the sitting room, darkness crept at the edges, the only light being the roaring fire in the massive hearth at the end of the room. For once, there were no slaves lying about, naked, for her pleasure. Just the *ingarmr*, or hellhounds as one would know them, chained to the far wall, gnawing on a suspiciously shaped limb.

A side table had been set with various sundries and tea but neither prince nor queen would partake in that tonight. Shelves lined the walls around the hearth, but they were not filled with books.

Instead, glass jars filled with body parts and odd specimens sat randomly, and several crowned skulls, conquered kings of old, stared ominously back at the room.

The queen stood by the fireplace, staring down into the flames. She was clothed in an emerald and gold dressing gown, her arms wrapped around herself as if shielding her from the cold. Gold tresses were weaved in a Viking braid, hanging over one shoulder. She did not turn to him.

He gave the customary bow. "My Queen."

Alcaeus was met with silence.

Finally, she said, "You gravely insulted me in front of my Court, Prince Alcaeus. You must know that cannot go unpunished."

"I would risk the insult again, My Queen, if it meant not letting the Alchemist dismantle our entire Court down to dust. Surely you understand you are playing with a power you do not understand. No one does."

She turned to him then with a calculated stare.

"Do not pretend I am unaware of what you are doing," she said quietly, "Do not pretend I do not see it."

"I pretend nothing, Your Grace. Please, educate me on what I cannot possibly know." He did not bother to keep the sarcasm out of his tone, enjoying the spark of irritation in the face of his passive disrespect.

"You're different! With her, you change! It is subtle but you have been mine for over a millennium; I see it. Now that you have absorbed Lord Saelish's powers, well, there can be only one reason."

Alcaeus narrowed his eyes to the implication. "You desired this, Ragna. Queen Mab is gathering her armies as we speak. The Unseelie King has been ever silent, his position unknown. The Changeling Kingdom has allied with the Seelie Court. Do not even let me begin on the state of the Were-Wildlands' Tribes and the Kings and Queens of Were! We are closer to all-out war than we have been for over a thousand years! Not to mention the continuous devastation the Sickness has wrought! The consequences of you slaying Oberon are creeping up on us! My actions towards the Alchemist are out of pure necessity. I cannot believe your behaviour is based on some misguided sense of jealousy."

Ragna glared at him, but then waved dismissively. "I have a surprise for that Seelie bitch, one that would surely bring her to her knees. Oberon serves me now; although he has lost a bit of his, shall we say, grandiosity?" she giggled, laughing at her own joke.

Alcaeus swallowed as his expression remained guarded, not sharing her humour. He had his suspicions that the Fae king's body was reanimated somewhere within the castle, most likely subject to Ragna's twisted experiments. But the issues stated were very real; ones he had tried, and failed, to get his mad fiancée to acknowledge.

Looking back at him, she sobered slightly, but the mirth was still in her eyes. "You are already mine in every way that matters, Prince. Even so, I am not without the foresight that you would do anything to usurp me. To take the vengeance you so desperately crave. Oh yes, do not think for a moment I have forgotten your true ambitions, even after all these years."

Alcaeus waited for it to appear, as it always did in these moments. A necklace suddenly manifested at her throat. Haunting white, a large orb surrounded by silver and iron casing, glowed eerily in the darkened room. Normally it remained safely hidden; only when she wanted to remind him of the real chains that bound him, did she reveal it.

A knowing, sickeningly sly smile crawled up her face. "Nothing you do will work, *ástin mín*. Yet I do so enjoy watching you struggle to fly with clipped wings, my noble owl. I dare say I can scarcely blame your hatred. It burns so much more passionately than love, does it not?"

The Prince of the Nightmare Court gave her a murderous glare and made a threatening step toward her, dropping all calm pretences. But the Norse Vampire just grinned, unbothered, and continued. "No, silly man. Even I can admit that I can be a jealous monarch, but I would not risk the ritual over something so trivial. The Alchemist is hiding something, something that will change the tides for the upcoming war. I will find out what it is. I should not have to tell you this, but to be sure—you will not fall for her, Alcaeus. Fuck that pretty little cunt if you must, but that is all. She is a toy. A plaything. Through you, I own her." Annunciating each clipped word, the queen squared her shoulders, demanding submission in its entirety. "She will never be yours. Nor will you ever be hers. The Alchemist is not our equal. So, keep your tricks and manipulations for her purely out of necessity, for the sake of the mark. You. Belong. To. Me. Do not make me take away that which I have given."

Alcaeus struggled to compose himself in the face of all the *Dauði Dróttning* had already taken from him, but a pair of gold and silver eyes flashed across his mind. Centring himself, he became the Master and Commander that he was, the bane of old gods.

"You need not worry, My Queen. My interests are purely for the sake of the realm. Nothing more."

"Good. Keep it that way." Ragna sauntered back over to her position by the fire. "I want that first mark, Alcaeus, and I want it by the third toll of the midnight bell tomorrow eve. Surely all your tricks have paid off by now. I grow sick of the Alchemist's bravado. She needs to be taken to heel. We need her fully marked before Yaldā Night, so we might utilise her for the great games. I want to see that Seelie bitch tremble before me. Do I make myself clear?" she demanded, turning sharply to face him. "If you do not, I will gladly give Melisandre to Mage Ilirhun or perhaps even to Lord Cyto; he is quite blessed in breaking spirits, and his creative methods of inflicting pain are unsurpassed."

"You have made yourself quite clear, Your Majesty. She will have the first mark," replied Alcaeus, jaw tightening at the prospect of Melisandre being at their mercy. "If that will be all, My Queen." Not waiting to be dismissed, he turned on his heel to make for the door.

"One more thing, My Prince."

He stopped but did not turn. She silently prowled to him, Alcaeus' body stiffening as she ran her hands down his back, before sliding them along his waist. Fingers searched him until they found the skin of his abdomen. The prince's hand snapped to hers, stopping them before they wandered too deeply.

"Once you have fully bound the Alchemist, we shall proceed with binding ourselves in matrimony. Too long have you put me off and too long have I allowed it. No longer will you defy me in this. You know the consequences if you do."

The warning was clear.

Alcaeus clenched his fists, but slowly gave her a nod over his shoulder. With the stiff back of a soldier at attention, he left the queen of darkness to her never-ending schemes.

CHAPTER 17

I stretched underneath the sheets, revelling in an unknown warmth behind me. Arms snaked around me pulling me against a very naked and muscled torso. I stiffened but a Familiar voice whispered in my ear with a gentle kiss, "Shhhh mikrós asvós, it is just me."

Relaxing into him, I raised my arm behind me and threaded my fingers into that thick walnut hair.

"Just you? You shouldn't be here," I gasped as he cupped my breast and pressed his groin into me from behind, his desire for me more than evident. My body roared fiercely in answer. "This has to be a dream."

"Mmm, perhaps." His other hand wrapped underneath me, continuing to fondle my breasts as his other hand moved confidently between my thighs. "The question is, do you want it to end?"

Moaning, I turned my face up to kiss him and pressed my rear back into his hard length.

"No."

Lifting my thigh slightly, I granted him access and his fingers slipped between my folds, caressing my clit before dipping inside me. He swallowed my gasp with a deep kiss, pressing me into the bed.

"Gods, Melisandre... you're so warm... so LET ME IN THIS GOD-DAMN ROOM OR I WILL LET THIS BEAST OF A DOG RIP YOUR FUCKING THROATS OUT!"

My eyes shot open, panting and disoriented. Yelling and growling resounded outside. Flying out of bed, I nearly ripped the fabric of my robe trying to shove myself into it. Yanking the door open, I barrelled into the sitting room just in time to see a very ruffled Elis pushing past the guards. Ares was already inside baring teeth and snapping at the guards, who were yelling something about 'having orders' and 'no one being allowed in'.

Elis slammed the door shut and placed his palm on the door. Vines shot around it, completely barring any possibility of opening it.

"AND STAY OUT!" He yelled, dusting off his hands as one would after a hard day's work.

Letting out an exasperated huff, he patted down his hair and straightened himself out before turning to me. Ares bounded towards me.

"Elis, I—Oof!" The big black wolf bowled me over, pressing his nose all over me. Whatever he smelled he gave a dark growl and whined in between sniffs and licks. "Ares get off, I'm fine. Seriously, let me up you big oaf."

Unrelenting, Ares laid down on top of me, whining into my hair. Giving in, my arms wrapped around his neck. I buried my face into his thick black fur. He smelled of forest and home. Thoughts of my library, the late day sun peeking through the kitchen windows, filled my mind. There was no fighting the tears that gathered in my eyes with how positively safe he made me feel. After last night, my emotions were quite surface level, making me far more sensitive than was usual for my character.

"I've missed you," I whispered, and Ares licked my ear but stayed still with me clinging to him.

"Get up off her, you bloody mongrel! It's my turn. I'm the best friend and you the pet–I outrank you. Now come off it." While one could take Elis' words for the jest it seemed to be, his voice was thick with emotion.

Ares let me up and as I came to my feet, Elis grabbed me by the wrist and yanked me into a backbreaking hug. What tears I held back hugging Ares, now threatened to spill over in his embrace. He had no idea how much I needed it. Or perhaps he did.

"I'm so sorry Mels," whispered Elis, his voice breaking. "I know... what happened. This was a part of the Nightmare Court I could have hidden you from, one I thought Prince Alcaeus would protect you from but... I couldn't. We are truly a barbaric people. If my prince had left even a single ounce of Lord Saelish, I would feed him to the Ya-Te-Veo plant, to be digested for over 100 years." We pulled apart but he kept me in his arms. "Queen Ragna is who she is and... would that I could see a more merciful king take her place so that you would be safe."

I quickly placed my hand over his mouth. "Shh, don't say that so openly. Not that I don't agree with you. Truly, I'm fine. It was a shock; I won't deny that. There is still much to process. But... Alcaeus did save me before anything truly scarring could happen. For that, I am grateful."

"I know." He hesitated, finding his words. "I may have sent him a message. The Queen has been forbidding Llyr and I from attending things where you are involved. Not that either of us wanted to attend the Gathering; it's a heathen practice only meant to stroke the egos of the powerful. But I kept a close ear on the servant's gossip as they came and went. I was worried sick when I heard the Queen demanded your presence. As soon as I heard fighting inside, I sent the prince a message with flowers... as is my way..."

I took his face in my hands and drew his forehead to mine, whispering, "Thank you."

"I will always be there for you, my dearest friend." We held each other for a moment longer before Elis jerked me back with an excited smile. "Come! I have been tasked with just the thing to take your mind off all the ludicrousness that wretched queen has put you through. Also, tell Alcaeus I get a special entryway ALWAYS to your quarters. Next time, I'll strangle his guards with poison ivy and turn their toilet paper into giant hogweed. That'll teach them that magnificence cannot be barred."

I laughed and agreed to his demands.

Dressing quickly and in my own clothing, I told Ares to stay in the room and guard it for me. He jumped on the bed and flopped down as it was probably a far cry from sleeping in the stables.

I followed Elis to the doors and, after removing the vines trapping the door, we were met with two very angry guards.

"Sir! I insist you get clearance from His Highness! We were told—"

Elis stepped forward, every ounce the lord he was. "For the last time—I am Lord Elis LeGervase; not only is my family the second oldest house in this Court, but my father is an Ealdorman on the council! I already received clearance the moment the prince put this woman in these rooms. If you had done your own duty, you would be aware of this! Now let us pass."

The guard shut his mouth, face tight but allowed us through. Elis jerked his chin high as he took my hand. He led me through many corridors and several courtyards. Once we were beyond the main buildings, I was finally able to breathe. It was a beautiful night, the air crisp and wonderfully peaceful, all things considered. As we strolled through the grounds, he chatted about what he and Llyr were up to; mostly discreet investigations in Court gossip and loose ends in order to better assist in my plight. The topic that delighted him the most, though, was Toby's newfound love, Sophie.

"Oh, Mels you should have seen the look on that poor boy's face when that little cherub of a girl gave him a kiss on the cheek!" He let out a delightful snorting giggle. "He brought her flowers! One's I created mind you, so they were DIVINE, and oh! I wish you could have seen it! Never has a boy reached the level of blush our Toby did! Oh, young love, Mels!" Elis gave a dramatic sigh and wiped an imaginary tear away. "Our boy is growing up."

"We've only known him for a few years, Elis, calm down."

He gave a dramatic gasp of outrage. "Did the great Creator deliberately make all Alchemists' sole purpose to piss on the beautiful things in life? It's love, Melly! L.O.V.E! Can you not manage a smidgen of excitement for the boy?"

I rolled my eyes. "It'll be wonderful until Toby steals her underwear or some such nonsense and gets caught because that boy cannot help himself. It'll just end in heartbreak or a good whipping or possibly even Ragna using it as a reason to doom us all."

Elis stopped dead and stared at me. "Negative Nancy, slow your steed please! Seriously, Mels, who hurt you?"

A snort escaped me, only to morph into laughter. I may be painfully cynical but perhaps I enjoyed it a little too much when I rained on Elis' parade.

"Fine, alright. Just... send those two my way so I can see this... this..." Rolling my eyes, I waved my hand trying to find the word, "budding love."

"Oh dear, my beautiful prince has his work cut out for him, doesn't he?"

I raised a bored eyebrow at him. "What on earth could you possibly mean by that?"

Elis gave me a sarcastic look and said, "Don't be obtuse, it's contrary to your nature. You know exactly what I mean. It's no wonder that it would take nothing less than a demigod to break down the walls of your heart, my dear."

"Love is for schmucks, poets, and the youth. Besides, if I had a penny for every moment you referred to me as 'irrevocably heartless', I'd be richer than Midas. Alcaeus could arrive at my heart's door and beat it till his hands were bloody. The only answer would be an echoing 'fuck off, thank you kindly' in return."

Elis snorted. "For once, I believe you. But I refuse to lose hope! We both know you can be a lusty little thing so perhaps said door opens a bit more south, hmm? If that be so, then we must quickly get you two alone! I can only imagine my sexy prince isn't just a godslayer in the arena but one between the sheets as well!" Dodging my slap, he laughed. "So, if that is who love is for, these 'shmucks and poets', as you say, which one would I fall under?"

"You need ask?"

"Hateful thing."

Unable to contain my laughter, I turned my face away but not before I caught Elis' answering grin. Little did my best friend realise that his prince had already broken past my ramparts, laying a mighty siege, and several times, I had almost surrendered.

It should concern me. Panic at succumbing to this Nightmare Prince should be eating me alive. Embracing my introversion, blocking out every attempt at seducing me, should have been my only response. But it wasn't. For I knew the moment Alcaeus caught me that fateful night, that somehow, someway, I would inevitably be his, even if it was just in body. Perhaps it was when I became aware that he was just as bound. Yes, more and more Alcaeus convinced me he was not the enemy. Elis certainly trusted him. What that left was something yet to be determined. Something about him called to me in a way that was inexplicable.

No, I was too old to pretend the density that plagued women of youth. Maturity demanded I admit our attraction; my dream was enough to prove that. It would be a foolish move to not acknowledge my vulnerabilities, and he was certainly becoming one. Declaring it publicly, however, well... it certainly wouldn't be today.

"Ah! We're here!"

The massive building, majestic and phenomenal, stood proudly and would have no doubt been included in the 7 wonders of the world were this the human realm. As it was, it was the second most incredible building I'd ever seen in the Otherworld. When applied like this, magic was a truly wondrous thing to behold.

"You'll be carrying your jaw in your cleavage, my dove, if you keep your mouth open like that. Wait until you see the inside." I shut my mouth, wordlessly following Elis.

He was not wrong.

I walked in and there were thousands upon thousands of books. Ceilings so high, they were almost lost in the shadows. The interior design loosely resembled the 17th-century in its architecture, but on a much grander scale. Elaborate hand-carved walkways connected different levels as far as the eye could see. On the ground floor sat huge mahogany tables surrounded by well-cushioned chairs.

All around were different models and structures, ones you might find at a museum, hanging in the air or on huge pedestals. Statues of different gods and creatures filled the spaces. In one open area there were a group of children, of varying different species, sitting up and staring into a 3D galaxy; not like a projection but as if they were truly floating among the stars. Their teacher, a silver-haired dark elf, reached up and grabbed a star, expanding it in her hands. From a glance, I could tell they were learning about nebulas, as she went through each stage of a star's life. My joy of learning had part of me wanting to sit among the children, despite knowing all I did.

"If you stop and stare at everything Mels, we'll never meet the head Sage, whom I just know you'll like. Come, come!" He grabbed my hand so I wouldn't stop again.

We walked for what seemed like forever, until the settings seemed to change into close quarters and intimate parts of the library. Finally coming to a stop at an elaborately carved wooden door, Elis pushed it open to reveal what looked like a private study.

It reminded me so much of my own library at home, I felt my emotions bubble up. Wall-to-wall bookcases, the shelves beautifully designed with little animals and creatures racing up the wood. A white granite fireplace with a small flame warmed the room. Large maroon velvet chairs that would swallow you whole when you sat down, were situated in front of the hearth. Lush rugs you could sink your toes into. Huge French windows sat behind a massive gold and mahogany desk, whose legs were roaring lion heads.

"Well, hello there! You made it!" A gentle and happy voice reached my ears, its gruffness showing age.

I turned to see an elderly man slowly climbing off one of the lad-

182

ders that slid between the bookcases. Snow white hair that was tied back with a leather thong, still managed to make a curly halo around his face. I also noted he wore the black robes of a scholar. Coming closer revealed delicate gold-rimmed glasses resting on his nose, with robins-egg blue eyes behind them. He had a full white moustache and a little patch of hair on his chin. His eyes had a twinkle about them, and they crinkled as he gave me a gentle smile as he stuck out his hand.

"And you must be the famous Alchemist everyone has been chattering about. It's truly wonderful to meet you, Lady Von Boden," he said, placing his other hand over mine warmly. "I am the head sage, Kevyn Michaelis Harrys. But please call me Kevyn."

My soul warmed in the face of this kind man, and I just knew deep down he and I would become fast friends.

"A pleasure to meet you, Kevyn. The library is most spectacular; I am speechless in the face of its magnificence."

He let out a loud ha! and said, "Oh gosh, wait till you have to clean it! But yes, this is truly my happy place and," he gave me a good look over the rims of his spectacles, "I think it's going to be yours too, no doubt. Come, let's sit and let me tell you how this monstrous place works. That'll be all, Master Elis."

I held back a snort at my best friend being dismissed like an annoying schoolboy. I wondered if Kevyn had the unfortunate task of having to teach Elis when he was younger. My friend rolled his eyes but gave me a wink before shutting the door.

"So," started Kevyn, as we sat down before the fire. "After Prince Alcaeus spoke with me, he and I both agreed that you should have use of my personal study. Less likely to be bothered here. Now, I tend to keep all of the rarest texts in here, and quite a few of my favourites I've snuck from the main hall." I smiled, raising an eyebrow at that. He leaned back, not a smidgen of shame on his face. "What? I am the Head Sage; it should come with some perks, don't you think? Anyways, you are free to come and go as you please but I'll need you to leave your mark so you can have access."

"My mark?"

"Yes, just a little bit of blood on the symbol on the door, which I have already readjusted so you can gain entry."

I stood and walked to the door, curious. Sure enough, Draconus Lingua runes littered the doorway in elaborate carvings.

"Dragon magic," I whispered in awe.

Dragons had little in the way of magical powers but what they excelled in was guarding their hordes with the strongest of magical seals; no one got in and no one came out, except by the dragon's command.

They must have a dragon on staff for it to be used here, I surmised.

Turning back to the sage, I said, "I apologise, Sage Kevyn. While I can read Dragon-tongue, there doesn't seem to be a lot of sense to this. Where do I—?"

"Oh, how interesting!" stated Kevyn, hobbling over to me. He walked with a slight limp, favouring his right knee. "Very curious. Do you see this here?" There was only an empty space to where he pointed, so I shook my head. "How about this?" I bit my lip, my face showing there was nothing to be seen. "Do Alchemists have no magical ability at all then? You're probably the only one other than myself to know how to read Draconus Lingua, but I daresay it takes a magical being to see the entirety of the ward."

"I see nothing but the carvings on the door and around the frame. You could rightly say magic and alchemy have never been friends."

He looked at me then, finger pressed against his lips, his other hand supporting his elbow.

"Well, tell you what, let's get you coded in, and I will guide you for that part. Afterward, you can fill me in on how I can assist you in whatever brilliant plans you have in overthrowing the tyrannical queen."

Staring at him in shock, I said, "Master Sage, even the prince hesitates to declare something so bold. Either you are truly a fearsome fellow or a brave fool."

He laughed. "Sweetie, when you've lived as long as I have, you'll learn that tyrants come and go at the will of the people. Let us not mince words—Ragna has had a revolt coming her way for centuries, especially after she made it clear to the rest of the realms she wanted to 'unite the land'. After conquering the other eleven kingdoms, King Alcaeus's being the last, she went and slew Oberon; the consequences of which we've been waiting to come knocking on our door ever since. So, in answer to you: I do not fear the queen. Not only is she barred from the library, but she also couldn't kill me if she tried and trust me, she has, and failed miserably."

This old Sage had rendered me speechless for a moment. But then the entirety of his words registered. "I'm sorry, did you say 'king'? Alcaeus was a king?"

"He is THE king, my dear, the one we have all been waiting for. Unfortunately, the Queen... Ah, well, I'm sure you'll learn soon enough. Not my place to tell." Before I could question Kevyn further, he lifted my hands to the door. The dragon letters came to life and began spinning. A pinch on each palm, the magic demanding blood so the door could know me. "Okay, now that that's settled, what can I do for you?"

I turned to face him, mentally prioritising my list before answering him. "I need all texts on telekinesis, a history of Vampire rituals and abilities, and anything on Ragna's specific history. I know she is a necromancer, but she also has telekinetic power. Twice now, she has caught me off-guard, but there will not be a third time if I can help it."

Sage Kevyn nodded, and it was then I noticed his little patch of hair on his chin was slightly crooked, making him that much more endearing.

"Perfect," he replied. "They will appear on the desk as I find them, which should take but a moment. I've already sent several stacks, as you can see, but I'll have to dig into some of the old archives; it's been years since anyone has been brave enough to request Ragna's history, so it'll take me a bit of time."

His mention of the books had me looking at the huge desk and, sure enough, half of it was taken up by tomes, scrolls, and leather-bound books. A happiness I hadn't known for a good long while filled me.

"Thank you, Kevyn! Oh and...um," I blushed red at my imminent request. "Could you get me anything on Alcaeus as well?"

He gave me a knowing smile with a twinkle in his eye, having the graciousness to just nod before taking his leave.

▽▽♂⚉♂⅚

I had lost track of the hours, sitting cross-legged up on the desk, shoes forgotten. It was imperative I began devising algorithms for telekinesis in order to combat the unseeing force. There was always a middle ground between science and magic, I just had to find it.

Perhaps there was a way to study magic at a quantum level... The quantum field theory is probably the best to start with, which could only explain the interaction rate of particles... and then we need to take into account the energy needed to produce a–

"Something tells me you would never leave here if I gave you the option."

Startled, I flung the book sky high, the rest of the stacks scattering. The voice had appeared right behind me, having whispered in my ear.

"By the MOTHER, what is WRONG with you!?" I gasped. "Give me some warning, damn you!" My hand snapped to my chest in an effort to prevent my heart from breaking through my ribs. My other smacked the surface of the desk below me in a subconscious effort to release some panic. "Fucking Vampires and their damned silent teleportation!" I growled. Having been so lost in my thoughts, I hadn't sensed Alcaeus appear.

Swivelling to face my intruder, I froze at the sight of Alcaeus bent over with a hand to his belly. His other hand held a book. Rich, masculine laughter filled the room. So stunned by it, I was at a loss for words as my annoyance evaporated.

"Oh, Melisandre! You should have seen your face! What a delight you are!" The laughter finally dying down, he reached for me.

"It's not funny, you wretch! This is the second bloody time— Mmph!" All thoughts scattered as Alcaeus's lips pressed firmly against mine, his tongue demanding entry. There was a desperation from him that wasn't present last time.

My mind went hazy as I opened for him. His fingers threaded through my hair, holding the back of my head so he could kiss me deeper. Alcaeus drank from my mouth like a dying man thirsting for water. Not breaking the kiss, his hands gripped my calves, pulling them apart so that my legs were on either side of his thighs. Reaching under one leg, Alcaeus pulled my hips to meet his, pressing me into him so my core could feel the pressure of his. A gasp tore through me as desire spread like wildfire throughout my body. Grinding his hips against me with deliberate purpose, I moved with him, lost in the sensation of him. Our hands explored each other in desperation, squeezing and groping, seeking skin.

Finally, he broke away, resting his head on my shoulder, breathing hard against my neck. He took a deep inhale as if sucking up my scent and then let out a ragged exhale. The prince held me tightly, no longer moving against me.

"Alcaeus? Are you alright?"

Nuzzling right underneath my ear, he kissed me there. "Yes," he whispered but said nothing more. I felt a shift in him, so I pulled back slightly.

"I don't believe you."

With a small smile, he said, "Ever astute, aren't you, *mikrós asvós*?"

"Only with you, it seems."

Alcaeus kissed me gently on the side of the mouth. "I would not have it any other way."

Pulling back, he took my hand and helped me off the desk. He didn't let go though.

"I hate to interrupt your research, but I am not sorry in the least. I want you, Melisandre, in all the ways a man wants a woman. I do not know how much longer I can wait and... I do not think Sage Kevyn would appreciate us christening his desk."

Trying to gather my wits, I shook my head. In hopes of distracting him before we took things too far, I said, "No, I don't think he would. Kevyn is wonderful, by the way. And –"

My surroundings seemed to flash and morph. "...what? Where...? How?!"

The room was no longer Sage Kevyn's personal study. It was a bedroom. My bedroom. Swaying, I stumbled, the world spinning slightly. Alcaeus wrapped his arm around my waist, steadying me.

"Careful, it is a little disorienting at first, but you will become accustomed to it."

Spinning around in his arms to glare up at him, I snapped, "There will be no 'becoming accustomed to it'! Honestly, Alcaeus we're going to have to have a serious conversation about forewarning!"

Raising an eyebrow, he asked, "Would you have let me if I had asked?"

I jerked my head back, my ire deflating in the face of his point. "Well, n-no but..."

Cupping my face, he kissed me again. "Not everything needs to be structured with prefaces and formulas, my love. It is not because of reason that I kiss you like this." Alcaeus's lips grazed mine gently, holding it for several moments. "Or like this." This time it was full of passion, hard, and deep. I was coming to love it when he kissed me in this way, as if demanding I submit to all of him while at the same time, he worshipped every part of me.

Yet, little alarm bells went off in the back of my head. "Wait, Alcaeus... just, wait. This is fast, so fast—" He lifted me up on the bed and I scooted back, laying down as he crawled over me. I stared up into his face, not immune to how deliciously those broad shoulders flexed and towered over me, caging me in. The masculine lines of his body made my mouth water, the promise of his weight pressed against me had my walls clenching with need.

"I must have you Melisandre, please." His voice was husky and thick with desire, sending shivers across my skin. Fingers traced along my neck, sliding down across my collarbone, finally dancing over my breasts. "For once, let go. Let me show you the effect you have had on me in a way words would only fail to describe. Allow me to get lost in you, as I have been since the moment I saw you."

I could take no more.

"Yes," I replied breathlessly.

This pull called to me so deeply and my reasons for fighting it were fast depleting. Perhaps my defences were weakened because of the previous night but regardless—I wanted Alcaeus's touch to wash away all the horrors, even for just tonight. To feel something good in this castle of horrors. To take the chance that he was not the enemy.

And I wanted only him.

CHAPTER 18

My shirt was held by a leather corset which was fastened in the back. Alcaeus flipped me over, his groin pressing into my behind, his hardness thrust against me. I gripped the sheets for leverage, pushing my hips back into him. His hands snaked up to my neck and then downward as he began unhooking the corset, his lips and teeth replacing where hands touched. I writhed, desperate to feel his skin against mine. As quickly as my corset was removed so my shirt followed.

Flipping me back over, Alcaeus's midnight-blue eyes feasted upon me and the hunger I saw had my toes curling. His passion matched my own. Slowly easing my pants and underwear off, leaving me only in stockings, he pulled his linen shirt off in one motion. Sliding off the bed, he stood and began untying the laces to his pants. Gazing down at me, the prince hooked his thumbs underneath his waistband, and they slid down strong thighs.

My heart surely skipped a beat. He was magnificent. Unabashed, his arms spread as he leaned against the posts of the bed, letting me take him in; the firelight illuminated every valley and sharp curve of strength. Every Greek statue was laughable, an outright lie, compared to the Vampire gladiator that stood before me. Carnal hunger burned through me until my limit was reached, and I sat up, reaching for him. I needed him above me, on me, inside of me. Muscles rippled and flexed as he leaned down over me, and my breath gave out at how much larger he was compared to my small frame. Holding himself up on one arm, his hand trailed down my chest, my abdomen, just brushing the top of my sex.

"You are perfection, Melisandre," breathed the prince, his gaze matching my own in fascination with the other's body. He dipped down to trail kisses over my chest until he took one of my nipples into

189

his mouth, sucking hard.

I moaned, the feeling of his hair tickling over me as I grew wet from the heat and force of his mouth. His tongue flicked my nipple and then swirled, eliciting a gasp. Alcaeus gave the same attention to my other breast, kneading and massaging one while sucking and licking the other. Threading my fingers through his hair, I pulled him up for a passionate kiss. I tried to pull him closer, but he growled into my mouth.

"So impatient, little Alchemist. Or should I say greedy?" He rubbed his cock along my folds, shamelessly teasing me, then pulled away.

I could have screamed.

"Alcaeus please..." I panted, running my hands up his arms and across the broad depths of muscled shoulders.

"Say it again," his voice rumbled against my skin, and I arched against him.

"Please..."

He eased on top of me and spread my legs further to accommodate his large size. Alcaeus slipped one hand underneath my head, his fingers gripping my hair firmly and pulling back so my neck was bare to him. At the same time, his other hand slipped between my legs, deftly manipulating my folds, sliding up and down, and then finally dipping inside me. Two long, thick fingers stretched me, and I gasped at the intimacy of him being in the most vulnerable part of me.

My fingers dug into the arm that held my head and I held onto him as he began to thrust his fingers deeper, in and out, curving upward with every thrust, massaging me from the inside.

"Oh, gods!"

"No, *mikrós asvós*, just me," He chuckled darkly and thrust his tongue against mine, his massaging tempo matching the dance of his fingers inside me.

Alcaeus broke the kiss, burrowing his face in my neck. I looked down and watched the muscles and tendons work in his arm as he fingered me. The sight was so erotic I moaned and clenched tight around him. He groaned and moved faster, his palm grinding against my clit. Pushing against him, my hips rose of their own volition as my desire started to peak.

"Come for me," he commanded, his hot breath against the shell of my ear as his hand worked its magic, propelling me into my climax.

I cried out. My body went taut, my walls clamping around his fingers which had pierced so deep, I was sure he could feel every flutter.

As I came down, Alcaeus removed his hand, only to replace it with the head of his cock at my entrance. Just then, a sliver of rationale came to me.

"Alcaeus are you going to bite—Mmm."

He kissed me hard, "Yes, little one, I will give you the first mark, but I promise I will make it exceedingly pleasurable for you."

Before I could respond, he pushed into me, and my breath caught. With a silent gasp, he filled me until his pelvis was flush against mine. I clutched his shoulder, my other hand holding his head to me. With small pants, my body adjusted to his size. Alcaeus moaned into my neck, his muscles tensing as he held himself still. I was no virgin, but I was petite enough that I appreciated the stillness. But with it came an intimacy I hadn't expected, blossoming as we stared at each other, becoming one. It felt right; like coming home after a long and harrowing journey. Like I had waited my whole life for this moment.

Slowly, he pulled back, only to thrust harder and deeper, bottoming out inside me. Pleasure with a twinge of pain gripped me; I wanted more.

"You're so deep. I can't..."

"Yes, you can, Melisandre. You were made for me. Feel me. Every bit of this is for you."

He continued moving that way, making sure I felt every inch of him. He cradled my head against his forearms, and he picked up the pace. My arms went around him, pulling him closer so his head tucked into the crook of my neck. I became delirious with the sensations, so overwhelmed I couldn't help the love bites I nipped at his shoulder. No longer withholding my voice as our coupling became faster and harder.

Lips and tongue played along the length of my neck, stopping where it met my shoulder. Alcaeus kissed and sucked, his tongue swirling, teeth scraping. Teeth that had become decidedly sharper. My already pounding heart skipped faster as I realised what was coming. A trickle of fear snaked through me, piercing through the haze of pleasure that clouded my mind.

"Alcaeus..."

"Yes, my love. It is time. Are you ready?"

"I..."

"Do you want this?" At my hesitation he pulled back slightly, so he could look me in the eyes. His hips stopped, throbbing cock still inside of me. "Melisandre, do you want this?" Alcaeus's irises had that geometrical silver pattern, making his eyes look like a galaxy.

Did I want to? I didn't know. There was such a dissonance between my heart and my mind, and I could admit I feared facing what my heart wanted.

But...if you are going to be bound to anyone, you must admit it's the Prince of Nightmares, Alcaeus, that calls you. Stop hiding. Stop running. For once, face your desires!

Emotion welled within me as I let go, finger by finger, of my life as I knew it. Taking a deep breath, I couldn't stop the tear that trickled down my cheek.

"Yes," I whispered.

"Do you want me?" The look on his face caused several more tears to slip free.

"Yes, damn you."

He kissed me deeply, thrusting hard and reigniting my desire. He moved with purpose until I was once again lost in sensation. Alcaeus placed his lips back to that spot, the same spot I remembered Elis having his mate mark with Llyr. Once again, his large hand grasped the back of my head firmly and pulled it back, putting me in a position of complete submission.

Placing a kiss there, he growled, "You are mine, Melisandre Von Boden."

Then he began.

"To thee, I give my mark, the first of three
That which was once unmade, made whole again
To thee I give my heart, my soul
As was proclaimed at the breath of first light
Return unto me as the stars align
One chord, one soul
To thee I claim ye bound for all eternity
Beginning to end, in darkness and in light
Death nor life shall tear asunder that which was made for none other.
Thusly to thee I bind."

I closed my eyes.

With a violent thrust, he shoved his cock deep into me at the same speed his fangs pierced my flesh. I screamed. Burning pleasure and pain spiralled down me and I orgasmed so hard I saw stars. Alcaeus climaxed as well, his entire body stiffening as he groaned against me. It didn't stop. My pleasure and pain kept going. Suddenly I couldn't tell whose body was whose. The world spun. Then a face from a chained memory appeared in my mind.

"MELISANDRE! WHAT HAVE YOU DONE!? STOP THIS NOW!"

"I cannot! I must fix this! I can heal you!" Transmutation light swirled around me.

"YOU KNOW NOT WHAT YOU DO! YOU HAVE BROUGHT DOOM UPON US! DO YOU NOT HEAR HER? MOTHER EARTH SCREAMS, CHILD!"

The earth trembled and the circle grew so bright I could no longer see.

"I CAN DO THIS!" I screamed. "I WILL SAVE YOU! I MUST MAKE IT RIGHT!"

Instantly, the world seemed to go still and silent as time came to a stop, and my mentor's face appeared before me. Sorrow and grief lined the edges and cracks of his weathered face.

"No, child. You shall walk the earth alone and bear the sins for what you have done."

My heart sank and I stared at him in confusion. "What? Master?"

With sad acceptance, he closed his eyes.

"Master!" He vanished.

All that was left in his wake were the screams and cries of agony and thousands of tortured faces.

I cried out, shoving away from Alcaeus. He let go before he tore my flesh with his sharp fangs, blood dripping down his chin. Horror and confusion marred his face.

"Melisandre, the screams... the faces... what—?"

"GET OUT! GET. OUT!" I screamed, shaking uncontrollably. *He saw. He saw it!*

He stood, brows dipping dangerously low, but he made no move to leave. "No! Not this time. I will not let you run! Talk to me, Melisandre! Tell me what I saw!"

I shook my head violently, backing into the wall, and then sank to the floor, hugging myself.

"I will not. I cannot." Tears spilled down my cheeks as I struggled to push down my memories, my guilt.

My shame.

Alcaeus stared intensely at me then, face shrouded in ancient mystery. Then he made for the bathroom, but came back after only a few moments. His face was cleaned of my blood and he was holding a hand-towel. Watching me curiously still, he grabbed a blanket from the bed and walked over. Gently, he wrapped me in the plush fleece. My fists gripped the blanket closer as I buried my head in my arms. But then arms wrapped around me.

"Don't!" I snapped, feeling trapped.

Alcaeus held his hands up placatingly, his tone soothing and gentle. "*Mikrós asvós*, I am not going to hurt you. I am just going to clean your mark. Then, allow me to take you to bed?"

I didn't respond, shutting my eyes as another wave of shaking overtook my body. His hands were gentle, and I didn't push him away when he lifted me up and cradled me to his chest. The warmth of his body was begrudgingly welcome, and I let my stiffened body relax, my rising panic slowly coming down. Alcaeus snuggled us under the covers, his back propped against the pillows and headboard.

It took me a few moments, but weariness finally gripped me. I laid my head against his chest and curled up in his arms. For a moment, I felt a faint beat, slow but sure. There it was again. I lifted my head and looked at his chest. Vampires weren't supposed to have heartbeats. Did they?

Just as I was about to ask him, Alcaeus said, "Will you not tell me what I saw, my love?"

My love. He's called me that several times. I tried to ignore the endearment.

"All of us have our secrets, Alcaeus. That is one that I will never part with. Not even Elis knows about what you saw."

He sighed. "Melisandre, I have walked both realms for nearly three thousand years. Among the gods, I am known as the Godslayer, the Divine Reaper. My sole creation was for the purpose of leading and fighting wars, battles. You must know the brutality, the depths of unspeakable savagery a life that lives by the sword brings. If you were privy to half of my countless transgressions, you would turn from me without question. No matter the heaviness of your own sins, there is nothing I would hold against you. Nor would I ever turn away."

"Are you saying you would tell me your deepest, darkest sins if I asked them?" His eyes narrowed but withheld his answer. So, I probed further. "Would you tell me what Ragna has on you that keeps you from destroying her, Godslayer, and stealing her throne?"

The Prince of the Nightmare Court now stared back at me, a shadow of guarded mystery replacing his expression. "You have the right to know, and you will. But I cannot. The time is not right."

I nodded my head sadly, knowingly. "I know. As such, neither can I share mine."

We sat there in heavy silence. Alcaeus let out a heavy exhale through his nose. Gently taking my chin by his fingers, our eyes met.

"I know you and I have much to do in the realm of building the bridge of trust. I also know that it will take more time than we have to reach that point. The best the both of us can do for now is be open to it. I told you at dinner that I would never stop working to earn your trust; I meant that. So, when you are ready, come to me; I will be here to hear your tale. Free of judgement. You bear my mark now, Melisandre. Your secrets, your sins, all of that which defines you, are mine to bear as well."

Emotions welled up in me and I placed my forehead against his. My entire life, I had been alone. Truly alone. Not even the brief moments my mother was in my life, nor Elis' or Toby's presence could alleviate the solitude that had plagued my every step. In fact, their presence in my life amplified it; a constant reminder of how different, and thus alone, my life was.

For the first time, this ancient, godlike-being opened a window to a possible connection I never thought I'd have.

"I can try." Was my whisper against his skin before laying a kiss against his brow. Pulling away, my heart clenched at the tenderness in those eyes.

"That is all I ask."

Alcaeus pushed a stray strand of hair out of my face, then kissed me gently. Wanting to sink into every part of him, I deepened the kiss, threading my fingers through his hair. It was as silky and as thick as I had imagined. Shifting, I straddled his hips, my legs splaying wide from the width of him. Strong arms wrapped around me, large rough hands sliding up my naked back. Feeling him grow hard against my core, I teased by gyrating my hips. In one smooth motion, I was suddenly on my back with Alcaeus's weight bearing me down into the mattress. He plunged his tongue greedily between my lips as he took control, those warrior thighs spreading my legs wide.

Then I bit him.

He jerked back, his lip bleeding a little. A mischievous grin took over my face.

"So, are you a one-and-done kind of man, or is the endurance of the Champion of Athena worthy of the legends? Something tells me you went easy on me the first time."

Alcaeus grinned, incisors flashing as he answered my challenge.

"The woman does not know what she asks for."

I licked the blood off his lips.

"Then make me regret it."

CHAPTER 19

When I awoke, the eve found me alone. Well, not quite. My face was buried in thick black fur and the soft snore of Ares was the only noise colouring the silence. Come to think of it, Ares was nowhere to be seen the previous night; I had no idea when or how he managed to sneak back in or where he'd snuck off to yesterday. Just like at my own home, he seemed to come and go as he pleased. Strange wolf.

I curled around him more snugly; my head was so full of what had transpired that I had to force myself to slow down, process one thought at a time. The prince proved the legends true and then some; I had never ached so deliciously in all the best ways. Not a single regret, however. My desire had lay dormant for too many years and Alcaeus had lit its flames without mercy. The memory of his lips against my skin haunted me, the way he filled me until I was nothing but shallow breaths and incoherent thoughts. Hiding my smile, I secretly accepted the fact I burned for him still.

Finally, my thoughts turned to the pressing reality that I now bore his mark and what that meant. The desire I had just felt turned to ash. My gut churned and nausea threatened. Perhaps some deep dark part of my twisted soul felt warmed, relieved even, at belonging to someone. To Alcaeus. The rest of me couldn't afford to take that risk with anyone. Brief flashes of those moments of intimacy, the way he looked at me with longing, gentleness, and a hint of sadness; those memories warmed me to my core. For the first time, I wished reality was different and that just maybe... but no. Last night had only determined the beginning of a war inside me; one of clashing desires as old dreams fought their way to the surface, only to be smashed down by the cold hammer of what was and what could never be.

This... romance was not meant for me. For over 600 years I had given up the idea of a happy ending with someone and I wasn't about to start fantasising now.

The place where he bit me was only mildly sore, but I didn't feel any different. I needed a mirror.

I wonder what the side effects of the mark entail... does it get more obvious with the second? There must be something in the books and scrolls Kevyn sent me that will tell me more about this 'Familiar' mark and bond. No more hiding and sulking about. Damnit, I should have asked Alcaeus before he bit me.

Stretching my limbs through the soreness, I was careful not to wake Ares, but the wolf beside me didn't even cease his snore.

"I most definitely concur about the sulking, although your face is quite endearing when you do."

I shot straight up.

"Alcaeus? What are you doing in my head? I thought we'd been over this!" I snapped out loud, thoughts scrambling in an attempt to build a mental wall to shut him out.

"I am afraid that won't work this time, mikrós asvós. The mark prevents any walls between us. It will only get stronger until it is completed."

Strangled angry sounds arose in my throat, grinding my teeth at this foreign threat to my mental privacy. I didn't know how, but I was revving up to psychopathically unleash my fury into his unprotected brainwaves.

However, he stopped me by saying, **"Save your concerns, Melisandre, I will not abuse this. Your thoughts are your own; I merely heard you talking to yourself by chance. A habit, I have noticed, that is just as charming as your beautiful sulking face. I will not intrude unless absolutely necessary. Eventually, we shall find a balance. Patience."**

"I see. Well then. Why don't we begin now?" Sarcasm dripped with every word. "Waking hours is never the time for this. Ever. Now—Go. Away."

His deep masculine laughter filled my mind. "Gods you are a grumpy one!" The sound of his joy filled me with satisfaction and warmth bloomed inside my chest. **"Ah, but one more thing,"** Alcaeus paused, and his tone became deep and gentle, **"My apologies that I**

was not there to wake with you as I would have liked. You slept so soundly and my presence was required elsewhere. Would you join me for dinner, and we can discuss your findings with your research? Oh, and we can also discuss your concerns about the side effects regarding the mark beyond the obvious one."

It was warming, the thought of our night together. Nevertheless, I was determined to put space between us. My brain could not stand a moment more of drowning in this obnoxious fog of oxytocin.

"Something tells me I hardly have a choice in the matter either way, so dinner it is. Still, I can hardly research when you continue to keep me from it. Go away."

A faint feeling of humour echoed in my thoughts and then he was gone. The sigh that left me was more of a groan as I scrubbed my hands over my face. This was a disaster, a catastrophe. Thoughts of explosive passion and sweaty exertions blew through my mind. Gods, what was I going to tell...

Oh, no. Elis.

With an audible groan this time, I flopped back down into the pillows. Ares, somehow, continued to snore.

I beg you Mother Earth, crack your tectonic plates and swallow me whole now.

Hearing movement outside the door, I called out, "Ada! Could you please have the largest pot or even cauldron of coffee sent up?"

My door smacked open. It wasn't Ada. Both Ares and I shot up in bed this time.

"You would treat me like a servant you –" Elis stopped suddenly, nostrils flaring as he inhaled. His eyes dilated. His jaw dropped to the floor as those perfect eyebrows went soaring skyward.

Oh no.

"Lord and Lady and all the gods of fertility, have mercy," he gasped. "You... and the prince..." He grasped dramatically for the nearby table while putting a hand to his cheek.

"For God's sake Elis, you and your theatrics! You knew it was going to happen. Hell, you encouraged it," I muttered, willing the bed to swallow me up before anything else came out of my best friend's mouth. "Let me clean up and I'll join you. Make sure Ada brings –"

"Coffee, yes I know," interrupted the Vampire. His gaze was distant, lost in thought. "Some whiskey too, we are going to need it..."

Voice trailing off and one last pensive glance back at me, he closed my door.

After showering and getting dressed, I came into my living room for breakfast and the wonderful smell of coffee. Elis was already seated, sipping his. I walked over and sat down, but Elis said nothing, his eyes indicating his mind was far away. Content with the silence, I dug into my food.

Finally, the growing tension broke away as Elis asked, "So, what happened to 'I'm not going to sleep with him for if I do, I would subsequently be throwing away all my moral standards? I'm quite positive marking a Familiar doesn't require sex."

I sighed deeply, in no way wanting to have this conversation, but also accepting it was inevitable considering who I was dealing with.

"Well... you see..." I fumbled, struggling but coming up with nothing. Frustrated, I rubbed my temples. "My research hasn't gotten that far yet, Elis, as I only had one night, and it kind of just... happened. Maybe I was tired of fighting the attraction and the mark had to be done either way. I know that now. May as well enjoy my doom while I can."

"Your doom? Pish posh! Anyone would be lucky to go out with a bang like that!" he said with a laugh.

"My god Elis! You're so—"

"Delightfully witty? Poetically handsome?" At my eye roll, his laughter quieted as he continued. "Besides, that better not be defeat I was hearing in my best friend's voice! Mels, my dove, there is nothing wrong with what you did. I'm just stunned you allowed it to get that far. You are the most immovable person I know." Leaning forward, he lost the smile as his eyes drilled into me, emphasising his point. Then he sat back and rubbed a long forefinger over full lips, his brows drawing together in consternation. "Yet, within a fortnight, my liege has managed to not only convince you to finally get the mark but thoroughly seduced you -Ah!" He put a finger in my face just as I went to dispute him, "Don't deny it! Not to me. Not when I can barely distinguish his scent from yours." Rolling his eyes, he waved his hands. "Anyway, I truly believed nothing short of a full-scale war had to happen before you would allow Alcaeus to bite you. Regardless of what I may or may not have encouraged, this behaviour from you is -"

"Worrying? Concerning? Divergent from all standing data?"

"Quite. It means the Nightmare Court is starting to get to you, in which case that would be our number one concern. Or, perhaps I don't know you as well as I thought I did. Perhaps there is more to my little troll that I did not anticipate." He grew thoughtful at this. "Our beloved prince, dare I say it, seems quite infatuated with you. I have no idea what to make of it."

The very inkling of the prince developing an emotional attachment to me caused me to freeze in all ways. Of course, certain actions and phrases Alcaeus used could be interpreted as such, but hearing my friend say it aloud forced me to become more aware of that possibility. I had accepted Alcaeus had motives far beyond my understanding and took his affection as a means to an end. To entertain thoughts of it being more than that seemed ridiculous.

Don't be a fool. Don't go there. I chastised internally.

Elis continued, oblivious to the impact that his implication had on me.

"Prince Alcaeus has been nothing but a powerful enigma in this Court; the mysterious Commander whom one admired from afar. You feared him. You respected him. You bow to his prowess in battle, and you never play chess with him unless you enjoy quickly losing. One does not dine with him unless it's a Royal Dinner, in which case he sits beside the Queen, a statue of propriety. As soon as it ends, he takes his leave along with the Captain of his Guard, Sotiris."

"But what about the gatherings? He made it seem like his presence was always required."

"Oh, but it is. Queen Ragna demands he take at least one life before he's allowed to leave. Typically, most Vampires indulge enough to fill their power reserves. Although it's not uncommon for casualties, to be sure. It's expected. Yet our prince is always finding ways around her twisted cruelty. So, Prince Alcaeus always makes one odd demand: one convicted prisoner. Words are spoken between them, I know not what, and then he will run Nemesis straight through them, stealing their essence. As soon as their body turns to ash, he is gone. He does not linger. And yet now, linger he does. For you."

Deep concern began to rise at the truth that was slowly coming to the forefront of my mind. I feared if I was to analyse Elis' words any closer, I would be faced with admitting to a futile connection due to an emotion I could not afford to have. I could not, would not think any further on this.

"Enough of this Elis!" I exploded, slamming my empty coffee mug on the table. "I will not sit here and speculate your prince's intentions or emotions when both would inevitably block my way to freedom and put us all in grave danger. I have neither the time nor the capacity to entertain fanciful bouts of romance. That is the last reason I am here. You know this! So please, let it go. Whatever ridiculous notions you have between me and Alcaeus, let it go. Please."

For once, Elis looked hurt, and I watched a metaphorical wall come up between us.

"Fine!" He bit out. "You don't want to hear it? Fine. But mark my words: one day Mels, true love will look at you square in the face, the kind of love that people only dream about. The kind of love you cannot breathe without. YOU, however, will miss it because you're too damn busy running away and hiding behind your books, your cynicism, your secrets—"

I gasped. "How dare you—"

Elis suddenly flashed before me, on his knees and in between mine. His hands grabbed my cold ones and held them tightly to his face.

"Because you deserve it! You deserve that kind of love, Melisandre! I don't give a damn what horrors you think you've done. I love you far too much to let you walk the worlds alone." He rested his forehead on my knuckles. "Please, Mels, don't harden your heart to the possibility you may have met your match."

My breath went out of me like an extinguished flame, and I felt like I got sucker-punched in the heart. Looking down at lavender eyes so full of care, of meaning, I could not come up with a response. Not one that would satisfy my adorably melodramatic friend.

Gently tugging my hands away, Elis released them, and I cupped his face.

Looking deeply into his eyes, hoping he could see all the affection I had for him in my own, my lips pressed against his lightly. It was not sexual in the slightest, rather, one of kindred spirits.

"Thank you," I whispered.

We looked back at each other in meaningful silence. As Elis began to stand, my door burst open, and Toby appeared with a smaller blonde girl trailing closely behind.

"Ms. Melly!" screeched Toby, his voice breaking, a clear sign manhood was not far behind him. "I brought er'! I brought Sophie!"

He dragged her straight up to me and I met the most crystal, Caribbean blue eyes I'd ever seen. I'd guess her age was around 13 or 14 but her Brownie blood kept her small. Her long white-blonde hair was braided and hung over one shoulder, tied with a ribbon that matched her eyes. A light spattering of freckles dusted her nose and blush had risen on pale cheeks. Sophie wore a pale grey frock with an apron over it. She looked like a mini version of Cinderella before the prince found her.

Oh, Toby was already irrevocably lost to us, and understandably so.

Giving us both a proper curtsy, she acknowledged Elis with a sweet 'milord' before turning to me fully.

"H-hello my lady. I-I'm Sophie. I, um, work in the kitchens." She looked down quickly when she started speaking, my own stare unnerving her, no doubt.

Elis had gone back to his seat and smiled at the exchange as he sipped his beverage.

"Well, it's certainly nice to finally meet the mysterious Sophie, whom we can thank for helping our troublesome Toby."

"Oi, I've gotten better!" Toby whined, but I shot him a knowing look and turned back to the sweet girl in front of me.

"Feel free to call me Melly too, Sophie. You are among friends, and we clearly owe you a great deal. Thank you for being a friend to my ward." She blushed harder, her eyes darting back up, and stared at me. That's when I noticed it. Realising what she was doing, she quickly looked down at her feet again. "Sophie, look at me. It's alright. I know my eyes can be a bit disconcerting, but they're harmless. I just want to check something."

She peeked up shyly at first, but then her gaze turned confident and curious. The light helped illuminate her eyes as I searched them.

There it was.

Barely perceptible but a slice in each iris; one silver and one gold. Someone far back in Sophie's lineage was an Alchemist. We never ventured out of our land, beyond the walls. It was forbidden. But someone did. The evidence was standing in front of me.

Emotion overcame me and my skin broke into goosebumps. For the first time in over 600 years, I stood among someone of my own kind.

"Oh Sophie..." I whispered.

"Yes, Ms. Melly, I-I was looking forward to meeting you because I too have Alchemist blood in me. My great-great granddad was one, is what my grandmother told me. We have always been instructed to keep it secret... but when the servants started whispering about an Alchemist being here and then Toby told me his guardian was an Alchemist, I begged him to take me to meet you! Um, I cannot do trans-tra-um–"

"Transmutations."

"Yes! I cannot do them. But I've always been able to sense something, more than any brownie can."

"What do you sense Sophie?"

She gave an embarrassed laugh and shook her head. "It's...it's silly but I can sense salt."

"Sodium chloride. It's not silly, Sophie. Had you been born as a true Alchemist; this ability is vital in maintaining balance in nature. Sodium is integral to all living things. You probably would have been close to the sea, maintaining its levels so sea creatures could thrive. Or even in medicine since it's part of the Tria Prima, where sodium represents the body. Very useful."

Her eyes widened in wonderment and then saddened at a reality that could never be. I grabbed her hand before she got lost in her thoughts. "Would you give me permission to see if you have an Alchemist's Mark?"

"Alchemist's Mark?"

I nodded. "All are born with it. I've never met a hybrid before so I'm curious."

"Oh, I see. I-I guess that would be fine."

Just as I was about to bring her to the bedroom so we could have some privacy, Elis stood and grabbed Toby by the shoulder. "Alright lad, let's give the ladies some alone time to get to know each other. Why don't we go grab some of those excellent tarts you so enjoy sneaking into your room come morning eh?"

"But—" Elis squeezed Toby's shoulder hard, "Ow! Alrigh' alrigh'. We'll be back in a smidge Sophs. Ms. Melly's more growl than bite, yeah? She's a good woman, though. You can trust 'er." A look passed between them before Elis quickly ushered him out.

Sophie's head whipped back around, but a sweet smile graced her face and her dainty pointed ears were red. Oh boy.

I rolled my eyes and gestured to her. "Now, every Alchemist is born with the Alchemical symbol associated with the element they are genetically tied to. It can be anywhere, though typically it's on the upper body somewhere. Are you comfortable with just undoing your dress to your shoulders?"

Sophie nodded as she was already untying her apron. She unbuttoned her dress enough that the sides slipped down her tiny shoulders and she held it to her chest. I checked in with her again.

"How do you feel? I'm just going to look, alright?"

"Okay."

Lifting her arms, I scanned her front and back, then her shoulders and collarbones. Nothing. As I rounded to face her back, I didn't see anything initially.

"Wait. Let's move closer to the fire."

As we neared, it became more visible but still oh-so faint. A circle with a horizontal line through it, right there in the middle of her upper spine. The symbol for sodium.

"There it is," I breathed in wonder as my finger grazed over a symbol I never thought I'd ever see on another person.

"It's there?! What does it look like Ms. Melly?" asked Sophie excitedly.

"Here I'll show you."

Pulling my hair to one side, I pushed the left side of my robe down and revealed my shoulder. Right on top was the same symbol, albeit a stark black against my own pale skin compared to the nearly transparent one on hers.

Her eyes widened and she went to touch it but stopped, glancing at me for permission. Giving her an encouraging nod, she touched the symbol. Small fingers traced the jet-black lines.

"Wow... but what does it do?" she whispered.

I smiled and said, "It gives us the ability to call and manipulate our chosen element."

She glanced at my chest. "But you have so many of them... Did all Alchemists have multiple symbols like you?"

"No, they did not. We are only born with one. I... am unique among our kind as I was born with all the primary elements. Now, I command many." I pulled my robe closed and turned back to the table.

"How many?" Sophie asked with fascination.

Pouring more coffee into my mug, I sat down and crossed one leg over the other as my eyes met her over the cup's rim.

"All of them."

205

A. R. Morgan

CHAPTER 20

Toby took Sophie back to the kitchens shortly after, with her promise that she'd be back to learn more about her heritage. Her excitement and wonder left me in a strange state of nostalgia and pensiveness. I had performed small transmutations to give her just an inkling of who and what we were. Her excited squeals, jumping up and down, her tiny hands clapping, cracked my normally stoic nature and had me laughing right back. Her joy was incandescent and infectious, her innocence provoking the same protectiveness I felt toward Toby. So out of place was this little Brownie girl in this castle of horrors, I had half a mind to ask Alcaeus to see her safely out of it. But her family had been here for generations. So, my opinion remained silent.

Who was this rebel among my kind who went against the biggest law put down by Mother Nature herself? Do not leave The Citadel. If one must, then never venture beyond Eladaria's Wall. And here I thought I was the only unruly outlaw among them. Perhaps we had been related.

Pondering these things, I made my way to the library, escorted by some of Alcaeus's personal guards. After their encounter with Elis, they relaxed a bit and no longer prevented him from coming in and out of my room. Alcaeus no doubt thought I'd make a fuss but, honestly, I appreciated their presence. Underestimating the queen proved to be rather unhealthy and I was keen on keeping everyone alive.

Once I reached the great building, I walked down the path Elis had shown me when we had first arrived. The magnificence of this place was something I would never get over and it was fast becoming my favourite place to be.

In no time, Sage Kevyn's door appeared before me, and I placed my hand in the middle of the seal. It flashed and the door gave way. Walking in, I noticed Kevyn sitting at his desk, writing with a massive feather quill that jerked and swayed with every word. It was obnoxious really, and it incited a chuckle out of me. He looked up upon my entering, eyes twinkling as his snow-white moustache lifted in greeting.

"Ah, Melisandre! Come in! Come in. I was just finishing up some correspondence." He hobbled over to me, his slight limp giving him a unique gait.

"I apologise if I've interrupted you. I was hoping to get to my research if that is alright?"

"Of course! That's why I added you to the seal, silly! You are free to come in and use the study at your leisure. Don't mind me, I'll just be pottering around and doing what I do." He gave my shoulders a squeeze and waved back towards his desk and the coffee table by the fire. Books and scrolls were suddenly there, neatly stacked as if waiting patiently for their reader.

"All the materials you left with previously. Anything else you need, just ring the bell at the door and say what you're looking for and it shall appear in due time. I'm off to teach several seminars so I shan't be back until quite late, but feel free to stay as long as you'd like my dear." His gentle smile was warming to my icy demeanour, and I melted under its cosiness.

"Thank you, Kevyn. You're a gem."

He booped me on the nose. "And priceless too!" Winking as he made his way out.

Taking a deep inhale of the smell of true joy that all libraries smell like, I began rifling through all the materials. Out of all that was here, only one book contained information about Vampire markings. Grabbing it, I made my way to the desk and removed my shoes. Hopping up on top, I sat cross-legged and began to read.

Hours went by. Time felt meaningless here. I had read about 129 different types of marks among Vampires, Fae, and Weres, but nothing regarding a Familiar's Mark. So I rang the bell as Kevyn had suggested, asking for more information on rituals and markings. Then I switched to discovering more of Ragna's history and finally, researching the components of telekinesis and necromancy.

By then, scrunched-up papers with possible formulas for the psychic ability littered the floor, others lying scattered around me. Journals lay open with furiously written notes of my different hypotheses regarding orientation, physics, and mind-magic connection. Somehow, Ragna was either able to control gravity or possibly electromagnetism; but if it was the latter, I would know instantly. Or, somehow, she can control the space between particles. Either way, I'd need to understand the source, range, and strength of that ability in order to manipulate it. Where magic ends, science begins.

Suddenly I was overcome with longing and aching, so much so that my eyes burned with unshed tears. I wanted something, needed... him. I needed to be near him, touch him, taste him. The sound of my broken moan snapped me out of my reverie. I shook myself violently, slapping my cheeks.

"Get it together, Mel!" I muttered to myself, breathing heavily.

I stood up and walked to the window, resting my forehead on the cool glass. Taking deep breaths, I willed my body to calm but the fire of lust continued to burn low. How very strange. In a singular moment, it felt as though my heart was breaking but my body was on fire. This had to be the Mark.

A sharp rap on the door had me turning to see the very man I was trying to understand walk through. For a prince, Alcaeus was dressed casually, all black leather and linen. His hair was pulled up halfway, as it usually was, with several strands framing his face. The cream button-down shirt he wore was open enough to see a silver chain disappear below. Sleeves rolled to his elbows, I noticed he carried a book in one hand. Several of his fingers wore rings. Slightly pointed ears also sported several silver rings and one ear had a cuff with a chain connected to the ring at his earlobe.

Seeing this gladiator of old in a library setting, with the firelight dancing along his golden skin and chestnut hair, silver jewellery glinting... did something to me. I narrowed my eyes and turned back around to the window.

"What are you doing here?" I asked, tiredly, my mind still battling my body for control.

In the reflection of the glass, I saw him stop and regard me for a moment. Then he walked over to the chairs positioned in front of the hearth and sat down. Stretching one leg in front of him, he opened his book.

"I am reading. Seemed an appropriate pastime in a setting like this, don't you think?" he replied, with one raised brow. The small lift at the corner of his mouth had me rolling my eyes.

"Indeed. And as you're well aware, this happens to be a massive 'setting' so perhaps you'd care to find your own space?"

"Oh no, I'm quite comfortable, thank you. Worry not, we Vampires are excellent at being masters of silence. Pay me no mind." Alcaeus turned to his book, subsequently ignoring me.

My glare at his relaxed form reflected back through the window, the lines of irascibility marred my face. Annoyed, I scratched my head while walking back to my research. The last thing I needed was a distraction; specifically, this distraction.

I had just gotten control of my biology too, I whined internally. Settling back up on the desk with a bit of grumbling, I reviewed my information, intent on getting back on track.

The amount of force it takes to throw 55 kilos into the air while applying enough pressure to keep the subject immobile would have to be immense. Could it be something akin to blast force? No, it must be some kind of diamagnetic levitation, maybe spices and leather, that rough beard against my—I looked up, realising Alcaeus's scent invaded my thoughts.

His scent.

Now, I may be a master at tracking the elements, but my abilities very much stopped at hyper senses. Very, very strange.

My eyes wandered back over to his relaxed form. The long lines of his body. Defined muscles in his forearms. Large, strong hands. Broad shoulders filling the tall-backed chair. The sharp lines of his jaw only emphasised by his scruff. Closing my eyes, I felt the memory of it.

Rough against my inner thigh, hot breath scorching my skin, as he'd crept closer to—my eyes shot open only to find Alcaeus staring straight at me, a knowing gleam in his eye.

I cleared my throat.

"So," I began, shutting my book, "I thought we were going to be meeting for dinner?"

Alcaeus shut his book, but his thumb still held his place. Amusement danced along his features. "We were. You failed to appear. So, I came to you."

"Wait," I squeaked, "that was last night?"

He nodded.

"Oh..." Suddenly disoriented, I wondered if Kevyn had ever come back. There was no memory but who is to say? Especially when my work consumes me so thoroughly. "Well, I apologise. It's not uncommon for

210

time to get away from me. Elis has more than once had to drag me away lest I accidentally starve myself."

Alcaeus chuckled. "It was no trouble. You certainly would not be the first to never want to leave here. It has been my escape as well."

That surprised me.

"A warrior escaping to a library? Colour me surprised."

"Athena is a goddess of wisdom, first and foremost. I am but made in her image. It is only natural that I am a philomath as well. Perhaps too, it is also the one place untainted by certain individuals." Meaning the queen.

"That's understandable. What are you reading?"

He looked down fondly at the leather-bound book he was holding. It was green with gold lettering. Judging from its condition, it looked well-read too.

"This is actually a human book I picked up on my travels to the human realm about fifty years ago. It's called 'The Hobbit'. It was written by a man named—"

"J. R. R. Tolkien! Yes, I know. It's one of my favourite human pieces as well. Did you read The Lord of the Rings? Or the Silmarillion? What did you think? Oh! And there are two other human authors you must read if you haven't: Musashi Miyamoto and Sun Tzu–Ah." My rant was cut short when it occurred to me what I was doing. Up on my knees on the desk, I was leaning forward in eagerness, bursting with excitement at the mention of human literature.

Alcaeus' cocked his head at witnessing this side of me, no doubt, and a smile blossomed on his face. "Tolkien was a brilliant human and gifted storyteller. The Norse gods are probably having the time of their life having such an incredible wordsmith among them. If only our problems could be solved with the destruction of one ring," he joked. "I am very fond of the other two humans you have mentioned. Zhenbai gifted me a copy of The Art of War, several years ago. Although, something tells me you and I both share a love of William Shakespeare as well." Regarding me thoughtfully, he continued, "Had I known you had such a love for human literature, I would have spent more time filling the library with them. As it is, I only have a small collection since my visits have been limited these past few hundred years, but you are welcome to it. I'm sure Sage Kevyn has a few books in his own study as well."

My cheeks reddened at his consideration. "Yes, well I am also very much in my element surrounded by literature of all kinds. We Alchemists are insatiable in this regard."

"Certainly not only?" he questioned, his voice darkening.

I looked at him pointedly, sitting back on my heels. "No, not only. As you well know."

Sexual tension elevated between us. My heart thumped against the bones of my ribcage. The lingering soreness where Alcaeus had bitten me was forgotten, replaced with a sharp warmth that raced through my blood and straight to my groin. I slipped off the desk. I had to know if what I was feeling was legitimate. I needed to know this wasn't just the Mark influencing me somehow. Slowly, I crept one foot in front of the other until I was one step from him, I stopped.

"Tell me, Alcaeus," I asked, my voice going sultry, "This mark you gave me, it's barely but a stain on my skin. Yet, it aches. Not just from pain but something more. Is it responsible for this ache inside me? This," coming toe to toe with him, I looked down into his eyes and slowly dropped to my knees, "overwhelming desire," I ran my hands slowly up his strong thighs, "...to feel you. To be near. Is what I feel really me? Or is this the beginning of my end?" My voice ended in a heavy whisper.

Leaning back, I looked up at him, half afraid of his answer. A midnight storm greeted me as I saw the battle of desire and apprehension in his eyes. He sat up and leaned forward so fast that I began to lose my balance. He snagged my wrist, keeping me from tumbling over. Alcaeus's grip was a shackle as we both intensely regarded each other. Slowly, he brought my hand to his cheek and placed it gently there. He closed his eyes, rubbed his stubble against my palm, laying a kiss there. Then he placed another one on the underside of my wrist.

"The Mark only enhances what we already feel for one another. With each progression, yes, it will get harder and harder to be apart from each other for longer periods of time. We will be so finely tuned to the other that if either of us is in peril, no matter how far apart we may be, the other will know immediately. Your pain will be my pain. Your excitement, mine. The Mark may have given you slight enhancement in your senses and that is from me. As we are not the same species and Alchemists are not creatures of magic, I do not know what enhancements you will give me."

"So, what I'm feeling is real?" I whispered. Not breaking away from where we touched, he reached out and also cupped my face.

"Yes, *mikrós asvós*, it is very real."

The bonds of my reservations shattered and I captured that inviting mouth with my own. Giving in never felt so good. I wanted him. Beyond words. The tip of my tongue teased at his lips, and he opened, allowing me entry. Tongues dancing as I moaned at the taste and heat of him. My hands ran up to his shoulders and I applied pressure, pushing him back into the chair. Our kiss broke and he looked at me questioningly. I was mesmerised for a moment at his glistening lips, wet from our kiss. They beckoned me, but my desire for something else helped me focus.

My hands glided down his large chest and firm abs as I scooted forward between his knees. I took my time, enjoyed every sensation his body revealed to me.

"Let me?" I asked huskily, as I nipped and kissed his inner thigh.

Alcaeus's acquiescence came by opening his legs wider, relaxing backward. I smiled at my small victory and slid my hands underneath his shirt. My hands revelled at the feel of muscles tightening underneath my touch as my fingers slipped underneath his waistband, brushing the tip of his already hard cock. Alcaeus's breath hitched and I made quick work of the laces, pulling them down just enough for him to spring forward into my waiting hand.

Looking up at him to catch his gaze, I ran my tongue from base to tip, tracing the edges before wrapping my lips around the head. That incited a growling groan from Alcaeus, who threaded his fingers through my hair and gripped my head. He didn't try to control me, however, as I began to work up and down his impressive length. The sheer girth of him was guaranteed to leave my jaw sore later but the unrestrained pleasure on his face made it worth it.

When his cock hit the back of my throat, I swallowed and relaxed, opening to him and taking him further until my nose brushed his abdomen. I held there for several moments, holding my breath.

"Gods, Melis—Ah!" Alcaeus gasped, his grip on me tightening. The masculine groans had me wet and aching and I knew he could take it no more when both of his hands grasped my skull and began a rhythm. I let go, holding onto his thighs, trusting him. Glancing up at the vulnerable sight of unadulterated pleasure in his expression, had my nipples peaking and my slit clenching with my own need. Alcaeus's muscles strained, his eyes closed, and teeth clenched, fangs on full display. The knowledge that I was doing this to him almost brought me to climax.

With a snarl, Alcaeus lifted my head, and his cock left my mouth with a pop. Tugging at my hair, I stood and he quickly removed my pants and underwear.

"Come here," he growled and spun me around, pulling me into his lap, my back against his chest.

Hooking his arms under my knees, he spread my legs wide. Then his fingers found my entrance and he slid them up and down through my folds, spending time rubbing and rolling my clit. I gasped and squirmed, whispering please repeatedly. I rolled my hips in motion with his fingers, my ass rubbing against the heat of his cock. When I could take it no more, he took himself and rubbed against my core, teasing me.

His breath was hot against my ear, and I felt the tip of his tongue slide up my ear and then down to my neck.

"Mmm, you are so ready for me, Melisandre. Is this what you want?" he asked, his voice thick as syrup. He took the head of his cock and tapped it hard against my clit, as if to incite my answer. With a yelp, I bucked in response, clinging to him.

"Yes! Yes... I want it," I whimpered, one hand holding onto his arm as I threaded my fingers into his hair behind me.

I felt his masculine chuckle as he slid inside me. I let out a choked moan as his cock stretched me and bottomed out as we went pelvis to pelvis. Alcaeus wrapped one arm around my waist as his large hand firmly gripped underneath my right thigh, keeping my legs opened wide for him. Then he began to move, and all thoughts left me.

This position caused Alcaeus to hit deep and I could no longer hold back my vocals. I prayed Kevyn was sage enough to keep busy a little while longer. The fear of him interrupting us was quickly swept away in the wake of the deep thrusts that rendered me undone.

My head rolled back on Alcaeus's shoulder, and he took that opportunity to pepper my neck with kisses and licks, right below my ear.

"You feel incredible," he whispered in my ear as his hips thrust faster into me, holding my hips up slightly and away from him so his own could do the work.

I held onto the nape of his neck as he nuzzled me. The feel of his hot breath against sensitive skin only drove me closer to peaking.

"Oh, oh! Please Alcaeus please!" I ground against him, meeting him thrust for thrust. My hand sought my clit and I began teasing it. My body tightened in anticipation.

"Come for me, my love, I know you are close. Come!" He commanded.

My walls clenched hard. Holding my breath, I let the orgasm take me while Alcaeus fucked me through it. My mouth opened in a silent scream. Spasming, my spine bowed. Blood rushed through me as my muscles fluttered and then I collapsed against him. He slowed only slightly, allowing me to recover before he began ramming back into my body. At the speed he was going, a second orgasm came swiftly, and just when I thought I could take no more I felt Alcaeus stiffen beneath me. He cursed into my hair and then the warm heat of his climax surged inside me.

Both of us lay there panting. Finally, he released my leg with a squeeze and kiss on my neck. Gingerly, I climbed off him. My knees gave out and I quickly grabbed for the coffee table, but Alcaeus's large hands grabbed me at the hips.

"Steady there, careful."

I let out a rather unladylike giggle and Alcaeus also began to laugh. Mirth filled the room as we put our clothes back on and readjusted ourselves. As our laughter died down, Alcaeus pulled me back into his lap and I curled around him, tucking my head into his chest and shoulder.

My body hummed in the afterglow, and we sat quietly, listening to the crackle of the fire. My mind felt clear, for once. As much as I didn't want to admit it, Alcaeus' arms were fast becoming one of my favourite places to be. Lulled by the now steadiness of his breathing and the quiet thump of his heart, my lids began to feel heavy and began to close.

"I have to go away for several days," Alcaeus said, breaking the silence.

I sat up and looked at him. "Why?" Realising that I was not within my rights to ask that, I quickly amended by saying, "Ah, stupid question. You are the prince so I suppose you have important things—"

"That may be, but you have every right to ask. You have the right to ask me anything, mikrós asvós," he said, squeezing my leg. "There have been several reports of seeing the Wild Hunt along our borders. The Hunt belongs to the Unseelie King, whose whereabouts are unknown at the moment. None of my soldiers are equipped to face the Hunt and so I must investigate this myself. I suspect I will be gone for several days."

"I see. Is the Nightmare Court on good terms with the Unseelie?"

"There is no such thing as 'good terms' when it comes to relations between courts, my dear. Just unstable alliances. As far as that goes, let us just say the Unseelie has more common interests with me than with their shining brethren. You could even say, at one point, their king and I were on friendly terms."

I looked at him then. "Friends? With the Unseelie King? The Raven and the Owl getting along? Absolutely not. I refuse to believe it."

Alcaeus laughed and said, "Friends is a very generous term, one I would never use in his presence. Allies, certainly. He is the only one to beat me more than once at chess."

"Ah, but you have yet to play against me," I challenged.

He raised a scarred eyebrow and then gave me a quick kiss. Before I could blink, he stood and the world fell away. When I opened my eyes, the spinning had ceased. Still being held against Alcaeus' chest, I turned my head to see the familiar surroundings of his own private study. In front of us stood the beautiful marble chess set with two chairs at either side. He set me down.

"Let us put your bravado to the test, my little Alchemist."

CHAPTER 21

Two days went by uneventfully. I spent all my time holed up in Sage Kevyn's study, still smarting from my aggravating loss in chess against Alcaeus. My pride had taken a devastating blow at being bested, although twice I had claimed victory. My accusations that he had let me win still rang in my ears, which reddened in embarrassment. He had merely baited me into another game, playing my ego like a fiddle.

He knows me too damn well already.

Having finished one book, I grabbed another one of the several stacks I had grown.

Toby came by often, bringing food and beverage. My ward, with his gift of gab, filled me in on all the kitchen gossip and whatever new skills he had learned. He always came bearing edible gifts, usually taken when the cook wasn't looking, I'm sure. I did attempt to continue his education during his visits, but the boy had the attention span of a puppy in the presence of squirrels.

Sophie, however, would often visit me after she was done in the kitchens, and we would spend hours talking about science and Alchemist culture. Most of the time though, I'd dodge her pesky questions and make her focus on meditation in hopes of strengthening her sense of sodium. I began teaching her the basics of a transmutation circle and memorising the symbols for each element. She was very smart and disgustingly optimistic. We Alchemists were a grumpy folk so, clearly, her Brownie heritage took over at some point. Nevertheless, I began to look forward to her tinkling giggle and how wide her blue eyes would get at every new piece of information. Her reactions turned up bittersweet memories of my own self when I first began training under my old mentor.

Sometimes Toby and Sophie would visit together. Oh, sweet Toby. He was lost to us in his unwavering infatuation with his sweet little friend. If there was a pebble on the ground, he would step on it before Sophie could even notice. That boy lived for her smile. For once, I could see the point Elis had been trying to make. I relaxed a little, taking pleasure as a bystander in the face of innocent love.

What a terrible mistake that was.

∇∇𝒹♙♂ᵒ𝔰

At the beginning of the third evening that Alcaeus was gone, I was summoned.

"M-my lady it's, um, it's the queen," Ada said, hands a trembling mess.

I slammed the coffee down. "The queen? Here? At my door?"

"No! Her steward is here to escort you! She asks you to tea." Sheer panic was on this poor woman's face.

"Right now?!"

"Yes! Right now!"

I swallowed all my curses. Whatever blissful relief I had been basking in from the queen's absence during my day was completely obliterated.

"Fine. You can tell her shit-stain of a steward I'll be right out. As soon as I finish my cup of coffee," I said, sipping slowly. Very slowly.

Ada paled and gulped. Looking as if she were about to argue with me, she stopped herself and hurried to the door. Trying to calm my nerves, I put my mental guard up. It's just tea, Melisandre. Just tea. I frowned. Pinching the bridge of my nose, my grumbling continued.

It's not just bloody tea, and you know it. Prepare yourself. And try not to unleash the next apocalypse.

After hearing the chatter between Ada and Oweyn start to escalate to shouting, I scooted my chair back loudly. Marching to the door where Ada had it cracked open with her head poking out, I yanked it back, startling them both.

"Unbecoming behaviour for a queen's seneschal, causing a scene in the hallway with my lady's maid, don't you think? Let's go. We shouldn't keep Her Majesty waiting." Sarcasm dripped with every word, and I walked past Oweyn.

218

The look on his face gave me more joy than biting into a freshly baked bridie. The steward straightened his vest and jacket with a huff and speed walked past me. He was so ridiculous I had to cover my laugh with a cough.

My mood became ever more sombre the closer we got to the queen's receiving rooms. Perhaps it was just me, but it even seemed to get darker, provoking me into searching my surroundings in apprehension. What I was expecting, I don't know, but it wasn't the brightly lit gold and cream sitting room that was before me.

As soon as we entered the empty room, Oweyn pointed to the couches and snapped his fingers at me like I was a dog.

"Stay."

"Go fuck yourself."

He whipped around and stared daggers at me. I faced him and the stare down began. His pasty skin was mottled red with anger. Any angrier and the heat would melt the wax right off his slicked-back, greasy hair.

"That will be all, Oweyn."

Straightening immediately, he gave me one last glare before bowing his head to the queen. Ragna's entrance was silent, and I finally looked at her. She was dressed in a beautiful midnight blue Victorian-styled day gown. Black lace delicately covered it at the bodice and in patterns down the dress. She wore several necklaces and a diamond tiara. A strange cultural switch in fashion but it did not hide the proud Viking she really was.

She rounded the cushioned chair opposite me and sat.

Gesturing to the seating in front of her, she said, "Please. Sit."

Apprehension filled me but I slowly took a seat, far away from her. My eyes never left her. Picking up her teacup she took an elegant sip before her eyes levelled with mine.

"I see my prince finally gave you the first mark. Show me."

My eyes narrowed at her command. This was not the hill to die on, so I slowly unbuttoned two of the top buttons of my black silk shirt. I pulled the collar down. His bite marks were still there, although sealed. From them, two faint circular black lines and patterns swirled around, making an imperceptible symbol.

At her smug smile, I quickly rebuttoned my shirt. Crossing one leg over the other, I placed my hands on either side of the chair.

"To what do I owe this great honour, Your Highness?" Try as I might, I couldn't keep the sarcasm out of my tone.

"You Alchemists truly have no respect for authority, do you?"

"We respect balance. We respect Nature's processes."

"Predators rule in nature, do they not? If that was so then you must respect that in this room, you are beneath me in the food chain."

"Even predators take shelter from the storm, Your Highness. Your mistake is in thinking my place is even on the food chain."

Her eyes narrowed. "No, you see Lady Von Boden, that is exactly what I am and have been trying to do. Understand what you are. Unfortunately for you, I am very tired of guessing."

I studied her. I knew what she was after. She wasn't going to get it.

"I am but a humble Alchemist, previously minding my own fucking business before you trapped an innocent boy in order to blackmail me into being your prisoner."

"Ah-ah," she held up a slender finger, "no lying, not even by omission. That's one mark against you."

My brows nearly smacked into each other with a frown, annoyance bubbling in my chest. "Don't deny it, Ragna. That is exactly what you did. If you are going to try counting whatever make-believe sins you've deemed I or my ward have made against you, we best get comfortable. It'll be a long night."

Ragna sighed, putting her teacup down. "You are a very intelligent woman, Melisandre," she said. "I knew you would see right through my plans the moment you stepped into Castle Fyrkat. Which was fine; the goal was merely to get you here. I also believe you knew how trapped you truly were the moment your ward was taken captive. I will not deny it—as soon as I had received word that the last Alchemist had been sighted, your capture was inevitable. I just needed to find a way to get you to leave your home as I myself cannot cross the Veil as Alcaeus can. To get you to come to Khaviel before anyone else could take you away from me.

"We are far past arguing over spilled milk. You are here. The Mark of the Familiar now manifests on your skin as we speak by my very own Royal Consort. So, let us discuss the real issue at hand: your cooperation. Now, being an intelligent woman, surely you understand what will happen should you continue to defy me." Her eyes hardened and the room dropped several degrees. "I will take everything you love, everything you cherish, and you will watch as I tear them apart, piece by piece. The hybrid boy? I personally will show him the meaning of pain;

I have even debated on handing him over to the Seelie Court, as a gesture of good faith to be sure, so that Mab can make an example of him. Oh, how she hates to be reminded that the purity of Seelie blood is waning. Their kind grows weak. For being a Court of Light, their creativity when it comes to torture and death is almost artistic–his screams will be the only thing you will hear for years to come." The gleam in her gaze was a clear warning. "You will be chained like the dog you are as you watch your friends become my puppets, dancing corpses who do all that I command. Is that what you want?"

Glaring back, I said, "A lot of words. A lot of threats. Helium has more substance than you, Ragna."

"You are mistaken, Alchemist. Those were not threats; it is your future if you continue to rebel, to defy me. There are two paths before you: submission or suffering. The choice is entirely yours." She leaned forward, snagging a grape from the mound of fruit in the middle, and slipped it between ruby red lips.

The movement loosened the necklace hiding in her cleavage and instantly my eyes were drawn to it. At first, it looked like a large opal but upon further inspection, it was just a strange glowing orb. A mysterious white substance moved from within like it was alive. Something inside of me screamed to go to it. My new Mark began to burn.

Before registering what I was doing, I was halfway across the space, hand reaching out as if to grab it. Snatching my hands back, I sat down instantly but my gaze never left the necklace.

The queen was just as frozen, staring at me in wonder. The orb continued to imprison my attention. Similarly, to how something in Alcaeus called to me, so too did this necklace except this was the Siren's song. I heard it clearly as if it was playing right in my ear. No, not my ear. My heart.

Ragna placed her hand over it and I almost cried out in desperation. In rage. She clenched it in her fist and mumbled something. A sharp stabbing resounded in my chest and I clutched it.

"Very interesting," purred the queen. "So, the Familiar Mark works like this too, does it? Most intriguing..."

Panting and still holding my fist to my chest, I gasped, "What is that necklace? What's in there?!"

She waved her finger at me again. "Nah-ah-ah, Melisandre! You tell me your truth and I will tell you mine. It's only fair."

I stared at her, seeing the unobtainable knowledge behind those emerald spheres. I wanted to gouge them out and extract them from her brain. If only that was a possible way of information gathering. The difference between myself and Ragna, however, was those fantasies stayed in the same place they were begotten.

A humourless laugh escaped from me. "You know what, Your Highness? Keep your truths. I'm quite fond of keeping mine." Coming to my feet, I squared off with her. "Let me make this abundantly and explicitly clear, Ragna: I owe you nothing. I do not belong to you nor will I ever. I am the daughter of the Mother, Creator of this earth as we know it. I answer to her and her alone. When you have the ability to stop the might of her storms, calm the wrath of her volcanoes, and keep winds from blowing then maybe, just maybe you'll have my attention."

I got up to leave. I didn't turn when I heard the porcelain shattering against the wall.

"Damn you, Alchemist! I will reveal your secrets even if I have to rip them from your flesh, layer by layer!"

Once at the door, I finally turned.

"You can try. In the end, it will not end in your favour."

"*Det som göms i snö, kommer fram vid tö!*" hissed Ragna.

What is hidden in snow, is revealed at thaw.

The threat hung thick between us as I swung the door open and escaped. Quickly, I made my way back to the library. Try as I might though, there was no running from the sinking feeling that Ragna's green fire sought to devour me.

CHAPTER 22

"The queen demands your presence at the banquet being held this evening," said Sage Kevyn, looking up from the message he'd just received.

"Of course she does," I muttered, only sparing a quick glance before continuing to write down my new findings. "I take it, it is only my name on the missive?"

Kevyn snorted. "Naturally. The queen demanding my presence at a royal banquet? Are you kidding me? My first thought would be the audacity," he scoffed, throwing the note into the fire. "I'm more than happy to make your excuses."

"Ha, thanks, Kevyn. Unfortunately, I cannot afford to give the queen any more ammunition against me. I can hardly keep my civility around her as it is."

"Fair enough. If you need a reprieve, you know where I am."

I looked up and smiled at him. "Thank you... I'm sorry but might I ask how you're able to just say no to Ragna? Are you not a part of her Court and thus subject to her authority?"

He looked upward, his beard slightly twitching as he considered my question. After a moment, he replied, "No and no. That is a very long conversation and probably for another time, but the short answer is that we Sages belong to and only answer to our own Order; we have divine immunity as our original purpose was to essentially be the historians and bookkeepers of the Otherworld. I am here to serve my dear friend, King Alcaeus. Does that answer your question?"

I smiled, nodding. Returning my expression, he went back to sorting books.

With great reluctance, I made my way back to my rooms to get ready. Relief filled me at my empty bedroom, which meant that Ragna had not taken it upon herself to once again dress me. Putting on a black silk one-piece jumpsuit which I then placed a silver and black under-bust corset over. Black boots and my hair in a large French braid with a few strands pulled out finished the look. Grabbing my staff, I transmuted it to a large-hoop chain that I wrapped several times around my waist. A stylish belt. They would never know.

Now, to wait for— "I'm here! I'm here, Mels! Alright, what am I working with?" Elis burst through my door, looking incredibly handsome in a black and lavender tapestry-patterned tailcoat. A matching waistcoat with a black shirt, and the silver chain sporting a large diamond rose gleamed at his neck.

"Oh, Mels...you look...great?" sputtered Elis, confused.

"Why did you say it like that? I'm perfectly capable of dressing myself occasionally, Elis."

My best friend was still looking at me like I'd grown two heads when Llyr walked in with Toby following closely behind.

"My love, we'll be late! Toby, your bowtie is crooked." Llyr leaned down to fix Toby's tie. I smiled.

"Boy, don't you look smart! They even tried to comb your hair. Poor Llyr." I chuckled. His unruly curls were miraculously slicked back, but one hadn't given up the fight yet.

"I beg ya, Ms. Melly, don't say nuthin'. This is downrigh' embarrassin' and bloody uncomfortable." Toby kept tugging at his jacket and shirt until Llyr gently slapped his hands away.

Elis rolled his eyes heavenward in silent prayer. His look slid to me, and he pointed between us. "That's your fault you know."

I held up my hands innocently. "I truly can't find fault in his statement. It is bloody uncomfortable."

"Ugh, hopeless, the lot of you! Come on now. Llyr is right, we'll be late."

⏶⏷⟋⟐⟐♂°ϛ

Castle Fyrkat's Great Hall was a sight to behold. Magnificent braziers roared, brightening the room. Long tables ran the length of the room. At the end sat the high table, elevated by a dais. Dancers and entertainers were in constant motion in the middle for all to see. Jovial music danced around the room, setting an uncharacteristically festive mood for the Nightmare Court.

Upon arrival, a footman led us to our seats. We were the last to arrive, save those sitting at the high table, so curious stares followed us. Elis, ever the social butterfly, made his rounds of greeting as he went by.

My back was to the wall and I was only a few seats down from the table's end, close to the dais. I could only suspect it was so the queen could keep a close eye on me. Elis, Llyr, and Toby sat across from me.

"All rise for the Queen!"

The queen and her entourage came through the doors and all in the room stood and bowed. Well, not all. Dressed in a gold gown that would make any red-carpet dress look like a cheap knock-off, the queen's matching gold and glittering stilettos clicked on the marble. Upon reaching her seat, which was being pulled out for her, she raised her arm.

"Welcome all! Tonight, we celebrate our very own Lord Cyto, ascending from his noble status of Lord to Master! We drink to you, my lord, and come the light of morn, I shall bestow a most befitting gift, one of your choosing as is tradition! Let the feast begin!"

The lord in question bowed deeply and everyone cheered. Distaste filled me as I remembered him from the Gathering. Beady eyes looked around and found mine. He smirked at the disgust I knew was blatant on my face.

I crossed my arms over my chest. My appetite had stayed in my room when I had left. Toby, however, had no such reservations and began piling food in his mouth.

"By the Mother Toby, slow down. You'll choke," I snapped. He grinned and kept eating.

The gentleman to my left chuckled and leaned his head near mine, though he didn't look at me. "The food is good. You should try it."

"Yes, thank you," I replied with strained politeness, making no move to pick up my fork.

He noticed and finally glanced at me. Doing a double take, he whispered, "You're the Alchemist. The Consort's Familiar."

"Not quite." I reached for my goblet, sniffing it. Ale. It would do.

"You are quite pretty! The rumours about you painted a portrait of quite the terrifying creature. As your dinner companion, I am grateful to find that I was misled."

Barely containing my annoyance, I let out a long sigh before swinging my attention to the man, taking in his features. Suave black hair with a white streak through it and a matching goatee. Chocolate eyes crinkled at the ends when he smiled. Clean bone structure. Definitely Vampiric nobility.

"Oh, forgive my rudeness. I am Jericho Sinclare, Lord of the Marshes."

"Pleasure to meet you."

"Oh please, the pleasure is all mine."

"Watch your money around Lord Sinclare, Mels. Man is a slimy gambler and a damned cheat. Hells, your money might be gone already," Elis muttered, downing his glass.

"Oh, Lord LeGervase, still bitter at losing a quarter of your fortune when we were at The Downs? I told you: you should have listened to your little fairy here. It's not my fault you choose passion over reason."

Elis looked downright murderous at the slight while Llyr shook his head, pinching the bridge of his nose. My own expression left little to be interpreted, but by some miracle I kept my comments to myself; I still had an ulterior motive, after all. Deciding we were due for a change in conversation before Elis vaulted the table, I turned to the Vampire next to me.

"My lord, would you be so kind as to educate me on the man of the hour? What is so special about Lord Cyto? How does one go from your average Vampire noble to master?"

Lord Sinclare finished chewing, wiping his mouth.

"Lord Cyto, Master of Pain. He is one of the queen's personal favourites, hogging her good graces for the last 150 years," he said with annoyance. "And, trust me, one doesn't just go from nothing to Master. The process is heavily based on breeding and lineage, personal power base, as well as political connections. Expanding your own pool of power and magic takes years and many sacrifices."

"Sacrifices? So, he kills what? Other Vampires?"

The lord grimaced. "We prefer to use the word 'consume' rather than kill; far more refined. A Vampire that is not from the direct line of a Champion, must consume a considerable number of not just Vampires, but any creature that holds significantly more magic than him. The strength of a Vampire can be seen in how powerful his thrall line is. But enough of that, lest I am overheard giving too much away – I would not want to spoil all the fun. Besides, it is enough of a shame that this pervert and his 'dolls' are being celebrated at all." His face soured immensely as he snagged his goblet, only to glare at the empty contents.

Intrigued, I leaned slightly closer and asked, "His dolls?"

"Yes, our Lord Cyto here really prefers them young. Very young. Once he is done torturing them, he turns them into thralls, forever his prisoner and under his command. Does not even try to hide his perversion. Twisted bastard," he said with disgust.

I looked over to where Lord Cyto was seated, and a coldness washed over me.

"Oh, and if you see to Lord Cyto's left, that woman? Horrid wench, she should not even be up there..." Lord Sinclare continued, but I tuned him out.

My mind was filled with all of the horrors Lord Cyto had probably inflicted on innocents, when a pair of Caribbean blue eyes and bouncing blond hair came through the doors.

CHAPTER 23

Sophie was carrying a huge pitcher, only a bit unsteady with the weight as she made her way around the room, dutifully refilling goblets. Her blue and white lace dress with her white apron made her look like Lewis Carroll's Alice. She was quick and discreet, flitting and weaving her way among the merriment unnoticed. Before long, she made her way to us.

Unease crept through me. I don't know why; Sophie had been a servant of the Nightmare Court her whole life. Her family had served for generations.

Sophie snuck up to an oblivious Toby. "Would you like some wine young sir?"

"Shoph—aack!" Toby choked, inhaling his food in surprise. One of Llyr's hands clapped against the boy's back.

Sophie giggled, leaning down to say, "Oops! My apologies little lord. Maybe when you're older!" She looked up and flashed me a bright smile. "Ms. Melly! You look absolutely lovely!"

"And you're a vision straight from a fairy tale. Never without your ribbon, I see."

She touched her braid, fingering the blue silk. "Nope! First gift Toby ever got for me! The first gift I've ever gotten, actually." Pink tinged her cheeks as she glanced down at the boy fondly.

Toby, having recovered from almost suffocating, looked up at her with stars in his eyes.

"Looks right pretty on ya Soph. Right pretty."

"Oi! Girl! More wine!"

Sophie jumped in the caller's direction. "Yes milord!" Turning to us, she gave a quick smile and hurried over to fill impatient lords' and ladies' goblets.

I didn't want to, but I let my eyes wander back to the dais to where Lord Cyto sat. He was speaking to the woman next to him, but then I saw him glance down. Black eyes followed Sophie's every move, his beaked nose flaring as she neared. My fingernails almost broke my skin as my fists clenched, no longer fighting the growing unease.

"What's wrong, Mels? Everything alright?" Elis looked over at me, concerned.

I just shook my head and leaned back in my chair, staring at my untouched food. Perhaps I was being paranoid. The room was full of Vampires; death, blood, horrors–that's what this Court was made of. This was a celebration. Not a Gathering. I took a long swig of my ale, stealing a glance at Ragna. Like Lord Cyto, she watched Sophie with a predatory gleam. I slammed my empty goblet down.

As soon as Sophie rounded to us again, this time on my side, I snagged her tiny wrist.

Wide-eyed, she looked at where I held her and then up at me as I pulled her close.

Leaning down, I furiously whispered, "Sophie, once you fill my cup, I want you to go back to the kitchens and stay there. Stay hidden. Stay out of sight. Okay?"

Confused, she shook her head, "Ms. Melly? What's wrong? Cook will yell at me, and I'd have to get one of the other girls to –"

"Sophie!" I cut her off. Letting my alarm fill my gaze, her own eyes widened at my intensity. "Do you trust me?"

She hesitated, blue eyes darting around the room until they landed behind me. The evidence of fear was in the dilation of her pupils, prey seeing the predators watching her. She gulped, bringing her attention back to me. "Always, Ms. Melly."

"Okay, please just go. Quickly," I squeezed her hand and let her go. She turned and hurried away. After I saw her slip through the doors, a sigh of relief drifted past my lips.

Turning back to my cup of ale, I looked across the table. Toby was frowning at me but didn't press the issue.

A new wave of dancers came, scantily clad, and music filled the air. Perhaps in any other Court, this would have been a sight to behold. I just wanted to be back with my books. I wanted to be back... in his arms. I smiled at the thought.

I miss him...

"And I you, *mikrós asvós*."

I didn't get upset that he answered. His presence in my mind filled me with warmth and longing. My eyes closed naturally as I spoke in a hushed tone.

"Today we are celebrating Lord Cyto becoming a Master Vampire. You're missing all the fun."

"Let me guess, the queen commanded your presence? Of course, she would." I could feel his mental sigh. **"Keep your chin up and head low. I am coming back."**

"You don't have to tell me twice. I just want to go home."

"I know, my love." With that, his presence disappeared, and emptiness took its place.

I looked over at my friends, chatting away. "Elis?"

He paused in his conversation with Llyr. "Yes, my dove?"

"When can we leave?"

"As soon as the Queen does, or she gives her subjects leave to do so. You know how Court etiquette can be."

"Well, some things were best left in the eighteenth century."

Elis snorted, raising his glass in agreement. I wrapped my arms around myself and began watching the entertainment.

After a time, the queen stood, holding her hands out to silence the room.

"Lord Cyto, in honour of your ascension I have promised you a gift of your choice. I ask that you name it now."

The lord stood, flipping the tails of his coat out, and straightened his jacket before he bowed deeply.

"My Queen! I am ever grateful for your generosity and consideration toward your most humble servant. I do indeed have a gift in mind." His smile was slow and vile. The queen sat gracefully back down, her attention on him. She waved for him to continue. "Well, Your Majesty, my... collection has grown rather small as of late."

She smirked as she examined her claw-like nails. "Always too hard on your toys, Lord Cyto. They break easily, you know. Most especially the young ones."

"Lesson learned. Well, I am in the market, as it were. My Queen, I humbly request a replacement." He placed his hand over his chest.

Ragna narrowed her eyes at him in consideration. Then she smiled.

My stomach sank.

No.

"Oh, my Lord Cyto, I have just the girl in mind."

She motioned for Oweyn. When he appeared, she whispered in his ear, and he vanished.

My heart began to race, and my eyes darted to Elis who looked back, panic in his eyes. Then we both looked at Toby. Elis looked back at me, and I slowly shook my head.

I mouthed, "You must take him. Take him away from here."

He looked helpless at me, then at Llyr, before finally nodding. He mouthed back, "I'll try."

But our time had run out.

The door that connected the great hall to the kitchens burst open. I tried to stand but a force suddenly pushed me back down. My ass hit the chair with a thud, my limbs sticking to the armrests like they were sewn to it. The damn telekinesis I had been researching.

Swinging my head to glare up at the queen, she gazed down at me with what could only be interpreted as satisfaction. The sounds of crying and struggling brought my attention back. Several guards walked in, one dragging a sniffling and shaking Sophie behind him.

No, please...

That horrible feeling I had; it wasn't a feeling. It was a prophesy come to fruition, and I watched helpless as it unfolded before me. Sick dread sank through me and I struggled against the invisible force, unsuccessfully. Blue eyes drowning in tears looked over at us then darted to the queen. Confusion and fear marred her innocent face.

Ragna waved her hand in Sophie's direction. "Your gift, my lord."

Sophie's eyes widened and her mouth fell open. "W-what? Your Majesty? What do you mean?"

Toby snapped to me, confused, looking to me for an explanation. "What does she mean...? Ms. Melly?" But before I could respond, the queen answered.

"You belong to Lord Cyto now, girl. Serve him well."

Suddenly, Lord Cyto appeared before her, his face alight with hunger and lust. I knew the moment she realised her doom because she began struggling with renewed fervour.

"No! Please! Toby! Ms. Melly! Help me please!"

"Noooooo!" screamed Toby as he jumped up to charge toward her.

"Stop him or I will kill the half breed myself!" cried the queen.

Elis tried to grab him, but Llyr got to him first. He grabbed Toby around the middle and dragged him back into his seat. Toby cried and fought but the Fae lord was much stronger.

What could they do? They had no power here.

I continued to struggle, trying to see if the queen was manipulating electricity while keeping an eye on Sophie.

Lord Cyto ran a hand down Sophie's cheek. She screamed. Her little feet lashed out, one after another, the first taking the Lord in the crotch and the second a guard in the shin. Before they could recover, she shoved herself away, launching herself in my direction. Somehow, one of my arms slipped free from the pressure holding me fast, moving aside just in time for the fleeing girl to crawl into the opened space. Her arms wrapped around my waist. Tight.

I wished that I could squeeze her just as desperately, but the queen's telekinesis still pushed against me, as if weights were holding me down.

Her face was red as tears streamed down her cheeks. I held her to me as hard as I could, my heart breaking.

She looked up at me and said, "Please Ms. Melly, help me! I don't care what you have to do, please don't let him take me! I beg you! I don't want to become a doll!"

My impotency skewered me like a trident to my heart, as once again, my options were having to choose between lives. I couldn't beat this force bearing down on me; not without stripping this room and everyone in it down to the atom. Even if I could do it without dismantling molecular structures, I couldn't take on an entire room of Vampires and a Champion without sentencing my own friends to death. That only left me with one option. One that I knew was going to haunt me forever. But what choice did I have? Helpless I may feel but powerless I was not.

Time slowed. I cupped her cheek and searched her eyes. My gaze slit to Elis, whose arms were around both his mate and my ward and saw the grief. He understood. Then, my attention switched to the struggling boy in his arms; Toby's face was desperate, pleading with me.

"Please, Ms. Melly! You can save 'er! You're the strongest person in the world! Don't let 'im 'ave 'er!" my ward cried out to me, clinging to Llyr's arms.

I looked up at the queen. Back she grinned, the cat who got the cream. Fury burned through me. Vengeance filled my eyes as I glared

233

back at her before closing them, readying myself for what I was about to do. What Ragna was forcing me to do.

Looking back to Sophie, I kissed her forehead. "Sophie, sweetheart. There is only one way I can help you," I said, my voice breaking. She stared back at me and then I knew she understood my meaning.

Peace came over her features and a tear rolled down her cheek. "I understand, Ms. Melly. It's okay. Do it. Please," she said, her sweet voice the only sound I heard among the cacophony of chaos. "Set me free."

Searching her face through a blur of tears, I nodded slowly. Placing my hand on her small neck, I shut the world out. Her pulse beat against my hand. Warm and alive. Clenching my teeth, I transmuted the blood in her jugular vein into a ball of coagulation; large enough she would be dead in minutes. The transmutation was so small it was imperceptible visually.

When I opened my eyes, Sophie was smiling at me. She had stopped trembling.

"Thank you," she whispered, squeezing my hand at her neck.

I could taste the salt of my own tears as I kissed her forehead again.

"Be free, little sister," I whispered back.

She was suddenly yanked from me, Lord Cyto grabbing her by the hair. She yelped and instinctively I tried to reach for her. Sophie didn't struggle. She didn't fight him. Just looked back at us with a smile on her sweet face.

I couldn't tear my eyes away from hers as I watched them leave through the main doors. Watched them close with finality. The sound echoed through me, as if that was the sound of life closing too soon on a life that had only just begun. Because it had. And I was responsible.

That was when I noticed my hand clutching something. The world fell away as I cracked my hand open. Blue silk ribbon peeked through. I sat there and stared at it.

Sophie's ribbon.

Vaguely, I became aware of Toby, still a struggling and sobbing mess in Llyr's arms.

"Why?! Why didn' ya save 'er? Why did ya let 'im take er'?! How could you!" Toby screamed at me.

I finally looked over at them, barely able to breathe. Elis' face was tortured as he tried to help Llyr hold Toby. The brown eyes that raged back at me swam with betrayal and horror. A look I knew all too well.

I was in such a state of shock that I could barely feel my own body. The invisible pressure finally gave way, letting me shoot to my feet. To run far away from here.

What had I done?

A furious, raging scream pierced the air and the doors burst back open. Neck flushed with anger and spittle dripping down his chin, Lord Cyto came to a stop in front of the dais. He threw down Sophie and she landed with a sickening crack against the marble.

She was already dead.

"SOPHIE!!" cried Toby, reaching for her.

"Llyr! He shouldn't see this! Don't let him see!" I yelled.

Llyr looked at me and then placed a hand over Toby's head and whispered magic. The boy instantly went limp, unconscious.

"She is DEAD, Your Majesty! That Familiar, the Alchemist," he seethed, pointing at me, "she killed my doll! I want justice. This was MY gift! MINE! And she took it from me!" I said nothing, but my face held no remorse, only my own fury and hatred. "Your Highness, I beg you to awaken this girl as my thrall! She was dead before I could bite her."

The queen looked bored. "Cyto, it is not my problem if you cannot control a little girl. She bested you. A Master Vampire. Is this how you want to be known? The Master Vampire who was outdone by a little girl? Have some pride, man. Besides, you know my reanimations only work on those that are slain by my hand, not of others. We shall find you another one. Now sit down and stop causing a scene. It is unseemly. Someone remove this," Ragna waved apathetically at Sophie's body, "thing from my floors."

Lord Cyto looked outraged and horrified but then he whipped around to me. Once again, he lifted a bony finger at me. "I will remember this, thieving bitch!"

Ignoring the fuming Vampire, I turned to Llyr and Elis, both of their pale faces drawn taught from sorrow.

"Take care of him. Tell him... I'm sorry."

Holding my hand out to Elis, I dropped Sophie's ribbon into his waiting one. I gave one last look at the girl lying on the ground, broken, burning the image in my mind.

I turned and left.

CHAPTER 24

Once clear of the great hall, I broke into a full sprint. Blasting through my door, I slammed it behind me. The pain was so great that no matter how fast I ran or how hard I breathed, nothing stopped the destructive emotions that swept through my body, suffocating me.

I had failed. Again. The only other Alchemist on this earth died by my hand this night. I slid to the ground, hyperventilating. I thrust my fingers into my hair, squeezing at the roots as an agonised moan ripped through my throat. Sophie was dead. She was dead because of me. My teacher. My friends. My family. They're all dead.

Because of me.

I stood suddenly, trying to rip my clothes off with an angry scream. I tugged the chain at my waist and threw it far away from me; while I didn't need my staff to transmute, it significantly amplified my power. In the state I was in, bringing down the whole of Idrisid would only be the beginning of the destruction.

I had enough blood on my hands.

Anything that could be touched was thrown. The sounds of breaking and shattering only fed my agony, my wrath. I screamed. I roared my sorrow to the heavens just as I let my sins this night sink into the depths of my soul.

Stumbling onto the terrace, I grabbed the balcony with both hands, my legs no longer able to sustain me. The weight of everything was too much to bear. I broke down into a sob, my tears falling to the stone. The stars glittered down at me, callous pinpricks of light, cold and so very far away.

"I'm sorry Sophie," I sobbed, voice cracking. "I'm so sorry! I'm sorry.... forgive me."

Closing my eyes, my body shuddered as I cried.

Warm, strong arms came around me, pulling me away from the balcony. I was enveloped in the smell of spices, leather, and forest. The heat of his chest came against me as Alcaeus pulled me toward him.

"It is I who should be apologising for the horrors this Court has put you through. I was not there, my love, and for that, I am sincerely sorry. I had just returned when I heard what happened," His voice rumbled against my hair.

I broke away from him, every fibre of my body screaming that I didn't deserve the comfort he was offering me. Jerking away, I backed up until my back hit the railing, my hand out.

"Stop it! Do not try to take away my shame! I did this! The queen she... gave her to him... and I... she... I had to... set Sophie... free," I gasped at the fresh pain cutting through me. And with it, explosive anger. Straightening, I narrowed my eyes at him through the blur of tears. "I killed her, Alcaeus. I just *murdered* an innocent, sweet, little girl! She didn't deserve this! Of all the people in the world, Sophie didn't deserve this end! She was pure and good! So don't you dare try to comfort me or take the blame! Her blood is on my hands just like theirs and I will face it, accept it, just as I did then! Toby *begged* me! He begged me to save her! He trusted me! Trusted me with her life, goddammit! He said I was the strongest person in the world but tonight, I just showed him that I...I was the weakest!"

The emotion proved too much so I turned, about to slam my fist into the stone in rage when Alcaeus suddenly grabbed my wrist and swung me back around. He took hold of my shoulders roughly, shaking me.

"Look at me, dammit!" He growled. "What you did for that little girl was mercy! A *mercy*, Melisandre! Zhenbai told me what happened; if not for you, she would have been strapped down and stripped. Raped and mutilated, trapped forever under Lord Cyto's control! How is what you did any different than when I have dealt the final blow to soldiers, enemy and ally alike, already dying an agonising and slow death on the battlefield? Death is a part of this life, *mikrós asvós*, even to those we consider immortals. It hunts us down and strikes when we least expect it; we do not always get to choose how or when. You gave Sophie the gift of a painless end and even as we speak, her soul flies to Elysium. I know it!" He pulled me to him, cupping the back of my head as I buried my face in his shoulder. "It was a mercy, my love," he whispered against my hair. "I have killed thousands in cold blood. I have slain even more to protect what is mine. Immortality. Fears. Me! There is a monster that lurks within me, within every person who has known bloodshed. Who has taken a life. I know the difference. Whatever sins you think you have committed, what you did tonight should not be counted among them. You are stronger than this. Do not let this break you."

I shook my head. "But it did, Alcaeus. This did. I feel myself cracking in the face of my actions."

"It shook you, but it did not break you. For if it did, I doubt we would all be here."

I pulled away from him then, studying his face with apprehension. Did he know? Did he know what I was?

"What...? What do you mean?"

"Do not look at me like that, my love," Alcaeus tucked my hair behind my ear. "We both know you are far more powerful than any Alchemist that has ever walked the realms. Why that is, I do not know. For now, know that you are not alone in this. I wish I could tell you that this is the worst side of Ragna, but I cannot. She is only just beginning. So, see this for what it was: another ploy to crack the great Alchemist. Until the truth behind your abilities is revealed, the queen will not stop her crusade." Silence fell between us. "If... if you would just tell me, Melisandre, I could—" began Alcaeus but I cut him off.

"No. I can't. You know I can't."

He let out a frustrated growl. "But you can! You can trust me, Melisandre!"

Done being pushed, I snapped, "What about you, Alcaeus? How am I to believe the legends are true—that you are the most 'legendary' warrior the worlds have ever seen' when, truly, you are nothing but a dog on a leash? The queen calls and you come! She commands you to sit and you obey!" He jerked away from me, shock all over his face before anger filled the lines. But I didn't stop. I could not. "What the hell is stopping you?" My voice began to rise until I was shouting. "How long does Ragna have to continue torturing me, take everything away from me, until you fucking. DO. SOMETHING?!"

Alcaeus took another step back and he stiffened, his face becoming stone. Closing his eyes, he took a long inhale. Then he looked back at me. His body language gave nothing away. The wall that now stood between us was impenetrable.

Finally, he said, "Remember, Melisandre—it was a mercy. You did not break. She can never break you." He turned away from me, but then turned his head in my direction. "Goodnight, *mikrós asvós*." Then he vanished.

I blinked, my mouth open. He didn't answer me. Hurt and betrayal crept into my heart. I shook my head, no longer having the mental power to think about it. Looking down at myself, my shredded clothes, I couldn't stand to be in them for a minute more.

∀∇ ♂ ⚉ ♂ °♭

After a hot bath and some fresh clothing, I made my way over to the hearth, noticing the gift Elis had given me. Laying in one of the cushioned chairs was the violin. Running my fingers down the case, I realised I could do one last thing for Sophie.

The violin was light and gleaming as I removed it from its case. After tuning it, I walked back out to the balcony where the moon lit up the space. Resting the instrument on my shoulder, I angled the bow on the strings.

Then I began to play a requiem.

The haunting melody swam around me, and I let my heart take over. My grief and sorrow were in every note, my anger and bitterness in each pull of the bow. All those turbulent feelings coloured the music as it rang out into the night.

By the time the song had come to a finish, my fingertips were protesting but I refused to stop; my heart demanded more. I decided that I would play another that embodied the sweet child I had known. A gentle and sweet tune, happy in its tempo began to fill the air. One that mimicked her tinkling laughter.

Just then, the sound of a piano in my head followed along with my violin. I almost stopped. Alcaeus was playing with me. Tears gathered in my eyes but I didn't let them fall.

While I felt hollow with grief, my anger and hurt by this man still very present, the sweetness of his actions warmed me with this peace offering. I focused on that instead. We were in perfect harmony as the rich resonance of his keys danced with the trill of the violin. That night we played together, with only the moon, the stars, and each other as our audience. Sharing the musical story of innocence and youth; of joy and friendship.

We played the tale of Sophie.

CHAPTER 25

"This is why I didn't want to teach you! You're too idealistic! Too arrogant! As if the very laws the Mother put down do not apply to you!"

"Please, Master Kian! Hear me out! I really think I'm on to something! This could work!"

My master slammed his cane down on the table of his workshop, the sudden sound making me flinch.

"That is enough, Melisandre! I'll not have this blasphemous talk in my home any longer! Get out!"

His gnarled finger pointed at the door, the finality of his anger leaving no room for argument. I sighed and my shoulders slumped in defeat as I turned towards the door.

"LOOK OUT!"

Swinging back around, my master was pointing straight at me.

"Master?"

Pain so sharp it stole my breath and seared through my abdomen. I looked down as blood began spreading across my rough spun shirt.

Snapping my eyes open, my body was already in motion, my hands wrapped tightly around the wrist holding the blade that was sunk deep into the right side of my stomach. I couldn't see who my attacker was in the darkness, but dreadful recognition cut through the pain when he spoke.

"This is for taking away what was rightfully mine! Tonight," he twisted the blade, and I screamed through clenched teeth, "is your last!"

My runes lit up as I transmuted the dagger, breaking the blade at the hilt. Lord Cyto lost his balance, and I placed both feet at his solar plexus, my kick sending him flying away. I rolled off the side of the bed, trying to get to the door. The Vampire was on me then, clawing at my throat. I punched him hard enough to hear a crack but with a hand suddenly wrapped around my neck, he threw me into the wall next to the hearth. I landed with a smack, breaking the low-hanging planter that hung there.

Soil spilled on me, and I coughed and groaned, my back and ribs screaming from the impact. My mouth salivated from the pain in my stomach as white streaks filled my vision. With a Vampire's speed, he was before me, sending a right hook plummeting toward my face. I tried to block it, but he still clipped my chin and my head snapped sideways. I saw stars. I also saw charcoal and soot, which gave me an idea.

Shoving him violently away, I scooted next to the cold hearth. Grabbing handfuls of soil, I threw it in. Cyto grabbed me by the hair and slammed my face down onto the marble. I tasted blood. The Vampire used his leverage to straddle me, his hands coming around my neck once again and this time he squeezed so hard, my eyes felt like they were going to pop right out of my head.

Pressing a hand to my bleeding abdomen so I could cover it in my blood, I then began reaching for the iron stand of fireplace tools, knocking them into the hearth. My other hand grabbed at Cyto's wrists. My main rune lit up as I sent a surge of electricity through him. He stiffened, his shoulders nearly hitting his ears. The smell of burning skin filled my nostrils and he cried out, stumbling away.

Coughing and gulping heaps of air, I turned around and put my hands in the fireplace. With a flash of light, iron, charcoal, sulphur, saltpetre, the steel still in my stomach, and several other elements came together.

Just as Cyto was recovering, I whipped around and pointed the loaded single-action revolver in his face. He looked down the barrel at me and smirked.

"You really think that is going to save you from me? Guns do not work on us, you stupid bitch!" He seethed but made no sudden movements.

Blood poured from my now empty wound, and I was beginning to get light-headed from the blood loss. I swayed slightly but I held fast. This opportunity would not go to waste.

"Human guns don't, no. A gun made by an Alchemist? I suppose we're about to find out."

He moved just a hair. I shot him. Cyto screamed. Blood and flesh spewed from the gaping hole where his shoulder used to be. His arm was dangling by a thread of tissue and ligaments. I was initially aiming for his heart but missed but... we'll keep that between us.

Grabbing his ruined appendage, he fell to his knees.

"You fucking cunt! Those bullets... what magic have you infused them in?!"

"No," I said, looking at the gun in my hand happily, "not magic. Alchemy. Or, for the slower ones–science. The bullets themselves have alchemical runes on them which react to your own body's elements. The bullets are, in essence, projectile transmutation circles. All living creatures are made of the same things, just different measurements. It was just a theory, but it looks like it worked explosively well!"

Chuckling with the coldness of vengeance, I dropped in front of the Vampire. I sank my hand into the ruined flesh, digging deeply. He screamed and went to shove me away, but I stuck the gun straight against his genitals. The Vampire froze, eyes widening in horror as I cocked the hammer back.

"You know, I am known to be a rather horrific shot; however, this one," I said casually, "I have no intention of missing." Then my voice dropped to a whisper as I went nose to nose with him. "This is for Sophie." I pulled the trigger. He jerked back, letting out an ear-piercing scream that probably woke the whole castle.

I didn't care.

Cyto writhed and shook on the floor, sobbing and moaning. I sat back and observed for a moment, watching my justice unfold. He tried to sit up, but I rose and shoved him back down with my foot.

I kept him pinned like that as he raised his head and spit, "This is far from over! The queen will end you! I am one of her favourite torturers! She will not let you go unpunished! You will suffer at the hands of the Dauði Dróttning herself!"

I cocked my head at him.

"Your biggest mistake was thinking that the queen is the most powerful person in this castle. She is not. Do you know who it is? Ah, you do." I smiled at his look of realisation, but my face held no humour. "You will not have a chance to kill me or hurt anyone ever again. Tonight, the demons will feast on whatever is left of you. Lord Cyto, your life," I cocked the hammer back for the last time, "is mine." With that, I pointed the gun at his head and squeezed the trigger.

I did not miss.

His head exploded, spraying blood, bones, and brains. My ears still ringing, I stumbled over to the bathroom, reaching the tub before I collapsed against it. Gritting my teeth, I placed a hand over the wound and a transmutation circle appeared. Miraculously, he didn't hit anything vital. Not that it mattered. With a hiss, I activated it, cauterising the wound. My body bowed at the pain as I screamed through a closed mouth. Eyes rolling, I slumped back against the copper bathtub.

As if someone had stuffed cotton in my ears, I could hear muffled voices in the distance.

"MELISANDRE! WHERE ARE YOU? MELIS-" the door burst open, and Alcaeus appeared. His eyes widened as he took in the bloody mess I undoubtedly was.

"Took your damned time," I coughed. "I thought this Mark was supposed to alert you or something. I couldn't even feel you in my head. Are our rooms not close to each-"

"Athena save us, you are injured!" Alcaeus rushed over and ripped my night shirt off and away, letting it drop to the floor in a wet heap. Reflexive modesty had me covering my breasts, but he pulled my arms apart.

"Alcaeus! I'm fi—"

"Shh, let me see." When he saw the cauterised stab wound, the bruising and swelling on my face and neck, his face fell into a fury and all the lines in his body went taut. He gently grazed the angry pink scar with his thumb.

"I'm alright, Alcaeus. He didn't stab anything important. I'm mostly healed, just sore. Most of the blood is his," I said in an effort to reassure him.

The soldier with the scarred face I'd seen in his study, appeared in the doorway. I went to cover myself again, but Alcaeus moved his body so that he completely blocked me from view.

"Sire, Lord Cyto—"

"Got exactly what he deserved. Had I gotten to him first, not even Hades could have kept his soul from me!" he roared. For the first time, I felt like I was seeing the gladiator that was Alcaeus Pallas. Knuckles white, jaw muscles flexing furiously, it was truly a sight to see him struggle to contain his anger. "Sotiris, have his body removed and burned in the courtyard. Let it be a reminder to all those who cross my Alchemist and try to take what is mine."

"Yes, Sire."

Alcaeus shifted and I saw the tall, hooded creature they called Cillian, appear. Then it spoke.

"Sire, I have finished unravelling the final spells," it said, voice deep but haunting, "this is not the work of the Vampire Master alone. Ilirhun's essence was present in the deafening spell and the psychic entrapment spell. That is why you could not reach her. I will re-work the spells and add a few runes that will alert you personally if someone tries to enter without permission."

"Thank you, Cillian. Do what you can."

The hooded figure vanished. Alcaeus turned on the shower and removed his shirt, leaving him only in black breeches.

"Hold on to me."

Lifting me up, he walked straight under the rain of water. He placed my feet down but held a firm arm around me so I wouldn't fall. Fingers threaded through the strands of my hair. I stared at his chest, unseeing. My mind was blank, and I felt nothing. I didn't have to look to know the water ran red as it flowed down the drain.

Touch felt good and I rested my head against his pecs as he continued to wash the blood and Vampire brain bits off me. The beat of his heart lulled me into a sense of peace. That calling I felt still tugged at me but being this close seemed to satisfy it.

"Thank you." My voice was soft enough I wondered if he'd heard me.

When Alcaeus didn't respond, I glanced up at him. His face was raw for once, the lines filled with anger and contrition. But when my head leaned back fully, his eyes met mine and a tender sadness filled them.

"This should never have happened," he whispered. "You are under my protection—"

"Shh, stop Alcaeus," I interrupted. "Do not blame yourself. You said it once; what the queen wants, the queen gets. Her subjects will continue to grow bolder. We just have to grow smarter." My words had the impact I was hoping for when the sadness lifted from his face.

Alcaeus studied me seriously, like he was putting my face to memory. "And here I thought I was the Champion created from the goddess of wisdom," he teased as his lips inched closer to mine.

"Perhaps I am merely taking a page out of your book, Prince of Nightmares," I replied just as warm lips met mine. The kiss was deep and soulful and it consumed me.

Ada's voice cut through the sound of rushing water and we reluctantly broke away. "I sent her things over to the residence as you've commanded, Your Highness. Horses are ready to go as well!"

"Thank you, Ada. That will be all."

She bobbed a curtsy but quickly looked back at me hesitantly. I gave her a small smile, indicating I was okay. She left, closing the door behind her.

"Where are we going?" I asked quietly as Alcaeus shut off the shower.

"Somewhere we can have a reprieve from the queen and her machinations, even for a moment."

"But Toby? Elis? Llyr? Will they meet us there?"

"No, they will remain here." Alcaeus shook his head at my attempted interruption, softly but firmly saying, "I have already commanded Sotiris and Cillian to keep watch over them personally while we are away. Toby is safe for now, so be at peace."

I was too weary to press him further. We dried off and dressed in the bathroom. Walking right past the servants cleaning the bedroom, Alcaeus led me to the outer balcony from my living room.

He jumped up on the ledge and let out a low whistle. For a moment, nothing happened.

Suddenly, a brilliant white Pegasus soared past, his coat and feathers gleaming in the moonlight. It swung around in a small arc until it hovered next to the railing. Saddled and ready, the flying horse waited patiently as Alcaeus climbed on. Then I heard a cry only a kelpie could make and looked to see my beautiful Zephyr flying above.

Alcaeus nudged his horse away so Zephyr could take his place. Climbing on, joy filled my heart as I hugged his neck.

"Oh, I've missed you, you big oaf! My boy!" I kissed his mane and gave him scratches to which he made happy noises.

"Come," Alcaeus said, "We must go now before anyone can stop us. Fly close; we can avoid any wyverns milling about, but we must stick together."

Without waiting for my response, the prince commanded his Pegasus into the skies, and Zephyr and I quickly followed behind.

∇∇♂⚫♂♌

We managed to avoid any wyverns or griffins. At one point, I finally succumbed to all that had happened, and I began to nod off. Alcaeus had then flown beside me, despite my loud protesting, snatching me right off my saddle, and promptly deposited me sideways on his lap.

With the winds blowing gently past us, the warmth and strength of him gave me a quiet peace.

"Sleep, mikrós asvós, you are safe in my arms. I will not let you go." Was what he had said to ease my slight panic. Exhaustion finally claimed me, my head tucked against his chest as one strong arm wrapped securely around my middle. My slumber was disturbed when we made the descent into the thick copse of trees below.

I was dimly aware of him carrying me into a small house or cottage, but sleep overtook me once more.

A. R. Morgan

CHAPTER 26

The chirp of crickets and the hoot of an owl broke me from sleep's clutches. The feel of warmth and soft skin teased my consciousness as I slowly began to wake and I pressed my face firmly into it. Cracking my eyes open, my arm was flung across Alcaeus's middle, and my face pressed against his lower ribs. A warm hand was pressed against my back, fingers occasionally making small, lazy circles on my skin. The bed was unfamiliar, and the sheets smelled fresh, if slightly unused. Pulling my arm back towards my chest, I brushed something hot and hard. Both of us were very, very naked.

"Καλημέρα, *mikrós asvós.*" Alcaeus's voice had that sexy gruffness that men do when they first awaken.

I lifted my head, causing the sheet to rise and with it, revealing a very hard cock that rested against his belly.

"Good morning to you too. Is that for me or is it a false alarm?" I asked, feeling his grin despite the fact I'm still buried under the sheets.

"He is always for you. Why—Ah, I see. That seems to be a distinctly human issue," he said. In one motion, hands grabbed me, sliding me up and out of the blankets. Alcaeus was above me, arms caging me in as his hair tickled the side of my face. "Do I look human to you?" Smile predatory, his jaw opened to display those deadly long, white fangs. Then ever so slowly, he leaned down and nuzzled my neck, pushing my face to the side. Gently, those sharp points grazed the delicate skin there without piercing it.

Maybe it was the fact that he could, or the primal instinct to submit to this dominant male in all the sensual ways, to be conquered by him, that had a fire exploding through my veins.

I gasped.

Alcaeus pressed against me with his weight as hands hooked underneath my knees to bring them upward. The width of him forced my

251

hips wide as my legs came up to accommodate. The hard length of him nearly bruised my core as he pressed against me. I loved every bit of the discomfort. My arms slid up his sides as he pulled away enough for me to look at him, travelling up to his shoulders until my fingers threaded through his thick hair.

"To be fair, I've only ever really known human men... in that way."

Despite my hold on him, he leaned down so our noses grazed.

"Then let me be the one to enlighten you on the benefits of having a Champion Vampire as your lover." He whispered, lining up the tip of his cock and thrusting into my wet channel. Not all sex needed foreplay; granted, the way he played my mind, I was already desperate to have him inside me.

I gasped and Alcaeus plunged his tongue into my mouth as he pressed his hips as deep as he could go. He stopped, unmoving.

"You're perfect," he whispered, studying my face.

I reached up and cupped his own handsome visage and one of his hands covered mine. Tenderness filled me and I wanted to live in that moment forever. This moment where we were one with each other. My resolve against this bond we had was cracking at an alarming rate and for the life of me, I couldn't be bothered to resist any more.

So overcome with a foreign hope that I'd never allowed myself to entertain, words were impossible. So, I kissed him, channelling all my feelings into it. Alcaeus responded with equal amounts of passion and fervour.

He began to move then, slowly drawing out until just the tip hovered in my entrance and then shoving forward, rendering me breathless each time. Reaching down, he grabbed my breast firmly, palming it with his entire hand before taking my nipple between his index finger and thumb. Rolling it, pinching it, he grazed over the sensitive tip. Tension began to build within me, but I needed more from him to get there.

"Please," I moaned as I slid my hands past his lower back while lifting my hips, pleading. His long torso made it a reach, and my breathing hitched when my actions pushed him deeper.

"No, *mikrós asvós*, I am going to take my time this morning. Right now, it is just you and me. Just us. So, I am going to enjoy every," thrust, "single," thrust, "moment." Alcaeus suddenly pulled out and flipped me over. His large body covered mine and I moaned into the pillow as his cock filled me. A large hand cupped my face to the side, and he kissed me, tongue mimicking every slow but hard thrust until my cries rose in his mouth. Pulling away, Alcaeus took that opportunity to kiss and nibble on my shoulder. My body was wound tight yet still, I needed more.

"More! Alcaeus more!" I begged. The feel of his smile against my skin sent a thrill through me.

Roughly, he shoved my head down on the mattress but pushed my hips up, ass in the air. Hot breath tickled my ear as he leaned down and whispered, "I think my little Alchemist likes it a bit rough in bed. But how far can she go? Let us test those limits."

He shoved himself back in violently, and a deep moan erupted from me. Rotating his hips in such a way his cock massaged every angle deep inside of me. My moans turned guttural. He continued that agonisingly slow but hard pace until he had me wailing out in frustration. I needed a fast, punishing rhythm. My orgasm teased me. I shoved back on him, trying to take control. That invoked a deep chuckle from him, his large hot hand sliding up my spine. Strong fingers gripped my scalp and yanked my head back. The pleasure-pain that shot through me almost sent me over the edge.

"My impatient little Alchemist," he growled in my ear. "I will give you what you want but you will scream for me. Scream my name, Melisandre!" Alcaeus began to move faster, shoving my head into the pillows. Setting a brutal pace that had me clawing at the sheets, but his hand held me down firmly.

Just as I was about to come, he slowed almost to a stop. I tried to thrust my hips back again, but he pressed down on me, his weight holding me still. As my orgasm slowly began to slip away, he started thrusting again. He edged me over and over like this until I became a begging and pleading mess. This time, he went harder, giving me every bit of that punishing pace I screamed for. My orgasm hit me like a freight train. Just as he demanded—I screamed his name.

▽▽♂⚬♂♄

There I was, being wrapped up in the warmth of him, my limbs jelly. Never in my life had I felt so complete. My heart wanted so badly to enjoy it, but the events of the previous night began crawling back into the recesses of my mind. Guilt. Shame. Anger. Grief.

Alcaeus felt the change in me and the arm that was wrapped around me, fingers trailing my skin, stilled. It was a bit irritating how in tune he seemed to be with my moods and it was entirely foreign to me. Elis was a nosy busybody but it was easy enough to deflect and distract him. I had no such tools with the Consort and something told me it would be futile anyway.

I pushed away, making a move to stand. He didn't stop me. The room was dark, save for the fire Alcaeus had started earlier. Walking to the oak wardrobe, I opened it to find some of my clothes hanging up next to his. I grabbed the silk black robe hanging there.

"Pray tell, what makes my little badger so sombre?" Alcaeus asked gently as he sat up, resting against the headboard. The way his arm casually held onto the back of it, the firelight dancing across his muscled chest almost tempted me back to bed. Swallowing hard, I tore my gaze away.

Tying the sash of the robe slowly, I hesitated a moment, resting my hands on the oak doors of the wardrobe. We had to talk. There was so much we needed to discuss. But where to start? It was imperative we addressed these issues, but I wanted to make sure we would. That required a tactful start.

My body turned slowly as I crossed my arms, leaning my back against the furniture.

"You never answered me that night," I began. "The night Sophie died. Instead, you left me with more questions. So far, my entire stay has been filled with nothing but infuriating mysteries. Even the answers only leave more questions. This isn't going to work if we continue this way. You know it. I know it. So, please, talk to me. Tell me. Why have you been so passive against Ragna?"

Jaw clenching, he looked away and then quickly left the bed. Grabbing a pair of trousers, he slipped them on. "Not all knowledge is for you to know, Melisandre."

My eyebrow curved upwards. "That is the last thing you should say to an Alchemist, prince. You call me 'little badger' but how little you seem to realise how apt that is. Nothing will stop me from digging for the truth, no matter the cost. Knowledge is my strength, obtaining it is my forte. Keeping an Alchemist ignorant is a very dangerous and an inevitably futile thing to do."

Running an agitated hand through his hair, he gave a sharp breath through his nose. Not looking at me, Alcaeus went to stand by the window, staring out into the darkness. His jaw ticked, shoulders tense. I couldn't tell if he was considering whether to tell me or trying to find another way to avoid the conversation. I certainly wouldn't allow the latter. But my temper would be ill served here.

Easy does it, Mel. Implore him.

"Alcaeus, please. You yourself expressed how important it was that we trust each other. That we be open to building it." The silence between us remained so I attempted to become even more vulnerable. "Sophie," I said, my voice cracking, "is dead. Because of me. Mercy or no, her only crime was being a recipient of my affection. Toby hates me and is forever changed. Who else do I have to lose before Athena's Champion decides to do something about it?"

His head snapped to me, and he stared at me long and hard. Then he went back to the window. Anger flared within me at his continued silence. I pushed off the wardrobe, taking a step towards him to further confront him. What he said next stopped me in my tracks, the flame of my anger extinguished.

"I had a wife and son."

Eyebrows raised, I could only reply, "What?"

"Her name was Cressida. She was half Vampire, half Unseelie noble. It was initially a political alliance I had made with the Unseelie King, Ruarc Ó Ceallaigh. Cressida was a hybrid but of a distant cousin to the king; she had no prospects in her own court and it suited Ruarc to give her hand to another Vampire where she could be safe from the prejudices of the Fae. So, the marriage took place secretly, binding our two kingdoms.

"Now, I am sure you are aware of the old gods' disappearance after The Great Battle, scurrying back from whence they came, presumably. Our purpose as their puppets of war was no longer needed. After a time of chaos and turmoil, the Champions eventually claimed their own territories and created their own nations. While many were content to rule within the boundaries of their own lands, Ragna was not. She had always been ambitious and a force to be reckoned with, even in the Megálo Kolossaío, where the Divine Games took place. No one could prepare for the extent of her thirst for power, however. Ragna had one goal– uniting the Vampire Champions under her rule.

"She began what is now known as The Conquering of the Twelve Kingdoms. She became known as the Dauði Dróttning, or Death

Queen. With the slain, so her army grew as she raised the dead to fill the ranks. She became unstoppable.

"When the news reached me that she defeated Ansanbosam, Champion of the trickster god Anansi, the need for allies and a larger army became imperative. Thus, the reason I married Cressida. What I didn't realise was that Ragna was saving my kingdom for last; the kingdom she wanted most. I had been so sure her plans for my kingdom were imminent."

I remained unmoving, entranced with Alcaeus' tale.

"But years went by with not a sword swinging my way. News had come that Ragna's armies had gone quiet after the eleventh kingdom fell. That she had returned to Idrisid, much to everyone's shock. Although I was wary, it came as no surprise to me that she would hesitate at attacking my borders; I had strategically picked my lands to give my kingdom the best advantage if war was ever at our gates. At my full strength, I had beaten Ragna several times in the games. She knew she would lose fighting me in my own territory even with her army of rotting corpses.

"Suspicion grew and for several years, our spies and scouts worked endlessly to unearth her plans. They found nothing. Eventually, so much time went by that we had been lulled into a sense of peace; we were still wary, yes, but she did nothing to cause concern. During this time, we had our son," Alcaeus paused, the last word clearly difficult. Drawing a deep breath, his Adam's apple bobbed as he swallowed hard. "Aleksei."

I carefully made my way towards the bed, easing down onto the mattress. I kept silent, wanting him to continue but not wanting to rush him.

"By the time Aleksei was seven, the concern of an invasion had been put in the back of our minds. All was silent in her kingdom of Khaviel, much to our relief. Now, I had respected my wife and cared for her deeply, but we were neither fated nor chosen mates; we never marked each other. My son, however," Alcaeus's face filled with a soft gentleness, the nostalgia clear on his features, "was the light of my life. Never had I felt so blessed by the gods. He had his mother's eyes and her smile, but he had my love of learning and my passion for strategy." The small amount of joy in his tone gave way to sorrow and regret. "Yet, my folly in believing in that false sense of peace ended up taking everything from me." I could see his reflection in the mirror, the way his eyes squeezed shut, the sharp lines, the muscles of his jaw ticking with tension.

"They came during the day, while the kingdom slept. Hundreds of thousands died. Even more fled. You see, the queen had become more powerful than I had imagined; powers like controlling her dead armies from afar, an ability she had not been given by the goddess Hel. They were not impeded by the sun, or any other limitations Vampires have. Ragna had managed to ally herself with Mage Ilirhun, whom you have met, one of the greatest sorcerers to ever walk our realms. Her powers had grown through the black magic he provided." Alcaeus nearly spit as if the mage's name was poisonous. "When the city gates were breached, I sent my wife and son away, into hiding." He paused, muscles bunching around his shoulders as his breathing increased.

You could see the beginnings of pent-up rage seeping through his posture. Suddenly, Alcaeus snapped and slammed his fist into the windowpane above him. "We were betrayed! To this day, I know not who... They should have been safe!" Taking a moment to get a handle on himself, he rested his head on his clenched hand. "I slew... thousands of her thralls, but as soon as one wave went down, another replaced it. They just kept coming. Ruarc's own forces were still on the way but they were too late. I was forced to retreat into the castle, but I never stopped fighting. Not even when I was the only one left standing from either side. Sotiris had been gravely injured; the rest of my men slaughtered. My sword would have sucked the very life out of Ragna if she hadn't walked into the throne room, dragging my wife and son behind in chains." Clenching his eyes shut again, the pain and agony so clear, my own eyes misted over.

"When...when I refused to surrender, she slashed Cressida's throat and swallowed her soul. Then she took my son in her vile hands, demanding I surrender myself to her. For the sake of my son, I did. For the first time in my life, I relinquished my sword. With blood magic, Ilirhun had me bound. Bound so I... I couldn't protect my son when Ragna snapped his neck and proceeded to tear his soul out from his little, defenceless body. My Aleksei," he said brokenly, "Never again will I feel his little hand in mine. Never will they know peace and joy in the fields of Elysium."

Hearing the gruesome details of his tragedy, I covered my mouth in horror. Sorrow filled me with the tale of his loss. It was all beginning to make sense; his hatred for her, how he refused to touch her. Why he had delayed consummating the marriage for so long. Yet, it did not answer my original question.

Alcaeus was a warrior, a Champion, one who would not appreciate pity, so I gave him none.

"My heart breaks for your loss, Alcaeus. I knew Ragna was truly a creature of nightmares, but the depth of her evil continues to know no bounds. I know you do not want my pity nor was I going to offer it, but you have my deepest empathy. But..." I took a deep breath. "It does not answer my question of what she has on you, why you seem to bend to her will; especially after all that she has done to you. What more could you have left when she's taken everything?" I asked, trying to say it gently, but I knew it pushed him.

His face twisted in rage and agony.

"After murdering my son, she cut off my wings. Being bound I could do nothing. Then, she placed her hand over my heart, cutting symbols into my chest with her own fingernail. Pain, like I had never known, exploded through me as she severed it in half."

I shook my head, trying to understand. "Wings? What do you mean severed? I don't understand."

He turned to me then, his hopelessness and grief stealing my breath away. Alcaeus's next words pierced through me, and I felt like the proverbial rug had been yanked from under me.

"She took my soul, Melisandre."

CHAPTER 27

"W-what? How...?" It felt as if Zephyr kicked me straight in the gut. I could barely get the words out as I slowly got to my feet. "How is that possible? How are you still alive?"

Alcaeus looked down, placing a large hand on his broad chest. The fingers there curled into a fist as he shook his head slowly. Strands of burnt amber locks fell across his anguished face, fury in every line. "All I know is she somehow severed half of my soul. She had it encapsulated, and it stays with her at all times. So," he cleared his throat, his voice hollow. "The man that stands before you is but half a man. Therefore, I am unable to go against her. She controls part of me. I am but a fucking puppet!" He flung his arms out and roared, his vengeance so palpable that goosebumps raced across my skin.

A weaker woman would have bolted from the room, his rage so great that it demanded cowering. Breath heaving, muscles so strained that veins popped, his attention snapped back to me.

"Over a thousand years, Melisandre, I have tried to retrieve the other half of my soul. I have tried everything. Many loyal lives were lost in vain to see me restored. All have failed. For a thousand years, I. Have. Failed!" The brokenness and rage that dripped in his voice had me reeling.

I had only been at the mercy of the queen for several weeks; it was unfathomable to have to endure her for over a thousand years. I ached for him, without a doubt. Perhaps if I were a meeker woman, I would have stopped the conversation there. As it was, I was so very close to wanting to hide away for as long as we could and try to help mend this brokenness in front of me.

Swallowing hard, my mind raced. Questions, ideas, solutions, and doubts were a chaotic cloud threatening to swallow me. So much of me wanted to go to him, comfort him, grieve with him. All of me wanted answers, a plan of action. A way to free him. To free us. A terrible thought stopped me.

"I'm sorry, Alcaeus... metaphysics isn't something I'm well-versed in. So... at any point, can she..." It was so upsetting that I couldn't finish. As if there were an apple piece lodged in my throat, I could barely swallow past the grief at his display of emotion.

"Yes. I suspect she could. Even with half my soul still inside me, I'd be trapped forever, my flesh under her command, the essence of me buried underneath the thrall she replaces me with. So much of what she does was forbidden when the gods were still in power here, but now that they're gone... Ragna is free to exert her madness," he spat, but his posture eased as he began to regain his normally stoic and graceful composure.

I tried to imagine this man gone from me forever. This beautiful and lethal Vampire. It should have been easy; loss was no stranger to me. Solitude was my habitat. But a sharp pain shot through my chest, clawing at my heart. Squeezing my eyes tight, I shook my head, my hands threading up through my hair and fisting it in an attempt to dispel the darkness of that thought. Somehow, in such a short amount of time, the Prince of the Nightmare Court had become something far dearer to me than any other lover I'd had. Alcaeus was before me in a flash, wrapping me up in his massive arms.

"But she won't, my love, she will not. Heed me: I am far too valuable to Ragna. She has desired me as her chosen mate for centuries. I am what she wants. Even as a thrall, she would only be getting a shell of a man. You cannot force a mating bond if you are already bonded to another."

"Well, I won't let that happen. She can't have you. I won't let her!" The look of surprise at my outburst on his face matched my own.

Instinctively, I pull away and cleared my throat, trying to put space between myself and my embarrassing display of attachment. Alcaeus's arms tightened, keeping me from retreating.

Lifting my chin up to meet his gaze, he studied my face before saying, "I am yours. Always. Never doubt that."

A knot formed in my chest, and I blinked rapidly. The situation was so intimate I was unprepared for the feeling of vulnerability.

When did this happen? When did we become this close?

Thankfully my stomach saved me by growling so loudly that both our eyes went wide as saucers.

The Nightmare Prince let out a shout of laughter. "Come. The weight of this conversation has stoked both of our hunger. I had the kitchen restocked before we came here. These lands are rich with game as well. Do you enjoy hunting?"

I snorted. "Only for information, as it were. I'm much more inclined to grow my food. I enjoy meat as much as anyone, though. I'm quite the proficient trapper should the need arise. Although, I am partial to fishing."

"Then I look forward to seeing your provisional skills. There is a river nearby where the salmon are known to run."

We headed to the kitchen which I found to be quaint and rather adorable. With a small cast iron stove, large tin basin, wooden counters, and no running water. Alcaeus went out to the well nearby to water and care for our mounts. I decided to have a look at what we had to work with food-wise. It was indeed fully stocked and, much to my delight, was filled with spices, oils, vinegars, and other dressings. In another cupboard were loaves of several different types of breads and baked goods.

I began pulling out cheeses, nuts, fruits, and some olives. A few dried and smoked meats, as well. Slicing up one of the loaves, I took a bowl and filled it with olive oil and balsamic vinegar for dipping. Something told me Alcaeus would appreciate that.

The man in question came back in with a bucket of water for washing and placed it next to the basin. My perpetual frown resumed its place at the sight of it.

"Honestly, Alcaeus, plumbing is a thing now. It wouldn't be that difficult to install it here. You Otherworld creatures' aversion to growing technology is most inconvenient."

He grinned. "It's been almost two-hundred fifty years since I have been back here. Besides, perhaps it is nice to go back to simpler times. Manual labour builds character."

"By all means, feel free to wipe yourself with banana leaves. I, on the other hand, am going to try to find some copper once we've finished eating," I declared, my hand waving to the assortment of food.

The prince raised an eyebrow at this, but then understood and an answering smile crossed his face. "I shall come with. I am eager to see more of the powers of a true-born Alchemist." Taking in the array, we sat and dug in.

There were a lot of embarrassing moments of affection; touching, sly glances, feeding one another. Although, eventually, I did attempt to bite his fingers when my shame could take no more. His laughter nearly shook the roof but after the second time, when my teeth scraped his skin, I made the unfortunate discovery that my biting him stoked the fires of his lust. Let's just say there ended up being more cleanup than just food.

Once recovered, I made true my word of hunting down some copper. Walking outside, the rising suns gave a warm orange glow to the foliage around us. Huge cedar trees surrounded us, the grass a rich green. The smell was lovely; fresh with jasmine filling the air. Asking where the well was, Alcaeus led me to it.

Kneeling, I closed my eyes as my fingers dug into the earth. The elements sang their song to me, and I sifted through their notes.

Magnesium... Silicon... Potassium... Aluminium... Iron... I pushed my senses farther, past the first layer. Sedimentary rock, where are you... Ah! I found you. Grinning at my discovery, there was a pleasing amount of copper ore sitting amongst the sand and mud.

Next, I searched for a stream, or the river Alcaeus referred to. Reaching out with my mind's eye, I sought out the moving hydrogen. Yes, there, about four hundred metres from me was a river. Wonderful.

Getting to my feet, I placed myself at the middle point between the cottage and the well. A transmutation circle with symbols that bound the copper ore below, appeared at my feet. Raising my right hand towards the house, another circle appeared above it. Lifting my left hand, a circle activated above the well. Feeling the energy within them, I adjusted each one ever so slightly until the algorithm was perfect. Without seeing, I knew circles also formed the pathway from the house to the river.

"A little more...yes, yes that's it," I muttered.

With a bright flash and a snap, pipes, water heater, and septic tank formed into place. The cottage jolted with the change and a cloud of dust burst from it. I opened my eyes to find Alcaeus grinning in wonder.

Delight at his reaction bubbled within but shyness overtook me. "Are you always so easily impressed?" I teased.

"When it comes to you, my dear, there are no limits to my fascination."

Blushing, I brushed my hands off. "This was nothing. Most adolescent Alchemists could have done this. Though, it would take more people."

He shook his head. "Nonetheless, it is incredible, isn't it? No other creature can do what you can do, the way you do it, and that is what makes it spectacular. Alchemy makes magic appear cheap in comparison."

"Can't argue with that," I replied, grinning.

Inwardly I warmed at the praise. Everyone was always so impressed with magic and it always seemed to overshadow alchemy. But Alcaeus seemed to see my abilities in a genuine light.

I grabbed his hand, squeezing it in mine as we headed back in to rest.

▽▽ ♂ ☖ ♂ ♄

The next day, Alcaeus went out to hunt while I remained, remodelling the little cottage with the prince's blessing. I was eager for this time alone as I had much to process.

While still grieving poor Sophie, I cringed at the knowledge that I wasn't there for Toby in his own grief. Yet, my presence would have only fuelled his anger and bitterness for my hand in it. Being so young, I could not expect him to understand the sacrifice and the mercy I did for her. Yet, even knowing this, my own guilt still clawed at me. Replaying the scenario a million times in my mind, did not lead to any other realistic outcome. One more precious life to add to the list of all those I had already taken.

Turning on the hot water at my self-made sink, I began washing the dishes. A mundane task, but it gave me something to do while I analysed our next moves.

Ragna would be furious that we left. Alcaeus was taking a large risk, whisking me away outside of the queen's wrath after I killed one of her favourite nobles. It would not be long before she forced either of us back. Escape was not an option, so I didn't even entertain the thought. Elis, Llyr, and Toby were still at her mercy as was Alcaeus. This was but an illusion of a reprieve before reality came crashing down upon us once more. The best I could do was use this time to come to terms with what happened the past week before we returned.

The closeness that was developing between myself and Alcaeus was

263

alarming, and I worried we were reaching the point of no return far faster than either of us anticipated. This almost physical pull was the most mysterious piece of it all and it unnerved me how little control I seemed to have in its presence.

However, I meant what I said—Ragna would not have him. Getting Toby and myself out of this was still my priority. Still, there was no denying that the thought of leaving Alcaeus to his fate was unconscionable, especially if I had the power to do something about it. That was the real question was it not? What could I do? What was I willing to do? How much more blood would be spilled before the terror of the Nightmare Queen's reign would be at its end? Was it possible to somehow regain Alcaeus's soul by means of stealth? Run off into the sunset while she's not looking?

I snorted.

Sighing, I mimicked the voice of my old mentor as I spoke aloud. "To have power but stand idle in the face of evil and unbalance, renders you unworthy of alchemy and is blasphemous to the Mother. Balance is all, Melisandre."

"He sounds like a wise man."

I whipped around and then hissed when my finger caught the soiled knife I was about to wash. Alcaeus was suddenly beside me, a large rough hand encasing my own. Large dots of blood were welling to the surface and sliding down the length. Raising up my hand to the level of his face, he looked down at me and said, "Careful, my love."

He held the look for a moment more before turning his attention to my injured finger. His pink tongue darted out, canines resting on his lower lip as he licked up the blood. I could feel the roughness of his beard as he wrapped his lips around my wound, sucking gently.

I inhaled slightly, my centre growing warm. Slowly, he pulled back, giving a gentle kiss to my now-healed index finger.

As arousing as this encounter was, it was also a painful reminder of something both of us had been neglecting on speaking upon.

"Alcaeus, we'll have to do the second mark soon, won't we?" I asked in a whisper.

"Yes." Was his only reply.

"Will we have to do it while we're here?"

"I think that would be for the best, yes."

I nodded, biting my cheek slightly. Growing concern from the last experience had me frowning and I pulled away. While the first mark was done, that did not mean I was anything less than thrilled about the second. The thought of it had my stomach in knots more than the first; the urge to run, fight, and defend my freedom at all costs was rising quickly within me.

Alcaeus let me go, although he said, "We have some time yet, *mikrós asvós*. We've only just arrived. Plenty of time to discuss what to expect this next time."

Crossing my arms, I looked up at him. "Yes, but how much time do we actually have? I can't imagine the queen won't retaliate. Even as we speak, all those I love are in grave danger from your actions."

"We have a few weeks at most. Ragna will not harm them. Upon my honour, I give you my word they are safe while we are here. She believes I took you away in order to finish the Familiar's Mark. And before you think it," he held his hands up in supplication at my scowl, "That is not the true reason. I wanted to give you respite. To give us the chance to spend time together without her constant scheming." Forcing my face to relax as I shoved my suspicion down, he continued to reassure me. "Zhenbai and Sotiris have things well in hand in my absence. Besides, I am sure you've come to realise she enjoys watching her victims break and she cannot have that pleasure while you're here with me. She desires this ritual to come to fruition above all else at the moment, so she'd be a fool to disrupt the process even now. Take peace in this."

I suspired, turning back to the topic of the second mark. "For now, I guess all we can do is be true to the path that has been set. I have already accepted the inevitable and I know we'll discuss more in due time but let me make this clear: all I ask is that whatever you see, you do not ask. Whatever you might think, don't. I will not negotiate this."

Alcaeus leaned back against the cabinets, cocking his head slightly as he studied my face. If the mood of the conversation weren't so sombre, I'd laugh at how he made the kitchen seem like a broom closet, dwarfing the space with his size. The cottage was certainly made more for someone of my stature and only made Alcaeus all the more imposing.

You could see it in his face how he weighed the situation, my words. I couldn't say for certain if my reply bothered him, as there was only a look of measured consideration.

Finally, he said, "All in due time."

"What do you mean? That answer should have been a simple 'yes',"

I retorted as suspicion rose in my tone. His raised brow only served to light the flame of defensiveness within me.

"You once asked me if I would tell you my deepest secret if you told me yours. I have. So now, it is only fair that you start to do the same. Do you not agree?"

Anger like a wildfire spread through me at the audacity of him. "Only out of willingness! Not out of a twisted sense of transactional fairness," I hissed.

Now it was his turn to display his anger, all in how he straightened, unfurling his arms. "Remember. Your. Words." His voice deepened with authority. "I have been nothing but understanding and patient for you, Melisandre. Yet here you stand, demanding your right to the privacy of your secrets when, just last night, you impressed upon me the importance of revealing mine." Alcaeus' stare bore into me as intensely as the truth of his words rang out.

Humility is and always has been a terrible pill to swallow. Maturity and pettiness warred within me as I clamped my mouth shut. My thoughts raced around my head. I thought about telling him, I really did. But playing that scenario in my head only caused me to clam up, the truth dying an ugly death in my throat.

"I can't. I'm not ready," I replied weakly. At his darkening expression, I quickly said, "You're right. I'm not being fair. But..." My swallow was loud, my words almost sticking to my mouth. "My secrets have never been uttered aloud; to do so would only bring more grief and destruction."

Alcaeus took several steps toward me, closing the distance, and put his hands on my shoulders. "Or it could save us! Show me who you really are. I am here. Unjudging." He looked around, hands going wide. "This place is safe. Please, *mikrós asvós*, let me in. Give me your truths." This time, he placed a hand at my cheek, the other on my upper arm.

Just tell him, I told myself as my eyes searched his. Tell the Prince of Nightmares your sins. My mind went back to that fateful day. The screams of thousands. The agony of millions. The silence of all.

Sheer panic crawled up my throat and, suddenly the room was far too small. Claustrophobia wrapped its ugly hands around my neck and I ripped myself away from Alcaeus.

"No!" I yelled. "No, I can't! I won't!" Resorting to my favourite emotion, I let anger take over. "Fair or not, those are my terms, take it

266

or leave it."

Alcaeus' face was thunderous now.

"Did you ever stop to think, Melisandre," he hissed, "that perhaps by keeping your secrets it has caused far more harm and left you and all those you hold dear exceedingly vulnerable? That maybe had you revealed the truth of what you are and what you're capable of, it would have stayed our enemy's hand? At the very least, telling me could only strengthen our alliance! What else must I do for you to trust me?!"

My jaw dropped and I met Alcaeus's glare with my own. "For being a creation of the wisest goddess, you are a fool to think that, when we both know knowledge is power and in the wrong hands, they would seek to wield it against you! You've already admitted Ragna possesses half of your soul; revealing my hand could also just as much backfire as it could help and that is not a risk I am, at present, willing to take! Take care of your own vulnerabilities before projecting onto mine!"

With that, I stormed out of the kitchen.

"Where are you going?" shouted Alcaeus.

"Out! And don't you dare follow me!" I yelled back.

The fresh air hit me and I inhaled it greedily in an effort to calm the adrenaline coursing through me. Once I was clear of all Vampire presence, I stopped for a moment, taking a minute to breathe in the trees and smells of the forest.

Water had always had a calming effect on me, so I made for the direction of the river. The night was bright as the two moons' light speared through the trees. Unlike the human realm where the night is inky black and the forest lay quiet save for the occasional hoot of an owl or chirping insects, the Otherworld forests were teeming with activity. Plants shone brightly in the darkness, their phosphorescent lights giving off a soft glow, a myriad of unearthly colours meant to attract prey.

I was about halfway to the river, so lost in the replaying of the scene I'd had with Alcaeus, that the snapping of twigs had me stumbling to a stop. Whipping around, my eyes searched hard at the brush and tried to sense any elements that could tell me what was stalking me.

A soft nicker and a short huff told me it was merely Zephyr. A giggle erupted from me at my paranoia. "Come on out Zeph, I know you're there. I've been awfully neglectful of late, haven't I?"

The big hulking beast of a horse gave a happy whinny, and I could hear him make his way towards me, crunching leaves and twigs. He was so dark I could barely make him out. Wings tucked neatly against his back, he nuzzled my hands, and I gave him kisses and scratches. Turning, we made our way closer to the sound of moving water.

CHAPTER 28

As soon as we arrived at the riverbank, Zephyr let out a screech of excitement and stomped into the water. I'd never witnessed him shapeshift into his true kelpie form; I honestly didn't know if he could since his mane dries instead of staying wet, and he didn't have the typical waterweeds intermixed in his hair that a pure Kelpie has. The coal black of his coat, his haunting melody, and being tamed with the bridle were the only indicators of his Kelpie lineage. Only twice have I heard him sing; a beautiful siren's song that drifts across the night in the presence of the full moon. Thankfully children never seemed to be on the menu for him as never once has he tried to harm Toby.

The moons shone bright, reflecting off the moving water. The night was an orchestra of creatures lighting up with the sounds of chirps, calls, and songs. It is when it's quiet that one should be wary. At this moment, however, the forest teemed. The sounds of the river soothed those emotions that chained my rationale. The elements all around me gave me a gentle awareness, calming the spirit of malcontent within me.

I sat at the base of a weeping willow, whose branches almost touched the banks of the river. They flowed gently above and around me, veiling me from anything outside. I loved willows; while all trees were created by the Mother, willows were the favourite among Alchemists for they gave safe haven from prying eyes.

The second Mark had to happen. I understood this. Yet, I couldn't help but wonder if by sealing myself to Alcaeus's half-soul, would I not also be bound to Ragna? Would that not cause us to become more vulnerable? Not only that but after all that I had done, so many years ago... did I still have a soul to bind?

The first bite seemed to work so yes, apparently you do have a soul

269

after all.

Rubbing my temples in frustration, I raised my head to see a very wet Zephyr come plodding towards me. Getting as close as possible without crushing me, he flopped down, successfully spraying water all over me.

"Oi, watch it! You big oaf," I grumbled.

In response, Zephyr let out a loud snort that blew out heavily and began munching on the grass we sat upon. His black eyes glittered, and he stretched his neck to nuzzle me.

I let out a long sigh.

"I...don't know what to do Zeph," I whispered. "All this knowledge and yet not even the 823 years I have been upon this realm could have prepared me for something like this. I liked my life the way it was, I miss it. I am not made for politics, wars, and intrigue let alone.... whatever the hell is going on between Alcaeus and me. Alchemists are just caretakers. Honestly, we're glorified gardeners really." I laughed at the thought and prayed the Mother wouldn't smite me for watering down my purpose.

One thing was for certain—with every passing hour, every minute, every second, the truth of who I was, what I was, was inching closer to the surface. I didn't know how much longer I could keep it in the darkness as I had for so many years. Alcaeus's pressure for my truths was understandably persistent. Was it safe to tell him? Could I trust him with a truth so powerful it would change the tides of fate?

Yes, I could trust him. *If* he was not chained to Ragna. My point I made to him still stands. However, I had to accept the inevitable—I could not hide forever. Perhaps it was time to stop being a pawn and become the master of my own damn ship.

After some time had passed and my thoughts were in order, I made my way back to the cottage with Zephyr. After finding some feed in the shed, I went to find Alcaeus.

The house was empty, dark, and cold. Debating on whether I should wait until he returned or find him myself, I concluded that a midnight walk was in order. Transmuting an oak branch into a walking stick, I tried opening my mind in search of him so that I might have a sense of direction. Nothing.

"Stupid, silly metaphysical nonsense and poppycock," I groused.

Grumbling to myself, I began heading away from the cottage. Forty-five minutes went by and no sign of the prince.

Continuing on, I began foraging a bit when suddenly I felt a tug in my chest; that call. I stopped. It was faint but it was there. Yes, this is what I felt whenever Alcaeus was nearby. The desire to be near him flooded me and I would have slapped myself silly if my original purpose wasn't trying to find him. Following the call, I walked through brush, trees, and thickets until the scenery opened up to a clearing.

The tall grass swayed gently in the breeze, the double moons hovering above, illuminating the area in soft light. The stars glittered like a spattering of paint against the black sky. There, in the middle was Alcaeus, in all his shirtless glory. Black breeches hugged his hips, low enough it displayed his pronounced Adonis belt. All of that chestnut mane was pulled back tightly. Standing preternaturally still, he held Nemesis, the sword glowing in his right hand.

Then he began to move. Like running water, his limbs moved with fluidity and grace. The sword arced and danced as though it was merely an extension of his arm. You could hear it sing as it sliced through the air with every precise movement. Thousands of years of training and discipline could be seen with every flex of muscle, every single step, and the control of stance. It was mesmerising.

I moved closer to watch and my breath caught as he increased his speed. The quick glimpses of his face showed he was calm and serene. This was truly the dance of the sword. Hypnotised, I watched the routine. In that moment I tried to imagine him with the wings he said to have lost; I had no idea what kind they could be but nonetheless, the thought itself made Alcaeus look like a battle angel. Truly, I had never seen someone so beautiful in their own element.

Alcaeus came to a sudden stop, his back to me, snapping me out of my reverie.

"*Mikrós asvós*," he said into the breeze, "you've found me."

Slowly, he turned his head to look at me. We regarded each other silently for a moment, so much to say yet neither of us felt the need to speak. Being in each other's presence was enough.

Alcaeus slowly turned to face me but did not approach.

"I believe I owe you an apology, my lady," he said. "It was never my intention to cause discord between us."

I studied him silently, making no move to respond. Hesitantly, he took a step toward me.

"Melisandre, I will agree to your request that I do not question

271

what I may see but you must understand–You are a powerful being, one so shrouded in mystery that I would be a fool not to be wary of the unknown. What we are doing has never been done before, thus we are attempting this blind. I should think," he paused, visibly choosing his words carefully, "that you most of all would understand that knowledge is our ally in this."

I stayed silent for yet another moment, contemplating my answer. Longing peeked out of Alcaeus's eyes as he studied me.

"Then," I finally replied, "we shall learn together."

Walking closer, I stopped when he was just a short distance away. The prince cocked his head curiously. "So, you will tell me–"

"You said, and I quote, 'in due time'. I agree with that. No more, no less. All will be revealed in due time. That I can agree to."

"But surely—" Before he could continue, I swung the wooden staff towards his head. Instinct took over and he deftly dodged. "Melisandre, what are you—"

I lunged at him again and he parried. I went at him head-on, swinging and thrusting my staff on the offensive, forcing him to give ground. Alcaeus caught on to my desire to spar and he grinned fully when he caught the glint of playfulness in my own eye. I was but a child with a toy, attacking a true warrior but I didn't care in the slightest. We Alchemists were not exactly made for battle but that did not mean I hadn't picked up a thing or two in the last century.

With grace, Alcaeus blocked every attack and parried perfectly, but made no move to put me on the defensive.

"Don't hold back on my account, Nightmare Prince," I teased.

"I would never," he teased, his lie causing us both to grin. "But if my *mikrós asvós* wants to have a go at me, who am I to stop her? I have been aching to know what my little Alchemist is made of."

With that, he parried my next thrust, smacking it away, slicing my poor staff in two. I grinned and my runes lit up as I slammed the staff to the ground, calling the tungsten ore deep below and transmuting it with the carbon and hydrogen in the soil. I gripped the wooden handle of my tungsten tomahawk and pulled it out of the ground just as Alcaeus went for the victory. The tomahawk was heavy, but successfully blocked Alcaeus's attack. He lunged and I rolled, my fingers brushing over the other half of my staff. Runes alight, I grabbed it with my other hand – now a long tungsten dagger. I circled him and he watched me like an eagle.

"You are truly incredible, mikrós asvós," Alcaeus said, his voice deep and silky. "And you have the heart of a warrior. My, what a Champion you have made."

"Distracting me with pretty words won't work, Alcaeus," I warned playfully.

He smirked. "Is truth a distraction then? Alright. Since you clearly want this to end quickly, I shall make it so."

Snorting, I replied, "If you think you can. Show me what you're made of then, Champion of Champions."

The corners of his mouth lifted, and he began to match my stance. Stark hunger was evident in his face, his eyes having bled black with that geometric galaxy glowing around where his irises would be.

Not waiting for another moment, I struck but as expected, he blocked my blow. I tried to swing my axe towards his open side but before I could blink, my tomahawk went flying, leaving me only with a dagger. Alcaeus grinned. To my shock, he stuck his sword into the ground and then squared me up. He was unarmed now and I with my dagger. I raised an eyebrow at him, and his only response was a grin and cheeky wink. I would have blushed had he not been on me in a flash, tackling me to the ground. The breath knocked from me, I stilled at the feeling of cold metal against my neck. I had no idea how he managed to disarm me so fast, his speed beyond comprehension.

Alcaeus had me fully pinned with his body weight, my legs on either side of his knees. His other hand held the back of my head, fingers weaved into my hair. I could feel both of our hearts racing, his breath warm upon my face.

"I do believe victory is mine," he teased, nose nuzzling my cheek.

"Ahh, but you have made a very fatal error, my prince," I whispered.

Alcaeus lifted his head to look down at me, confusion on his face. "Oh? And what error has the Champion of Champions made?"

I pushed up slightly, so our noses brushed. "Never let an Alchemist touch your heart."

He glanced down at my hand, fingers splayed over the thick muscles there, covering his thumping heart. Alcaeus looked back up at me and his face became very serious. Tossing the dagger away, he cupped my face. Looking deep into my gaze, his thumb caressed my cheek, then my lips.

"It's far too late for that," he whispered.

Then he kissed me, plunging his tongue deep, conquering me in one fell swoop. We kissed like the world was ending tomorrow. Clothes came off quickly, hands exploring each other desperately. His large hands grabbed and massaged my breasts firmly as he kissed and licked his way along my neck. Those kisses travelled downward, worshipping my chest before continuing his path. With the same fascination I had when watching him practise with Nemesis, my eyes devoured him when he finally reached his goal. Our eyes met and butterflies erupted in my stomach as I watched his thick, hot tongue reach out and taste me. I moaned. His thumbs spread my lips wide as he explored me.

Nearly ripping up the grass clenched in my fists, I gave in, one hand sinking into his hair when his tongue pushed inside me, before sliding back up to swirl around my clit. Flicking it back and forth, I nearly came undone. Alcaeus held my thighs in a bruising grip as I bucked when he pushed me to climax. But, instead of calming down, it only stoked the fire within me. Lifting my legs even more, I invited him in. I needed him inside me so desperately.

"Please, Alcaeus, I just want you inside of me. Please," I moaned.

Without hesitating he moved back up, then lined himself up with my entrance. His thrust felt divine but so overwhelming from my already stimulated core. I screamed into his mouth, the pleasure so immaculate as he stretched and filled me. Alcaeus groaned loudly, igniting me further.

"Elysium has nothing on the feeling of being inside you," he growled, pushing deep until he was flush against me. "Ahh, yes."

I rolled my hips over and over, working him. He moaned and thrust back. I hooked my left leg around his and pushed his left shoulder while pushing off the ground with my other leg. We rolled until I straddled him. My lover's grin turned into a gasp when I rolled my hips again, grinding hard into him. He was so deep I could scarcely breathe, and I took small, short breaths to adjust. Then I began to slowly ride him, left hand on his chest to brace myself, the other behind me on his thigh. Alcaeus slid his hands up my belly and cupped the heavy weight of my breasts, teasing my nipples until they peaked. I moaned and rolled my head back, straightening my spine even more, to take him deeper.

Looking back down at him, his face was filled with desire but also something else I couldn't discern.

"What is it?" I asked breathlessly. I slowed slightly, wanting to hear his answer.

Alcaeus sat up, coming face to face with me although his head was a bit above mine. He kissed me deeply and said, "The sight of you riding me, the moons and stars behind you, lighting every perfect curve and angle of you, will stay with me until my very end. No language possesses the ability to describe the perfection before me."

I was grateful he kissed me again before I could truly process the depth of his words. For if I had, my heart would have truly been lost to me in that moment. Reclining once more, he grabbed my hips firmly and thrust hard. I cried out, grabbing onto anything I could. He thrust again harder and then began pistoning in and out of me. I bounced, bracing myself on his chest as he brought me closer and closer to orgasm. I couldn't speak, so lost in the sensation of him that it consumed me. I came with a shout, stiffening and contracting around him.

Alcaeus rolled us so I was on my back once more. He slid back inside me and hooked his arms underneath my knees. Whatever calm euphoria from my orgasm that was left over was immediately forgotten as my hips were lifted.

"Oh! Oh! Alcaeus!" I cried out, the angle he had me at made my eyes go wide, my hands grasping and clenching, my fingers sinking into the ground.

He continued to thrust until I came again, eyes rolling into the back of my head. He also came with a shout, one arm letting go of my leg and slamming his hand down next to my head, fingers digging into the grass. He hissed and ground his teeth as his hot release flooded inside me. I was boneless as he rocked slightly before collapsing on top of me.

Slowly, I became aware of the sounds of the night creatures chirping away, and the silent peace of the forest. Studying the stars, I knew there had never been a more peaceful and fulfilling moment in time throughout my life.

Alcaeus's face was nuzzled in the crook of my neck, and I threaded my fingers to the back of his head, gently stroking. My thoughts drifted to what he had told me, all that he had lost. The queen wanted this man, this demigod laying in my arms. She tried to break him by murdering his family and tried to control him by cleaving his soul in two. Yet here he lay with me, in the safety of my arms. I hugged him to me tighter.

It was then I knew: there would be no running away for Toby and myself. Not without Alcaeus there beside me.

A. R. Morgan

CHAPTER 29

"So, who was this wise person you were quoting in the kitchen several days ago?" Alcaeus asked, breaking my concentration on the book I had been reading.

Along with our things, the books I had been studying in Sage Kevyn's study had magically been appearing over the last few days, much to my excitement. The Principles of Magic was a rudimentary read but I was hoping it contained clues on the fundamental nature of telekinesis as I could not rely purely on quantum physics alone.

"He... was my mentor. My teacher," I replied softly.

Alcaeus sat down next to me on the chaise in front of the cosy fireplace. Candles had been lit, giving the room a warm flickering glow. The smells of the forest, parchment, and herbs floated around us as rays of the setting sun filtered through the small windows of the cottage.

My toes touched Alcaeus's thigh as he made himself comfortable and he grabbed my foot to place in his lap. His strong hands began to massage my instep. Letting out a sigh of happiness, I rested my book in my lap. Sinking a bit deeper into the couch, my eyelids fluttered shut while I enjoyed his ministrations. The strength and warmth of his large hands had me melting.

"Would you tell me about him?" he asked.

I didn't answer right away, rather glanced down at the book laying in my lap as I tried to remember my old teacher. No matter how much time had passed, there was still a dull ache in my chest whenever I remembered.

"Master Kian was the best Alchemist I had ever had the honour of knowing. Brilliant and wise, he was also an absolute curmudgeon, even by our own race's standards. He was known for pushing the boundaries of our society, always questioning the ridiculousness of those in power. It took me an entire year to convince him to train me."

"Ah, things are beginning to make sense now," Alcaeus said with a smirk.

"What do you mean?" I asked, raising an eyebrow at him.

"Why, the origins of your merry nature, of course." Now a full-blown smile, he laughed as I smacked his shoulder playfully. I couldn't contain my answering smile, so I turned away from him to hide it.

Continuing his wonderful attention to my foot, he said, "Jests aside, I have always wondered how Alchemist society functioned. What it looked like. For years, I searched for any information that I could. During my hundred and fifty-eighth year as king, several neighbouring kingdoms were facing droughts and plagues, and many came to me to find solutions. There were legends of a people that could control the elements and manipulate them. They were Masters of Science and innovation, living in a hidden city of gold, silver, and riches. Engineering technology that was so far from our own advancements that I desperately sought to find them. I surmised that these Sons and Daughters of the Great Mother must have the knowledge to prevent thousands of deaths."

I chuckled and shook my head at the fanciful legends and the colourful imaginations people had. "It was no city of gold and diamonds, although the Citadel was something to behold," I said, nostalgia thick in my voice. "Our economy was purely reliant upon inner trade. Society was based on the four primary elements, with subclans falling under their born-element sign; if your element was iron, you would be a part of the Metal Clans, living in the Earth District, etc.

"As the Mother intended it, we all functioned together as one living organism." I couldn't quite hide the bitter edge in my voice as I said that last part, being the outcast that I had been. Not wanting to dwell on it, I continued. "Theoretically, had we been allowed beyond the Citadel, we could have brought balance in the face of natural disasters. However, in some cases, those very disasters are necessary to bring a better quality of life. Only the oldest and wisest Alchemists were allowed to make those decisions. I will be honest with you and say that the Elders would have most likely let nature take its course. Fear of death due to loss correlates with emotional attachment - to be one with the Mother is to accept death as part of the cycle of nature. All living things must sacrifice themselves for the benefit of all. At least, that's what the Council of Elders would tell you."

Indeed, while Alchemists were nurturing in many ways, their society as a whole was as brutal as nature itself could be.

Alcaeus sighed, "I cannot say that surprises me; you are servants of Mother Nature, and she is a cruel mistress oftentimes. Nevertheless, one should not discount the finality that death brings to those who are not of her realm. Immortality can often blind someone to the necessity of death. Something tells me, however, that you may have struggled with this?"

I smiled, although it was a smile that held its own bittersweetness.

"I have always had a soft spot for the less fortunate, the weak. I know what it's like to be viewed in society as unwanted and unnecessary. Long ago, I believed that perhaps instead of letting nature take its course, as it were, we should merely change the laws themselves. Needless to say, that was highly frowned upon, even by Master Kian," I cleared my throat, deciding to change the subject as I already felt I was revealing too much. "So, did you ever manage to find an Alchemist?"

If Alcaeus noticed my discomfort or deflection, he did not show it.

Instead, he replied, "Interestingly enough, I did manage to make contact with an Alchemist once, through writing. One of my informants contacted an exile, from what he told me, and we exchanged responses. The Alchemist never gave me a name and I could only trust the integrity of my informant, but the information they gave proved invaluable to engineering new technology that led to a respite for the people. I was most indebted to them and sought to meet but my informant received no response. Many years later, there were rumours the entire society had disappeared."

A sombre mood descended upon us, the crackling of the fire seemingly louder in the silence. I could feel how badly Alcaeus wanted to ask me what happened. Pulling my feet from his warm hands, I rose. Tucking my book under the crook of my arm, I headed towards the bedroom with the intent on drawing a bath; yet, truly just wanting to escape. I paused at the door when Alcaeus asked me the dreaded question.

"What happened, *mikrós asvós*? Why did they disappear?"

Looking down at the ground hard, I tried to decide what to do. After a moment, I looked up at him and I could only imagine the emotions he saw on my face as I was about to reveal to him that which I had never revealed to anyone before. One sentence was all I could manage and all I would say for now.

"They disappeared," I said, my voice breaking, "because of me."

Shock and confusion filled his face, but I turned and left before he could question me further.

▽▽ᕧ♌ᕯ°ᕹ°

As morning came, Alcaeus slipped into the bed beside me, his warmth enveloping me. His chest came against my back as he enfolded me in his arms. Kissing me gently on the temple, he nuzzled my hair as he inhaled my scent.

"No matter what happened in the past or the future, no matter what you have done or will do, I am with you, my love," he whispered.

My heart sputtered at those words as they penetrated past my once impenetrable walls, the shame and guilt I'd carried for hundreds of years. I squeezed the arms around me as tears filled my eyes.

I shook my head, turning towards him. "You don't know–"

"I care not."

"Truly Alcaeus, you don't understand—"

"I do not need to."

Just as I was about to try again, he kissed me. My tears spilled over when my eyes closed, trickling down the side of my face as I lost myself to the feel of his lips on mine. Slowly, he pulled away.

Midnight blue eyes searching mine, he said "In due time, remember?"

Another tear slipped out and I nodded, kissing him gently once more.

A loud knock on the door startled us out of our moment and Alcaeus quickly sat up but placed a hand on my chest, preventing me from doing the same.

"It is Sotiris. A moment, my love."

He quickly dressed and went out to meet him. As soon as he was out of the room, I jumped up, grabbed my silk robe, and quickly tiptoed out of the room. I had no doubt they could hear me with their heightened sense. Apprehension crawled through me, and my intuition told me our time of peace had come to its end.

The front door was cracked open, and I could see Alcaeus's back through it.

"...urgent, Your Highness. The queen demands you back at once."

"What for? Did you not tell her what I instructed you?" Alcaeus's voice sounded impatient.

The other Vampire, Sotiris, let out a sound of frustration and said, "I did, even Cillian attempted to assuage her. We have tried to keep her at bay, but she is holding Lord LeGervase hostage, Sire! She demands both of your presence before she releases him."

My heart dropped and I swung the door all the way open.

"We're going back, Alcaeus. Now." My demand left no room for argument.

The scar-faced Vampire's eyes widened but he gave me a quick bow with a grumbled 'my lady'.

Alcaeus swore but nodded. "Get things ready for our return. Tell the queen we will be back by nightfall."

"But Sire, the sun—" attempted the other Vampire, but his liege cut him off with a wave of his hand

"I'll be fine, Sotiris." A measured look passed between him. The usual cold demeanour I'd only ever seen from his captain, was replaced with sincere concern.

"Yes Sire, I'll be off then." Giving an appropriate salute and a polite nod to me, the captain took his leave.

As Alcaeus came back inside, that same thought worried me. My hand snagged his, stopping him as he went to walk past me.

"Will you be alright, Alcaeus?"

"Yes, I'll be fine. It may slow me down and drain me, but my sun curse was relieved when Ragna... I'll be alright."

I hesitated for a moment, then nodded in understanding. I began dressing but stopped when I felt Alcaeus come up behind me. Turning around, I took in the concerned look, the tightness around his mouth.

"Alcaeus? What's the matter?"

"We must do the second mark and we must do it now. I thought we would have more time to spend together before performing the ritual. I had planned to wait as long as possible until you were ready. However, it will protect us and validate the reason I gave her, initially. It could buy us time, much-needed time so we can focus on getting Lord Elis released."

Giving a deep sigh, I nodded. His reasoning was sound, but it didn't help in the slightest to appease my churning gut, the fear that began to snake up my insides. I felt the metaphorical shackles tighten around me.

"Alright, let's have it done then. I... I'm not sure what you'll see—" I began but Alcaeus cut me off.

"It does not matter for I will not ask. If you choose to tell me afterward, your truth will be safe with me. I must warn you though, *mikrós asvós*, this time you will share blood with me at the same time I take from you. I will say the words for the ritual, and you will repeat them after me. Do you understand?"

Here we go. We were doing this. I closed my eyes and rallied. I faced him with only resolute determination on my face. My steady gaze was free of fear or hesitation. I would trust this man. I would trust him.

"Yes."

The relief on his own face was evident. "Good, now come, sit with me."

Alcaeus sat on the edge of the bed and motioned me towards his lap. I went to him. Turning me away from him, the prince grasped me around the waist, and pulled me onto his lap. He was still tall enough that his head was a few inches above mine and I could feel his warm breath against my ear. He slowly edged the lapel of my robe away from the nape of my neck until it went past my shoulder. Pulling my hair to one side, I felt him run his nose up the side of my neck and then gently kiss his way back down until his lips came to rest on my mark. I leaned back, relaxing into him.

He raised his right arm and pulled his head away. When his arm came back, blood dripped from the bite on his wrist.

"Now, once we say the words, drink from me as I do to you. You must be sincere, Melisandre, or this could go awry. You must believe the words with every part of you. Do you need a minute?"

No, as I had decided in the field when we made love under the stars, I was done running.

"I will not back down, Alcaeus," I whispered as I turned my head to look back at him. "I trust you."

His face softened and filled with something I couldn't decipher, but planted a sweet kiss. "Thank you," he said against my lips and kissed me once more.

I turned back around and brought Alcaeus's wrist to me, waiting for him to begin. He wrapped his left arm firmly around my waist and I felt his lips once more at my mark.

"Melisandre Von Boden—

To thee, I give my mark, the second of three.
That which was once unmade, made whole again
Together our blood doth flow
Thine in mine, mine in thine
The thread in which our souls thus bind
As was proclaimed at the breath of first light.
Return unto me as the stars align
One chord, one soul
To thee I claim ye bound for all eternity
Beginning to end, in darkness and in light
Death nor life shall tear asunder that which was made for none other.
Thusly to thee I bind."

He paused, waiting for my response. I grasped onto his arm and closed my eyes, bringing forth my feelings for him so that my words might ring true. For a moment, concern flashed through me in fear of forgetting the words but, much to my surprise, they began to flow naturally.

"Alcaeus Pallas—

To thee, I give my own mark and accept thy claim.
That which was once unmade, made whole again
Together our blood doth flow
Thine in mine, mine in thine
The thread in which our souls thus bind
As was proclaimed at the breath of first light.
Return unto me as the stars align
One chord, one soul
To thee I claim ye bound for all eternity
Death nor life shall tear asunder that which was made for none other.
Thusly to thee I bind."

I wrapped my lips around his wrist, the coppery taste exploding in my mouth just as I felt him strike, fangs sinking deep. The sting made me double-down on Alcaeus's arm. Then white light and stars exploded in my vision, and I felt like my consciousness was being sucked in through a vortex.

"May I present Alcaeus Pallas, Champion of Athena, undefeated winner of this year's Theïká Paichnídia!"

Gods and goddesses alike cheered the warrior coming through the door of the great hall. The massive room glowed and glimmered with celestial beauty as fires roared in massive hanging braziers. The man in question walked down the marble steps, his massive bronze and gold feathered wings trailing behind him. An olive wreath graced his head and his golden skin all but gleamed against the white toga he wore. With a white glowing sword at his side, he came to a stop in front of a woman dressed for battle, whose eyes were deep oceans of wisdom and cunning. Her golden spear glinted and there was a great owl at her side.

"I honour you, my master, teacher, and creator," Alcaeus said, kneeling before her, "for the blood I have spilled in the sands of the Megálo Kolossaío, and the lives sent to Elysium, Hel, and Valhalla. Victory is yours, Athena, daughter of Zeus!"

Another cheer went up and then all quieted when Athena raised her hand, commanding silence. "Thank you, my blessed creation," she said, her voice rich and filling the room although she did not shout. She placed her hand upon his bowed head. Then she turned to address the rest of the hall. "Let us remember that the true victory is the peace we have achieved among us! Divine beings from other realms united, here and now. Together let us celebrate our differences and learn from our losses and our failures. For right now, all the realms are in harmony; for that is truly the power we, the Divine, hold. I ask you to raise your glasses and toast to peace, prosperity, and wisdom!"

Everyone raised their glasses and cheered, drinking deeply as the merriment continued and music filled the room. Dancers and performers filled the space, and all was joyous.

Alcaeus moved away and towards his place as Champion. As he approached his table, a woman dressed as a shield maiden cut him off. No one seemed to notice the woman, whose face held black-painted symbols of war. Her blonde braids reached all the way down her back, occasionally touching the two battle axes sheathed along her belt. She was nearly as tall as Alcaeus, her frame supple yet strong.

Athena's champion stiffened, wings flaring slightly. Giving a slight, customary bow, he said, "Greetings, Ragna Heldóttir. Blessings to you and praise to our makers."

"And to you, Champion of the great Gyðja viskunnar. A most im-

pressive feat. It cost my goddess much to put me back together after our battle.”

“Good to see she completed your recovery in time for the feasts.”

“Yes, reanimation is her forte after all. I think she did a wonderful job; do you not think so?” Ragna held up her arms and with sultry grace, slowly turned in a circle for him to observe.

“Indeed, all your limbs seem to be intact.” The Greek warrior’s face stayed emotionless.

The Shieldmaiden beheld him with rapt adoration. “Well, you certainly tried your damndest to make sure I went back to her in pieces but, worry not, I hold naught against you. Your prowess in battle is awe-inspiring, Alcaeus. But if you are so concerned with my limbs then, I wonder,” Ragna stepped into him, noses nearly touching as she ran an elegant finger along his chiselled face, “Why don’t you check to see for yourself? It would be a shame to leave it with just a kiss.”

Alcaeus snagged her wrist as her finger travelled downwards and leaned closer in, dark eyes boring into her emerald green ones.

“I have told you before and I will say it again, Ragna: the answer is no. That kiss was a mistake. This is your third attempt at getting me into your bed and it will not work. I have yet to forgive you for killing my servants in order to sneak your way into my quarters. Go try your feminine wiles on Bréanainn, Macha’s champion. Rumour has it he likes dead things,” Alcaeus growled.

Ragna ripped her hand away, eyes glittering with temper. Yet a smile curved on her perfect lips adding to the cold lines of her face.

“Deny me now, Alcaeus, but heed me: I will have you. Together you and I could create something beyond being the lackeys of tyrants. Already you have slain the gods Sobek and Ayar Cachi! You have proven we are capable! We are better than them! You desired me once, Godslayer. By your own confession, you have grown weary of the collar of servitude around your neck. It’s not too late!”

Alcaeus bared his fangs at her, pushing past her, but then turned back and snarled, “One kiss does not equate genuine desire nor does a moment of weakness justify treason! Keep your blasphemous thoughts and treacherous hands away from me Ragna!” With that, he whipped around and stalked off.

But the Viking Champion merely stared longingly after him with a sly smile still upon her lips.

The world swirled, and I was suddenly back in the bedroom at the cottage, both Alcaeus and I breathing heavily. I pulled away from him and he let me go. Anxiety shot through me as I took in the look on his face, searching it desperately, trying to find some indication of what he had experienced.

"What did you see, Alcaeus?"

He shook himself, midnight blue eyes glittering with the geometrical design. His full lips were tinged with my blood.

"You were so hated, mikrós asvós. How could you have been so hated by your own people? The mark on your chest, why did everyone shun you for it? Yes, we agreed I would not ask but," Alcaeus shook his head, a hand sweeping through his hair in agitation, "my mind is struggling making sense of that vision... of the cruelty. It seemed as if you were merely walking and yet people threw things at you, calling you mutant and murderer. They attacked you."

Ah, I knew of the memory he spoke. "That is a perfect conversation to have on the way back to Idrisid, for it is a long one," I said, quickly pulling on my clothes. The wardrobe swung open a little too fast as I began pulling the contents out. "And, don't worry; that is a memory I am ready to explain." My teasing smile was answered with one of his own.

"And what of my memory? What did you see, Melisandre?"

I stopped fumbling with my bag, my fingers running over the seams while recalling the dream-like memory. "I saw you at a feast, celebrating your win of the *Theïká Paichnídia*. Ragna stopped you and... made her intentions known."

"Ahh, yes. That was the moment I sealed my fate, I believe. But you're right, let us save that for our return. Do not concern yourself with packing; Cillian can transfer it all there with magic."

Hesitating, I searched around to make sure I wasn't missing anything. The idea of transferring things via magic was so foreign but perhaps it was more convenient. As I turned back to the wardrobe, the sight of the now-darkening seal where my shoulder met my neck, stopped me. Intricate ritualistic gold and black swirls and runes I did not recognize, came together in a large circle. The outer part of the design was still very faint, but it was what was inside that made my eyes widen.

An owl whose wings faced downward, the wing tips touching creating a circle. Inside the circle of wings was the alchemical symbol for the philosopher's stone.

CHAPTER 30

The sun was bright on our backs as we tried to drift in and out of the sparse clouds around us, our mounts quietly gliding through the air. When I went to get on Zephyr, Alcaeus had grabbed me around the waist and threw me onto his own Pegasus. So, we could 'talk', was his reasoning. Of course I protested but once the warmth of his chest seeped into my back, the comfort of his firm arm around my waist, and the heart-stopping kiss efficiently silenced me.

"So, Ragna has always been a scheming bitch, has she? It was so long ago, your memory, and even then, she could not keep her hands to herself." I tried to keep the bitterness out of my voice but only just.

I felt the rumble of his chuckle and he replied, "Yes, as you have probably come to realise, Ragna cannot tolerate the word no nor accept defeat. Granted, that is the burden of all creatures created in the gods' image. I slew her twice in battle; once, slicing her to ribbons and scattered her pieces over the arena. The other, she only stood amongst the sand for mere moments before Nemesis relieved her of her head. Unfortunately for me, the goddess Hel was a powerful deity – Ragna's deaths did not last long. However, instead of instilling fear or caution, it only seemed to inflame her desire for me."

"Yes, she is a few sandwiches short of a picnic, that one," I mumbled under my breath, but Alcaeus laughed, although there was a hollowness I felt with equal measure.

"Ragna," Alcaeus paused, as if searching for the right words, "held firmly to the belief we were enslaved, empty puppets to our creators, just flesh for slaughter. For many of us, we took great pride in our masters. Being a Champion was what we were created for—warriors like the world had never seen. We were demi-gods in our own right, our blood unblemished by the human condition, as many half-gods were. But Ragna never saw it that way. Slaves, she would sneer. Nothing but dogs whipped to come to heel at our masters' sides, sent to the slaughterhouse every single year, she would say. So much so that soon enough, the Twelve Champions were split, and her secret rebellion began to brew."

Brows furrowed, I turned my head to him slightly and asked, "Did your prospective gods treat you so poorly it would instigate that kind of insurrection?"

"A majority of them. Contradiction will always be the nature of the gods, as they are both kind yet cruel, merciful yet demanding of their will. My own mistress, Athena, was unrelenting and ruthless in my training. Yet, the core principles of those lessons started in the mind, in conquering oneself. She understood that little came from breaking me, but rather in teaching, challenging, and refining. A warrior's will and the strength of their integrity when faced with impossibility–that is what won battles and wars.

"But Hel," I felt Alcaeus shake his head as he sighed, "made Ragna look like a child in comparison. The Norse goddess cared little for the dealings of the gods and men, so the creation of Ragna came as a surprise to all. My mistress was quite suspicious of it. It was also speculated that Loki himself had a hand in her making. Regardless, I have no doubt that Hel's and Loki's treatment of Ragna lived up to her claims. The cruelties Ragna endured, well, I would rather not say out loud."

Surprised, I asked, "Is that pity, or dare I say, compassion in your voice for her?"

"Compassion? No, most definitely not. Pity? Only in as much that I understand, as I did back then, the origins of where the seeds of her insanity were sown." Suddenly his voice dropped and there was the unmistakable undercurrent of old anger. "Nothing will keep me from my vengeance, least of all misplaced pity."

I sat in contemplative silence, glancing back to where Zephyr flew close behind. It saddened my heart to know he flew so loyally beside me, back to a city where we were surrounded by enemies. Even my beautiful Kelpie was not safe. Ares, however, seemed to come and go as he pleased, a mysterious phenomenon I would at some point find an answer to.

Alcaeus cleared his throat. I braced myself for what I already knew he was about to ask.

"Now, will you tell me what I saw this morning, my love?"

Oh, how I did not want to. I shifted in my seat, uncomfortable but not due to the saddle. If there was anything that I was truly terrible at, it was discussing my past.

"You know, not even Elis knows what I am about to tell you. He would be as green as the vines he commands if he knew that you knew something about me that he didn't. He takes being my closest friend quite seriously. And jealously," I teased, hoping my deflection would work.

Alcaeus moved the arm around my waist, his broad hand sliding over to splay across my abdomen as I felt him lean down. The tip of his nose brushed against my ear.

The chill in the air made his breath hot against the shell of my ear as he whispered, "Yet I know many things that Elis does not." His hand dipped, his pinkie teasing the waistline of my pants, sliding back and forth.

My heart began to speed up in anticipation. When his hand sinfully cupped me, Alcaeus pushed my pelvis firmly against his.

"I know for a fact he does not know your inner heat; how wet you are for me, or how you squeeze tight around my fingers; my cock," he growled, dancing his fingers along the walls of my channel. His thick erection pressed so hard against me it almost hurt. Yet, being the deviant I was turning out to be, the discomfort only spiked my arousal. Knowing how much he always seemed to desire me was quickly becoming an addiction.

Fingers spread my lower lips and I let out a gasp as he began to flick my nub over and over. Then he slid two fingers back inside and I lifted my hips off the saddle slightly, allowing him more access. My head lolled against his chest and shoulder, helpless against the desire his expert hands stoked.

"See?" he whispered. "Only I know this tight little hole. How you drip for me. How you spread your legs so willingly for me. Only me."

"I... do not... Ahh! Spread... my... oh... my legs—"

"Your body sings the truth, *mikrós asvós*," he rumbled against me.

Suddenly his hand disappeared, coming to grab my breasts, massaging them roughly. I ground my backside against him, tilting my head back and exposing my neck. A hot thick tongue licked and kissed me from shoulder to ear, his beard rough against my sensitive skin.

"The sun is draining me, Melisandre. May I..." he trailed off, and I felt the scrape of incisors against my jugular. He teased but did not break the skin.

Apprehension filled me.

"Will it... will it be the third marking?"

"No," he whispered against my skin, "just giving me sustenance, replenishing my power that the sun diminishes, as is our curse."

"Will you be able to... see into me, like when we do the marking?"

"No."

"Then... alright. Get on with it," I said hurriedly, bracing myself against him.

"Shhh, relax. I won't let it hurt," he smiled slightly, "too much."

There was little warning before his fangs pierced my flesh. At the same time, fingers slid back into me with purpose. With steady, deep movements, he played me like a fiddle when I felt his teeth leave my neck to allow the blood to flow from the punctures. Sucking deeply, Alcaeus' movements became faster, harder. I cried out, the sensation of his palm against my clit becoming too much, my peak coming too fast. My climax hit with a crash, and I was careful not to thrash for fear of throwing his Pegasus off-kilter.

Alcaeus swiped his tongue along the wound and lifted his mouth from me. He was panting, leaning his head against mine.

"Alcaeus? Are you alright?"

"Yes, Melisandre. It is just that your blood is... exceedingly rich. It was like drinking from the Ancient Powers themselves."

Confused, I breathlessly said, "But you've tasted my blood before during the Marking."

He lifted his head. "During the ritual, I do not consume your blood. It is more infusing my fangs with power and injecting it into your bloodstream. Being the first time, I could only take a little lest I risk becoming blood-drunk."

Holding onto the pommel, I turned my neck side to side. Surprisingly, I was not sore. "Did you taste bitterness and annoyance as well? I refuse to believe my blood would be unstained by my best characteristics," I joked.

The prince chuckled and replied, "Well, after seeing your memory, I could certainly understand why. Enough deflecting, mikrós asvós." He squeezed his arms around me then briefly ran his hands up and down my thighs as I relaxed back into him. "I am replenished and feeling more myself than I have in hundreds of years. Come. Tell me." At my hesitant sigh, he encouraged, "Please, my love."

I took a moment before answering, deciding on the best place to start. "Yes, it was true. I was very much an outcast in the Alchemist society. I was... clanless, technically. My mother tried very hard to keep me with her but when I became of age, among other reasons, I was cast out."

"Why were you cast out?"

"Because," I struggled with wording, unprepared for how difficult talking about myself was, "I was born without a primary element. You see, every Alchemist is born with a singular element, tied to their very DNA. It's rare but sometimes a child is born with two or possibly three. But never four. Nor would it be the primary elements themselves. Only the originals possessed them. But," I paused, still trying to decide how much I should reveal, "I was born with all four primaries, as well as the ability to control and transmute atoms in their entirety."

"So, that symbol—"

"Yes, yes, all that rubbish," I sighed, feeling weary. "So naturally, the one thing I could manipulate first was creating lightning. Just little sparks of electricity at first, but once I learned the structure of how lightning is created, I became quite adept."

"'Naturally', she says," Alcaeus chuckled. "I cannot say I would not love to see a demonstration in the future. Still, that does not explain why your people made you into an outcast. I would think it would make you revered among your kind."

"One would think. I certainly wished for it every day of my youth. Unfortunately, my ability to control atoms meant the ability to transmute anything, but as no teacher would take me since I was the equivalent of pure untamed magic. I would destroy things when I tried to fix them. Everything I touched became a catastrophe. I," I swallowed hard, my eyes going hazy at the memory, "hurt people when I would only try to help them." Alcaeus' tightened his arm around my waist, kissing the back of my head. It was the encouragement I needed. "It was not until I accidentally killed a man that my stance in society went from just being the odd duckling to criminal, deviant of nature, a monster." My words caught in my throat but a deep breath kept me steady. "He was beating his daughter, you see. She also happened to be the one person who ever showed me kindness," I said, nostalgia thick in my voice. "I was quite young, merely a juvenile. But because I could never leave well

291

enough alone and was bound and determined to be a hero, I ran over to stop him. I just remember seeing all the blood on Edenia's face. When I grabbed the fist responsible for it, the man exploded into a mist, the concussion sending Edenia and me flying. It broke three of her ribs and she was in a coma for months, or so my mother told me afterwards." I shook myself off, clearing my throat but I continued. "I was lucky to escape with my life that day. Kept under lock and key until I came of age and the Elders came for me. Right before guards broke down our door and beat my mother to death, she told me to find Kian Ardahvans. They shoved me out of the Citadel's shining gates so that I might fend for myself within Eladaria's Wall, no longer a 'threat' to society."

"And that, I presume, is where you found your Master Kian?"

"After several years scraping my way in the wilds, yes, I did manage to track that old bastard down. Spent another year relentlessly begging him to take me, train me. Finally, I accidentally destroyed his garden trying to pull the weeds. He told me he refused to go one more minute putting up with the 'snivelling daughter of mayhem and chaos incarnate' so I better be 'damn ready to get your arse whipped by the devil of education'." I laughed at the bittersweet memory and said, "Personally, I think he was just trying to save his begonias, as they were the only ones left standing if I recall."

Alcaeus squeezed me affectionately and I noticed that we had begun to descend.

"He sounds very much how I would imagine a teacher would need to be, teaching a student like you, mikrós asvós," he said, letting out a laugh when my elbow found his ribs. Then he sobered, holding me close. "I am very sorry for what you had to endure, Melisandre. It is not pity, so let down those hackles. It is empathy. It is anger on your behalf. What I would have done to have protected you from it. Yet, at the same time, it is your story. The story that has made you irrevocably you and I would not change that even if The Fates themselves came to me demanding it."

"And if they offered to give you the other half of your soul back? Would you humour them and change me then?"

"What use is my soul if the you that I know now is not in it?"

I blushed so deeply at that heart-stopping statement, butterflies exploding in my chest. I crossed my arms and took on my usual frown, completely at a loss at what to do with all this happiness.

Alcaeus saved me from the need to respond when he kissed my

head and then pointed ahead.

"Look."

Below us spread the sparkling city of Idrisid, the massive Sanguine River encompassing around it. It was truly breathtaking, especially from this angle. One could even say tragically romantic. Flying upon a pure white Pegasus, in the arms of a Vampire Prince, certainly added to the idea.

However, as we drew closer, anxiety and dread began to rise. The truth of the matter was that behind this magnificent city and its glorious castle, was the horrible reality that my best friend sat imprisoned and was at the mercy of a demented and jealous queen. So, too, was there a little boy who held me responsible for killing his first love. The peace, serenity, and safety of the last couple of weeks found in Alcaeus' arms were but a dream. The true nightmare was about to begin.

CHAPTER 31

Alcaeus flew to my balcony, letting me off in my room before taking our mounts down to the stables. Neither one of us wanted to make a scene and we were both weary; well, I certainly was. Nevertheless, after getting cleaned up, I immediately demanded Ada take me to Elis and Llyr's quarters. I needed to see them.

When we arrived in front of the double doors of Elis and Llyr's wing, I paced left and right behind Ada, crossing and uncrossing my arms. Nervousness and impatience clawed at my insides. A million thoughts crowded my mind; I had yet to figure out a solid plan for getting Elis released beyond playing the queen's game, abiding by her rules.

We gave her the second mark; surely that had to count for something? However, I reminded myself, *when it came to the queen, nothing one did ever seemed to matter. Ragna got off on the suffering her manipulations and control caused.*

Then my mind jumped to another pressing issue– Toby. Did he understand my position? Why it was better that Sophie died by my hand rather than Lord Cyto's? Could he? Was I asking too much of a child?

I guess we are about to find out, I thought to myself just as a maid answered the door.

We were led into the sitting room, already prepped with tea and finger foods. Pale gold and blues coloured the room, a gentle background compared to the number of flowers that filled the room. Except, instead of beautiful blossoms and floral scents, they drooped and dulled in colour. Sadness filled me as I walked over to a particularly full vase, lifting a withered blossom up with my finger.

They were dying. Which could only mean that Elis was suffering, incredibly weak.

Anxiety rose and panic threatened to peek its unhelpful head, but I squelched it down and schooled my features.

"Melisandre, thank goodness you have returned," said a weary voice.

Spinning around, my jaw dropped slightly. Llyr, a child of Spring and Sunshine, was pasty and muted. Even his clothes looked like he'd slept in them for a week. He looked downright haggard. I walked towards his outreaching hands. Those beautiful healer's hands were icy and dry.

"We came back as soon as we could. How is Elis? Alcaeus took us away from the queen's wrath after Lord Cyto—"

"Yes," interrupted Llyr, "we all heard. It has been the talk of the town these last few weeks. Not that I would dream of doubting your capabilities, both Elis and I were worried sick for you. As it was, I could barely hold Elis back from skewering the lord's corpse with his beloved vines," he said wistfully, although there was a note of sadness too. "While I will admit that the world is better off for his death, the timing could not have been worse. It is my belief that Queen Ragna imprisoned Elis as an act of retribution for killing Lord Cyto."

There was a weight in my throat that swallowing wasn't helping. "We suspected as much. But her lackey made the very unfortunate decision to come into my room and stab me. The inevitable consequences of his actions lie within his own decision-making. Ragna's lack of control over her own subjects lies at her feet as well."

Llyr waved his hand in the air. "No, no, I would not possibly fault nor place blame upon you, my dear. It's just," he paused, exasperation heavy in his tone, "Please sit. There is much we must discuss."

Clearing my throat as I made a move to the settee, I asked again, "How...how is Elis? And Toby? How is he?"

Straight copper hair slid over his saddened face, but Llyr did not respond, just looked at me. Several different emotions played out on his face, and it told me all I needed to know. Nodding in understanding, I reached for the teacup that had been placed out on the coffee table between us.

"Melisandre," Llyr leaned forward, making no move towards the refreshments. His voice was a harsh whisper. "I must tell you this in utmost confidence and secrecy."

I scooted closer, placing my tea down. "I understand, Llyr. What is going on?"

"I," he glanced quickly back at the door, scanning the room before turning back to me, "have been making arrangements to sneak all of us out of Idrisid. Out of Khaviel. We are at the brink of war, Melisandre. Yet, I have been unsuccessful at reaching my contact with the Seelie Court; the dark magic here overpowers any light magic I am able to do. None of my letters have been responded to; I strongly believe they might have been intercepted."

"I don't see how escape is possible, Llyr. Elis is sitting in the dungeon even as we speak. If I was not concerned about your and Toby's safety, yes, I could probably break him out. However, I am not willing to trade one life for another. Besides..." I looked down at my hands twisting in my lap. "Things are a bit more complicated now."

The Fae noble gave me a questioning look. "What do you mean?" Then understanding blossomed on his face. "Ah, the Nightmare Prince."

Stiffening, I nodded. "While we were gone, we completed the second mark. I do not know what that means or what it entails beyond this desperate feeling that I cannot, will not, just leave Alcaeus to face Ragna alone."

"Rest assured, my dear, I included Alcaeus in my arrangements."

I shook my head. "No, he cannot... he would not be able to leave. Ragna has something on him that forces him to remain here. No please," I started, stopping Llyr from questioning me. "It is not for me to say. In a safer place and with Alcaeus' blessing, I will confide in you but this... I cannot. Suffice to say, leaving with him is not an option at this time."

"I see," replied Llyr, his look pensive. Then he leaned forward again and asked hesitantly, "May I... may I see this Familiar mark?"

Unbuttoning my black blouse, I pulled the collar past my right shoulder. Llyr stood and sat next to me. He leaned in, placing a hand on my arm. Suddenly, his spring green eyes widened, and he gasped, not in surprise but almost horror. Apprehension filled me.

"What? What is it? Why are you looking at me like that?"

Llyr continued to stare, his already pale face losing whatever colour he did have.

"Sweet Goddess... Melisandre, oh my dear girl... that is not a Familiar mark."

"Excuse me?"

"A Familiar's Mark would have an inscription around the sides, just here. It would be in Alcaeus' mother tongue, and it would have only his seal. Your mark is written in a language I have never seen. I would wager it to be in one of the Original Tongues. Yes, the owl is indeed his sigil, but it would not be..." he struggled to find the right words, "like that. And that symbol there—I take it is yours, which makes little sense. It is so elaborate, and, in terms of contracts and magic, this would fall under the category of the divine; only the gods were capable of a binding like this.

"Are you sure it is not because I am an Alchemist? Surely that could change its appearance. Have you ever seen—"

Llyr held up a hand, stopping my interrogation. "I am sure that could play a role in its design, but there is nothing in it indicating your role as a Familiar. Could it be...?" He gasped, his hand coming over his mouth. He stood and began pacing, running a hand through his hair. "No, no, no not possible... but if it is? No, it cannot be, it is too unlikely," Llyr continued to mumble to himself.

Irritation bubbled through me. "Llyr, what in the devil is going on with you? Just tell me!"

He jerked around, eyes wild and intense. I had never seen the favourite ambassador of the shining court so out of sorts. It was starting to concern me. He shook his head, then waved his hands in dismissal.

"There is only one possible way to get the kind of mark I am thinking of, and it is simply not possible. Anyways, nonsensical thinking will only deter us now. Just... ask Prince Alcaeus," he said, grabbing me by the shoulders, "ask him about it. Verify it is indeed a Vampire's Familiar's Mark. He will know. Right now, however, I must finish telling you what I have done since we do not have much time."

Gesturing back to the couches, Llyr and I sat back down.

"Now, as I said, my missives to The Outer Court, where the Summer Court lies, have gone unanswered. The Inner Court, too, has been unresponsive. Which left me with one alternative, one that I would not have done if it were not so imperative. I..." he swallowed hard, in clear discomfort. Apprehension wriggled in my stomach. "Well, I may have ties, albeit very fragile ones, to the Unseelie Court as well. War is on the horizon, and they have yet to declare a side. Although, historically, they have only ever declared for themselves. Nevertheless, it has come to my attention that Prince Alcaeus possibly had an alliance with King Ruarc many years ago."

"More like over a thousand, Llyr. Surely it is null and void by now. He told me about it while we were away."

"Yet, as history reads, King Ruarc failed in upholding his vow of protection to King Alcaeus. His failure arguably caused the fall of Alcaeus' kingdom."

Realisation dawned on me.

"You are calling upon the alliance treaty," I whispered, "You are calling upon his debt to Alcaeus."

"Yes, I am. We Fae are bound by blood and magic, our very immortality chained to the deals that we make. That is why we as a people hold the prejudice that all Vampires are honourless in this way, breaking vows as soon as it no longer benefits them. Fae may be cunning of tongue, perhaps oft times earning the moniker of tricksters, but it is because once we have made a vow, it cannot be broken until the agreement is fulfilled. Otherwise, we forfeit our very souls, becoming enslaved to the one we broke our oath to, forever exiled from Tír na nÓg." He shuddered; the concept visibly unsavoury to him. "So," Llyr sighed, "I have sent a message to the Unseelie King himself, pleading our case and requesting assistance in our immediate evacuation. Strictly speaking, you...belong to Alcaeus which means that that vow also now applies to you."

I shook my head in disbelief and replied, "Llyr, that is an astronomical leap let alone reach! Not only that, but the queen would also see King Raurc's interference as an act of war. Ragna sees me as her property, and we don't need to be reminded how vehement she is about theft. Giving her a reason, any reason, to start this is the last thing we should be doing. Besides, how on earth would King Ruarc even get to us?"

"Magic, my dear. You forget the magic. You see, while Mage Ilirhun overpowers almost all forms of light magic, he is only an expert at dark magic. The Unseelie Court IS dark magic. Comparatively, the mage is but journeyman level in the face of the masterful skills of the Champion of The Mórrígan. I hardly doubt that slimy, oath-breaking, ogre shite of a mage noticed when I slipped my letter into the flames of Lord Cyto's pyre. Only through the flames of death can one send messages to the Dark Court. Remember that, Melisandre."

Surprise and a half smile accompanied my response, "Llyr O'Cananach, I dare say that is the first time I have ever heard you bad mouth anyone. Certainly, well deserved. Although, I am shocked you did black magic, Llyr. I thought you could only perform light."

"For my love, my Chosen Mate," He whispered, his stare haunted and sincere, "I would do anything. Anything, Melisandre. Even if it means doing things that... I may come to regret later."

At that, I frowned at the hint of guilt that crossed his face.

Suddenly his eyes filled with tears. "I know that what I am doing goes against the hundreds of years of diplomatic skills I have accrued. That my very own beloved queen would see this as treason and that keeping the peace between the kingdoms of the Otherworld is a priority over everything, especially personal matters but... but my mate's life is at stake. Please understand—neither Elis nor I regret being here with you, with Toby, and doing all we can to protect both of you but staying is suicide. We both know this."

All I could do was nod because what he said was true. I sat in contemplative silence as Llyr continued.

"Elis' position at court has fallen greatly, although he would never willingly admit it. It has made him vulnerable, weak, and easily preyed on. The queen has always respected old bloodlines, but she has little use for a Vampire whose powers are of living things. They do not strengthen that of the Nightmare Court." Llyr's face scrunched in frustration. "Of all of us, I should have protected Elis better. I should have—" his breath caught, his tears now flowing freely, "I should have been able to get him released. I failed. This queen is riddled with insanity; logic and rationale are twisted and mutilated to serve only Ragna. So that leaves us with only one option, and I will be damned if I do not try. I must try, Melisandre!"

I understood; was in vehement agreement with Llyr. Yet sorrow filled me with this very sad truth—that they would need to leave without me. My heart clenched painfully at the idea of leaving Alcaeus, to possibly never see him again. Just as Llyr could not leave Elis to his fate, neither could I with the Prince of Nightmares.

I went to reach out to him when I felt the air shift and my hand shot out to transmute the oncoming projectile. Strips of paper and toothpicks exploded from the book that had been thrown at me, scattering all around Llyr and me.

"I HATE YOU! YOU KILLED SOPHIE! I FECKING HATE YOU!" Toby screamed at me from the doorway, his face bright red and puffy. He had been crying, struggling to keep the snot in his nose.

I jumped up, moving towards him. He let out a roar and came at me, fists flying. I barely caught them before Llyr was behind him, holding him by the arms.

"Toby that is enough! How dare you hit, Melisandre! Calm yourself!" Llyr shouted, trying to wrestle him under control.

While I understood Toby's rage and I certainly did not fault him for it, his show of violence stoked my ire, my anger growing with every foul word he spat at me. "It's alright, Llyr. Let him go. If he thinks trying to beat me into a bloody pulp will bring Sophie back, let him try."

"Feck you!" Toby spit, only slightly stopping his thrashing. "You fecking killed 'er, Ms. Melly! Why?! She was me best friend and ya fecking took 'er away! I was gonna marry 'er one day! Now I can't and it's ALL YER FAULT! Why couldn't ya just kill the evil man instead!? Soph didn't deserve what ya did ta 'er! Yer a GODDAMN VILLAIN!"

The words cut deep, the hurt igniting my anger further. Before I lashed out, however, one fact hit me.

Confused, I looked up at Llyr. "You didn't tell him? He doesn't know about Lord Cyto?"

Llyr just shook his head and continued trying to reason with the angry child.

I looked deep into those red, swollen brown eyes that were filled with rage. I ripped my shirt up to expose my stomach, where the two-inch keloid scar of where Lord Cyto had stabbed me lay red and angry against my pale skin.

"Look at it! Look, boy! That man, who was going to torture Sophie for the rest of her sweet life, the one who preyed on children's innocence? This was a gift from him," I spat, pointing to the scar. "He tried to gut me like a fish. Now, why would he do that Toby? Why?! Answer me!"

Toby's face fell, shocked. In a tiny voice, he choked out, "I don'... I dunno why he... He...did tha' Ms. Melly? He did tha to ya?"

"Yes!" I hissed, shoving my shirt down. I leaned over him, my eyes boring into his.;

"He shoved a 6-inch blade right through my damned liver, Toby. Tossed me around the room like a Sunday salad! Just when he thought his stupid idea of killing me was working, I made a gun. And you know what I did?! I BLEW HIS FUCKING HEAD OFF! Yes," I panted, "I did, in fact, kill him. Exactly as you've just asked."

Breathing heavily, my voice went to a level of deadly quiet. All the fight in Toby had been replaced by fear and apprehension. "I'll ask you again, boy – Why would Lord Cyto want to kill me? Why do you think I killed Sophie?" I added, trying to stoke the boy's prefrontal cortex.

Toby just shook his head, remaining tearfully silent. I knelt then, looking up at him, although my voice still held the harsh intensity to it. "There are things in this world that are worse than death, Toby. Things that make you wish, no, desperately beg for the relief that only death can bring. Sophie knew this, she understood it. She knew that Lord Cyto would cause her unimaginable pain and suffering. So, she begged me to release her from her fate; there was no way out for her otherwise. You need to understand this! Just as she did! We are living in the court where nightmares are made! Where your worst fears become reality! Only the strong survive here, the weak are controlled and at the mercy of the powerful. Sophie didn't belong here; she belonged in fields of flowers and butterflies, where the waters–" my voice broke but I swallowed and continued, "the waters were as blue as her beautiful eyes." Tears threatened then, and I looked down as I tried to gather myself. Toby needed to understand the reality of what we were up against, and he needed to accept the truth, right now, before he too became a casualty of the Vampire court. "I swore a vow, Toby, that I would bind myself to the royal consort in exchange for your crime of theft to be lifted –"

"But I didn't–"

"It doesn't matter whether you did or not! Do you not see that now, boy?! It doesn't fucking matter!" I paused, wanting the effect of those words to sink in. "What matters is what Queen Ragna thinks, what those in power think! It means that you were never free, that my agreement did not keep you safe! No, you were still a pawn in Ragna's machinations." My hand went to my hip as my other pinched my nose to keep my tears in check. "After what happened to Sophie, I also realised that it could have been you. She could try to give you to one of her damn lackeys, to torture and maim and mutilate!" I crouched, grabbing those tiny shoulders. "But I will never let that happen because you are my ward, Tobias Greenley! Mine! You are my child!" I cried brokenly.

Coming to a stand suddenly, I turned my back to him, unable to let him see me so emotionally out of hand. I held my face in my hands, squeezing out tears. Then I pinched the bridge of my nose again, taking a deep breath in an effort to calm myself.

Finally, without turning around, I whispered wearily, "Go ahead, call me the villain. I never have, nor would I ever, claim to be a hero. I am not a good woman, Toby; my sins run so deep I doubt I have a soul anymore. But one thing I know for absolute certainty: I would rather give you a gentle death than see you in the hands of someone who would hurt and break you to the point you were only a shell of a living being... who would take away everything I love about the little Birmingham boy I met in London." My confession was met with silence and my heart sank.

My eyes closed, too filled with grief and anger. Anger that I had to watch this child lose his innocence so brutally and that I had a hand in it. Anger that I did not know how to be soft and nurturing, a gentle mother figure this boy so desperately needed. Self-hate began to eat away at me, and I felt the walls my heart normally hides behind start to rise up.

That was when I felt a slight pressure on my back. I stilled. Slowly the pressure deepened, and I recognized it as Toby's head pressed against me. I let out a ragged breath and looked up at the ceiling, fresh tears welling in my eyes.

Toby sniffed and said, "I'm still righ' angry. So angry wit ya. But... yer the closest ta real family I've ever known. I don't understand everythin', but all I see when lookin' at ya is Sophie. Dead. I'm tryin' Ms. Melly..."

So overwhelmed with emotion that I was unable to respond verbally, I just slowly nodded my head.

He let me go and said, "Gonna just... need some more time, Ms. Melly. We're alright, I just... need time."

I turned my head slightly towards him and nodded my understanding but did not turn to watch him go.

The room was thick with emotional tension so I quickly excused myself once Llyr told me that he would notify me as soon as he heard anything regarding the Unseelie King.

"Be on the ready to leave at a moment's notice. We will only get one window of opportunity," he had said.

I did not have the heart to tell him I would not be going with them but, nevertheless, I had agreed.

As I walked briskly towards my rooms, I focused on my next order of business—First, I needed to grill Alcaeus about this damn mark. Second, figuring out how I was going to rescue the Lord of Flowers from the clutches of evil incarnate.

303

A. R. Morgan

CHAPTER 32

Acceptable behaviour in Alchemical Society never included reactive, emotionally charged responses. One never made decisions out of rash impulse, motivated by feelings. That was how bias happened, how the balance of nature became corrupt. Personal agenda, desire, and passions were cancerous self-serving motivations that harmed the collective.

That is what the Elders once had us believe. Emotional attachment was only acceptable with your Natural Match, that which The Mother deemed at the time of each Alchemist's birth. Even then, an Alchemist's purpose was to maintain the natural order, and to birth the next generation of philosophers and scientists. Parents raised their children by the strict code set forth by our ancestors so very long ago. Affection became limited after age five, which is also when one began rigorous studies. All played their part. All but me.

I had been the anomaly. I had felt deeply, with great passion. In the face of injustice, flames of retribution burned in my veins. Breathtaking scenery led me to tears of awe and witnessing an injured soul stirred an ocean of empathy. I once craved a connection that was deeper than what was acceptable. My beginning was spent desperately bottling it all up, doing everything I could to become a proper Alchemist and philosopher. To fit in. My mother would tell me to envision a steel box within my mind and to fill it with all my feelings. Imagine locking it with the strongest lock and not touching it. I tried so very hard, but time and time again, I failed. Just as I felt like I was failing now.

My row with Toby had already left me in an emotional state; now, I was itching for a fight. And Llyr had pointed directly at one—Alcaeus' deceitful behaviour regarding the Familiar's Mark.

Trying to push down the wrath building within me, I walked

quickly and with purpose towards the tower that held our rooms. Hurt from the betrayal stung with annoyance and a flash of queasiness had me clenching my teeth as I tried to swallow it away.

I was not telepathic, nor did I have any idea how to tap into the neurological 'gift' that was supposed to come with this mysterious mark but, nonetheless, I unleashed my thoughts.

How dare you lie to me! We had a deal! You were to tell me the truth! I do not know if you can hear this, Alcaeus, but by The Mother, I will rip the truth out of you if it's the last thing I do!

No response came and perhaps it was for the best as I was on the edge of verbally screaming my answers.

At the appearance of his study, I reached for the door. Locked. Snorting and with runes flashing, the doorknob fell to a hundred paper-clips bouncing on the floor. I slammed it open, only to find the room empty, the fireplace cold.

"Can I help you, my lady?"

I whipped around to see Tomwyl standing there with a bewildered look on his face as he took in the damaged door. He looked in far better shape than when I had last seen him, a crumpled bloody heap on the floor.

"Where is he, Tomwyl?"

He shook his head, confused. "My lady? His Highness is indisposed at the moment."

Glaring up at him, I asked again. "Where, Tomwyl? His highness and I have urgent business."

Brows furrowing, he replied, "I was unaware of his appointment with you, my lady. He is currently attempting to secure Lord LeGervase's release, I believe."

Grinding my teeth, my fire went out a bit at that. Damn him.

"Fine, I understand. I need to see Elis. Would you be so kind as to direct me to the dungeons?"

"My apologies, Lady Von Boden, but the queen has prohibited any visitation between you and the lord upon pain of death. His majesty has requested I inform you to wait for him in his rooms as well as," the steward cleared his throat, clearly uncomfortable with what he was about to say next, "trust that he has all in hand."

At his mention of trust, my eyes widened at the audacity. "Well, you can tell your hypocritical Prince his idea of trust is bullshit," I hissed.

Walking past him, I ignored his call out and made my way to the library.

▽▽ ♂ � ♂ ♗

My mind stewed. I stalked the aisles of the bookshelves like an angry animal and people were quick to move out of my way. Dirty looks and curses flew past me, but I ignored them as I came to a stop in front of Sage Kevyn's door. I raised my hand to knock but the door swung open.

"Melisandre! It is lovely to see you– oh my, that look tells me something is afoot. Come, come. Inside."

The sage ushered me in, quickly shutting the door behind us. The fire was ablaze, as they usually were in this palace. I went to take a seat, but a visceral memory of my time with Alcaeus in this very spot had me veering away, arms crossed and pacing.

It took me a moment to realise the wise old man had taken a seat at his desk, carefully regarding me. He made no move to begin the conversation, just watched.

Turning to him, I asked, "What do you know of Familiar Marks? Or Vampire marks in general?"

"I know as much as one can without being a Vampire myself," He replied thoughtfully, "although there are many different kinds of marks between the species. Truly, marks of any kind are all considered magical contracts."

"Then why do you not see marks among the Fae? I've only seen it among Vampires, witches, sorcerers, and the like."

"Fae do give visible marks but only if they possess powerful magic. But the Fae are unique in that their promises are inherent, the consequences of not keeping their word having direct consequences to their souls. Morality and ethics are quite different for each magical creature and so marks were created in those species to bind them to their word. Words themselves have power but if, say, the promised were to meet an untimely end, then the promisor could be free. The rate of murder would inevitably spike. Thus, the importance of marks."

I considered this as I stopped pacing, finally coming to sit in the chair facing the desk.

"That would explain Elis and Llyr's mating mark."

Sage Kevyn nodded. "Quite so. When one finds another, they desire to spend the rest of their immortal lives with, a Chosen Mate's Mark is made between the two."

An idea popped into my head, and my stomach turned a bit at the thought. "Um, do you by chance know how it works? Are there words exchanged? I read a book on markings but that wasn't mentioned."

He raised a silver eyebrow at me, and a little light of misplaced understanding twinkled in his blue eyes.

Thankfully, he did not inquire further but answered, "Why yes, of course. All marks are a ritual in their own way. Most especially mating marks. As you could probably guess, Vampires infuse the essence of their power into their bite after they have said the mating words. Here," he got up from his desk and hobbled over to his bookcase. Tapping his lips as he searched, he gave an 'ah!' and grabbed a tome. Flipping through it, he came back over to me and gave me the book. "There it is. This is what is said during the mating ritual."

Skimming over the words, I read:

Oh my Chosen
To thee, I bind myself
Accept my mark and giveth yours
Together forever under moon and sun
Our souls do we bind for our hearts already beat as one
Let me not stray from thy side, nor thou from mine
And we shall both vow, to love and cherish
And hold thee in all loyalty
This do I vow
My word to you, my bond

These were not the words Alcaeus and I used. A strange flurry of disappointment and relief swirled within me, but my frustration of finding no lead in this mysterious mark heightened.

I shot up and began unbuttoning the top of my shirt.

"Melisandre...?"

"Sage Kevyn, please take a look at this mark. Have you ever seen anything like it? Llyr told me something about it being of the Old Tongues?"

I shoved my shirt collar below my shoulder, looking up at him. Brows furrowed he tilted his head to look.

"My, that is very complex. These markings..." Kevyn muttered, sounding puzzled, "they are ancient. It has been several thousand years since I have seen them. Unfortunately, the mark is incomplete so I cannot say for certain exactly what it is. Llyr is most correct but...Yes, this owl is indeed Alcaeus but," I heard Kevyn inhale sharply, "that's... it is... oh my," he whispered sharply.

Suddenly he grabbed me by the shoulders and swung me around to face him. Eyes wide and penetrating, the lines of his face taut with tension.

"Whatever you do, do NOT show this to the queen! This is not a Familiar mark, and she will know it immediately. I have only seen the ancient runes surrounding it once before, very, very long ago. Even now the gods are up to something... No," he said sharply as I went to interrupt, "I will not speak of it for fear the darkness would carry it to the queen. Trust Alcaeus! He knows what he is doing. Keep it hidden, my dear!" He shoved my shirt back over my shoulder and I rushed to rebutton it. Sage Kevyn rubbed his hands together anxiously, clearly deep in thought. "Yes, and we must tread carefully. Also, while you were away, I did some research of my own on your issue with telekinesis."

He went back to his desk and after opening several drawers, placed a pile of parchment on top.

"Here. This should help you break down the magical aspect of it so you can negate it. If my theories and calculations are correct, that's all you can do. In the meantime, I have a visitor I need to attend to so I should be on my way. Leave a note if you need anything else."

Sage Kevyn grabbed his long robe jacket hanging on the back of a chair and headed for the door. He stopped abruptly before turning back to me. His crystal blue eyed stare was full of ominous seriousness. "Remember Melisandre: do not let the queen see."

The door clicked and he was gone.

Pacing a bit, riddled with the desire to see if Alcaeus was back but now also terribly curious as to what Sage Kevyn had discovered, my curiosity finally won out. Sitting at the desk, I pored over his notes.

"Of course!" I exclaimed. "How the hell did I not see this before?! It is not telekinesis as we know it but rather... Perhaps the magic itself can control molecular structure, similar to what I can do... and she can change its velocity and thus resulting in a larger pressure? She would need to in order to reanimate dead tissue. Telekinesis and necromancy, of course! Dammit! I don't have time to break down the components of her magical manipulation of physics!"

Coming to an abrupt stand, I scrubbed my head in frustration, my hands becoming fists on my scalp. My mind raced as I tried to think of alternatives. Coming to a stand next to the window, I watched the wind beat against the trees, leaves scattering. Suddenly a stick flew at the window, smacking it with a bang. A bang that triggered an answer.

"Aha!" I half shouted; half laughed. "Of course! Force is a vector quantity! All I must do is negate or possibly change its course from A to B... perhaps by slowing down the intermolecular forces the magic cuts through, assuming magic has a tangible structure." I rushed back to the desk, grabbing the pen and some empty parchment as I began to write out several equations to validate my theory.

The hours ticked by, and flames burned low. Finally, I was satisfied with my theory although eager to try it out. I wondered if Alcaeus could perform the same magic or if perhaps, he knew someone I could test it out on.

Alcaeus.

The thought of him reignited the anger at his secrecy. As if the gods themselves had heard me, a gentle knock sounded at the door.

"Come in."

Ada's mousy head peeked in.

"Begging your pardon milady, but you asked me to inform you when the prince had returned. He is waiting for you in his study."

Getting up, I compiled all the papers together, placing them inside the desk. This was the safest place for my research; the last thing I wanted was the queen to catch wind of it.

"Lead the way, Ada."

For being so small, Ada was brisk of pace and if I was not paying attention, I was at risk of losing her. When we finally did arrive back at the study, she bid me farewell and left. The door handle had been repaired it seemed. As I reached for it, I stopped, having heard music coming from within.

Not the piano I missed hearing him play, no. This was more modern. More like the music I would listen to in my own library back home. Opening the door slowly, I looked around.

The swaying notes of *The Way You Look Tonight* were now crisp in the air, giving the room a warmer vibe. The object of my ire had his back to me, a glass of whiskey in one hand as he stood, watching the flames in the fireplace crackle and dance.

As much as I wanted to enjoy the long lines of his back and the perfect fit of his pants, I would not be swayed.

"Alcaeus!" I snapped, slamming the door shut. He still did not turn to me. "How dare you! How could you?! You swore you would tell me the truth, always! You promised me! Both Sage Kevyn and Llyr confirmed that this mark—"

"Dance with me."

CHAPTER 33

"This is not a Familiar Ma—I beg your pardon?" I sputtered to a halt, believing I had misheard him.

"Dance with me, *mikrós asvós*. Dance with me and we will talk."

He finally turned; his handsome face unreadable. Slowly he set down the tumbler as he stalked toward me.

I placed my hands on my hips, squaring up. "Absolutely not! Not until I have some goddamn answers—Alcaeus! Unhand m—Oh!" The prince snagged my hand and pulled me against him, his other arm going around my waist tightly. One would think our height difference would have made this position awkward but, somehow, it worked.

The smell of him, feeling the strength of his arms affected me instantly. I had resisted when he had grabbed me, but as he began to sway to Tony Bennett's crooning, my body begrudgingly relaxed.

"I really don't like you right now." I whispered, tempted to slam my heel down on his foot.

"So, the Fae noble and our dear Sage told you it was not a Familiar mark?" He asked, ignoring my statement.

I glared up at him. "Indeed, they did. Sage Kevyn also confirmed that, um," I cleared my throat, "it is not a Chosen Mate's mark either. What in the hell are you up to? Explain yourself!"

To my ever-growing ire, he had the audacity to chuckle at this.

"Disappointment?" He had the wisdom to quickly continue speaking before I could respond. "They are correct, it is not a Familiar Mark. Nor is it a Chosen Mate's. Melisandre, do you truly believe I would make you my Familiar?" He slowly twirled me in his arms so that my back was pressed against his chest, his arms caging me as he swayed us to the music. Leaning down, his voice rumbled against the side of my head, "Are my feelings so unclear to you, even still?"

"I do not possess the powers of telepathy that you and your kind so clearly do," I hissed, "nor am I able to decipher what your motives are anymore! It's not a Chosen Mates so now your feelings are even more confusing. If I am not your Familiar then what is this? What are you scheming Alcaeus!?"

I tried to pull away but still, he held me to him, even as I was turned back around. Except for this time, we stopped dancing. Instead of answering right away, he studied me with a tenderness that threatened to pacify my anger. Fingers trailed gently over my face as if he were trying to memorise the lines.

With his thumb still caressing my lips, he said, "I have been bound in more ways than I have the capability of confessing, my words and truths imprisoned by Ragna and her sorcerer. I have never lied to you, but I am at the mercy of forced omission, mikrós asvós. With desperate reliance on your intuition and intellectual fortitude, I ask you to continue searching for the truth. This mark is something more, something deeper than a Chosen or a Familiar Mark. What I can say is this," He slid his fingers into the collar of my shirt. I do not know when he managed to unbutton my top two buttons. He slowly revealed my mark, caressing it.

"You have desperately feared the shackles of this oath, frantically trying to break free from it. I know it well; it has been a constant presence in our connection. Yet if only you knew that this was the key, the solution we have been looking for. But if you cannot believe that," he cupped my face fully now, "if even at the very end, you lose all faith in me, I beg you to trust in this: our song has been written in the stars, our fates tied together. I have watched over you for far longer than you could possibly know. Though my soul may be in pieces, my heart in its entirety is yours, always. May the gods strike me down now if you believe this false – I love you, Melisandre. I've loved you for a very long time."

The world stopped as soon as his confession fell from his lips. All the frowning tension in my face dropped as my eyes widened. The pull between us vibrated with intensity. Warmth, joy, surprise, and disbelief all warred within me. For a moment, I begged time to stop. To let this be real. Let this be a reality where I can say yes. Tears filled my eyes as I pictured what could be. What I wanted to be. To let him in without fear. To no longer walk this earth alone.

Yet my cursed rationale forced me to face the cruel reality that clawed through the vestiges of happiness. Regret spilled over. Upon its wings, a biting sorrow as I turned away from a dream, I had never dared dream.

Pushing my arms out, I spun away from his grasp.

"No! We cannot Alcaeus! This is insanity! You cannot feel this for me! She will kill you! Ragna's vengeance and her wrath will decimate whatever chances at freedom we have! You know we cannot go down this path! This is a death sentence! Think about your soul!"

"Undoubtedly, our path is fraught with danger and risk! Once the mark is completed, it will be impossible to hide it; but when that happens, we will be free! And we will be unstoppable! Yes, for now, we must move with utmost secrecy, covert with every measure of the feelings we have for one another. Still—"

I waved my hand in finality. "No, Alcaeus, no! We cannot afford this love! When she realises you will never truly be hers, she will destroy you! Or force you to her! If only to prove that, if she cannot have you, no one can! I will not... I cannot bear to see—" I choked on the last of my words, unable to say it. Even thinking about it brought about that reality with a cruel vengeance. I thought of Sophie and what came of her for even having the light connection she did with me; how it was manipulated and twisted till one of us was destroyed. I covered my face with my hands, fighting back my emotions.

"My love, please," He begged as I felt his hands around my shoulders, but I shook my head, pushing them away yet again.

At the cost of everything, I knew I had to convince him to let go of this notion of love. I had so many questions, especially about how long he claimed to have loved me, but right now, we needed to control ourselves or suffer irrevocable consequences.

"No! Stop. Stop it!" I looked back up at him. "Promise me you will not love me! You've been calling me 'my love' and I have let it slide, but no more! I am an Alchemist, for the Mother's sake! My biological design has no place for this type of sentiment! That has never been my fate, no matter what you say! There is no happy ending waiting for me, in this life or the next! I accepted this long ago and so should you! So, give up Alcaeus. Whatever this mark is, have done with it but do not, I beg you, do not risk everything by making the mistake of loving me!"

Before I could react, the prince ripped his shirt off and grabbed my wrist.

"Look, Melisandre! Do you see it?!" He jerked, pointing to his chest. Black swirls stood stark through his chest hair. My eyes widened. A twin mark to mine, right above his heart. I had just seen him the day before and it had not been there. Had he masked it with magic?

Suddenly, he pulled me forward so the hand he held smacked against him. Alcaeus moved it to cover the mark and I felt the beating of his heart. Stronger than ever before, a war drum declaring its presence.

"Did you know that a Vampire's heart does not beat, even living ones? Why do you think even humans refer to us all as the Undead? Yet there is one reason and one reason only that life can enter the chambers of their heart. You know another Vampire whose heart lives!" Alcaeus declared earnestly.

I swallowed hard. I did. I did indeed.

"Elis' heart..."

He nodded, the corner of his lips lifting. "Yes, it does. And why does it beat, Melisandre?"

"Because... because of Llyr," I whispered, my eyes once again filling. "But I thought...?"

A breathtaking smile broke across his face. "Yes, because of Llyr." He stepped closer now, gazing down at me. "His heart beats because he loves him."

I began shaking my head again, placing my other hand against him to push myself away but all the fight in me had waned. He placed his other hand on mine, holding me to him.

"Only a Vampire who loves does its heart beat true. I could no more stop loving you than I could cease its tempo. It beats for you, your name its only song."

His words filled me with both euphoria and despair, words I had always desperately wanted to hear yet I knew they could not be mine.

"You said you've been watching over me and have loved me longer than I could know. So, how long? For how long did you know me?" I asked desperately.

Alcaeus lifted my hands up and kissed them before he answered.

"I knew the moment of my creation, almost three thousand years ago, another had been made just for me. For thousands of years, I waited until hope had all but left me. Then, several hundred years ago, I first felt the call of your presence and laid eyes on a beautiful lone woman, sleeping with a book on her face, resting against one of the biggest hybrid Kelpies I had ever seen, in the human forests of Scotland. Since then,

I have watched over you, doing my best to keep the Otherworld from your door."

Words abandoned me at the realisation that Alcaeus had known of me, protected me, yet concealed himself.

"W-why? Why did you not reveal yourself? The woods! You knew who I was! Why did you pretend otherwise?" I asked, scrambling to understand, trying to comprehend what he had revealed.

At this, his face relaxed, and mirth danced across the lines.

"Come now, *mikrós asvós*, can you truly tell me you would have welcomed me with open arms? Especially after Lord LeGervase would have undoubtedly told you who I was. No, I think not. You were in hiding. Revealing who I was, what I was, would have only made you run. And I needed you here. When the time was right, all would have been revealed to you. I would have very much liked to woo you, court you properly. Seduce you. Maybe even take you on what humans call a 'date'. But, alas, Ragna was one step ahead of me; I fear my feelings for you blinded me. An amateur mistake I deeply regret."

"And that is exactly what I am afraid of," I replied solemnly. "That your feelings for me will be your demise."

"Or they will be the strength that I need to give me the fortitude to slay my enemies and protect the woman I love," he whispered, leaning down to kiss me.

I closed my eyes as his lips brushed mine, giving in even for just this one moment. My heart exploded, deepening the kiss as my arms flew around his neck. Alcaeus pressed our bodies together tightly, running his large hands up and down my back.

Suddenly, something made my consciousness ease back into reality. "The woman you *love*?"

It was the last voice I expected to hear, making my stomach plummet and ice swallow my insides.

It was the voice I should have expected the most.

CHAPTER 34

Ragna's incredulity sliced through the air, shattering the illusion of whatever reality we had tried to make.

We spun around and Alcaeus pushed me behind him, shielding me. Ragna's eyes burned; her cheeks sunken with rage. For just a moment, I swore I saw sorrow and grief flicker in that fiery emerald gaze. Yet it was quickly replaced with unimaginable fury.

Guards surrounded her, filling Alcaeus's chambers. Mage Ilirhun stood silently behind her, ready to do her bidding. Most likely he was the reason we did not hear their entrance. Beyond the open door, advisors and nobles peeked in. Shock ripped through me at the one person I did not expect to see standing next to the queen: Ada.

Wringing her tiny hands, she dared not look at me, the little traitor. It was my mistake for forgetting where her loyalties truly lie. Where the prince's own guards and men were, I did not know, but the answer to that did not bode well for us.

Fists clenched; her lips curled with barely contained outrage.

"Did the word 'love' fall from my intended's lips? Surely not," she scoffed as she stepped forward. Alcaeus' glowing sword appeared at his side and swiftly he drew it. An answering call of steel and a whistle of spears resounded in the space as the guards faced the threat.

Pointing his sword at her, Alcaeus demanded, "Where are my men, Ragna?! What have you done to Sotiris? Where is Cillian?!"

"Your right-hand man will never serve you again, sweet prince. Nor will he ever see the afterlife or reincarnate. His power is mine now. His soul was a fine wine, aged so perfectly. Powerful too. And your pathetic lich fled when we tried to imprison him. In fact, several of my nobles have mysteriously disappeared, including Lord Zhenbai." the queen hissed. "They have abandoned you, Prince of Nightmares! But I digress." Ragna's face morphed into unimaginable anger. "Truly, my intended, my future husband would not deliberately betray his queen by falling IN LOVE WITH HER AFTER I EXPRESSLY FORBID IT? Must I slay another, Alcaeus? Were the souls of your family, your best men, not enough of a lesson for you?!"

"Sweet Mother," I gasped, my heart clenching in horror upon hearing the demise of Alcaeus' second-in-command.

"THE GODS CURSE YOU RAGNA! You will not touch her! This you will not take from me! Not this time, not ever! I will rip the other half of my soul out before I even let you close to her! MELISANDRE. IS. MINE!" Alcaeus roared, baring teeth.

His presence seemed to amplify tenfold and even I felt his power fill the room. Ragna appeared unfazed, her own power answering back. My skin buzzed as the magic crawled over my whole body. Those who had been eavesdropping as well as Ada, scattered. The amount of power in the room would have driven lesser creatures insane.

I moved to Alcaeus' side, refusing to let him take the brunt of her ire. Ragna's gaze darted in my direction. She pointed a black-clawed finger at me.

"You deceitful snake! *Hóra*! The arrogance in thinking you can take what is mine! You are no different than that mongrel piece of filth you call your ward! Too long have I allowed this insolence, this treasonous behaviour to go unpunished! Consider the boy's life forfeit!" Ragna screeched sharply, her voice a blade against my ears.

I should have been fearful of threats. Perhaps I should have cowered before her if only to keep Toby safe. If only I had been wiser, the kind of Alchemist my society had attempted to beat into me.

"It is you who has no right to Alcaeus, you murderous bitch! Look at you! Hiding behind children and your own subjects, using them as shields to try and command me! You call yourself a warrior, a shield-maiden worthy of Valhalla? Ha! You can't even get a man to love you without ripping out half of his soul! You want me, Ragna?!" I goaded, stepping in front of Alcaeus who tried to pull me back, but I threw him off, getting so close I was now staring up at Ragna. "You want me to bow before you? Force me to do your bidding? MAKE ME YOURSELF, YOU WEAK PATHETIC WASTE OF AIR!" I shouted.

The Queen of the Nightmare Court did not respond with equal

320

challenge. In fact, I was not prepared for the cocked head, the narrowing of eyes, and the psychotic calm smile that turned her face from cruel to terrifying. The prince grabbed my arm, once more trying to pull me to him. This time I let him, naturally easing into the shelter of his embrace.

"I do believe I shall, Alchemist." She whispered. "Bring them!"

Black armoured hands grabbed me, pulling me away from Alcaeus as spearheads pointed dangerously close to my neck. I felt movement at my back.

A white sword arced through the air, its razor-sharp edge singing at it sliced through metal, flesh, and bone. The knights around me fell to the ground with screams of agony. With predatory speed, Alcaeus thrust his sword directly at the queen's throat. His aim would have been true, but it stopped just short; the tip penetrated her throat only just, yet no blood welled. Her face was a cold, calm mask of confidence.

The sword began to shake, and Alcaeus roared again, fighting whatever it was that held him back. Suddenly, Nemesis clattered to the ground and the Nightmare Prince curled around himself, almost going down to one knee as he let out a strangled groan. A strange green glow emanated from him.

"Alcaeus!" I cried out, reaching out to my lover only to be pulled away yet again. I jerked to see Ragna holding a hand over the shining orb hanging from her neck. It too glowed green. That is when it dawned on me. The necklace, the one that called to me like a siren that day when Ragna met me in her sitting room, contained the other half of Alcaeus' soul. That was how she was controlling him.

Ragna vanished, taking Alcaeus with her. Before I could protest, I was dragged out of the room and marched to the great hall. My joints ached from being pulled in multiple directions and I tried to shake off the hands that held me, but to no avail. They continued to lead us into the throne room where Ragna was already seated.

However, it was not her that my eyes trained on. It was the little boy and a thin man chained to a post that had been erected in front of the dais.

Elis and Toby.

Toby's shirt was in shreds, his back a red mess of flesh and blood pooled at his feet. He had been whipped until the bone peeked through. He was still half human and at this rate, he would die if he was not attended to.

Just as we came to a stop, I caught motion to my right as Llyr broke through the crowd. He was out of breath and holding my staff. Desperately looking for Elis, he found him with a strangled sob. A hand covered his mouth at his mate's broken and beaten body.

The queen rose from her throne just as Alcaeus, a thick magical chain around his neck with his arms bound, was brought before her. With a battle cry, he broke the chains around him and then began tugging at the collar. Quickly, Mage Ilirhun said something, and a magical cage came around him. The prince spat a volley of insults in Ancient Greek. Gone was the calm and collected man I had known, the chained prisoner that had been caged for over a thousand years coming to the surface.

I turned to my best friend and ward, struggling against the guards. A large crowd had gathered around, soldiers keeping them far back from the scene. Ragna put her arms out.

"Nobles and Councillors of the Nightmare Court! Here before you, is your *beloved* prince." She spat his name as if it tasted bitter in her mouth. "He has committed grievous treason by betraying his queen, disobeying my commands! Too long have I allowed my dearest prince his freedom. What could have caused this heart-breaking betrayal you might wonder?" Ragna raised her hand and pointed to me. "This Alchemist has seduced your prince and has turned him against me! He has protected her from my wrath but no more!"

Her gaze dropped down to where the two were chained. The pillar they were chained to disappeared, causing both of them to drop. Toby cried out, the fall awakening him, and his shoulders began to shake. Elis groaned as he sat up on his knees, reaching out for Toby but stopping when the Queen began addressing him.

"Elis LeGervase, you have aligned yourself with this traitorous criminal! Time and time again you have stood up for Lady Von Boden; there is only one queen here and it is not HER! I told you to know your place! Your mate has been begging me to release you, making promises he has no business making with me in an effort to save your life! Stand and look at him! I want you to look into his eyes while you receive your punishment. And you, boy! Nasty little thief! Your time is at an end! You can thank your irresponsible guardian for your demise!"

"No!" I screamed with rage. "No! You will not touch them, Ragna!"

"Please, Your Majesty! I beg you! Spare them in the name of the gods, spare them!" Llyr cried out, dropping my Alchemist's Staff. It rolled towards me and I called to it, gently transmuting the floor at an angle.

Toby managed to stand and limp to Elis, wrapping his arms around the Vampire's middle. Tears streamed down Elis' face as he wrapped a hand around Toby's head, holding him. Finally, I was able to rip free of the guard's hold, grabbing my staff. I swung it around making my runes glow. The marble floor changed as spikes shot out, impaling the guards. Screams and shouts arose from the crowd, and I heard more guards moving in but they stopped, hesitating at seeing their fallen comrades. Changing the floor back, I faced toward the dais.

Preparing for the inevitable force that Ragna had bested me with, I tuned into the feel of the environment around me. Compounds, molecules, atoms... Electrons. Energy.

There.

The molecules across the room moved with unimaginable speed. I put my hand up—they slowed. The energy that they carried passed through my field of control and began to dissipate.

Fifty kelvins...forty...thirty...

Energy kept trying to flow into the perimeter I had created, to fill that void. I kept cycling it back to the periphery.

The wall of molecules in front of me slowed to absolute zero. I felt them separating into their elemental atoms; subatomic particles barely held together for now, as the forces that kept up their cohesion ceased within the boundary I'd created. Ragna's telekinetic force hit but immediately dispersed.

My theory had worked.

"What... ?" Ragna gasped, confusion all over her face.

Yet, I had no time to dwell on my small victory; I had to get Toby away and heal his wounds. I trusted Llyr to get Elis away.

"Toby! Come to me now!" I urged, starting to walk towards him.

He turned in Elis' arms, a precious little smile of relief on his face and he nodded.

"That's it, my boy. I'll get you out of here," I whispered.

He began to take a step. I matched it. I looked up at Elis and he looked at me. Our bond shone through his eyes. Then his face fell, jaw going slack. I looked down at Toby whose face also went slack as blood gurgled past his white lips. He choked and sputtered.

I stopped breathing, my heart freezing in my chest. Time seemed to come to a stop.

An agonising scream came from my right, and I glanced that way, only to see Llyr clutch his chest and collapse. Jerking my gaze back, that was when I saw it.

The tip of a blade was thrust through Elis and emerged through Toby's neck.

Emerald green eyes appeared behind them.

A triumphant grin on Queen Ragna Heldóttir's face.

CHAPTER 35

"No..." I could barely hear my broken whisper, shock hitting me like an ice-cold wind.

Ragna jerked the sword out from their bodies, the blood of my loved ones spraying from the blade. They both crashed to the floor before I could reach them. I do not remember moving but I was on my knees before my fallen ward and the Lord of Flowers.

I dropped my staff next to me, my shaking hands hovering over their bodies in horrified disbelief. I almost could not bring myself to touch them, as if doing so would make it real. The sensation of soft brown curls slid through my fingers. Tears spilled down my cheeks. My fingertips touched Elis' cold and lifeless face.

"No, no no no," I chanted silently, over and over.

A numbness began to spread over me, a cold so deep I thought I would never know warmth again. The world seemed to slip far away. All I could hear were the echoes of their voices.

"Yer a terrible shot, Ms. Melly!"

Toby's cheeky grin and twinkle of mischief in those brown eyes.

"I love ya Ms. Melly... yer the closest ta real family I've ever known."

Then, lavender eyes and honey curls filled my mind.

"I will always be there for you, my dearest friend."

That sparkling smile. His comforting embrace.

"I love you far too much to let you walk the worlds alone."

A piercing voice forced me back to reality.

"Stand aside, Alchemist. I will not allow you to continually come in between me, and what is rightfully mine to claim. This is the Nightmare Court thus all souls who die within these walls are mine to devour! I command death here!"

I felt the tip of her sword press against my jugular, the blood on the sword dripping down my neck. Elis' blood. Toby's blood.

Crack.

"Death, you say," I whispered. A wildness began to seep into my veins. I looked down into Toby's lifeless eyes.

Crack.

Elis' eyes were closed, his perfect lashes unmoving.

Crack. Crack.

I let out a humourless chuckle.

"You do not command death. You play at death. Like a child with a gun. You don't know what death is, or its meaning. You are nothing but a puppet-master pulling the strings of rotting flesh." I scoffed, my voice a hollow, deadly calm.

Slowly meeting Ragna's gaze, I wrapped my fingers around my staff. With my other hand, I grabbed the blade at my throat. With a flash, it disintegrated into metal dust. Ragna stumbled back, a wariness beginning to creep into the strained lines on her perfect face.

"I am the Champion of Hel! Daughter of Loki! Death," she spat as she raised her arms wide to display them, "is in my veins! I WILL take their souls, or I will sever yours as I did with the Great Owl! As is my right! Watch, Alchemist! See what the Dauði Dróttning can do!"

I felt her power then, reaching for their bodies.

No. Never again.

SHATTER.

I thrust my staff toward her, transmuting the air, as she had against me, blasting her towards the dais. She smacked against the steps with a bone-crunching thud, her gaze whipping to me.

"DEATH HAS NO POWER HERE!" I bellowed. "FOR I. AM. LIFE!"

Unleashing the hidden power within me, I slammed my staff down and massive transmutation circles exploded out from above and below, vertically and horizontally. They appeared all around us, creating a massive cage. My outer clothes disintegrated from the power, my runes all over my body exposed, shining as if lit by purple fire.

Guards rushed the circles. Only allowing two in, I instantly adjusted the runes in my mind. The two that came through dropped instantly; the circles liquifying their bones the moment they had crossed the circle's barrier.

"STOP HER! BY ALL MEANS, STOP THAT ALCHEMIST!" screamed the queen.

Several more tried to breach it, but promptly exploded into ash and dust. Terrified screams filled the room once more. Mage Ilirhun stepped forward, placing a hand close to the circle. I knew he was testing for magic, yet he would sense none. This was not magic. This was pure and raw energy, the symbols that commanded all things into being. Magical runes appeared around his hand, and he touched the glowing transmutation circle. His hand shook going through it. At first, nothing happened. Suddenly, the runes disappeared, and his hand exploded into dust. He screamed, falling back and hiding his wounded appendage within his cloak.

I positioned Elis and Toby out flat. Then I arranged the bodies of the paralyzed guards to parallel them. Standing in the middle, I held my hands out, my left hovering between the guards. My right towards Elis and Toby. Raising my hands, four glowing circles appeared underneath as well as above the four bodies on the ground.

Ragna paced; her eyes wild. I looked over to see Alcaeus staring at me in wonder and horror.

Let him see. Let them all see the meaning of dealing with the last Alchemist, Daughter of Mother Earth!

Closing my eyes, I focused on allowing the might of all alchemy to course through me and into the circles. The glowing purple symbols began to tick like clocks; the guards clockwise and the ones surrounding Toby and Elis ticking counter clockwise.

Each circle above my ward and friend held the symbols of life and creation. Those on the guards—death, and decay.

Oxygen, hydrogen, nitrogen, carbon, calcium, and phosphorus.

The body of the guards began to shrivel and age in their armour as their life force and bodily fluids were slowly transmuted into Toby and Elis. The bodies of my loved ones began to repair, cells multiplying at great speed. The blood beneath Toby began seeping back into him. The gash on his neck began to scab and then seal. Very carefully, I continued to adjust each symbol on each circle as they continued to heal, carefully closing off each one until the restoration was completed.

Sulphur, potassium, sodium, chlorine, and magnesium.

Putting my forearms together in front of me, pressing them together so the tattoos created a full transmutation circle. It glowed brightly as it activated. Then, I lifted my arms high in a V, palms facing the sky. Energy buzzed around me, every molecule, every atom. Focusing on it, I concentrated on building up the energy, using my own body as a capacitor. Sparks began to zap over me. Electricity began to dance across my skin. I walked slowly so that I was standing in between Toby and Elis, their bodies fully healed.

Waiting.

As electricity began to generate faster, currents began forming around me, shooting out in different directions. The buzzing became louder. The transmutation circles that faced the people surrounding us began to pull energy from their bodies. People began crumpling, attempting to crawl away. I didn't care.

I needed to get the voltage just right.

"Air, earth, fire, water. May what was done be undone. Turn back the sands of time. For lives were lost unjustly, their death serving no purpose to the Great Circle. Fix the cycle which hath been disrupted. I am of the Mother, who created me, and with her power, I shall restore the balance. By the power of the stone and The Elixir, let the breath of life flow once more!" I cried.

I slammed my hands down onto their chests and lightning struck both of them, causing their bodies to jerk upwards, meeting my palms. Life flowed through me and into them.

Suddenly, all the circles around us disappeared. The air felt heavy, still charged. For a moment, nothing seemed to move, as if I had stopped time itself. The power inside me dimmed until, finally, it went silent.

"Live," I whispered, holding my breath. Then, underneath my hands, I felt it.

Thump, tha-thump, tha-thump.

I let out a broken sob, relief shooting through me. Toby coughed, bringing a hand to his neck.

"Ms...Melly?" he croaked.

"I'm here, my sweet boy. You're okay, you're going to be just fine," I said, smoothing back his hair as I kissed his forehead several times. Elis groaned, his hands also coming up to his face. Cracking his eyes open, purple irises stared back at me.

"I should have known it would be your face I would see when I arrived in hell," Elis joked, his voice also hoarse. A desperate laugh escaped me. At the sight of him opening his eyes, I took his face in my hands and kissing him fully.

"Mmmph! By the gods, I really am dead," he said against my lips.

Pulling back with a laugh, I wiped away my tears. Elis sat up and cupped my face. Then his eyes went wide.

"Llyr," he gasped. "Llyr!"

I pointed to where his mate had also sat up, hand on his chest, checking for a wound. It seemed the healing of his mate healed Llyr as well. Elis tried to get up but stumbled. I went to help him, but Llyr was already at our side. Toby's arms went around me.

I hugged him to me, then gently said, "Go with them, Toby."

Toby squeezed me a bit harder but then complied, moving away from me. The three backed away from Ragna, moving toward the door. The room had cleared during the event and only a few soldiers remained.

"How... ? How is this possible?!" gasped Ragna. The syphoning of energy I had pulled when doing the transmutations had laid her out, weakening her, and she was shaking as she lifted herself halfway off the floor. "No Alchemist in history was capable of resurrection! How can you possibly give life to the dead? You are no god!"

I turned to her then. The cage around Alcaeus was gone and he was slowly moving toward me. The look on his face told me he knew what I had done and why I could do it. Yet, instead of fear or horror, only fascination, warmth, and dare I say it—love, filled his gaze.

Before I could answer, Mage Ilirhun spoke. "Oh, Lady Von Boden, you have been hiding a great secret indeed," his raspy voice deepened in revelation. "You possess the Philosopher's Stone! That is why! It is the only logical explanation! The Elixir of Life! It all makes sense! You slayed your own people to create the stone! Show it to me! Where is it?" He demanded; his tone maniacal. Ilirhun beat his staff upon the ground in eagerness. Ragna's eyes were wide, excitement filling her face.

I stared back at them. Alcaeus was only a few feet from me when I replied.

"I do not have the stone."

The mage threw back his hood, revealing a tattoo-riddled face and bald head. His sockets were empty of eyes. His flesh looked rotted away, his teeth fully exposed. "You lie! That is impossible! You have it!"

Switching my gaze from them to Alcaeus, I looked at the hand he reached out to me with. I looked deeply into his eyes, knowing my own were filled with guilt, shame, and a resolute acceptance.

"I do not have the stone," I repeated. Taking a deep breath, I braced myself as I was about to confess what I had never uttered out loud. "I am the Philosopher's Stone."

CHAPTER 36

"Well, well, well," cooed Ragna, and we both turned to her. She looked completely triumphant. As she should; the greatest weapon in the Otherworld was standing in her throne room.

I took Alcaeus' hand then, curling my hand into his large warm one and finding immediate comfort.

"It is time to finish the Familiar ritual–" Ragna stopped, staring not at me, but at the incomplete mark between my neck and shoulder. Her jaw dropped, exposing her fangs. Her face went white, and veins popped on her forehead. "No... It cannot be... That is not the Familiar Mark! Alcaeus! What have you..." her eyes widened with comprehension. "That is... Fated... NO!" She screamed, her hands fisting her golden hair. She fell to her knees, keening as if in grief. "How could the gods be so CRUEL! He was supposed to be mine! MINE!"

Alcaeus turned to me, wrapping me up in his arms. My own slid up his chest, my hands cupping his face.

"My love," he said hurriedly, "we must complete the mark now!"

I nodded quickly, as he sliced the mark on his chest, blood welling and dripping down. Ragna's screaming sorrow faded out in the background as I gazed into my Vampire's eyes.

With speed, he began:

"Melisandre Von Boden –
> *To thee, I give my mark, the last of three.*
> *That which was once unmade, made whole again*
> *Together our blood doth flow*
> *Thine in mine, mine in thine*
> *The thread in which our souls thus bind*

As was proclaimed at the breath of first light.
Return unto me as the stars align
One chord, one soul
To thee, I claim ye bound for all eternity
Beginning to end, in darkness and in light.
Death nor life shall tear asunder that which was made for none other.
Thusly to thee I bind."

Rushing, I began, "Alcaeus Pallas, to thee—Alcaeus? Alcaeus what's wrong?!"

His face suddenly contorted; teeth fully bared. Shoving me violently from him, I fell to the ground. Spinning, I looked up at him only to see the green glow emanating from him once again. Turning to Ragna, who was still on her knees with one hand buried in her hair as if to tear it out. She glowed brightly, gripping the necklace tightly. Alcaeus cried out and I turned back to him, slowly getting to my knees as I reached out for him.

"Alcaeus...? My... my love," I whispered brokenly. "Stay with me."

He groaned, sinking to his knees. Beating the ground with his fist, the marble broke and splintered. Those beautiful midnight eyes snapped to me.

"Always... remember... *mikrós asvós*," he choked out, as if there was a vice around his neck, "Remember that... my heart... beats... only... for you."

With that, he let out a screaming groan. I backed up, trepidation crawled up my spine. Still, I tried to break through the curse that held him. "No! Alcaeus! Fight it! You must fight it!" I turned to Ragna. Tears streaked her face as rage and jealousy consumed her form.

"LEAVE HIM ALONE!" I screamed, getting ready to transmute the floor around her to throw her off balance.

"He... is... mine..." Ragna bit out each word, slowly coming to look at me with bloodshot eyes. "The Norns promised me...THEY PROMISED ME HE WOULD BECOME MINE!"

Something grabbed me by the throat with a crushing grip.

Alcaeus.

However, the man I knew, the one who had been slowly filling the void in my heart, was no longer present. He was gone, replaced by the puppet of the queen.

Eyes filled with green fire looked vacantly back at me, his face slack with apathy. With speed I could not even comprehend, Alcaeus' other arm shot out, hitting me straight in the solar plexus. Suddenly, I was airborne. I hit the ground with a crack, my head snapping back. Then I heard the song of Nemesis.

"Slice her up a bit my love. I already made the mistake of underestimating her once; we cannot have that again. We need her ready for Yaldā as the games are fast approaching! Shall we test the limits of the Stone's regenerative abilities? Come! A few hacked limbs should do the trick!" Ragna babbled psychotically. Then she turned to me, the look of a woman who knows she has won. "You will need to kill him if you want to get to me," she said slyly, "and we both know you cannot do that."

An emotion I have never felt before, born of violent grief and frustration burst through me. The stone inside me flickered, trying to come to life. While the stone held an unimaginable amount of power, my own body had so little energy left to tap into it. Yet, still, I took a step toward the necromancer queen. I would kill her the old-fashioned way.

Just as I had turned my back to the prince, I heard the distinct notes of Alcaeus' sword. I dodged and rolled, coming to my feet. I grabbed my staff just in time to raise it above my head to block the blow. Barely able to defend against the speed of his attacks, my arms were soon covered in slashes. My grip was slippery from my own blood.

The white blade glowed in mockery, a cruel reminder of my powerlessness against it. With speed and efficiency, Alcaeus came after me. This was not like the time in the field; it quickly became evident now how much he had held back.

I heard Toby's cries behind me, unnaturally cutting off, but I had no time to see why.

Blocking another blow, I was too slow for the next. Blood loss and cut muscles were making it difficult to keep hold of my staff. Trying to bend my ribs to the side, his blade swung upwards, slicing the side of my ribcage. The momentum had me spinning before landing hard on my back. My staff went flying, clattering away from me. My side burned as I felt the blood flow.

The blade came down and I rolled, but this time Alcaeus pinned my outstretched arm with his foot, keeping me from fully escaping. I cried out, desperately punching and pushing his leg while pulling at my arm. For fear of my arm breaking, I began to transmute the ground; a spike through the leg would do it. Before I could complete it, however, my Mark burned like a thousand suns and I screamed.

Alcaeus raised his sword above my trapped appendage.

"Wait! No!" I cried out, thrusting out my other hand to stop him. I curled around myself when I saw the sword fall.

Clang!

The blow did not come. I looked up to see an obsidian-black sword blocking the prince's attack. A black boot kicked him squarely in the chest, shoving him away.

A strong arm lifted me up, pulling me against a broad chest. Before I could see who held me, Alcaeus was back on the attack, sword swinging.

My rescuer parried with ease, all the while maintaining a death grip around my waist, angling me away from the fight.

"*Gu leòr!*" the stranger's thunderous voice snapped.

Black smoky tendrils darted out from behind me, wrapping fully around the Nightmare Prince. My lover struggled like the mindless puppet he was but could not break free.

Sheathing his sword, the mysterious man holding me slid his other hand up and around my neck firmly. I squirmed in his iron grip.

"Release me!" I snapped, to no avail. My wounds burned and I whimpered against the tight hold. His chest rumbled with quiet laughter. Pressing his lips to my ear, his warm breath made me shiver.

"I will do no such thing, little one. Llyr has bargained and I intend to claim what is mine. Do not fret—we shall soon be free of this wretched place."

I looked to see Ragna storming towards us, battle axes in hand. Zombies began filling the room, answering their master's call.

"Ruarc Ó Ceallaigh, Champion of The Morrigan," Ragna growled out. "Intruding upon my lands! How dare you show up here, unannounced and uninvited! What possible reason could the Unseelie King have for invading my realm?!" She spat. "This is an act of war!"

My eyes widened, remembering what Llyr had said to me.

Be ready.

Ruarc began walking backward. My feet dangled but I had stopped struggling.

"War has ever been at your doorstep Ragna, when you slaughtered one of my nobles and imprisoned my ally. By all accounts, I should be

334

taking King Alcaeus! Unfortunately, your tampering with his soul has cheated me out of it. You owe me this debt, Ragna Valdis Heldóttir! Attempt to stop me and I will unleash the Wild Hunt on your city at this very moment and not even your army of corpses can stop it!" Ruarc challenged.

For the first time, Ragna showed fear. Lowering her axes, she glared a promise of retaliation but made no move to stop him. Alcaeus too had stopped fighting, staring blankly back at us. My heart clenched at the sight of him. I began to struggle once again.

"No, I cannot leave him!" I cried. "Alcaeus! Come back to me! Fight her!"

The hand at my neck slipped around to the back of my head, fingers slipping into my hair. Fisting the strands, the Fae Champion jerked my head back, forcing me to look up at him.

My eyes widened.

Unearthly beauty mixed with monstrous features stared back at me. The left half of his face was angelically beautiful, his eye an intricate swirl of aquamarine blue and sparkling gold. Perfectly straight nose, and full lips. The other side of his face was as black as ebony, the eye a monster yellow with specks of red. His nostril was uneven as if someone had tried to cut it off, and scars riddled that side of his face. Ruarc's hair was longer than my own, thick and wild, like a fountain of bright red blood flowing down his body. Upon his head sat a black crown made of obsidian, raven feathers, and burnt elder branches.

"He is lost to you, little Alchemist! Let him go!" He growled down at me.

"No! I will not give up on him," I whispered, a tear escaping me.

He tracked its path and then looked back into my eyes. "Your friends have already gone through the portal, as must we." The Unseelie King turned to Ragna. "Until Yaldā, Queen of the Nightmare Court. May the best champion win."

Immobilised, I could do nothing as I was dragged backward, Alcaeus still bound by shadow.

I had to try one last time.

"Alcaeus!" I screamed. The green glow around him dampened and he shook his head

Just as clear eyes found mine, we disappeared into the darkness.

THE END.

Thank you for reading **The Heart of an Alchemist.** I sincerely hope you enjoyed it! If you did, feel free to:

- Help others experience the same by writing a review on Amazon, Bookbub, or Goodreads!
- Head over to my website, armorganbooks.com, to catch up on the latest news and extra content!
- Like my Facebook page– https://www.facebook.com/ARMorganBooks/

Read on to see a SNEAK PEEK of the next in the series

THE SOUL OF A CHAMPION

PREVIEW

I'm not sure at which point I lost consciousness. Perhaps it was the blood loss, or perhaps it was going through a magical method of transportation; Alchemists do not do well with magic, after all.

The first thing I came to realise was laying prone, comfortable despite being met with resistance when trying to move. Instinct kicked in as I struggled against whatever limited me.

Bound.

Someone had shackled all four of my limbs to the four posts of the bed, leaving my body spread eagle. Looking down, I wore nothing but my undergarments–a black brassiere and panties. The extensive energy my body emits when the Stone is activated has an annoying habit of disintegrating clothing, unless it's something I have modified specifically for its use. Thankfully, I had the foresight to at least wear the right undergarments.

The covers beneath me were soft and luxurious and I virtually sank into the mattress.

At least my prison is more comfortable than that of Castle Fyrkat, I thought dryly.

Looking around, my eyes squinted in the darkened room. A roaring fire was the only source of light, illuminating the room in a warm glow. Thick drapes covered the windows and there were elaborate tapestries hanging from the walls in my view. Mahogany furniture with Celtic designs dominated the area. Lifting my head up further, I was able to make out a circular marble table with what looked like a matching chess set and two stools beneath it.

Testing my bonds again, my arms pulled but there was no give. Yanking my legs, I tried to swivel but failed. Exhaustion permeated both body and soul. My heart was weary. The metal chains crawled with magic; my alchemy useless against it. Clenching my jaw in frustration, my eyes closed against the feeling of helplessness.

Suddenly, I felt the bed dip toward the end, near my legs. I snapped to attention.

The Unseelie King was before me. He was shirtless; half his torso black as ebony, making it difficult to discern against the shadows in the room. But the monster yellow eye on that side glowed back at me, just as the aquamarine one on the left, twinkled. His right hand possessed sharp black talons, stark against the white sheets, while the other hand was beautiful. Elegant, even. Movement had me tensing and tugging at my bonds as he began crawling slowly towards me. Closer still, I noticed his body littered with keloidal scars. Muscles rippled and tightened as he positioned himself over me. To my ever-blessed relief, he wore pants.

"Unlike the Vampire Court, I am not entirely ignorant of the ways of Alchemists. I know a thing or two about keeping them chained. You, however, are still somewhat of a mystery I have been looking forward to unravelling."

End of Preview

ACKNOWLEDGMENTS

What a journey this book has been. As I stated before, this book was truly inspired by Kevin Harris, who was a brilliant author and writer himself and the most delightful librarian I have ever known.

I would also like to thank my parents, my beautiful daughter, and my BFF Scott for supporting me in all that I do and going above and beyond in helping me achieve my dreams. I love you very much.

To Elsa and Wes Dolan, for taking the time to help me edit and format this book and giving me the encouragement and constructive criticism, I needed to make this happen. The brilliance of both of you gave this book the creative edge it needed. You both will forever have a special place in both my heart and my life.

To Mel Wright, for being the eagle-eyes I needed and being my rock by keeping me going.

Kyle Maupin, for taking the time to give me all the advice I needed and assisting in writing those difficult battle scenes; I've learned much in proper writing from you, and it was priceless.

Nick Blankers, aka Edgecrusher, for lending your genius in the ways of physics and world-building; I will always cherish our hours of talks of metaphysics, quantum physics, and goofy hypothesis talks. You bring out my inner geek and I couldn't be more ecstatic.

Angel Turan - though we no longer walk the same path, you were one of my biggest cheerleaders and biggest inspirations in its art and design. Your thoughts and insights were invaluable, and I will forever be grateful.

Last but certainly not least, to all those who have taken the time to read and review this book - I did it for you guys. Thank you for giving this book a chance.

ABOUT THE AUTHOR

A R Morgan can be found in the wilds of the Pacific Northwest, surrounded by her many fur-babies. She is a lone mama bear to a smart and courageous cub, who has been her biggest cheerleader and reason for pursuing her own dreams. When she is not writing three different stories at a time, or sticking her nose into twelve different books, you will probably find her gaming or spending time with her daughter. A collector of curio and relic firearms, she can also be found finding peace at the local range.

Ms. Morgan has a background in Criminology and Psychology from Washington State University and has an intense love of languages, mythology, folklore, and legends.

From the age of five, she began writing her own stories, her overactive imagination desperately needing an outlet. Once in adulthood, authors like Laurell K. Hamilton, Keri Lake, Kathryn Ann Kingsley, J. R. R. Tolkien, George R. R. Martin, and Brandon Sanderson only fuelled her desire to pursue her own creative path of writing epic romances filled with fantasy, folklore, myths, and legends.

The Heart of an Alchemist is Ms. Morgan's debut novel.

Made in the USA
Columbia, SC
20 January 2024

df17325e-9435-4f67-9447-2bb3706e6bcdR01